The Girl in Times

"Part mystery, part romance, part family drama … in other words, the perfect book."
Daily Mail

The Summer Garden

"If you're looking for a historical epic to immerse yourself in, then this is the book for you."
Closer

Road to Paradise

"One of our most exciting writers … Paullina Simons presents the perfect mix of page-turning plot and characters."
Woman and Home

A Song in the Daylight

"Simons shows the frailties of families and of human nature, and demonstrates that there's so much more to life, such as honesty and loyalty."
Good Reading

Bellagrand

"Another epic saga from Simons, full of the emotion and heartache of the original trilogy. Summer reading at its finest."
Canberra Times

Lone Star

"Another epic love story—perfect reading for a long, lazy day in bed."
Better Reading

By the same author

FICTION
Tully
Red Leaves
Eleven Hours
The Girl in Times Square
Road to Paradise
A Song in the Daylight
Lone Star

The Bronze Horseman Series
The Bronze Horseman
Tatiana and Alexander
The Summer Garden
Children of Liberty
Bellagrand

The End of Forever Saga
The Tiger Catcher
A Beggar's Kingdom
Inexpressible Island

NON FICTION
Tatiana's Table
Six Days in Leningrad

Paullina Simons

INEXPRESSIBLE ISLAND

The conclusion of the *End of Forever* saga

HarperCollins*Publishers*

HarperCollins*Publishers*
The News Building
1 London Bridge Street,
London SE1 9GF

www.harpercollins.co.uk

First published by HarperCollins *Publishers* Australia Pty Ltd in 2019

This paperback edition 2019
1

Cover design by HarperCollins Design Studio
Cover images: Houses of Parliament, London © Lee Avison/Trevillion
Images; hands by Paullina Simons; Part title illustrations by
Paullina Simons; Author photo by Tatiana Ryan
A catalogue record for this book is
available from the British Library

ISBN: 978-0-00-744169-3

Printed and bound in Great Britain by
CPI Group (UK) Ltd, Croydon, CR0 4YY

MIX
Paper from
responsible sources
FSC
www.fsc.org   FSC C007454

To my four children
"L'amor che move il sole e l'altre stelle."

"What punishments of God are not gifts?"

J.R.R. Tolkien

The Two of Them

WAY DOWN WE GO.

"Julian, I'm going to tell you a story," Ashton said, "about a rider and a preacher. The rider bet his only horse that the preacher could not recite the Lord's Prayer without his thoughts wandering. The bet was gladly accepted, and the holy man began to mouth the familiar words. Halfway through, he stopped and said, 'Did you mean the saddle also?'"

"That is not a story about a rider and a preacher," Julian said. "It's a story about how to lose a horse."

"Ashton, why aren't you eating my *Kjøttkaker*?" Julian's mother said.

"Oh, he doesn't like it, Mom," Julian said. "He told me when you were in the kitchen. He doesn't care for your Norwegian cooking."

"Julian!"

"Ignore him, Mrs. C," Ashton said. "I love your meatballs. You know he's just trying to get a rise out of you."

"Consider me risen. Why do you do that, son?"

"Do what, Mom, joke around?"

"Mrs. C," Ashton said with a mouth full of *Kjøttkaker*, "the other day your son told me I was like a brother he never had."

"Julian!" yelled his mother and five brothers.

"Jules, remember to look both ways before you go fuck yourself," said his brother Harlan.

"Funny, I was about to say the same thing to Ashton," Julian said. Ashton laughed and laughed.

Julian's mother made Ashton's favorite for dessert: *lefse*—rolled up sweet flatbread sprinkled with sugar and cinnamon.

"Ashton, did Julian ever tell you the story of how he stumped a mystic when he was thirteen?" Joanne Cruz said. "Eat, eat, while I tell you. A pillar of the church was visiting our parish, a revered Augustinian monk, a man of prodigious theological output. He gave a lecture and then invited some questions. And your skinny friend, his voice still unbroken, stepped up to the microphone and squeaked, 'Um, excuse me, why did Jesus weep for Lazarus when He saw him dead, even though He knew that in a few minutes He would raise Lazarus from the dead?' The monk thought about it and said, 'I do not know the answer.'"

Ashton, wiping the cinnamon sugar off his face, smirked. His shaggy blond hair needed a cut; his happy blue eyes gleamed. "Even I have the answer to that, and I'm no wise man and certainly no monk—pardon me, Mrs. C. The God in Jesus may have known, but the Man in Him wept because Jesus was both—fully human and fully Divine. And to mourn the dead is the human way. Next time, Jules, ask *me*. I have an answer to everything."

Fast forward.

"If you wake up first, don't go out there without me, like you did yesterday," Ashton said. They'd been camping for days. "Promise you'll stay put?"

"I don't know what you're all up in my grill about. We're camping, not caving."

Fast forward.

"Oh my God, what happened, Jules? We've been looking everywhere for you. Everywhere but here. You don't know what you've done to us.

"Julian, say something!

"You're going to be okay. You're going to be okay. Help him! Help him!

"Why did you do it, I told you not to go, why do you never listen, why did you leave without me?"

I'm sorry, Ashton, Julian wanted to say, but couldn't speak. *I don't know what happened.*

Fast forward.

"My buddy Jules over here used to be a boxer," Ashton said to Riley and Gwen the night they met. The boys were groomed and shaved, wore jeans paired with Hugo Boss jackets. "You should be impressed, ladies." The girls were young and sparkling. "He was nearly untouchable in the ring. He hit his opponents with shots that could've brought down mountains. Yes, he was a magnificent fighter but a flawed human being. Whereas now, he's precisely the opposite—lucky for you, Gwen, and I mean the word *lucky* in the most literal sense—ouch, Jules! What are you hitting me for?"

"Lucky Gwen," Riley said after a beat, turning her smile to Ashton.

A flirty Gwen scooted over to Julian. "Well, I *am* feeling pretty lucky, I must admit."

Fast forward.

"Do you know any boxing jokes?" asked Riley. They had settled into a booth, ordered drinks and snacks. It was their first double date.

Julian did. "Did you hear what Manny Pacquiao planned to write on Floyd Mayweather's tombstone? *You can stop counting. I ain't getting up.*"

The girls laughed. Ashton laughed, even though he'd heard the joke before.

Fast forward.

"Riley, don't try so hard," Ashton said. "Women have no need to appeal to men by *also* being funny. They appeal to men already, you know what I mean?"

"Go to hell," Riley said. "I'm funny."

"No, no, my love. It's not an insult. You're under the mistaken impression that men *want* their women to be funny."

"No, no, my love," Riley said. "It's you who's under the mistaken impression that women *don't* want their men to be funny."

Julian nodded approvingly. "That was funny, Riles."

"Thanks, Jules. Ashton, you should try being more like Jules. Because unlike you, see, he is actually funny."

"Fuck you, Jules."

"What did I do?" Then Julian added, "You know, Ash, if you can stimulate your girl to laughter, and I mean real, head thrown back, deep throated, full and loud laughter, perhaps she will become more open to you and you can stimulate her to other things."

"Fuck you, Jules!" And later: "All right, I'll try to be funnier," Ashton said. "Let's try it Julian's way."

"Said the bishop to the barmaid," said Julian.

To be funnier, Ashton told a joke. "Joe Gideon says to the masseuse, 'Excuse me, miss, how much do you charge for genitalia?' and she replies, 'Oh, the same as for Jews, Mr. Gideon!'"

The four of them threw back their heads and laughed. They loved L.A. and *All That Jazz.*

Fast forward.

"Yes, I'm moving to London. It will help my dear old dad, and you know how close we are. Kidding aside, though, I've always wanted to live in Notting Hill. It's on my bucket list. Of course I'll still keep the Treasure Box. Why would I give that up? It's my life."

Fast forward.

"Yes, I'm selling the Treasure Box. Don't look so deflated. It's just a store. I'll get another one if I really want to be tied down again. Right now I'd like to travel, see the world. You in, Jules? Where have we been besides London? Nowhere, exactly. Want to go to France? We have the time. What do you say, we can be two free men in Paris, so we can do our best, maybe feel alive." Ashton grinned, humming, drumming. "Because you're a very good friend of mine."

Fast forward.

"She is going to break you," Ashton said as they were coming home one night, unconscionably intoxicated. "I told you she was going to bust you open, and did you listen? You never listen to me, because you think you know everything, you think you're the only one with gut feelings."

"You sure you're talking about me?"

"She turned to you, eyes blazing," Ashton continued, "like you were her enemy in the ring and said, tonight, I *keel* you. And so far, nothing you've done has stopped her from fulfilling her promise."

"Why am I even here?" Julian said.

"You're like my dad, you both keep asking, why are we here," said Ashton. "Why is anything here is a better question. Not why do *you* bother to exist, but why does anything bother to exist at all?"

"Because. The art of living in this world," Julian replied, recalling Marcus Aurelius, "is to teach us that whatsoever falls upon man, he may be ready for it—that nothing may cast him down."

"Some things cast you down," Ashton said. "Bow out, Julian. As if you have a choice. Admit when you've been defeated. Forget you ever loved her. That's what I had to do." His head was bowed. "Forget I ever loved them."

"Let's go to Paris, Ash."

"Okay, let's. But first come with me to the wedding in York."

"I can't." He had a lot to do to get ready for the equinox.

Was this the end? Were these wretched memories Julian's life passing before his eyes?

No, he realized.

Not *his* life.

Their friendship was the beginning of everything.

How could Ashton be the one on whom the tempests fell.

Run along, my only friend.

Rewind the reel, rewind.

Part One

London Pride

O'er fields and towns, from sea to sea,
Passed the pageant swift and free,
Tearing up, and trampling down;
Till they came for London town.

Percy Bysshe Shelley

1

Anonymous

"ANYONE CAN STOP A MAN'S LIFE," DEVI SAID, QUOTING Seneca, probably thinking he was being comforting, "but no one his death: a thousand doors open onto it."

Don't speak to me. Don't look at me. Leave me alone.

He had begged her, *begged* her not to, yet Shae still left him behind.

"Stumble up from your river of loneliness," Julian heard Devi say. "We know you're in sorrow. But you're not alone. Ava and I are with you. You're separated from your heart, yes, but don't think of how little you did for her, think rather about how much she did for you. Her love for you saved your life. That man would've killed you and desecrated you. And then killed her, and desecrated her. To give you a chance, she warned you, and then threw herself overboard. By sacrificing herself, she saved you. Even though you were lowly and unworthy. Take the gift from her and live."

"*I* was unworthy? Did you hear my story?"

"Of course," Devi said. "You should have never gone. You had no business going anywhere in the state you were in, in the state you're still in. You should've waited until next year, or the one after. Or not gone at all. You were no good to her. You were in no shape to help her. That she helped you despite yourself is a testament to how her soul feels about you even when you least deserve it."

"*I* least deserve it."

"Stop rephrasing and repeating everything I say."

"Why are you still talking to me?" Julian said. "Go away."

You promised Mother no matter where I go, you would follow me. Did you mean it?

I didn't promise it to your mother. I promised it to you.

Shae tried to take him with her. She jumped. But as always, he ran out of time, even for death.

Ava sat in horror. Nothing made her feel better, not the story of the frantic mother, not the bravery of the sainted Maori who stayed by Shae's side to the end. "Kiritopa's glory was in the union with that woman and my child," Ava said.

Julian lost three fingers on his right hand. He nearly lost four. After multiple surgeries, the doctors managed to save his pointer. Steel screws now held it together. It was a robot finger. The pinky was gone, the ring and middle fingers sliced off below the second knuckle. Your fingers for your life, Devi said. Julian gave Devi the finger, but it was more like he gave Devi the nub.

In the corner, Ava sat weeping. It's like the first time all over again, she said.

Julian's body was a mess. Electrocution flowers. A weakened heart. Along with the amputated fingers, he had suffered numerous other injuries during his cagematch with Tama: a broken nose, a cracked cheekbone, a concussion, a dislocated shoulder, a shattered radial bone from blocking that fucking *mere* club, torn ligaments in his knees, a fractured fibula, and a dozen cracks in his knuckles and hands and the bones of his feet. He was black and blue from his forehead to his shins.

Slowly, his body healed.

There were things that didn't heal.

You say to her be my goddess, and she agrees and opens her legs. What a burden you've put on her—and you. She must be what she is not. You must be what you're not. She is not a goddess.

Goddesses don't die.

Julian lived inside the silence, inside the silence of the ocean with her body in his arms.

"Is there a purpose to my suffering, an end to my despair?"

Devi got up and said no.

"What will I find at the end of my story?" Julian said another day, another mute afternoon. "Will there be a recognition of my labors, a list of my shortcomings?"

Devi got up and said yes.

Julian searched for the power within. He and Ava were catatonics, her sitting in his hospital room by the window, him sitting in his bed, both barely rocking, trying to draw the power from silence. He kept staring at the space above his palm where his fingers used to be.

Your fear that she will cease to be—will recede, will vanish into the vanishing point—has been allayed. Hallelujah. She is not vanishing.

You are.

∞

My life is wind, Julian thought when he finally returned to the apartment after six weeks in the hospital and six weeks convalescing at Hampstead Heath. He would've stayed longer, but they kicked him out. He would've stayed the rest of his life.

Instead he came back home.

My eye will see no more good, because he will not return to this house, neither will any place ever know him. Julian stood by the mantle in his empty apartment in Notting Hill. Their heads bent, Ava and Devi stood with him. They were always with him. They went with him to York to bring Ashton's body back, they flanked him at the funeral, they were with him now. To the end of his days, Julian would complain of the bitterness in his soul. He preferred a drowning death rather than his life. The Lord didn't take away my iniquities. I still sleep in the dust. *You will seek me in the morning, but I won't be here.*

Because *he* wasn't here.

Because she wasn't here.

Devi tried to lighten the mood, as only Devi could. He made food, brought Julian tiger water, told Julian things. They sat down with Ava; they broke their bread; they had sake and egg rolls with twice-cooked pork dunked in chili soy sauce; they sipped Ga tan, a Vietnamese chicken soup. And then Devi talked.

"My own son was raised a Catholic, too," Devi said. "But by the time he was grown, barely a trace of any teaching remained inside him. A remnant of faith turned out to be nothing but empty space."

"It's not just your son," Julian said. "That's how I lived most of my adult life. I had a fairly religious upbringing, which I attempted to discard when I went to college. My father's family were loud devout Catholics, but my mother was a silent Lutheran Norwegian. Except for my near-constant search for answers to life's unsolvable riddles, I felt more akin to her than I did to my *Dia de los Muertos* relatives. I went to a secular school with other kids who felt the way I did. Any mention of church was met with an eye roll. We talked video games, football, boxing, music, movies, girls. God never entered our language except in blasphemy. Until I met Ashton. He didn't go to church, but he had faith."

Devi nodded. "That was my son, too," he said. "A typical boy, growing up in London, not listening to his dad. He wanted to be a photographer. I thought it was frivolous. He thought I was hopelessly old-fashioned. He was embarrassed by me. After his mother died, all he did was party."

Julian nodded. Ashton, too, except for the dad part. Dad left the family, found a new life back in England, and didn't return for his son, not even after the mother died. Ashton shuttled between a dozen foster homes until UCLA.

"Then as now, it's difficult to tell by a man's life and actions whether or not he is a believer," Devi said. "Religious thought and teachings are so disconnected from daily life. A man can go one week, then another, and soon through his whole existence and not encounter God in his dealings with himself or other people."

"Maybe when new life is created?" Ava said.

"Despite the requisite exclamations of Oh my God, often not even then," Devi said. "The only time man usually comes into contact with faith or his lack thereof is when life ends."

Julian lowered his head.

"You can conceive without God," said Devi, "you can give birth, marry, live every Sunday, every Good Friday, every day without God, but it's difficult to confront death without God—especially for the living. We don't know what the dead do when the door closes, and darkness or light swallows them. But we know what we the living do when tasked with the burden of their burial, ritual, funeral, memorial. We have a hard time with it. A man dies quietly in the hospital. Sometimes his family is present, sometimes not. A priest is often absent, for the man has no priest and has never been to church, at least not willingly. After some medical to and fro, the body gets taken away. The funeral director brings it to a place most people rarely enter. There it lies for a few hours or days or weeks until the family decides whether to bury or cremate. Cremation is now the most popular option, for it allows the body to return to dust without any theological fanfare. I once knew a man who had made his own funeral arrangements, planned for his own disposal. He died alone in Dover, and by the time his sons arrived, a few days later, his body had already been cremated."

"How do you know?"

"I went to Dover and sat with him before he died," Devi said. "His sons didn't know me at all. They were presented with a cardboard box filled with their father's ashes and another cardboard box that held the last of his earthly belongings. His drugstore-bought reading glasses. His disposable cell phone. The Timex watch he had since the '70s. His thirty-year-old wallet, in which there was a ten-pound note, a National Health card, a credit card, one nearly expired license, and an old magazine about eagles. That was all. The sons kept the ashes and threw the other box into the trash on their way out. There was no funeral, no memorial, no wake, no dinner. Perhaps they went to the pub for a drink, I don't know. There weren't even any secular words to remind anyone of the man's life, why he lived, what he meant, who loved him. There was nothing."

"Why are you telling me this?" Julian said.

"That's how you die without God," Devi said. "Anonymously. But that is not how Ashton lived. And it's not how he died."

Julian wept.

2

It Didn't Have To Be This Way

LITTLE BY LITTLE, THE APARTMENT STOPPED CONTAINING traces of the man who was gone. His clothes did not remain in the empty closets, the smell of his open cologne did not linger over his dresser, his toothbrush and razor did not lie in his unused bathroom, and the old expired coconut water, courtesy of the delicate and tormented Riley, was no longer in the fridge.

The things Ashton left behind:

His accounts and insurance policies, all to Julian.

His poster of Bob Marley, which Julian tried to give to Zakiyyah, but she refused to take it.

A photo of him and Julian high in the Sierra Madres, nineteen years old, backpacks on, baseball caps on, arms around each other, beaming for the camera.

A scribbled saying on the side of the fridge. If it hadn't been in Ashton's large bold hand, Julian might've forgotten who'd written it. It was from Don Marquis and it said, *"My heart has followed all my days something I cannot name."*

∞

Julian still walked through London looking for the Café with the Golden Awning.

When he grew tired, he would find a bench, and sometimes that spot would be by the church at Cripplegate. Unmoving he sat, looking across the canal at the preserved crumbling stretch of the London Wall. He hoped that through lack of motion, he would eventually regain his strength. It hadn't happened yet. He wasn't growing handsome. He was getting older, grayer, thinner, flailing his helpless arms, clenching and unclenching his mutilated hand, shuffling his feet, all splintering aching bones. The Q'an Doh Cave, once a place of hope and salvation, had become nothing but a stalagpipe organ without a church, playing out the last of its quiet dirge, not in absolution but oblivion.

∞

Julian didn't hear from Riley.

A few times he tried to get in touch with her but remained blocked on her phone. Indirectly—through her parents or Gwen—the path to her also remained closed, and Riley remained purposefully and utterly unreachable, in the level desert sands of Snowflake, Arizona, working on herself or hiding, which amounted to the same thing.

How is she, he would ask her parents.

Not good, they would say. How do you think she is?

No one asked how he was, not even Gwen.

And it was just as well.

Julian didn't hear from Riley, but oh did he hear from Zakiyyah.

During some inopportune time during late London mornings she would call—when it was the dead of night in L.A. He knew it was her by the relentless mournful yawp of the neutral ring.

For hours he would sit at the island, elbows on the granite, eyes closed, phone pressed to his ear, and try not to hear the unendurable lament of a stricken woman—now married to someone else—the up and down modulation of outrage and anguish, punctuated every few minutes by a desperate, hoarse refrain. "It didn't have to be this way."

Zakiyyah didn't require Julian to speak. She required of him nothing but the phone squeezed to his ear.

"It didn't have to be this way!"

"It didn't have to be this way..."

After weeks and months passed like this, she stopped calling.

Her silence deafening, Julian reached out to her himself.

The new husband answered her cell phone. "It's not a good idea for you to talk to her anymore," he said. "Especially in the middle of the night, when she should be sleeping, or doing other things. It's just making her feel worse. We are trying to have a baby, and this is screwing up all our plans."

"It doesn't have to be this way," Julian said, feebly trying to argue, to persuade, to convince.

"Maybe," the husband said as he hung up. "But that's the way it is."

Julian didn't call her after that. His pose remained the same, even without the phone at his ear. Head bent. Eyes closed.

It didn't have to be this way.

A line of love.

A line of hate.

It didn't have to be this way.

A line of grief.

A line of rage.

It didn't have to be this way.

Zakkiyah recalled the days.

The years.

The joy.

The fights.

The life.

It didn't have to be this way.

She talked of L.A. with him by her side.

The bars, the hikes, the Space Mountain rides.

She talked of London, where she thought things were great.

But they weren't, Z, Julian wanted to say. They weren't. Things were already in a spiral, and I couldn't see it, and you didn't want to see it.

It didn't have to be this way.

She sobbed for the future that was so close, yet never came.

Sometimes exclamation.

Sometimes a whisper.

Sometimes he could barely hear her.

It didn't have to be this way.

Z...Z...please, you're going to be okay.

But now that she stopped calling, he heard her nonstop, a raw siren wail in his head.

I will never love another man like I love him, never, she said.

He never heard from Zakiyyah again.

He never heard from Riley again.

It didn't have to be this way.

∞

Every morning when Julian woke up, he was cold. And when he looked outside, it was raining.

He never left the house without an umbrella.

On the weekends, if he ventured out at all, he wore his waterproof boots.

He pretended he went to work. He got up in the morning and put on his suit and walked to Notting Hill Gate station and rode the Circle Line all day. He'd change for another train somewhere, get off at a stop he'd never gotten off before, walk around, staring at the coffee shops, maybe have some lunch in a pub, read, and head home.

There was no way Julian could go back to Nextel with Nigel still there. It was impossible. Julian knew he could never face him, which was a blessing for Nigel, really. But in August Julian heard that Nigel died of acute alcohol poisoning. Julian wanted to thank someone but didn't know who.

After Nigel's death, he returned to work.

He stayed until October. He only stayed as long as he did because he liked the reactions of civilized people to his mysterious deformity.

"How did you say it happened?"

"I fought a Maori warrior to the death."

And they would look benevolently at his slow-moving body and say, sure you did. But you won, right?

"Right. Otherwise I wouldn't be standing here telling you about it."

"Of course you wouldn't. Malcolm, come here. Jules, tell Malcolm what you just told me."

"I fought a Maori warrior to the death."

"A Maori! Roger, come here, listen to this."

Julian enjoyed being mocked. It reminded him of the old days. But soon even that got old.

After he took the payout and resigned, he spent the winter hanging around the boxing gym. Nobody mocked him there. You couldn't shock those people with fucking anything.

"A Maori warrior? Bloody hell, that's fantastic! Omar, come here, listen to this. Our Jules fought a Maori."

"He did? Is that how you lost half your hand? Incredible. But he got it worse, right? Or you wouldn't be standing here telling us about it. Dead men tell no stories. Rafa, come take a look at Julian's hand, he fought a fucking Maori warrior."

"No fuckin' way!"

Julian had been going to Nextel in his leather dress shoes. They were soggy and misshapen because the puddles by the Underground, near Fitzroy House, never dried. It was like being in his water-logged fur boots on the Antarctic ice, sitting in the boat, drinking whisky with Edgar Evans, talking about igloos in barren lands. The shoes never dried in England, all sodden near Sainsbury's where Julian still bought his milk, reflexively, despite knowing he would never drink it, because he didn't eat cereal. Ashton had been the one who had cereal.

Ava, who had moved into Ashton's room, made no comment about Julian's dairy purchases. She just threw out the milk when the expiration day came.

Sometimes when the weather was not great in London and the wind howled, Julian would remember something he didn't want to in the damp chill and double over. That described his life pretty well. Always trying to avoid remembering something he didn't want to.

Once in Invercargill, where the wind also howled in freezing circles, Shae said why are you always like this and he said why are you always like *this*. They fought like they'd been together a long time, and weren't on their best behavior anymore, smiling and making compliments, telling each other little jokes, asking cute questions. There was no flirting and no courting. There were no questions. Because they already knew everything there was to know, and it made them sick inside. She knew she was going to die, and he knew he was powerless to stop it.

Once, even longer ago, the blistering London wind broke his and Ashton's umbrellas. Cracked them in half. He and Ashton had a good laugh about it. They reminisced about living in a place where it never rained, where, with a million others, they used to sit in traffic on the Freeway or the 405 and curse their life, thinking they had it so tough, the sun always shining, them having to drive everywhere to drink with friends, tell jokes to their girls, buy books at Book Soup.

And now Julian walked with his head down and no umbrella as he battled the rain, waiting fifteen minutes for the train, the Circle Line so slow. He had a different life now, a life in which every day by Notting Hill Gate, an eight-year-old girl offered to sell him a red rose and said, for your sweetheart, sir? To make her happy?

And every day Julian bought one.

His floor was strewn with three hundred dead roses.

∞

Ava would wave him on. "Go," she'd say. "Go out for a walk. Go look for your golden awning. I have much to do. I'm seeding a vegetable garden in the back so next summer you can have your own tomatoes."

"Next summer?" They stared at each other, saying nothing. What was there to say? "I don't like tomatoes."

"Who asked you."

In the evenings, she stayed up with him. Late at night, Julian would sometimes become talkative, tell Ava things she could bear to hear. Mostly he told her stories of mothers and daughters. He told her about Aurora and Lady Mary in Clerkenwell, about Agatha and Miri in the rookery, about Aubrey and Mirabelle in Kent. He didn't tell her about Mallory in the brothel. The mother Anna was dead, the girl murdering men, burning in flames, blackening her soul. Nothing about that story could be told.

And he didn't talk to her about Shae and Agnes because it wasn't a story yet.

It wasn't still life yet, like a bowl of fruit.

Ava wanted to know what each girl looked like, what she sounded like. She wanted to know if she danced, sang, if she told jokes. She asked Julian to reproduce her daughter's best moments on the stage. She bought the plays and highlighted Mia's spoken portions and asked Julian to recite them for her, but recite them standing up, just as her daughter would have.

Ava never asked about her death. "I don't know how you can do it," she whispered to him one night. "How you can do it over and over."

"That's not why I go," Julian said. "I go to watch her live."

He kept missing something, Ava said. That's why he kept failing, he wasn't seeing an important detail, wasn't paying attention to some essential part of Mia's existence.

"If only you could point me to what that might be," Julian said.

"She was such a good girl," Ava said. "She and her dad had the best time running our place on Coney Island, Sideshows by the Seashore. That child was a born carnival clown; she tap-danced, sang, did stand-up, a juggling act; she never left his side." Ava smiled in remembrance. "She used to do this thing at the end of every show: after the curtain fell and she would thank people for coming, she'd fling out her arms, take the deepest bow, and say *Make it real, make it last, make it beautiful*." Ava wiped her face. "We had the happiest life, the three of us," she said. "Until Jack had a heart attack and died. But for twelve years before that, we were in paradise."

Death did that, thought Julian. It ruined fucking everything.

∞

Ava spent hours Skyping on the computer with her friends back in Brooklyn. It allowed her to be close to Julian if he needed something, yet still be plugged into her other life. Julian usually put on his headphones so he wouldn't hear the details of her private conversations, but one afternoon when he didn't, he heard something garbled in her speech that didn't sound right. He put down his book and walked out into the hall. Disjointed words were spilling out of Ava's mouth. The cadence was normal, but nothing in their content made sense. He heard someone's voice crying, help her, help her! Ava, what's wrong with you?

Julian ran inside the bedroom. Ava was sitting with her back to him, tilted to one side. She had stopped speaking almost completely except for one word she kept repeating over and over. "Once," she kept saying. "Once once once once once once once."

"Ava, what's the matter?" Julian said, turning her chair to him and staring into her unfocused eyes. "What are you saying? Can you sit up? Just hold on to me, I'll call the doctor."

"Only *once* more," she said, gripping his arm as she fell sideways. "Once."

3

Once

AVA HAD A STROKE. SHE LOST HER MOBILITY, AND SHE LOST her speech. She was kept in the hospital until the doctors decided there was nothing more they could do for her. Either she was going to get better on her own, or she wasn't. "She *is* close to eighty," the on-call genius said.

So the fuck what, Julian wanted to say. He *once* knew a treasure hunter who scoured thousands of miles of London's underground sewers looking for his vanished father, and he was eighty. He *once* knew a man who helmed a whaleship in the Antarctic ice storms, who flensed his own seals—among other things—and he was eighty.

Devi and Julian decided to move Ava to the Hampstead Heath convalescent home. It was familiar, clean, and the nurses were kind. "Plus it's not far, and we can visit her," Devi said.

Yes, said Julian, studying Devi. What did Ava mean by *once*? Was it the rantings of an unwell woman? Julian wouldn't have given it any more thought, except it had been the only clear word out of her mouth after everything else got muddled.

∞

"How am I going to make the trip two more times?" Julian said to Devi in a black cab, on the way home from Hampstead Heath. "I don't mean in a whiny sense. I mean in an actual physical

23

sense. All the bones in my body are unstable, like I'm about to fracture."

"Why are you still boxing nonstop if you are such a fragile creature?"

Julian shrugged. "Plus I'm handicapped now." He raised his right hand, as if Devi was confused by what Julian meant. "No matter what *I* want, I don't know if my body can survive two more trips."

"That's good," Devi said. "Because you can only go back once."

Julian stopped feeling sorry for himself. "Twice, you mean."

"Once."

"You don't think I can count to seven?"

"I don't think you can, no."

Julian stared at the back of the driver's head, wondering if he should close the little window between them before he continued. He decided to plow on. "You said seven times. I didn't imagine it." Julian was almost sure the dry-witted Devi was messing with him. "I've gone five. 1603, 1666, 1775, 1854, 1911. That's five. Next is six. I suppose if I fail again, then will come seven. That's twice more. One of us can't count."

"That would be you."

"What are you talking about?"

Devi signaled to the driver to stop by Marble Arch. They paid and got out, and when they had walked a little way down Bayswater Road, the cook spoke. "Her seventh and last incarnation is as Ava's daughter, Mia. In L.A. With *you*."

Julian waited for more.

"With *you*, Julian."

"I don't understand."

"But who are you that is hobbling next to me? Aren't you Julian?"

"So?"

"Where are you going to go?"

"You mean it won't come again?"

"That's not what I mean. It *might* come again. What I'm saying is, you can't be there when it does."

"Why?"

"Because you're already there."

Julian stopped walking.

"Come with me," a sighing Devi said, pulling on Julian's arm. "Let's go inside the park, walk through the fountains in the Italian Gardens. It's a nice day. For the first time in weeks, it's not raining."

The diminutive Asian man held on to Julian as they ambled in the blinding late February sunshine, both shielding their eyes from the blinding waters of the Serpentine. Or was it Julian who was holding on to Devi? Where did he go wrong, where did he go so far off the path? They didn't speak until they found a secluded bench under a barely budding tree near the ducks on the Long Water.

Kneading the beads in his hands, the Hmong shaman stared at the people ambling by, at the ducklings swimming after their mothers.

"There's a fallacy in your approach to this," Devi said. "I can see you're shellshocked, but you don't have to go back even once more. You're still a relatively young man. You have a little money now. You could travel a bit. There are places other than London and Invercargill. You can run a boxing gym. I see the way the other guys listen to you, spar with you, even with your mangled claw. They like and respect you. You have a knack. You could use your skills to remake men who need your help into better fighters and every day be around what matters most to you. What a gift to yourself that would be—every day to be around what you love. You can do that here, or in L.A. Your mother, I'm sure, would prefer to have you back. You might meet someone. The long-suffering loner is a popular option with some women. So much is still possible for you, Julian. Going back is only one of your choices."

Motionless, Julian sat.

"When you first met her," Devi said, "you thought you had forever. And the first time you went back for her, you thought you had forever. The second time at the Silver Cross, you were afraid and didn't know of what. The third time, you felt doom but didn't know when. The fourth time with Mirabelle, you knew exactly when. And last time, for the first time, Shae herself knew what was coming. How did that work out? What's next for you two, I do not know. What is left for you to show her and for her to show you? Perhaps how to live amid death, as we all must learn. But"—Devi folded his hands—"*if* you choose to go back, it will be for the last time."

The ducks in the Long Water were flapping, splashing. Somewhere a baby cried. Two women walked by, wrapped around each other. A man and woman perched on a bench, licking around the same cone of ice cream.

"You said seven."

"Did you listen to a word I said?" Devi exclaimed. "Why do you keep repeating things over and over? You *had* seven."

"The first time doesn't count."

"Why not?"

"Because it was just my life. I lived it."

"It may have been your life, but it was her last life. That counts, no?"

"No." Julian's legs felt numb, the nubs on his hand pulsing.

"All the other times you've crossed the meridian and gone back in time," said Devi, "you entered *her* life, not yours."

"So?"

"Julian, you can't breach a life in which you yourself exist."

"Why not?"

Devi tried to stay patient. "How can you be inside a time in which you already are?" He enunciated every word. "In that one unique, singular spacetime, she exists in *your* world. You do not exist in hers."

"What's the difference?"

Devi sighed. "What are you going to do with yourself when this old crippled body crawls out into Los Angeles and encounters the younger, spry, horny you chatting her up in Book Soup?"

"That's the other guy's problem."

"Instantly it will become your problem. It can't happen is what I'm saying. There can't be two of *you*," Devi said. "You get that part, don't you? One body, one soul. Not two bodies, one soul. Not two souls, one body. Not two souls, two bodies. One body. One soul."

Julian sat. "What do I do with the other me?"

"There *is* no other you!" Devi said. "There is only *this* you. Right here, where your soul is, on the bench by the Serpentine. Your soul cannot be divided. You are not—what's the thing that's all the rage these days—you're not a Horcrux. You are not a clone, a body without a soul. You can't compete with your material self in the material world, you can't co-exist with yourself in Los Angeles. How can you be so hostile to the thing that's obviously true? Only one of you can touch her."

At last Julian understood.

He wasn't prepared for it. It was like another thing had been severed.

∞

In the middle of March, in the middle of the night, Julian banged on Quatrang's door.

"This has to stop," Devi said, half-asleep in a black silk robe, letting Julian push past him and inside. "I have a life. I have to function during the day. I'm not a nocturnal like you."

"What do I do, Devi? I don't know what to do. Help me."

"Would you like me to give you something to help you sleep?"

"Are you saying you don't know how to help me save her, how to help me change her fate?"

Devi spoke low. "Yes, that's what I'm saying. I don't know how to help you change her fate."

"But seven is not enough!"

"Seven is not enough," Devi repeated dully. "Look what you're doing, you're making me repeat things, infecting me with your disease. Once more is not enough for you. Six journeys through time is not enough for you. Seven weeks is not enough for you. And if you had seventy times seven, what would you say? Would that also not be enough? And if you had seventy thousand times seven?"

"It would also not be enough," Julian whispered.

"Seven weeks to change your life and hers," Devi said. "Seven days to make the world. Seven words on the Cross. Seven times to perfect your soul so when you finally meet God, you're the best you can be. Don't be selfish, Julian. Think of her. You'd rather her immortal soul spin and toil for eternity? Over and over, trying and failing?" Devi shook his head. "Now that sounds like nothing but suffering for the sake of nothing but suffering. Look at yourself—your bones are crumbling. You are turning to dust before my eyes. Your body can't take even one more time. But long gone are the days when you swore to me you were never going back, and I pretended to believe you. You've really gone out of your way to answer a question I of all people didn't need answered: how does a man live when he must live without the thing he can't live without? Poorly, that's how. So go—for the last time go—and do what you can."

"Like what?"

"To have something you've never had," Devi said, "you must do something you've never done."

This is it, ladies and gents!

Make it real.

Make it last.

Make it beautiful.

4

The Importance of Being Julian

THE RIVER ENDS. HIS MAKESHIFT DINGHY GRINDS AGAINST A muddy decaying bed. Julian turns off the headlamp to find the light, but there is nothing to see and nowhere to climb. Dusting himself off, he turns his headlamp back on and proceeds down the dried-out riverbed. It's better than walking on ice, that's for sure.

After a long time, the tubular walls of the cave get smoother, grayer, and the rocks under his feet disappear. He bumps his ankle against something that feels like iron. He leans down. It is iron. It's a single rail. If it was a live rail, he'd be in real trouble. He wonders why it isn't live. He walks and walks and walks. To look for the light, he once again switches off the headlamp. Finally, in the dark tunnel ahead of him he sees a faint yellow glimmer and hears some distant noise.

The tunnel empties into a train station. He pulls himself up onto a platform in a cavernous space, all of it in near total darkness except toward the opposite end around a blind curve. Julian recognizes the station. He's been here many times, a thousand times. In case there's any doubt, on the wall, a red circle with a blue line through it tells him what it is.

It's Bank.

It's the Bank tube station in the City of London. He is on the Central Line platform, with its unmistakable sharp bend (the station was built around the vaults of the Bank of England). Julian can almost hear the shriek of the screeching wheels as the train turns the corner. Another day, that is, not today, because today there are no trains because the rail is cut.

Just past the curve, he sees a cluster of ragamuffin people spread out on the platform near the exit to the lobby that leads to the escalators that lead to the street. They're jammed together and sunk to the ground amid a few lit lamps. From the lobby, he can hear a single voice talking, modulating up and down the octaves, as if giving a soliloquy. Intermittently, the voices on the ground laugh.

It looks as if the crowd might be using the Underground as a bomb shelter. Which would explain why there is no live rail. The rail is cut at night, because people sleep in the Underground.

Julian pats himself on his proverbial back. Finally, he has guessed his destination correctly.

It's London, during the Second World War.

To fit in with the times, Julian bought a three-piece Armani suit, two sizes too big. No one wears fitted suits in the 1940s. On his feet are waterproof combat boots. On his head is a newsboy cap, the kind even King George liked to wear. Julian kept his hair curly and longish, slicked back, away from his forehead, and he shaved, though after time in the cave, his stubble feels an inch thick as he runs his hand over his face.

He steps into the lobby between the platforms and languishes at the rear of the crowd, trying to catch the voice echoing off the tiled tubular walls.

On the platform, some are already lying down, covered by blankets as if this is where they will sleep, but in the poorly lit lobby, people are sitting cross-legged on the floor next to their bags and sacks and coats and pillows. They're listening to the voice in front of them. Lit by a kerosene lamp, near the stopped escalator, a singular girl stands on a makeshift stage—a wide door ripped off its hinges and laid flat over some two-by-fours. She stands on top of the door, her long strands of dark hair spilling out of a blue headscarf. She looks tall, larger than life, because she's up on a stage. She wears rags like the rest, a skirt with a frayed hem, a falling apart sweater, and torn boots. But the beige wool fits snugly over her breasts, her neck is white, her skin translucent, and her huge eyes blaze as she gestures with her hands to amplify her words. There's a diamond smile on her face.

Already Julian is warmer. Shae never smiled. Not in the beginning, and certainly not at the end.

The young woman is reciting a humorous ditty about romantic love. It takes Julian a few moments to recognize it as a pretty solid paraphrase of Oscar Wilde's *A Woman of No Importance*. Her captive audience is moderately amused.

"Oh, the *Ideal Man!*" the woman yells cheerfully. "Let me tell you about him! The *Ideal Man* should talk to us as if we were *goddesses*. He should refuse *all* our serious requests and gratify every *one* of our whims. He should encourage us to have caprices, yet discourage us to have goals. He should always say *much* more than he means and always mean much more than he says. He should *never* run down other pretty women. That would show he has no taste. If we ask him a question about *anything*, he should give us an answer only about ourselves. *That*, ladies and gentlemen, is the *Ideal Man!*"

From behind the crowd collected at the girl's feet, Julian raises his voice, steps forward, and speaks.

"*Cecily?*" he calls to her, switching to his own paraphrase of *The Importance of Being Earnest.* "Is that you? The dog cart has been waiting, my dear. Are you ready to leave with me at last?"

With barely a pause the girl squints into the darkness, her hand at her forehead like a visor. "Algernon, is that *you*? Finally, you're here. Come quick! Are you planning to stay until next week? I hope so, though my mother will be *very* cross to discover this is so. She doesn't like the way you abruptly left me not long ago."

Julian takes a few steps through the curious crowd. "I left *you*? You mean, *you* left me. And I don't care about your mother,

Cecily. I don't care about anybody in the whole world but you. *I love you.* You will marry me as you promised, won't you?"

The girl laughs like a church bell. "Algernon, you *silly* sausage. *Now* you want to marry me? Don't you remember we were already engaged to be married, and then I broke it off with you?"

Two more strides forward. "But why would you *do* a thing like that, Cecily?"

"Well, it can hardly be called a serious engagement if it's not broken off at least once. But I forgive you, Algernon."

He crosses the concrete floor on which people sit and laugh and clap and jumps up onto the wobbling makeshift stage.

For a moment he stands, and she stands, in silence. For a moment it seems as if they both have forgotten their lines. Pulling off his cap, Julian presses it to his chest.

We, the drowned, are rising up for air.

He falls to his knees in front of her, to hide his exhaustion, to show her other things. "What a *perfect* thing you are, Cecily," he says, staring up into her baffled face.

The girl looks him over, his suit, his decidedly out-of-time hair, the newsboy at his breast, the dark beard flecked with gray. "Oh, my, Algernon, I see you've neglected to shave."

"Who can shave at a time like this?" Julian says, and the crowd murmurs, *hear, hear.* "No one is shaving. That's how you know how shaken the men of London really are."

Hear, hear, the crowd responds emotionally.

The young woman stares into his bottomless haunted eyes. A breath of animation passes across her face. Coyly she smiles. "You may be unshaven, but aren't you a little *overdressed* for the occasion?"

"Why, yes, you're right, I *am* a little overdressed," Julian says. "But I make up for it by being *immensely* undereducated."

The people laugh. Julian continues. "*Josephine*, do you know that this is the last time we will see each other? After this, I must leave you. I will not be staying for the rest of your performance. The dog cart *is* waiting, my dear. It is so painful parting."

Confused, the girl mouths *Josephine?* "I agree, Algernon," she says. "It *is* painful to part from people one has known for only a short while. The absence of old friends one can almost tolerate. But even a momentary separation from someone whom one has just met is *unendurable*."

He is still on his knees, gazing up at her. She flushes, blushes. He doesn't. He barely even moves. His eyes roam her face, her body. She is fair of skin and dark of hair. She is doe-eyed, pale-pink-lipped, long-necked, bosomy, beautiful. She is like she always is. Grimy in the Blitz, living underground, washed out in drab dress, her inner self is still a shining city on a hill.

Julian wanted a fairytale ending. Instead he is down on his knees. He stares at her open and unashamed as if he already *knows* her. He stares at her with eyes that have seen her. "Before I go, dear Cecily," Julian says, his voice cracking, his gray eyes full, "I hope I don't offend you when I state openly in front of all these good people that to me in every way you seem to be absolute *perfection*."

The audience cheers.

She swallows, stammers. "I think, uh, your frankness does you credit, Algernon."

"Ever since I first laid my eyes upon your wonderful, incomparable face," Julian says, "all those years ago, Cecily, in another life, I have dared to love you—wildly, passionately, devotedly, hopelessly."

The people on the platform are raucous with delight. He can barely be heard above their whistling and applause. His Cecily is frozen.

"Uh—I don't think you should tell me you love me *hopelessly*, Algernon." Her voice is croaky. "Hopelessly doesn't make much sense, does it?"

"It's the *ideal* word." Dropping his cap to the ground, he rises to his feet.

"My dear romantic boy—"

Julian steps forward. Before she can finish, he takes her into his arms and kisses her, in a prolonged open kiss. He kisses with lips that have kissed her. There is nothing tentative about their embrace.

The crowd goes wild. Her arms rise astonished to his elbows. Her soft warm lips kiss him back.

"Oh my," she says.

Louder! Louder! the crowd cries.

"There is no other girl for me," Julian says. "There never was."

And in reply she says, "*Ernest*, my love, I *know*."

Louder! demands the crowd.

"My dear," she says, breathless but louder, "please tell me your name is *Ernest*. It's always been my *dream* to marry someone named *Ernest*. There's something in that name that inspires absolute confidence."

"Cecily, are you saying you could not love me if I had some other name?" Tenderly he holds her wrapped head, touching the strands of her hair, pressing her body to him.

"What—what other name?"

"Julian," he replies.

"You mean *Algernon*?"

"Do you mean you couldn't love me if my name was Julian?"

She is still in his arms, but weak in the legs. Her lips are parted. Her breath is shallow.

"I might respect you," she says, "I might admire you, but I'm afraid that yes, I could not give you my undivided attention…"

"We'll just see about that, won't we?" Cupping her face, he tilts his head to her. They kiss again. They kiss full on, and they don't stop.

Tottering, she finally finds the strength to push him away. It's impossible to talk above the roar of the crowd. Julian and the girl have given the embattled citizens something better than a play, something better than comedy. They have given them life masquerading as art, life real and poignant, an eerie revelry blooming in the dungeons below the blacked-out city.

"Hey, you, why don't you get off there," a tall, unhappy-looking guy calls out, elbowing his way forward. "I mean—get off that door. Two people are not supposed to be on it. It's not safe. Are you all right, my dove?"

Julian's arm is still around the dove's waist. Dove pulls away, brushes Julian off her sweater.

"I'm fine, Finch," she says. "Finch, this is..."

Julian stands. She knows his name. He's not going to help her with it.

"Julian?" she says uncertainly.

"Yes. Julian."

Julian and Finch do not shake hands. Julian brings his right hand behind his back to hide his missing fingers. Before he can ask dove what her actual name is, or what her connection is to the gangly humorless fellow, Finch asks where Julian has come from. He simply might mean tonight, but Julian replies with "Wales!" as confidently as he would say Simi Valley.

"Oh, my goodness," the girl exclaims. "Finch, another Welshman! I'm gobsmacked. Finch is from a small city called Bangor. Where are *you* from, Julian?"

But of course Finch would be from damned Bangor. The only place Julian knows besides Bangor and Cardiff, which is too big and easily disproven, is Rhossili, where Edgar Evans hailed from. So that's what he tells them. Rhossili.

Wouldn't you know it, Finch's entire family hailed from Rhossili! For some reason this pleases the girl *tremendously*, though it doesn't please either Finch or Julian *remotely*.

"I haven't been back for years," Julian says.

"I should think not," Finch says, "because you don't sound at all like a Welshman." Though Finch is probably thirty, he looks as if he shaves sporadically at best. His short hair is carefully parted to the side, and his triangular brown eyes are intense and hostile.

"Yes, lost my accent—"

"You sound almost American, frankly."

"Don't know what *that's* about. Have the Americans come to London...?"

"Maria and I are getting married," Finch blurts, "at Christmas."

Look how much information Julian has gathered from just one short sentence. All sentences should be so brief and informative. Her name is Maria. She is getting married. To the annoyed string bean named Finch. At Christmas.

"Well, Finch," Maria says, "let's not count our chickens just yet. It's almost two months away. There's a war to get through between now and then. Plus, I'm still waiting for that ring you promised."

"I told you I'll get it, dove. Now come," Finch says, extending his hand. "Don't stand on that thing with him. Look, it's teetering. You will fall. Remember last week? You almost fell."

She takes his hand and jumps down, turning back to Julian. "Do you want to come meet our friends?"

"Would love to."

Finch yanks her hand with irritation.

"What, Finch?" she says. "We can't be impolite."

"Why not? We don't know him!"

An older woman stops Julian, grabbing him by the elbows. "Young man, you were *terrific*," she says, squeezing him approvingly. "You gave us all quite a stir—why, me and my friends was saying we haven't felt so aquiver since the Great War when we was young women ourselves. Where did you learn to act like that?"

"Who says I was acting?" Julian says. Both Finch and Maria spin around to stare at him in the tunneled darkness.

"I don't like that man," Julian hears Finch say to her as they walk down the platform. "I don't like him at *all*. I have a good mind to deck him."

"Finch, calm down. It's in good fun. He's just playing with you. Do you want him to continue trying to get under your skin? Keep this up."

"Kissing you like that was playing with me? Who does he think he is?"

"That was *acting*, Finch."

"You heard him, he said it wasn't. And I didn't know that Oscar Wilde called for that sort of passionate ... *acting*."

"What you don't know is a lot, Finch."

"I have a good mind to deck him. Why are you laughing, dove?"

"I wasn't laughing. I was nodding."

"I could do it. You don't think I could do it? I could. I played a fighter in *Jack Dempsey's Life* last year, remember? I know the moves. And what's he going to do? He's crippled like Wild."

"Yes, Wild will love him."

5

Wild

Adjacent to the main passageway between two subway platforms is a small secondary walkway, rarely used. There, Julian comes face to face with a group of vagabonds who have made themselves an abode in the Underground. A dozen people, women and men, young and old, in suits and dregs, sit on stools and benches or lie across the half dozen bunks that line the walls. A bony twentysomething woman sits in an armchair at a wooden table, doing a jigsaw puzzle. Four or five kerosene lamps hang off the bunks; there's a bookshelf, a clothes line, a coat stand; boots on the floor, purses and bags; a large oval mirror propped up against a wall; scarves and hats draping the posts of the beds; and weary faces staring curiously at Julian.

"Who the bloody hell *are* you, mate?" says a grinning blond man, stepping up to Julian. "You nearly gave our Finch a heart attack with your kissing. Well done!" The man is in his early thirties, floppy haired, good looking, but missing most of his right arm. The sweater hangs loose above his elbow. He gives Julian his left hand to shake. Gratefully Julian stretches out his own left hand.

"I'm Wild," the smiling man says. Julian is not sure if he is hearing a name or an adjective. The man doesn't elaborate. He is fit and strong, able-bodied in every way except for the missing arm. "How do you know Folgate?"

"Is that her last name?"

"Wild, leave him alone," Maria says. "Stop interrogating him. Let him meet the rest of the gang before the siren goes."

"*Is* the siren going?" Julian asks. He wishes for no sirens. He wishes for it to be 1942 or 1943, after the terrible beginning and before the terrible end, somewhere in the drudging middle. Please, no sirens.

"Fine, Folgate," Wild says, "but *I'm* going to introduce him, not you. You are atrociously long-winded, as if there isn't a war on. Listen up, everybody!" he yells. "We have a new member…"

Finch protests. "No, we don't!"

"Julian, gang. Gang, Julian." Self-satisfied, Wild turns to Maria. "That's how it's done."

Rolling her eyes, she pushes him in the chest. "Go away," she says. She is familiar with him, unafraid of him, and not in love with him despite his brazen good looks. "Julian, come here and meet Duncan." Duncan is a big guy, at least 6′5″, with a gruff voice and a lamb-like demeanor. He's deaf in one ear and can't serve, Maria says, but like many of their friends, he's a volunteer in the Home Guard, the London Defence League charged with doing whatever is required to help the city get through the nighttime attacks. During the day, Duncan works the docks at Wapping.

"London Defence League?" Julian asks Maria. "You're not part of that, too, are you?" He thought only men could join the LDL. Before she can reply, Duncan and Wild pull him away.

"Folgate, the war will be over before you're done introducing this man. Stop being in love with the sound of your own voice."

"Leave him alone, Wild," Maria says. "Let me—"

"This isn't the stage," Wild continues. "Julian doesn't give a toss about Duncan's deaf ear. I just showed you how to do it. Again, watch and learn. Julian—Nick Moore. Nick—Julian. Nick, say something."

"Fuck off," says Nick, a spindly albino chap, spread out on a lower bunk, smoking and not getting up.

"That's all you need to know about Nick," Wild says. "He knows only two words. Right, Nick?"

"Fuck off."

Nick works at the Ford truck and munitions factory in Dagenham, Maria tells Julian, which at the moment is closed on account of being nearly burned to the ground. So at present Nick is working the Wapping docks with Duncan.

"Julian, do you want to come with us when we go out?" Wild asks.

"Absolutely not!" says Finch, idling close by.

"Sure," Julian says. "Where are you going?"

"Finch, after losing Lester, you well know we could use an extra pair of hands." Wild waves his stump around. "We're a Rescue Squad, Julian. We call ourselves the Ten Bells Watch. Ever hear of the Ten Bells?"

"The pub over in Bethnal Green?" Julian knows that pub. It's not too far from Devi.

"Yes! Good man. When the umpteenth bomb fell into the transept of St. Paul's, and all the stained glass was blasted out, the church got itself a group of volunteers called the St. Paul's Watch whose only job was to douse incendiaries. Well, we're a group of volunteers who douse the incendiaries that fall near Ten Bells."

Julian laughs. "Pub saving is so often overlooked during war."

"My sentiments exactly!" Wild studies Julian with an approving grin.

"Is that where you're all from, Bethnal Green?" Julian doesn't want them to be from there. Bethnal Green gets incinerated during the Blitz. "Does anyone have a newspaper?" What year is it? What month is it?

Reaching into one of the bunks, Wild pulls out the *Evening Standard* and tosses it to Julian, saying to Maria—

But Julian has stopped listening. The paper hangs from his hands.

It's November 8, 1940.

His shoulders turn inward. He couldn't have come at a worse time, a worse month, a worse year. He can't even look up.

The math in his head is brutal. He almost wishes he were back in Invercargill where he did no math at all.

"Are you okay, Julian?" Maria says solicitously.

The 49th day is Boxing Day, the day after Christmas.

She peers into his face.

This can't be the way it ends. It just can't be.

Getting himself together, he takes a deep breath, lifts his head, and smiles.

"I'm fine," he says.

"You want to meet some more people?"

"Sure."

There are a surprising number of men in their motley crew considering all men under 42 must be conscripted. Uh-oh, a wilted Julian thinks, he's only 39, could he, too, be conscripted, before he remembers his missing fingers, his wonky eye, oh and that he has no ID and is not a British citizen. Never mind. Anxiety and logic make strange bedfellows.

With vigor, Duncan takes over hosting duties. He wants to be the one to introduce Julian to the girls, he says. "You got yourself well acquainted with Maria—as we can all attest—but we have other beauties with us, too, who unlike her are currently available. Here are the lovely Sheila and Kate. They're sisters *and* nurses. They're like sisters of mercy," Duncan adds with a mischievous grin, "and I've been asking them for months to show me some mercy." A bald thin smiling man in his sixties jumps out from a lower bunk and cries, "Duncan!" to which Duncan rolls his eyes and sheepishly says, "Sorry, Phil." And quieter to Julian: "That's Dr. Phil Cozens. He's their dad, unfortunately." He sighs. "Over by his side is their mum, Lucinda. When you talk to her, don't mention the war."

Julian smirks. Isn't that line right out of *Fawlty Towers*? But Duncan is not joking. Lucinda, a stout, gray-haired woman, sits on a low bench, knitting to keep her hands busy and chatting to Phil about a trip to the country in the spring. If they book their travel now, she says, they can get a hefty discount.

Julian has no time to shake his head at the idea of planning
a holiday for the coming spring while sleeping underground in
the middle of 1940 London before he's shoved in front of "sexy
Shona," the driver of the medical services truck, and Liz Hope,
"who is a virgin," Duncan whispers, dragging Julian away—past
the mute woman working diligently on the jigsaw puzzle.

"Who's that?"

"Frankie, the bone counter. Never mind her. She doesn't like
living human beings."

"The *bone* counter?"

"I said never mind her!"

Peter Roberts, or "Robbie," has his nose buried in a *Learn
French in Two Months* book. He is a 60-year-old journalist on Fleet
Street. Formal and stiff, he stands up to shake Julian's hand. He is
clean shaven and sharply dressed in a suit and bowtie, which he
carefully adjusts as he gets up, even though it's perfectly straight.
After he shakes Julian's hand, he sits back down and reopens the
French reader. His posture is impeccable.

"Here, Robbie, let me fix that for you, it got crooked again,"
says Wild, flicking up one end of the bowtie.

"When are you going to stop playing your games, Wild,"
Robbie says, calmly rearranging his neckwear.

Robbie's family is in Sussex, Duncan tells Julian, which is
unlucky because recently south England has become "bomb
alley."

"Where is safe?" Julian says to no one in particular, glancing
behind him for a glimpse of Maria's amiable face.

"Here, mate," Wild says. "Home, sweet home."

Julian acknowledges the lived-in, semi-permanent appearance
of their quarters, the books, the coats, the lamps. It's like a college
dorm. "You live here?"

"*Nice*, right?" Flanking Julian, Wild grins. "We're by the
emergency stairs, so we have our own private entrance. We have
Phil on call, several nurses, who also happen to be his daughters,
a chemical toilet at the end of the platform, and even our own

warden. True, he's not especially friendly, but if we throw him five bob, he watches our stuff when we're gone."

Julian clears his throat.

"No, no, whatever you do, don't cough," Maria says, flanking him on the other side, pointing at Phil Cozens. "Even if you're choking. Even if you're sick. Especially if you're sick. Phil assumes it's TB and good old Javert throws you out."

"Maybe it *is* TB," Finch says, hovering over Maria. "Also, he doesn't like to be called Javert, dove."

"She calls them like she sees them," Peter Roberts pipes in, his nose in his French lesson.

"Hear, hear, Robbie!" says Wild—and the air raid siren goes off.

Julian's heart drops. Except for the knitting Lucinda, everyone else stops talking and moving and listens alertly, though no one looks crushed like Julian. "Maybe it's just a warning?" he asks.

"It's always the real thing," Wild replies. "Once or twice a day for some minor shit, and twice a night for the really terrible shit. For the stray bombs, they don't even bother alerting us anymore. Last week, we had our first all clear day since September. The Krauts couldn't fly. We were never more grateful for crap British weather than we were that day, weren't we, Folgate?"

The squad revs into action. Even Frankie leaves her puzzle, gets her coat and goes to stand by Phil's side. The bone counter goes with the doctor? She has the stony demeanor of a mortician. Duncan grabs the sticks and cricket bats piled in the corner next to the umbrellas. In less than two minutes, eight of them are ready to head out. Peter Roberts, Lucinda, and Liz remain behind. So do Nick and Kate. "I'm working a double tomorrow at the docks," says Nick.

"I'm working a double tomorrow at Royal London," says Kate.

Liz says nothing.

"Julian, are you coming?" asks Maria.

"Of course." Why couldn't she be one of the ones who stays behind? Why couldn't she be Liz.

A peevish Finch addresses Julian. "Do you have ID? You can't go outside without it."

"I lost my ID."

"Then you can't go."

"Who's gonna check it, Finch, you?" Wild says, pushing Julian past Finch and toward the stairs. Finch runs around to get in front of them.

"What about your ration card, got that?"

"Lost that, too," Julian replies calmly, despite the fact that Finch is crowding him in the narrow stairwell. "Do I *need* my ration card? Are we going out to eat?"

"He's got you there, Finch," Wild says.

"He won't fit in the jeep," Finch says.

"He will," Wild says. "We'll tie Dunk to the roof."

"Try it," Duncan says, his huge frame towering over Wild.

"Where's your gas mask?" Finch demands. He's being petty and rude and doesn't care. "Because you can't be outside if you don't have one. It's the law."

"Pipe down, archbishop!" Wild says to Finch. "Jules gave his to a dying child. That's why he doesn't have it. Right, Jules?" Smiling, he adds, "You don't mind if I call you Jules, do you?"

"I don't mind," Julian says, scanning Wild's open face.

From his trench coat, Wild produces a gas mask. "Here, take mine. We'll get you another one. Just go to the council tomorrow, say you lost yours."

"Council won't give it to him without ID," Finch says. "You can't go without yours either, Wild. It's the law."

"Blimey, shut up, Finch!" Wild yells. "Folgate, of all the guys out there, why him? You'd be better off with Nick. The man never says a word."

"Fuck off!" says Nick.

"Or old Robbie."

"I'm married, thank you," Peter Roberts says, glancing up from his French book. "Married thirty-five years."

"Us, too," Lucinda says, glancing up from her knitting.

"Married thirty-five years. But my Phil is clearly intent on making me a widow, the way he keeps going out there in the mobile units, risking not just his life, but our daughters' lives as well. Why are you going again, Phil? You just went yesterday. You, too, Sheila."

"I'm a doctor, Luce."

"I'm a nurse, Mum."

"They have plenty of other doctors, other nurses."

"No, they don't."

"I told my kids—peace, war, no matter what, we're staying together," Lucinda tells Julian. "No one is getting evacuated."

"And here we all are, Mum," Sheila says. "Staying together. Going out together on the Mobile Unit. Mum, Kate, want to come? So we can all stay together?"

"Don't be cheeky," Lucinda says. "Someone has to stay with your sister."

The siren continues to wail.

"Mia," Julian calls out, "you don't happen to have an extra coat for me, do you?" Why is he always grubbing for a cloak?

The passageway quietens down. The pitched warble above is the only sound.

"Why did you call me that?" she says. "No one calls me Mia but my mum."

"*Yeah*," Finch says. "Her name is Ma-ri-a."

"You can pronounce your own girlfriend's name?" Wild says. "Well done!" He throws Julian one of his coats. "Here, take mine. Let's go."

"I don't mind you calling me that, by the way," Mia says quietly to Julian in the stairwell. "I just wanted to know why you did, that's all."

"I knew someone like you once," Julian says. "Her name was Mia."

Mia smiles. "Yeah, but did she look like me?"

"She looked just like you."

He doesn't meet her questioning eye as they climb the stairs.

6

Musketeers

THE STREET IS COLD AND DARK. JULIAN BUTTONS HIS COAT.
They feel their way down Princes Street, down the block-long
granite sidewall of the Bank of England. The Rescue Squad jeep
and the Heavy Mobile Unit medical truck are parked behind
the bank on Lothbury. Julian doesn't know how anyone can
find Lothbury. He cannot see his hand before his face. In the
blacked-out city, the streetlights are off, and the windows are
covered with curtains. The night sky is under cloud. Finch gets
behind the wheel of the jeep, Duncan rides shotgun, Julian, Mia,
and Wild pile in the back. Phil, Sheila, Shona, and Frankie ride
separately in the HMU van.

Julian had gambled on where he might end up and has
read a bit about the Battle of Britain, about the bombs and the
ruins. Here's what he didn't read about: under the night sky, the
relentless air raid alarm is an insanity maker. It's an echoey, up
and down howling of a million wolves. Julian doesn't know how
everyone doesn't plug up their ears and scream. His compatriots
seem a lot calmer than he is, even the girl.

Especially the girl.

"Where are we headed to tonight, dove?" Finch says to her.

Leaning over Julian's lap, Mia sticks her head out the window
and listens to the drone of the enemy plane engines. Julian sucks
in his breath and closes his eyes. *Do any of us really know where
we're going, C.J.?*

"Let's drive to Stepney," she says, settling back between Julian and Wild. "Something always falls near the docks." She glances at Julian. He attempts to affect a neutral face. "Stepney, Wapping, Bethnal Green, Shadwell. All of East End is in pretty bad shape. Where are you from, Julian?"

"The East End," Julian replies. "The East End originally," he amends, knowing he won't be able to fake a "been there, seen that" indifference to the coming destruction. "I've been away. Is Finch going to turn the lights on?" Finch is driving without them.

Mia shakes her head. "Can't. Not allowed."

"He plans to drive all the way to Stepney in the dark?"

"That's one of Finch's many gifts," Mia says.

"You mean his only gift," says Wild.

"Shut up, Wild."

"Finch knows the city like a blind man," Mia says.

"And drives like one," says Wild as the jeep rattles over a pothole.

"*You're* not in the Rescue Squad, are you?" Julian asks Mia. Women aren't allowed to join the Home Guard, he refrains from adding. It's for their own safety.

"I am," she replies. "From the side. I'm with the Women's Voluntary Services."

"So what do you do?" Stay in the truck? Keep it running?

"Anything. Everything. Depending on what needs doing. Tonight, for example, you can help by being security with Dunk and Wild until the police come."

Finch scoffs. "What's *he* going to be able to do? You might want to put a glove on that hand of yours, mate. Might appear more menacing."

"He'll act menacing," Mia says. "You're a pretty good actor, right?" Lightly she nudges Julian. "They liked you tonight. They've been getting quite bored with me. Maybe we can put on something else for them if we make it out alive."

If we make it out alive? She says it so carelessly. It's a good thing it's dark, and she can't see the expression on his face.

With the streets empty of vehicles and people, it takes Finch less than seven minutes to get from the Bank of England to Commercial Street, where he pulls up to a curb and idles the engine. Even though it's cold, everyone leaves their windows rolled down. The rumble of a hundred enemy planes is not distant enough.

It takes Julian a few moments to figure out that the squad is waiting to see where the bombs will drop. But what if the bombs fall on Commercial Street? he wants to ask. What if the bombs fall on the jeep where they sit and wait? The rising and falling of the piercing siren has not stopped. The sky flares up, followed by the sound of thunder. The night air is suddenly not as dark. In the brief bursts of light, he can see Mia's calm, focused face.

Lightning.

Thunder.

Rise and fall of the wolf howl.

Like fireworks at a state fair, one two three, a dozen flares all at once, still at some distance downriver. The sound of long booms and sharp cracks gets nearer, grows louder. The bombs whistle and explode. It's one of the most unnerving noises Julian has ever heard. He can't help himself. Turning slightly, he leans against Mia. He wants to cover her with his body. Why would anyone be out in this awful ruckus? It's like being out in a category 5 hurricane.

Lightning is followed by instant thunder over the buildings a few blocks away. Brick-busting explosions, plumes of flame, smoke.

There's screaming.

"Now we go," Mia says.

Finch shifts into drive and races the jeep around the corner, to one of the narrow residential side streets.

Between rows of terraced houses, two bombs have fallen in the street. Choking dusty wreckage rises in the air and small fires light up the cratered holes in the smashed-up homes, windows blown out, doors blown off. The street is littered with brick and wood and glass. There is some human exclamation, but not much on balance, not very much at all, considering. As they get out of the vehicle, Julian hears someone say, rather calmly, "Bloody hell."

Three women covered in black ash stand crying. One of them holds a small child. Wild immediately goes to her and tells her to move away from the house. She refuses. There's a fire in her kitchen, she says, and she just had the cabinets redone, "last spring!" The fire brigade is nowhere to be found. Julian feels that the woman's renovated kitchen might not be the brigade's priority. Four other houses on their street need dousing, and on the next street, the fire already rages. Julian can see it over the rooftops. Because of the fire, there is now light. Night is now day. It's a perversion of what's good in the world.

From the back of the jeep, Wild grabs one of the buckets filled with sand and runs into the woman's house, through the gaping hole in the wall. He heads to the kitchen.

"What is he doing?" Julian asks Duncan, watching Wild fling sand on the woman's cabinets. "By himself, with one arm? Why don't you go help him?"

"You go help him," Duncan rejoins. "Wild used to be a fireman. Who else is crazy enough to run inside a burning house? Don't worry about him. He's wearing a flameproof coat. He knows what he's doing."

The HMU with Shona at the wheel and Phil Cozens shotgun pulls up to Finch, patrolling the street to assess the damage. Finch gives Phil the all clear—meaning there are no injuries at the moment requiring the doctor's immediate attention. This does not seem credible to Julian.

"Duncan, go!" Mia calls, gesturing down the street. Standing next to Julian, Duncan doesn't move. "You're needed there, not here," she says, stepping over the bricks in the street to get closer to them. "Wild will be fine." Julian resists the urge to give her his hand. "Julian, will you go with Duncan, please? The valuables in the bombed houses need to be protected from looters." She must see Julian's expression because she shrugs. "War brings out the worst in some people. Though not that many, fortunately. But if they do come, it's immediately after the bombing. They hurry to get here before the police do."

"The thieves like the jewelry," Duncan says, "but prefer not to put themselves in any real danger."

Mia nods. "Somehow they always manage to find the street with the least catastrophic damage."

Julian glances up and down the block. "This is not catastrophic damage?"

Mia chuckles. "I thought you were from the East End? This is nothing. No real fire, no major casualties. Go, you two. Take the cricket bats."

"Don't need a cricket bat," says Julian.

"I'll take one," Duncan says to Mia. "But I don't need him. I'll be fine. What's he gonna do?"

"Wait, where are *you* going?" Julian catches Mia's arm. "Don't wander off," he says, holding her. "It's not safe." The planes have droned off farther west. But the street is full of flying debris, of falling unstable beams. The air raid siren continues to howl.

"What do you think I do, sit in the car and knit like Lucinda?" Mia says. But she hasn't disengaged from him.

"That sounds wise."

"Wise but not helpful. Look at that poor woman." Mia points down the block where a dusty disheveled older woman stands wailing. "I'm going to help her get her things out before the house falls on her head."

"Oh, you shouldn't do that," Julian says earnestly.

Mia chuckles, as if he is being *so* funny! and rushes off. Julian fights off the urge to rush after her.

Duncan smirks with amusement.

"What?"

"Nothing. Stay put. Watch over Wild. He should be done soon." Both men shake their heads as Wild swats one-armed at the remnants of the flame, using blankets and a piece of cardboard. "He's bloody mental," Duncan says with gruff affection. "As if the mother is going to be able to warm up the milk for her baby in that kitchen. What's the difference if her house burns down now or is demolished in a week? There's no repairing it. Kitchen cabinets! Mental, I tell you. Stay with him, okay?" He walks away.

"If you need help, holler," Julian calls after Duncan, who turns, glances at Julian's fingerless hand, and says yeah, I'll be sure to do that.

A minute later, Wild comes to stand by Julian's side, smelling of heat and smoke.

"How did you do?"

"Not great. There's no saving that kitchen."

"You knew that going in, though, didn't you?"

"I did," Wild says. "But you gotta do what you can. What are you standing guard for?"

"Doing what I can."

"Duncan left you alone? That fucker."

"Not alone," Julian says. "With you. We're going to protect this house together, Wild."

"Nah," Wild says. "I'm no good in a scuffle. Not anymore. I know my limits."

"No, you don't."

"Sometimes those bastards bring sticks and bricks. We need Duncan. Duncan!"

Julian stops him. "We don't need him, and he's busy besides. Just stand on my right, will you? And look tough."

"I got no problem looking tough," Wild says, moving around to Julian's right. "But usually only Duncan can take care of the looters."

"Tonight, you and I are going to take care of them."

With skepticism but no fear, Wild points at Julian's hand. "You want my glove to cover that up? As it so happens, I have an extra." He grins.

Julian shakes his head. "I want whoever comes to see my hand. It acts like an anesthetic. It lulls my opponents into a false sense of confidence in their own strength. My missing fingers become my lucky fingers." He smiles.

"Okay, say they're lulled. Then what?"

"Then, you and I will solve problems together. We'll get creative."

"I can't use a bat."

"Do you see a bat on me?" Julian says. "But you should carry a knife, Wild." Recalling Edgar Evans's Bowie knife that saved his life even as it nearly ended it.

"I'm a righty. Can't use a knife with my left hand."

"Sure you can. I was a righty, too. Once."

Wild appraises the severed half-hand, the man. "You want to show me how?"

"Not in the next five minutes. Have you got a hammer at least?"

"For you?"

"No, for you."

Wild shakes his incredulous head.

"What, you can't even swing a hammer left-handed? You just spent fifteen minutes whacking a useless kitchen cabinet!"

For now, knifeless and batless and hammerless, Julian and Wild stand shoulder to shoulder on a pile of bricks and wood. The siren wails up and down. What has Julian's girl gotten herself into? Doesn't she know it's the end of the line?

"Stepney has it worse," Wild says as they wait. "Anything near the river is a shambles. That's how you gotta look at everything—some poor fucker somewhere has it worse. Like: sure my arm is gone, but that's why the good Lord thought to give me a spare."

"How'd you lose it?"

"Don't want to talk about it."

Julian glances at Wild's suddenly distorted face, at his body struggling not to double over, and looks away.

The ambient light from the nearby fires illuminates the street. In the glimmer, Julian's eyes search for Mia. He spots her a few houses down, comforting the old woman who has stopped wailing. His gaze steadies and rests on her. When he blinks, he catches Wild staring at him.

"Who *are* you?" Wild says. "It's like you know Folgate from another life."

"That must be it." He nudges his new friend. "Heads up," Julian says quietly. "On my ten."

From the left, three young guys appear stealthily out of the darkness, heading for the house in front of which Wild and Julian stand. "See, if you hadn't put out the fire in the damn kitchen, they'd walk right past us," Julian says to Wild, and louder to the trio, "Move along. You have no business here."

"And what business do you have here?" one of them says.

Wild shows them his Home Guard badge.

"Step out of the way, cripple," an intense-looking chap says, approaching them. "You too, old man," he says to Julian. "You don't want to get hurt."

"*You* don't want to get hurt," Julian says.

"Nice one, Jules," Wild whispers.

"Thanks, Wild."

The three boys laugh. They taunt Julian. "What are you going to do, swat at us? Point at us with your pointer?"

"He can't even make a V sign!"

Julian turns his body sideways and kicks the talking bloke straight in the chest. The guy falls backwards. His head hits the bricks. "Move, Wild," Julian says, and to the attackers, "Go on, you two. I told you, you don't want to get hurt."

The two young men menace Julian, both edging to his right, where they assume he is weakest. One guy swings a stick. Julian catches the stick in the crook of his right elbow and chops the guy on the side of the neck with his open left palm. The boy reels, is thrown off balance, and now Julian is armed. He hits the guy once on the forearm and even harder across his shoulder, all secondary but debilitating injuries. He squares off against the remaining youth. "Did you see how gently I tapped your friend's arm with his own stick?" Julian says. "I could've bashed him in the face. And then he'd be dead. But, the night is still young. So what would you like to do? Run? Or fence?"

The dude clearly has learned nothing. He swings. Julian blocks, and kicks him in the knee. Howling, the guy drops to the ground. The entire confrontation has taken no more than twenty seconds.

Wild is overjoyed. "Finch, Dunk!" he yells. "Come here. I can't fucking believe it! Did you see that?"

"He hit the dirt with such a beautiful thud," Julian says with a light smile.

Finch and Duncan run over. Finch is not overjoyed. "No reason to knock them out like that," he says dourly. "The cops will be here soon."

"And now there's less for them to do," says Julian.

"Don't listen to a word Finch says, Jules," Duncan says. "That was amazing."

"You got lucky, that's all," Finch says. "You caught them off guard."

"You're right, I did," Julian says agreeably. "Otherwise I wouldn't stand a chance." He winks at Wild.

Wild throws his one arm around Julian. "Jules, you've been baptized by fire. You're now officially a member of our Ten Bells Watch. Finch, go get him a Home Guard badge."

"I can't get him anything without an ID."

"Get him an ID, too, Finch, or I'll beat you with his stick," Duncan says cheerfully.

Finch points to the groaning men. "What do you propose to do with them?" he says to Julian.

"Get me some rope, Duncan," Julian says. "More may be coming, and I don't want to worry about these three."

"The rope we have is not for tying up delinquents," Finch

says. "The rope is for rescues, for saving lives. In case people are trapped and need to be pulled out."

"Yes, thank you, Finch," Julian says. "I know what rescue means. I don't need a lot. I do need a knife, though."

Duncan brings him a tangle of rope and a knife.

"No one here knows how to tie a knot," Finch says. "So I don't know what good the rope will do you."

In half a minute, Julian binds all three men's ankles and wrists with handcuff knots. Grimly Finch looks on, while Duncan and Wild celebrate. "We finally found our third musketeer, Dunk!" Wild says.

"We sure did, Wild."

"So what was I, then?" says Finch.

"Aww, you're not a musketeer, Finch," Wild says. "You're more like Richelieu."

Finch ignores the mockery. "I think you made it too tight," he says to Julian, "their circulation will be cut off."

"That'll teach them to loot houses," Julian says, kicking one of them in the ribs. "Bastards."

When Mia reappears in the street, Wild and Duncan call her over and interrupting each other tell her what happened, while she listens, twinkling approvingly at Julian. "He did that, did he?" she says. A disgusted Finch storms off.

"Folgate, Julian's going to show me how to use a knife and a hammer," Wild says. "And tie a handcuff knot."

"Okay, let's pipe down, Wild," Julian says. "I'm not a magician. You can't tie knots with one hand."

"Who says?"

"As you were, boys," Mia says. "But, Duncan, I need you. That woman is trying to drag a trunk the size of a cupboard out of her house. It's too heavy for her, and it's too heavy for me. I tried, but I can't move it."

"I'll help you, Mia," Julian immediately says, handing the stick to Wild.

"There you go," Wild says. "Jules will help you, *Mia*."

"Shut up, Wild," she says.

"Yeah," says Julian. "Shut up, Wild."

"Folgate, are you sure you don't want Finch to help you move some heavy furniture?" Wild says, not shutting up—just the opposite.

"Shut up, I said! Of course I asked Finch first, but he's busy. Pay no attention to him, Julian, come along."

Leaving the boys snickering behind them, Julian and Mia make their way through the debris on the street to the old woman's house. "They're impossible," she says. "Don't mind them. They're just teasing."

"I know," Julian says, inexpressibly pleased to be teased. "And I don't mind."

"So you know how to fight?" Mia says.

"I got lucky."

"Sure you did," she says, giving him an amused up and down. "I think it's us who got lucky when you found us. I can't tell you how badly we needed someone like you. Now that Lester's gone, Duncan's the only one facing the thieves. Nick comes sometimes, but he doesn't like to fight. Wild likes to, but can't. Hard to find someone who likes to and can."

"Who says I like to?"

"I don't know." She squints at him. "You have that look about you."

Julian squints at her in return, takes a breath. "Glad to help. Who is Lester?"

"One of us. He died last week," she says. "A blast got him."

At the house, Mia holds the kerosene lamp to light the way, and together she and Julian locate the woman's half-open trunk in the debris of her partially destroyed home. The woman stands out in the street, shouting orders in a trembling but grateful voice. Near the spilled-out trunk lie necklaces and photo albums, a torn and dusty wedding veil, a child's baptismal gown.

"Thanks for helping me," Mia says to Julian as they collect the valuables. "Look how precious these small things are to her."

"They're not small," Julian says. "They're irreplaceable."

"I guess. Often, finding these items is what matters most to these poor people. Not the house, but the wedding rings."

Before he can respond, the all clear sounds. It's an intense, one-note, high-pitched shriek, and it lasts one interminable minute. Julian can't express the relief he feels for the blessed silence that follows. "Mia, you don't do this every night, do you?" he says as they drag the trunk over the bricks. *Please* tell me you don't do this every night.

"We try for every night. It doesn't always work out." She chuckles. "Sometimes Nick and Wild and Dunk get so drunk they can't go anywhere when the siren calls. Finch judges them pretty harshly for that. He never overindulges."

"In anything?"

That makes Mia blush for some reason and hurry past it without replying. "And the week Dunk had a concussion, I didn't go. It wasn't safe." She shrugs, calmly acknowledging the reality of certain disadvantages of being a woman during war. "The thieves bring big wooden sticks. It's a good thing all scrap metal, including tire irons, has been requisitioned by the city. Otherwise they'd be swinging iron, not wood, and we'd all be in a lot worse shape."

After they pull the trunk out into the street and leave the old woman sitting on it, Julian looks Mia over. "Are you okay?" He stops her from walking. With his thumb, he wipes a trickle of blood off her forehead.

"Tonight was nothing." She smiles. "It's not always this easy."

"This was easy?" Three houses destroyed, valuables lost, families homeless, looters. Seeing her quizzical expression, he coughs. "I mean, of course it's been worse, but surely this wasn't easy."

Mia tells Julian that once Duncan had to battle six guys on his own.

"Well, I can attest that's certainly not easy," Julian says.

Sometimes parachute mines float down, she tells him, and when you get close to them, they explode and rip you open. That's what happened to Lester. "Have you seen them?" When Julian shakes his head, she continues. Sometimes the incendiaries fall and everything is aflame and no one can get out. "Have you seen any of that?"

Julian nods. That he has seen, everything on fire and no way out. "People get caught under walls and broken glass."

"Yes. Children—the few that are left—get trapped in the houses with their mums and grandmas and aunts. The older men and the kids can't help. They sit nearby and watch their loved ones die under rubble no one can move or in a fire that's out of control."

"Are you afraid of fire, Mia?" Julian says, mining her face.

"I'm not *not* afraid of it," she says, undisturbed by his scrutiny. "It's not my favorite thing."

He wants to ask her what her favorite thing is but doesn't. What if she says it's Finch?

"Today we helped a little," Mia says. "But sometimes we can't. Are you ready for that, to do everything in your power and still not be able to save the lady under the rubble?"

"No."

He will never be ready for that.

7

Folgate

MIA BRINGS HIM A MUG OF HOT TEA FROM THE REFRESHMENT truck. Julian must look as if he needs it.

"Where are you really from?" she says, looking at him calmly but questioningly. "Forgive me for saying this, but you look like this was your first bombing."

"No, no, not my first," he says hurriedly. "But I told you, I've been away. Just came back recently."

"You'll get used to it," Mia says. "We all did. We had to. What a time to come back, though. Why didn't you stay where you were? Where were you, Wales?" she asks, sparing him an answer. "Bet it was safer."

"It's true, Mia, there are magical dangers here," Julian says. "But this is our last stand."

"By *our*, you mean London, right? Not…" She flicks her finger between him and her and smiles, like a joke. And he forces a smile in return, like a joke also.

They remain at the site until almost daybreak. Eventually the fire brigades arrive and the police, and the rescue services, who remove the possessions from the blasted-out homes. The Incident Officer appears in an enormous truck. Finch works closely with the IO and without Finch's meticulous itemization of damages, the IO's job would be much harder. Finch is indefatigable. Hours after the all clear, he is still interviewing people, taking down information, even comforting them occasionally, if awkwardly. He tags what's been found, he lists what's been lost. He catalogs everything. He is like a less genius and less genial George Airy.

"Finch does this every night?" Julian asks Mia, a grudging respect creeping into his voice.

"Day *and* night," she replies. "This is his full-time job. He gets paid by the Bethnal Green Council. There's bombing during the day, too. You don't know that either, East Ender? When did you get here, yesterday?"

"Hardy-har-har." Sipping the tea that has cooled down much too quickly, Julian chortles and sputters, pretending her question is a rhetorical jest. Daytime attacks, too? Julian thought Wild had been exaggerating.

After the anarchy of the bombing, the organized, measured response to the madness makes Julian feel worse, even more out of sorts. He is used to punch for punch, slam for slam, kick for kick. He is not used to clipboards and quiet conversation after a wholesale demolition, not used to pale slim cordial indispensable women casually sifting through the debacle on a stranger's behalf, looking for lost dolls and pearls.

In the blue icy pre-dawn, things look more surreal, not less.

The IO's men spend hours loading the truck with items that have been recovered and tagged to haul to the storage depot or the "strong room." Mia, Julian, Finch and Duncan continue to bring the valuables out into the street, one by one, little by little, precious toys, a fire truck, an heirloom Bible. Mia advises the dispossessed families to keep what's most dear to them on their person, not to lose sight of it. The face she presents to the families is one of unflagging optimism and kindness. It's going to be okay, she keeps saying. Your things will be found. The council will find you a new place to live. The shelters are warm and there's food. Don't worry. Keep your chin up. Don't panic.

She's a far cry from the frightened and desperate woman Julian found in Invercargill. Mia lives amid death, yet has not been ruined by the knowledge of her own death. *Poor Shae*, Julian thinks, bowing his head as if in prayer.

Julian, you're a fool.

The Inferno is no place for pity.

In the past, he tried to look too far ahead, and now he's being punished by being unable to look ahead even one more day.

Punished or rewarded?

We may be hopeless, Mia. But we're not broken.

"Who are you praying for, Julian?" Mia says, coming up to him. The face she presents to him, too, is one of unflagging optimism and kindness.

His expression must confuse her, because she averts her gaze. "Do you want to sit, rest your feet a bit? You look exhausted. They'll be okay, they're used to it," she says when she sees him scanning for Duncan and Wild. "Let's sit."

He and Mia huddle on the debris. Now that the fires have been doused and there's hardly any warmth, the slush is turning to ice. Julian wants to put his arm around her. She seems so cold. He gauges how far Finch is from them, whether he can see them. He's quite far and paying them no attention, but Julian decides not to antagonize the man any more than necessary, though he yearns to draw her to him, to embrace her.

"Maybe we should all go inside the strong room," Julian says, "and leave the trinkets outside."

"Why, are you tired of living?" She says it in jest.

"I'm not *not* tired," he replies, wanting to fall asleep right then and there, on top of a crumbled house, next to her. He has been in the river, in the dry beds, in the tunnels, in the flames, awake for weeks or days. "What are we waiting for?"

"Finch," Mia says. "It's at least another hour before he's done. He drives us back."

Julian's head bobs forward. Feeling her gaze on him, he shakes to stay alert.

"You got nowhere to go," she asks. It's not a question.

"I got nowhere to go."

"So come back with us. We have room. The more, the merrier. Come back."

What Julian wants is for her to go with him. Come with *me*, Mia. Come *away* with me. Away from this madness.

But come with him where, the hospital in Scutari, the demon fire, the deepest ocean? "Are you sure?" he says. "You look pretty full up at Bank. And your boyfriend doesn't like me."

"Can you blame him?" Mia smiles, self-aware but jokey. "Don't worry, you've made a friend in Wild. You'll be fine. He loves the girls but doesn't usually take to the boys like he's taken to you."

"There's no place for me," he says.

"Sure, there is," she says. "At night, you'll be with us, and during the day you can sleep in Robbie's bunk. He leaves for work at seven."

"What about you, where do you sleep?"

"Who wants to know?" She smiles. "Just kidding. You saw where. One of the top bunks is mine. All the girls are in the top bunks."

They exchange a glance. "For safety?" he asks.

She nods. "At Bank, we haven't had any problems with assaults and whatnot—touch wood, as Mum would say—but other places have had some trouble, and it's always better to be safe."

Always better to be safe, says the fragile girl whose life has been threatened and snuffed out up and down the centuries, now sitting in the rubble caused by high explosives, the rubble to which she has traveled out of her soul's own free will.

"You don't have a house in London," Julian asks, "a family?"

"I had both," Mia replies. "The house got bombed, the family left. Of course I could go to a proper rest center up on Old City Road, but they're overcrowded, and I don't want to stand in the street all day with my blanket, queueing for a space. Finch and I did that back in September. Bollocks to that, we said after a day." Mia takes out a cigarette, offering one to Julian. At first he refuses, and then accepts. Why not? They light up. Her lighter says *sad girls smoke a lot.*

"You don't seem sad," Julian says, inhaling the smoke, coughing, inhaling again.

Mia concurs. "I'm not sad. But the girl who died, she was sad. It was hers."

"Why was she sad?"

"Because she died."

He likes the camaraderie of smoking with his beloved over bombed-out ruins in a war. In *the* war. It's not the worst thing they've shared, by far. "None of you has a home?"

"Robbie has a home," Mia replies. "In Sussex. Liz has a home in Birmingham. But those places are getting hit pretty hard. Phil Cozens has a home, but he doesn't sleep there, because he's paid to be on call at Bank. It's not too bad at Bank, really. You'll see. They've spruced up many of the Underground shelters. Bank is like a fine hotel. There's even a refreshment center." She smiles wistfully, glancing down the street for the refreshment truck that's long left.

"Do you work?" Julian asks. "Or is this your day job, too?"

Mia has a different day job. She works at the Lebus Furniture Factory on Tottenham Court Road. She sleeps until ten or eleven in the morning and then goes in. Her boss doesn't mind; he knows why she is up all night.

"Do *you* work?" she asks, looking inside Wild's cloak at Julian's well-made suit, now dusty.

"I did. I had a restaurant on Great Eastern Road. It's gone now. Along with my flat right above it."

"Restaurant? I'm so hungry," she says. "What kind of food did you make, Cornish pasties? Shepherd's pies?"

"Beef noodle soup. Squid with garlic. Shrimp rolls."

"Tell me about it. Don't spare any details."

When Finch spots them sitting on the broken pile next to each other, he looks upset, even at a distance, even in the early light. But Julian takes the cue for how to behave from Mia. She doesn't move away from him. So he doesn't move away from her. Julian is not the keeper of her relationship with Finch. If he's overstepping his bounds, she'll let him know. But Julian doesn't think he is overstepping. Something about the way she kissed him back when they pretended to be Cecily and Algernon. As if she had been longing to be truly kissed.

While they wait for Finch to finish up, Mia tells Julian bedtime stories, and he nearly falls unconscious to the sound of her achingly familiar soft breathy voice. She's known most of the Ten Bells gang since primary school. She, Shona, and Finch grew up together on Folgate Street in the back of Spitalfields Market, and in September were made homeless together. For the first few weeks, they roamed the streets like beggars, and then found the passageway at Bank.

Shona, the medi truck driver, is a tough cookie, while Liz Hope is the opposite. "She is a soft cookie. Like a sponge cake." Liz began a promising, bookish career at the British Museum, but now that the Museum has shuttered indefinitely for the war, she's out of a job and out of sorts. Sometimes she volunteers for the church truck, serving refreshments to the dislocated, but mostly feels she's not doing enough. "She can't help it," Mia says. "People are not going to change just because of a little bombing. The truth is, Liz is terrified of the bombs. Going out into the darkness during the attacks is not an option for her."

Liz seems like the sanest of the bunch. "Why can't you be more like Liz," Julian says.

"You mean chaste and shy?" Mia is grimy yet shiny. She smiles. Every time Mia smiles, Finch manages to see it from wherever he is. Maybe because she lights up like a firework.

"I mean safe and underground," Julian says. "But chaste and shy, too, if you want, sure."

"You want me to hide from life in the dungeons?"

"Not from life," he says. "From death."

"There's nowhere to hide," she says. "A month ago, a bomb fell near the entrance at Bank. It killed twenty people and left a crater in the road so large it had to be spanned by a makeshift bridge. The Bank of England was untouched, though."

"Maybe we should hide inside the Bank of England." Julian says *we* but he means *you*.

Liz likes being part of the squad, Mia says, but because of her agonizing shyness has a hard time speaking up in a group setting. And a group setting is how they live these days. There is no private setting.

"So how do you and Finch make it work?" Julian asks, looking at his hands instead of at her. "In a group setting," he adds carefully.

There is a longish pause. "Biding our time is how," she replies. She returns to talking about Liz, glossing over his silence with a brisk "What option do we have?" as if she can read his thoughts.

Who's got the time to stay put, to linger?

Not you.

Last week, Robbie started taking Liz to work with him on Fleet Street. She now proofs his articles for the *Evening Standard*. She's never had a boyfriend but has had a paralyzing crush on Wild for years, and after his accident last summer, if anything, loves him even more because he is less perfect and therefore more accessible to her and therefore more perfect.

Wild's real name is Fred Wilder. "Isn't that funny? Wild is *Freddie*. He's been trying to rebel against his plumber name since birth." As if the moniker weren't punishment enough, his parents had named his younger brother Louis. "So one brother's a plumber, the other a French king. I mean, that's Wild's life in a nutshell."

"Where's Louis?"

Mia shakes her head, glancing around for Wild, as if he might be nearby and can hear. "We don't talk about Louis."

"Ah," Julian says. "Okay." Beat. "So, tell me about you."

"What about me?"

"You've told me about Liz, about Shona, about Wild. What's your story?"

"I told you."

"I mean, other than the war."

"Is there anything other than the war?" she says. "I almost don't remember." Before the war, she strived for the West End stage, but that's been put on hold, like everything. "Two bombings and my beloved Palace Theatre on Cambridge Circus has been boarded up!" she says with indignation. "As if people don't need entertainment during war. They need it even more, if you ask me."

Julian agrees.

"Do you know that theatre?"

"I do," he says. "Once upon a time, a man loved his wife so much, he built her the most magnificent theatre in all of London, so she could go to the grand opera any time she wanted."

"Yes!" Mia exclaims, staring at him in amazement. "How do you know that? No one but me knows that."

"And me."

Warmed and softened, Mia tells him about her work at Lebus, the furniture factory, becoming especially animated when she describes what they've started building for the war. "We take the hollowed-out frames of double-decker buses and paint them red. No engines, no transmissions, just the frames."

"Like the cargo cult planes in Melanesia," Julian says pensively.

"The what?"

"Never mind. Continue. Why do you do that?"

"We paint on the fake windshields, the wheels, even the numbers on the buses," Mia says, "and we place them around the outskirts of town, where they're easy to spot. The Germans bomb our decoy buses, while inside the city, we get to carry on with our business."

"Aha. Like building film sets. Except for real life."

"Yes, precisely! Fake buses for real life."

Julian and Mia continue to sit together on top of the crumpled exterior wall, hunched over, their feet on the window frames. They're covered head to toe in mortar dust, even their faces and mouths. She tightens her headscarf under her wool hat, breathes into her gloved hands.

Her mother is up in Blackpool with her Aunt Wilma, her three cousins and their seven kids. Aunt Wilma is atypically British. She is not calm. When the bombs started falling in September on a daily basis, Wilma became hysterical. Her vocal panic traumatized her grandchildren, Mia's second cousins. "And don't think that my mum doesn't mention every chance she gets that her sister is a grandmother *seven* times over and my mum not even once." So Wilma packed up the family and shuffled off to Blackpool where their family is from.

"Why didn't you go with them?" *Why, why,* didn't you go with them.

"My life is here." She draws the coat across herself. "I'm with my friends, so I don't care. I'll admit that when I first saw the Luftwaffe fly overhead with no Spitfires or Hurricanes in sight, I thought I was watching my own destruction." She peers at him. "Kind of the way you're acting today."

Julian says nothing. His eyes lock with hers. "Like I'm watching whose destruction?" he says quietly.

Mia sputters and moves on. "The first bomb that hit our house blew the roof off," she says.

"The *first* bomb?"

"Oh, yes. The brigade pulled my mum out from under the dining room table, the table fine, my mum fine, and she yells to me, Mia, I told you it was a good table!" The young woman smiles in remembrance. "The council said they could do nothing for us, and we should consider ourselves lucky that we had a roof over our heads, and I pointed up to the open sky and said, do you have *eyes*? What roof? The chap got mad and left." She laughs. "After we got bombed, we got free refreshment for two days. At first, Mum said it was nice and we should get bombed more often. We had the Emergency Londoners' Meal Service. We had our bath in the mobile bath units—I call it the human laundry—and did our washing in the mobile laundry that was parked a block away from us on Commercial Street. It was cold in our house without a roof, but it was still September so it wasn't too bad, and we were together. Aunt Wilma was next door with her kids and her kids' kids, and Mum liked that. Truth be told, I liked it, too. I'm close to Wilma's youngest daughter, Kara. She and I were born the same year. She's like my twin. She's funny."

"Funnier than you?"

"Like, who even could be?" Mia smiles. "But then a bomb fell on Wilma's house, and all the wood and glass ended up in *our* living room, and then it rained for a week straight, and that wasn't funny. So Mum agreed that maybe it was time to go and my aunt said, you *think*? After they left, I stayed for a few days alone in the house, but then another incendiary fell, and, well, you know." Mia hops up and extends her hand to him. "You want to go see what's left of my house? Come on. We still have a few minutes before Finch is done. It's just around the corner."

They hurry to Commercial Street. "The bombs have torn all the leaves off the trees," Julian says. "That's why it looks like winter."

"Silly boy," Mia says. "It looks like winter because it's actually winter."

Folgate Street is a short narrow road between two large wide thoroughfares, Bishopsgate and Commercial.

Not much is left of Folgate. Most of the two dozen homes are rubble except for the four corner ones. They have craters inside them, and only partial roofs, but families continue to live there. Even milk and newspapers continue to be delivered, the milk in tins.

In the middle of Folgate, Mia's flattened house is black cinder and dust.

"Mum said she'd be back as soon as she had my aunt and cousins settled," Mia says, "but I telegraphed her to say not to bother. Where is she going to go? She can't live at Bank with me. I admit, I'm a little jealous of Lucinda and her family. Sure, Lucinda's a nutter, but Sheila and Kate have their mum. It was nice when Mum and I were together and could wash our clothes in the laundry truck. Of course then the gal who'd been driving it died. Her lungs got filled with dust. It's her lighter I'm using." Mia smokes another cigarette as they walk back, slowly. "When my house collapsed, I walked away. Mum taught me to do that. She said, eyes forward, and never look back; otherwise, you'll be carrying the weight of that house with you the rest of your life."

If only Julian could heed that advice.

"What's Wild's story, Mia? Tell me quick, before we return."

"Okay, but you can never tell him I told you," she says. "He lost his arm when he was trying to save his brother. A bomb fell during one of the early attacks in July, and Louis got trapped in their burning house. Wild tried to get him out. Louis kept telling Wild to go, but Wild wouldn't leave him. Then the wall frame shifted, and he got stuck. He couldn't get even himself out. Wild watched his brother die as their house burned down around them. He barely escaped himself. The firemen had to cut off his arm to save his life. Their parents were outside in the street, while their two sons were trapped inside."

Julian lowers his head.

"It wasn't great," Mia says. "It's still not good. Being a fireman was all Wild wanted to be since we were kids, and now he's got no brother, no arm, and can never be a fireman. Can you imagine?"

"Yes," says Julian.

8

Tales of Love and Hate

HE DOESN'T NEED TO USE ROBBIE'S BUNK BECAUSE WILD offers him his. Julian sleeps like the dead, all day and through two sirens, as he learns when he wakes up. At night the Ten Bells collect in the alcove. They've eaten and drunk elsewhere, but Wild somehow divines that Julian is starving and shares some bread with him and the rest of his small bottle of cheap whiskey. The gang appears to be in good spirits, except for Finch, who looks as if he can't believe Julian is still around.

"Why are you giving him your food, Wild?" Finch asks.

"I share my food with him, Finch, because that's what Jesus would do," Wild replies, mock-solemn. "Who are you serving?"

"That's not what I mean, and you know it. He could use some charity, obviously. I mean, where is the man's ration card?"

"Or what, he'd eat like a king if he had one?" Wild says. "Hey, all you kingly ration-card holders, who wants some whalemeat? Delicious whalemeat right here! And look what else I might have for you with your royal ration card. I have one ounce of creamy butter, freshly churned. Now, Jules," Wild says, his one arm hooking around Julian's neck, "when you find your card, you will get one pat of butter a week. But it's your choice how you use it. You have free will during the war, and don't ever forget it. You can eat your pat of butter all at once or you could spread it out over seven days—like Finch."

"*Everybody's always pinching me butter,*" Mia sings with a naughty wink. "*They won't leave me butter alone.*"

"Come on, dove, don't joke like that," Finch says. "It's not proper."

"Who won't leave your butter alone, Folgate?" Wild says with a naughty wink himself, not letting go of Julian's neck. "Put a name on it, will ya?"

"Do you see what I mean?" Finch says to Mia.

"Just having fun, Finch," says Mia.

"Just having fun, Finch," says Wild.

"Someone, explain to Finch what fun is," says Duncan.

"How is making fun of me fun?" says Finch.

"In so many ways, Finch, I can't count them all," says Wild.

Carefully, quietly, Julian pats Wild on the back, two gentle pats, hoping no one will notice, not even Wild.

The men and women in the alcove circle around Julian to make him feel welcome. "Don't worry, Julian, it's nice here at Bank," Shona the driver tells him, speaking in a loud, guttural twang. She is narrow of eye and body. Her hair is tied up with a head scarf. "But it would be even better if we had a place to keep chickens and pigs. Then we'd really have something. What I wouldn't give for some extra bacon and a chicken."

"We're not allowed chicken and pigs in the Underground, Shona," says Finch.

Shona ignores him, continuing to address Julian. "Hyde Park has a piggery, right next to where the buses park for the night."

"Exactly. A park. Not the Underground," Finch says.

"But, Shona, darling," says Duncan, his gruff voice softened to a quaver, "if we had somewhere to put your chickens and pigs, Wild would kill them, cook the shit out of them, and eat them before you had a chance to say where is my little piggy."

"Dunk's right, Shona," Wild says. "That's exactly what I would do."

"You can't have chickens in the Underground," Finch doggedly repeats, in the deep black underground where beneath a gap in the busted pavement human beings have made themselves a home.

It's chilly in the tunnels. To repay their hospitality, Julian shows his new friends how to make a Swedish flame. Out on the empty eastbound Central Line platform, he uses a small axe (not an ice axe) to make six vertical cuts in one of the wood logs, as if he's slicing a cake. He makes the cuts not all the way through, leaving the log with a few inches intact at the base. He pours two spoonfuls of kerosene into the center of the log and throws a match after it. The log burns for over two hours. They leave it standing, warm their hands and faces over it, make hot water, make tea, and then fit around it right on the platform, as if having a campfire.

Wild happily starts referring to Julian as Swedish.

As in, "Swedish, where did you learn to do that?"

And, "Swedish, what else do you know? Anything, for example, that might be useful to Folgate?"

"Shut up, Wild!"

"Shut up, Wild!" Finch says, and then quieter to Mia, "It's because you were singing that butter pinching song that he talks like that."

"Believe me, Finch, it's not because of that song," Wild says, turning to Julian. "Swedish, where did you learn to fight with your left?"

The young people on the platform sit around the burning log, sipping tea and whiskey. Their eyes are on Julian. Mia sits next to Finch. Her eyes are on him, too.

"You can learn it, too, Wild," Julian replies. "Show them your mangled right claw, and while they're gloating about how they're going to lick you, wallop them with your left. You don't even need to make a fist. Though you can."

"That's not what you did."

"I trained for a long time to learn to fight southpaw. Also, to be fair, last night I didn't fight."

"What was it, then?" Duncan says. "Those three were down on the ground before they knew what hit them."

"Like I said."

When he sees Mia smile, Finch points to Julian's missing fingers. "One of the real fights didn't go so well for you, eh?"

Julian shrugs. "As they say, Finch, dead men tell no tales. And I'm still here. Make of that what you will."

"Oh, tell us, Swedish!" Wild says. "Don't hold back. We love a good story. Nothing better in the dungeons during war than to drink awful Irish whiskey with friends and listen to a rousing tale of mayhem. The only thing better than a story about a fight is a real fight."

Everyone seconds *hear, hear,* even the girls!

"But I suppose that's too much to ask," Wild adds wistfully. "So, tell us what happened."

Julian shrugs. "I got into it with a guy."

"What guy?"

"A guy who wanted a fight. He grabbed my knife that dropped on the ground. I jerked my hand just enough, or he would've taken it off at the wrist, and I would've bled out. That knife was like the fucking guillotine—excuse me, ladies."

Julian! Watch out! Unsteadily, he reaches for the cup of whiskey in Wild's hand.

"Maybe you shouldn't have left your knife lying around like that," Finch says.

"You're right, Finch," Julian says. "I definitely shouldn't have."

"That is a *terrible* story." To everyone's surprise, the man who says this is Peter Roberts. They didn't think he was even listening. He is a few feet away from them at the table, at his customary spot next to Frankie the puzzle maker. "Young man," Roberts says sternly, as if scolding Julian, "don't you know that the human capacity to contemplate life, to feel, to tell stories, is holy? It comes from the immortal soul. No animal does it, sits around the fire and tells stories. Only humans. And what you've just told us is not a story. You've merely summarized some distant events without passion or prejudice. There was nothing real in it, and therefore we felt nothing. For shame."

Wild grins, knocking into Julian. "That's a first, Swedish. With your deeply inadequate storytelling skills, you've roused the previously silent Robbie. The bowtie journalist claims you can do better. What say you?"

Julian takes a long swig of whiskey. Finch complains about how much of the common liquor he's drinking. Julian promises Finch he'll get more. But for now, he's sufficiently langered to tell them a proper story. He has many. Which one would they like to hear first? He's got one about a hanging in Tyburn. He's got one about murder in a brothel. And he's got one about a fight to the death at sea.

The kids look to Peter Roberts for guidance. The dignified man considers his choices. He's even put down his French lesson book! "Robbie," Mia says, "would you like to come over here and sit with us by the fire? Duncan, go help Robbie with his chair."

"Don't you dare, Duncan." Getting up, Peter Roberts grabs his own chair. "I'm sixty, Maria, I'm not an invalid. Someday when you're sixty, you'll understand."

"Swedish," Wild says, "why did you flinch just now when Robbie said that?"

"Why are you always studying him, Wild?" Finch snaps. "Who cares why he flinched? Who cares why he does anything," the man adds in a peevish mumble.

"Finch, shh. Robbie, come," Mia says. "Guys, make room."

Peter Roberts sets his chair in the circle among the young. "Since there may not be a tomorrow," he states philosophically, "Julian might as well start with the sea battle."

The young women grumble, pleading for something more delicate, all except the tough-cookie Shona, who doesn't do delicate, and Frankie, who remains with her puzzle and offers no opinion.

The boys shout the girls down. "No one wants a soft story, ladies," Wild says.

"Don't worry, Wild," Julian says, "even my soft stories end in death."

"Is there any *love* in your stories?" Liz asks quietly, leaning forward. The gang gasps. Liz has spoken! Liz opened her mouth and spoke to a stranger in a public setting! They cheer. They raise a glass to Julian for making Liz speak and for getting Peter Roberts to put down his French book.

"If only we could separate Frankie from her puzzle, then we'd really have something," Kate says, glancing over to the table. Frankie blinks but doesn't respond.

Julian smiles at Liz. "What kind of slapdash story would it be, Liz, if it wasn't about love?" he says. "Yes. Every good story is about love."

Now they *really* want to hear.

"Even the death at sea story?" Liz asks. A romantic tremble animates and beautifies her plain, freckled face.

"Especially that one," Julian says. "Because that one is about the truest love of all. A love that just is, and asks for nothing back. It's easy to tell a story full of sexy words about beautiful people loving each other in sunny climes."

"I wouldn't mind hearing *that* story," Mia echoes, sounding like someone who's rarely seen either.

Julian doesn't dare look at her, lest he give himself away. He continues to address Liz. "But just try telling an imperfect story about ugly damaged people loving other ugly damaged people and see how far you get."

With the Swedish flame burning between them and whiskey and nicotine burning their throats, Julian begins by telling his newfound friends about the frozen cave. Bound by grief, he embarked on a perilous journey to find the secret to eternal life. He tells them how long he walked along the river until he was blocked by a vertical cliff of ice, hundreds of feet tall and smooth like a sculpture, with no way to climb it or break it. No way in and no way back. He lay down on the ice and went to sleep, and when he woke up, the mountain was gone. It had melted into the river and refroze. The only thing left from it was a small mound with a circular opening, like an icy halo. "It is called a moongate," Julian says. "So I walked through this moongate and continued on my quest. This is before I knew," he adds, "that the life I looked for, I would never find."

"What did you really travel to the end of the earth in search for, Swedish?" Wild laughs. "It was some girl, right?"

Mia, Mia, my heart, my dearest one, you are the one.

"What do you call the cliff?" Wild asks when Julian doesn't answer.

"Mount Terror," Julian replies.

"Fuck, yeah!"

"Fuck off!" says Nick.

Finch scoffs.

Mia jumps to her feet. "Wait! Stop speaking, Julian."

"What a *splendid* suggestion, dove," Finch says.

"Your story is too good to waste on us wankers."

"Thanks a lot, Folgate," Wild says.

"I, for one, would enjoy hearing the rest," Peter Roberts says in a measured baritone. "The man has finally got around to telling a real story. He began at the beginning and was continuing capably until you stopped him, Maria."

"That wasn't the beginning, Robbie," says Julian. "Not by a long shot."

"You'll hear all of it, Robbie, I promise you," Mia says. "Follow me. Bring your chair."

Mia leads Julian and the rest to the escalator lobby where a hundred Londoners have collected for the night, spilling out onto both platforms. "These poor folks are *starving* for entertainment," Mia says. "You saw how fired up they were last night. What do you say? Let's give them a story. Some drama, some comedy, a fight. You'll lift their spirits, make the time pass. What could be better? I wish we had enough drink for them. They would so enjoy a little sip of whiskey."

"I'll get some," Julian says. "I'll get some as soon as I can."

"Sure you will." Mia smiles, as if she's heard a lot of promises men have not kept. "We'll do it interview style, okay?

I'll ask you questions and in your answers you'll tell them what happened."

"Thank you, Mia," Julian says, gazing at her, "for explaining to me what an interview is."

She giggles. "You're welcome, Julian." She hops up onto the makeshift stage. "Ladies and gentlemen, come closer," she yells, motioning the Londoners to her. "Gather round. Tonight, for your listening entertainment, we want to present our new series of tales. They're called...what are they called, Julian?"

"Tales of Love and Hate."

"Tales of Love and Hate!" she exclaims. "Tonight, we'll start with the first of—" She glances at Julian. "First of how many?"

"First of five."

"Tonight, we will start with the first of five, called 'The Death Match at Sea,' or the mystery of how Julian nearly lost his hand. I'm Maria Delacourt. Please welcome to the stage, my co-star in *The Importance of Being Earnest,* Julian Cruz."

There's tepid clapping.

"Thank you, ladies and gentlemen, for that *smattering* of applause," an unperturbed Mia continues. "Rest assured, when you hear the story of this fight, you will be standing in the aisles." She leans to Julian. "Am I overpromising?"

"Underpromising, I reckon," Julian says.

"Why don't we have a real fight instead?" a man in the back says.

"Yeah," another man says. "Now *that* would be bloody entertainment."

"Well, it wouldn't be fair for me to fight Mr. Cruz," Mia says. "He wouldn't stand a chance." She winks at Julian. "How about if we begin with a story, and then we'll see what we see. Prick up your ears, give Julian your full attention. You won't be disappointed."

And they're not.

Raptly they listen, gasping at the horror of being vastly outnumbered by murderous men with evil intent in the middle of an ocean, gasping even more at the girl's shocking betrayal. Even Mia loses her put-on composure. "Did she *really* do that?" she whispers, wide-eyed.

"She really did," Julian replies, studying her face.

"How could she do it? I thought she loved you."

"She did. But she didn't want to die."

"Julian, why do you keep staring at me, as if I have the answers to my own questions?" she whispers. "Did you forgive her?"

"What do you think?"

"You fool, I think you did."

Julian ends the story of his Valkyrie, the chooser of the slain, with Tama's demise, not with the actual end, which is too cruel for this setting and these people. Probably too cruel for any setting. Ending it early makes it almost a happy ending. Masha at the Cherry Lane was lost and then was found, just as she had always dreamed of.

The crowd applauds with gusto. Wild cheers wildly. Even Peter Roberts claps, his face flushed and satisfied. The only one who doesn't clap is Finch.

"Well done! You definitely want them more ecstatic at the end," Mia says to Julian, grabbing his arm and raising it together with hers as they take their bows. "That's how you know you've done your job."

"I agree, it's always good to end ecstatically," Julian says, squeezing her fingers. Blushing, she doesn't return his gaze.

"Fight! Fight!" the crowd keeps yelling. "Show us a real fight! A boxing match! There must be some plonker in your group who'll fight you. Come on! Give us something!"

"We're not going to do that," Mia tells the audience. "But if we're still here tomorrow, God willing, and you return, we might have some whiskey for you…and we'll tell you another story—which one, Julian? The murder in a brothel?"

"That one's good."

"Okay," she says. "Are there any details to the brothel story besides cold-blooded murder?"

"Oh, one or two," Julian says, making Mia blush again. He smiles. She smiles.

"How about a hot-blooded fight right now, Swedish?" Wild yells from the sidelines. "Finch over here just told me he'll fight you."

"You bet I will," Finch says. "I'll kick his arse. He won't know what hit him."

"Finch is dying to fight you, Swedish!" Wild yells. "What do you say?"

"Fight! Fight!"

The howl of the siren sounds. There's a collective groan of disappointment and misery. The bad part of life has intruded on the good part of life.

9

Cripplegate

"ARE THE DOORS OF ST. PAUL'S STILL OPEN?" JULIAN AND MIA are walking briskly down Whitechapel. Earlier that morning, they rode with Shona to the Royal London Hospital to get resupplied with bandages and antiseptic. With Julian carrying the heavy canvas bag, they're headed back to the jeep on Commercial Street, where Finch is undoubtedly steaming and waiting.

"Sure, it's open," Mia says. "Why, do you want to hide inside?"

"Yes," Julian says. "Inside the Bank of England, inside St. Paul's. Inside the Stock Exchange. Inside Monument." Inside things that don't fall. Things that *won't* fall. The gods of the city have cloaked the Bank of England and St. Paul's in an invisible shield, as if the mystical dragons of London jealously guard its greatest treasures.

"I've never seen London like this," Julian says as they walk, "without its people."

Mia nods. "It's like a ghost town. But believe me, the people are still here."

"Yes," he replies, not looking at her. "They're just ghosts."

The rain turns to ice. Frozen pellets drop out of the sky and pound Julian and Mia like gunfire. He notes her falling apart boots as they hurry down the street.

"Did you know," he says to her, "that if you run in the rain instead of walk, you won't get as wet?"

"You're pulling my leg."

"I'm serious. If we run, we won't get as wet as when we dawdle and take in the sights. Want to try it? Here, give me your hand."

They race down Whitechapel to where it crosses Commercial Street and duck into a covered archway at Aldgate East tube station to catch their breath and get out of the hailstorm for a minute.

"I don't know, Swedish." Mia laughs. "I'm pretty soaked."

"Well, you started out soaked," Julian says, "so it doesn't count. Try it when you're dry. Run through the rain. You won't get as wet."

"If you say so." She is full of good humor.

His newsboy hat on, her winter hat on, they resume their dash up Commercial Street, slowing down when they realize they're almost at the jeep, parked at the usual spot near the Ten Bells pub.

"Hey, so where's the best place for me to get things?" Julian asks. "Things that aren't rationed."

"Like on the black market? They cost a lot."

"I didn't ask that. I asked where to go."

"Find the back of a lorry," Mia says. "Not in the center of town, or where you need to be good." She points to the police station they pass on Commercial. The sign on its door says, "BE GOOD. WE'RE STILL OPEN."

Mia tells him to try north Cripplegate. "Though I should warn you, if you haven't been that way recently, you're in for a nasty shock. But if you manage to get beyond it, in the back of Smithfield Market there's a lot of stuff being sold off lorries. Watch out, though, because Finch doesn't like that stuff."

"What doesn't he like, whisky, bacon, wool blankets?"

"All that." She pauses. "But also be careful because stray bombs are always falling, even during the day. You keep forgetting that. They fall without a siren. Are you looking for something in particular?"

"I promised Finch good Scotch whisky, so that's one thing I'm getting."

"You're not going to win him over with that."

"Trust me, nothing I do is going to win him over," Julian says. Mia bites her lip. "What else should I get? What would your friends like?"

"Bacon rashers. Eggs. Anything out of ration would be good."

"What about you? Would you like something?"

She gets flustered. "I wouldn't mind putting on a costume and singing a song. All the girls would love some nylon stockings, even tough old Shona, even Kate, who pretends to be hard but that's only because she doesn't want people to think she's soft and take advantage of her."

"Is she soft?"

"Nah, she's hard."

"What about you?" He pauses. She blushes. "I mean...would *you* like some nylon stockings?"

Not answering, she points to her thick black hose. "I wouldn't say no. We're saving our money to go dancing sometime. And to the cinema. *Gone with the Wind* is playing at the Empire. They're charging something exorbitant for it like half-a-shilling, and it's always sold out now that there's only one show a day, but we're definitely going. I wouldn't mind some nylon hose to go to the pictures. We're planning to take a day off from the war for it. Would you like to come, too?"

"Would love to," Julian says. "What else?" He points to the soles coming off her boots, the mud leaking in. "Maybe some new boots?"

"Good luck finding a pair of those."

They've arrived at Finch's vehicle.

Finch sticks his head out. "Where have you two been?" he says loudly, almost yelling. "We've been waiting an hour!"

"We got bandages, Finch. Show him, Julian. And we got caught in the downpour."

"I just bet you have." Wild wakes up just in time to quip and grin.

Julian raises his hand in a goodbye. "You go on without me, Finch," he says. "I'll be back tonight—maybe. Today, I have things to do."

"Take all the time you need," Finch says. "A week, a month."

"No, don't go by yourself, Swedish." Wild starts to open the door. "I'll come with you."

Julian stops him. "Another time, Wild. Don't worry. I'll be fine."

"Will you come back?" says Wild.

"Fuck, I hope not," Finch mutters.

"Hey, aren't you going to ask me my boot size?" Mia calls out to Julian.

"Nah, I'm good," Julian says, waving. Around seven and a half, right, Mia? It's all he can do to not blow her a kiss.

∞

Julian has seen London unpaved and swallowed by a great fire. He's seen London in the muck of the rookery and in the white gloved elegance of Sydenham. He's seen the impoverished Monmouth Street and the well-to-do Piccadilly. He's seen London in the present day, teeming and open, lit up and loud, Ferris wheels, museums, white marble houses, black doors, green parks, red coats of the Grenadier guards, everything familiar and right as rain.

Julian has never seen London like this.

A sore evil has ravaged the city. Bitter hail has mixed with smoke and blood, it has blackened the air and the sun, destroyed the things that were good, left behind jackhammered ruin.

Julian, who knows London so well he can walk it in his dreams, loses his way without any street signs.

Julian loses his way without any streets.

North and west and east of St. Paul's, blocks of the old city have been cremated into skeletal dust. Nothing whole is left standing, nothing.

As he walks shellshocked through the deserted plain, Julian sees that the destruction of the cramped city around St. Paul's has exposed the church from all sides. In somber marble immensity, it rises above the ruins of the city that once teemed at its feet. No more alleys and skewed close-up perspectives from which to admire St. Paul's majesty. Yes, London has been brought to its knees, but the unbowed cathedral looms on its solitary hill, seen for miles from the ground and the air—now more unprotected than ever.

The area between St. Mary le Bow and Cheapside is a wasteland.

But because the British are the British, there's an arrow on Ludgate Hill in the middle of the devastation, and a sign underneath it that reads: *Berlin—600 miles.*

At the church of St. Giles, Cripplegate, the statue of John Milton has been blown off its plinth, the bell tower destroyed, and the roof of the nave blown in. The walls have survived somehow, but the rest of the church lies broken on the ground.

The area around St. Giles, like St. Paul's, has been bombed out of existence. There's almost no Roman wall left where Julian hid his money. It's dust like all the rest. Only a short, damaged chunk of the wall remains.

The stone with the little cross Julian etched into it stands exposed almost at the break. The graystone is loose, having been dislodged from its neighbors. Julian barely needs a chisel. As he's pulling out the stone, there's a loud rumble nearby and an explosion. It startles him, and he drops the boulder, almost on his foot. The stone falls and hits another. Both of them crack into smaller pieces.

For a long time, Julian sits on his haunches and stares at the weathered and dried-out leather bag with the dulled gold silk ribbons, stares at the shiny coins inside, forty-one of them, still gleaming. There is no stashing it away anymore for later. There is no later. He is never coming back. It's impossible to believe, impossible to accept. There's another explosion, another stray bomb detonated. It breaks his reverie. Black smoke, flames. The fire engine sirens slice through the silence. Julian grabs the purse with the coins in it, doesn't bother closing up the hole in the wall, glances at it once last time, and walks away, leaving it for good.

10

Blood Brothers

THAT NIGHT JULIAN RETURNS TO BANK A CONQUERING HERO. He has been to several gold dealers on Cheapside, shopped around, got the best price, and sold two of the coins for three hundred pounds each, half of what they're actually worth but decent enough in the middle of a war. He has been to Smithfield, has strolled past all the lorries. He returns carrying a breakwater stormcollar raincoat as a gift to Wild for taking his cloak, and sackfuls of gifts for the rest; Julian, a blackened bearded wartime Santa Claus.

"The whisky is in!" shouts Wild in his new raincoat, jubilantly running up and down the empty platform. "The whisky is in!"

"Are the boots in?" Mia asks shyly.

He smiles at her. The boots are also in, black leather, brand new. She beams. Julian wants to kiss her. But Finch is watching.

He's brought them bacon and dry sausage and ham that's not in a tin. He's brought more kerosene, boxes of matches, a knife for Wild, a straight razor to shave with, he's brought soap, new gloves, a yellow wool cardigan for Mia (Wild: "How did he know what size to get you, Folgate? Did he measure you out with his hands?" Julian: "Lucky guess." Mia: "Shut up, Wild!"), toothpaste, and bottles of ODO-RO-NO liquid deodorant. He's brought three blankets that don't itch. He bought all that he could carry. That night he makes another Swedish flame, uses Wild's new knife to cut up the meats, they pour out the excellent

Scottish whisky and for five minutes sit by the fire on the empty Central Line platform, drinking and smoking and joking around like they're nothing but young.

Then the warden walks up to Julian with a police officer by his side. Julian looks up at the two men hovering over him. He debates whether or not to stand up. He really doesn't want to. All he wants is what they've just been having.

"You got your ID on ya?" the warden asks Julian.

With a shake of his head at Finch, Julian reluctantly rises to his feet.

"You heard the guard," the officer says. "You're not allowed to be down here without your ID and your ration card."

"I need a ration card to be in the Underground?"

"Stop mouthing off. You have it or don't ya? Because I'll have to take you in if you don't have it."

Mia and Wild are by Julian's side. "He's with us," Wild says. "He's with the Rescue Squad."

"Yes," Mia says. "He's with the Home Guard. His house got bombed. He lost everything."

"What are you two, his solicitors? Sit down. Mind your own business."

They don't move. Julian is grateful, but he steps forward, away from them. He doesn't like to be flanked by friends when he's being confronted by enemy combatants.

The rest of the squad jumps to their feet and comes to his rescue, too. Slowly, Finch rises so he's not the only one sitting.

"He helped us out, leave him alone, Javert."

"Don't call me Javert."

"He'll show you his friggin' ID card tomorrow."

"He's helping in the war effort, what do you think he is, a spy on the inside?"

"Jules, offer Javert some whisky, he's ornery because he hasn't had any."

"Enough out of all of ya!" the policeman bellows.

The only one saying nothing is Finch.

"You want to see my ID card, officer?" Julian says. "Why, of course. That's not a problem." Reaching into his pocket, Julian produces the card, the best National ID card money can buy off the back of a truck. "There you go." Julian Cruz, it reads. Address: 153 Great Eastern Road. Occupation: journalist. "I work at a small financial publication near Austin Friars," Julian says. "Well, worked. A parachute mine fell on Throgmorton Avenue."

Mia listens to him in impressed puzzlement. "I thought you told me you ran a restaurant?" she whispers.

"Like you, I wear many hats." Julian found out that not only is 153 Great Eastern Road still standing, but there is no restaurant there. And he prefers to make his white fibs as truthful as possible. To mollify the public officials further, Julian even produces a ration card, with someone else's name etched out and his own stamped in. The cop glares at the sheepish warden, who in turn glares at Finch.

"Thanks for wasting my time," the officer says to Javert as they skulk away.

The squad descends on Finch.

"Was that *your* doing?"

"Finch, did you rat him out?"

"I didn't!"

"Finch, you fink, did you tell Javert that Swedish had no ID?"

"I didn't!"

"Finch, you're such a Berkeley hunt," Wild says. "We don't do that to our own. Why would you do that?"

"He's not my friend, he's not my own, stop calling me names, and I didn't."

"I'm disappointed in you, Finch." That's Mia. "Apologize to Julian."

"It's fine, Mia, don't worry," Julian says. "Finch made a mistake. He misunderstood. I said I misplaced it, not lost it. Good thing I found it, though, right, Finch?"

"I'll burn first before I apologize to that tosser," Finch says, skulking away.

∞

There is Coca Cola, and Bing Crosby, and jitterbugs and calm confidence and good humor.

Carry on.

Carry on.

Carry on.

The young keep life going. They help the city at night, they sleep, rush to work, paint fake buses, they unload freight ships and bandage wounds. And in the evenings, they stay young. They argue over petty slights, learn to fight and how to wield knives, they drink, sing, and entertain others trapped with them in the cave. They do dramatic readings from newspapers, from history books, from memory diluted with whisky, they butcher Shakespeare and Dickens. On Sundays they read Charles Spurgeon's sermons. They have drunken discussions about the meaning of life and argue about where more bombs have fallen, Shadwell or Lambeth. Sometimes they dance. They're close, yet afraid to get *too* close. They live like men in the trenches.

∞

Early one morning after they've come back from another pulsing all nighter, and the others have gone to work, or are asleep like Mia, instead of going to sleep himself, Julian takes a bottle of whisky and two mugs out onto the empty platform where Wild is lying down, humming and smoking, unmindful of the Central Line trains that screech to a stop in front of him every fifteen minutes. He sits up, Julian drops down next to him, pours them both a drink, they clink, and sit together in their solitude, resting their sore backs against the wall of the station.

"Awake all night, and awake all day," Julian says.

"I'll be asleep soon," Wild says. "There's something soothing about the trains skidding and leaving." He pauses. "Folgate told you, didn't she? About me."

They sit. "Told me what?"

"Whatever. It's fine. Just don't talk to me about it."

"Wasn't going to," Julian says. "Did want to talk about something else, though. So what's up with Finch?"

"Do you mean what's up with Finch and Folgate?" Wild laughs. "What, you don't think they're meant to be?"

"Just asking. How long have they been at it?"

"Hard to tell," Wild says. "For a long time they seemed like brother and sister, at least from the outside. I think he's been carrying a torch for her, though, since primary school."

"And she couldn't find anyone else?" Julian is incredulous.

"Sure, she did. But she kept coming back to him."

"Why?"

"I dunno. He was pretty good to her."

"And that's what you want in a guy you plan to marry."

"Yes, and he liked her, and he was around. I mean *always* around. The other chaps got tired of him hanging over them. And she never told him to go. She could've. But she didn't."

"And she agreed to marry him?"

"Ask *her* why she did that, mate. I'm not privy to Folgate's innermost thoughts. A woman's heart is a mysterious thing. I don't know why it beats. He asked her a few months ago, right after Dunkirk. And she took a few months to say yes." Wild chuckles. "Duncan and I said to her, were you waiting for him to die so you wouldn't have to give him an answer?"

"How did she respond?"

"She walloped us."

"And you?" Julian glances at Wild. "You and she were never an item?"

"Me and Folgate? Nah."

"Why not?"

"What, you're trying to match us up?" Putting down his drink, Wild ruffles Julian's hair. "When I first met her, she was going with a friend of mine, so she was off limits. And then she was never without a fella, and I was off doing my own thing. We're like family now. It's almost obscene what you're suggesting."

"You know what's obscene?"

"Yes, yes, I know." Wild laughs. "Finch laying his filthy hand on her. Anyone but you laying a hand on her, right?"

Julian doesn't reply.

"How do you know her, Swedish?" Wild asks, picking up his stein and tipping the whisky into his throat. "I know I keep asking." He wipes his mouth with his sleeve. "But you keep on not saying. She says she's never met you before, yet you two act like you're the oldest of friends."

For a moment Julian is silent. "Like you and me?" he says.

"We're men, it doesn't count. We can make friends with anybody."

"I suppose." Julian stares down the tunnel, wishing for a train to come and derail his angst. "But about the other thing… does she like me?"

"Who wouldn't like you, Swedish?"

"Well, Finch, for one."

"Because you're trying to pinch his butter. You won't leave his butter alone." Wild rattles his empty cup.

Julian pours again, they clink and drink. "So if she likes me," he says, "why hasn't she broken up with him?"

"You're like a dog with a bone, aren't you?" Wild says. "Why? Because she's known him since they were in nappies, and she's known you since yesterday, that's why. As you appeared out of thin air, you could vanish into thin air. You're an unknown quantity," he adds. "An amusing quantity, but unknown nonetheless." He burps. "But also, do you know what I do when I want to ask a girl a question? I ask the girl. I don't ask her plastered friend who knows nothing."

"I don't want to put her on the spot."

"Yes, but making love to her in public in front of her beau, such as he is, is not putting her on the spot?"

They clink.

Julian sighs. "You think I should leave her alone?"

"No, mate. I think you should ask her a question."

Minutes pass. After a while, Wild speaks. He doesn't look at Julian. "You got any brothers, Swedish?"

"Yeah," Julian says. "I got five."

"Five! Fuck me. So lucky." Wild raises his cup. "What are their names?"

"Brandon, Rowan, Harlan, me, Tristan, and Dalton."

"Amazing. How was that growing up?"

"Awesome. Loud."

"I bet. And your mum handled it?"

"Mom is Norwegian. Nothing fazes her."

"Do they all have kids now?"

"Yeah. Like fifteen all in all."

"Unbelievable. Where are they all at, Wales?"

Julian clams up.

Wild misunderstands. "Your brothers, are they still alive?"

"Yeah." Julian doesn't say more. "I'm sorry, Wild."

"But I know you lost somebody, too," Wild says, his voice quaking. "I can tell. Who was it, that girl on the ship?"

"Yes," Julian says. "The way you can't talk to me about your brother, I can't talk to you about her."

"I could tell you ended your story too soon. Is that who Folgate reminds you of?"

"Something like that." They both drink like they need it. "But I'll tell you this," Julian says. "I had friends growing up, though none of them especially close because I didn't need it, you know? I had my brothers. But when I was eighteen and went to college, I met a guy named Ashton. I don't remember a time in my adult life when he was not by my side, through everything, no matter what. My mother called him her seventh son. I was never closer to anyone than I was to him. He was my blood brother." The memories, just behind his eyes, had not faded. Only life had faded. Julian moved through the days in the dark; he had lost his sight. But he remembered everything, as if he could still see. "I can tell you about him, if you want."

"Oh, yeah?" Wild says absent-mindedly. "I like that name, *Ashton*. Never heard it before. What was he like?"

"He was a good guy. He was a great friend." Julian inhales. "You remind me a bit of him."

"I'm not surprised, because I'm a *great* guy. So what happened to him?"

"He's still somewhere, over the earth. I'm sure of it."

"My brother, too," Wild says. "Awake all night, like us."

"Drinking, talking about girls, uncovering the mysteries of life."

"Knowing Louis, probably just drinking, Swedish."

Side by side on the floor of the Central Line platform, Wild and Swedish sit, finishing the whisky, telling each other stories of those they lost and couldn't save, of those they left behind.

11

Mia, Mia

A GIANT EXPLOSION ROCKS BANK. LOOSENED PLASTER tumbles to the ground, a pipe dangles. It feels like an earthquake. Some women scream, but in the Ten Bells passageway, things stay remarkably calm.

"Fuck off!" says Nick.

"That was close," says Peter Roberts. Lucinda keeps knitting as if she didn't hear a thing. Peter Roberts and Lucinda behave as if they're in the library, and books have fallen off the shelves, books that are somebody else's problem. Frankie picks up her puzzle pieces from the floor, one by one, and carries on.

"Don't fret, Folgate," Wild says to Mia. "Finch is by your side, looking out for you. Put your arm around your girl, Finch, make her feel better. If anything happens, he'll be sure to write it down. He'll itemize every infraction against you and present it to the Incident Officer."

"What do we say to Wild, Nick?" Finch asks the supine man.

"Fuck off!" says Nick.

"Precisely," says Finch.

"You're letting Nick do your dirty work, Finch?" Wild says. "You're not fooling me. You're as dirty as old Brentford at Christmas."

"Are you happy we're all together now, Mum?" Sheila asks Lucinda.

"Yes," Lucinda replies without inflection. Most have settled into feisty defiance or resigned resolve. Lucinda has made a deliberate effort to remain nonchalant. The biggest fear for many British is to spread unnecessary panic. "Eight million people cannot become hysterical," Lucinda tells her girls when they refuse to match their mother's sanguine disposition.

"Our mum's way of dealing with the war is to ignore it," Kate says to Julian. "She acts like war is a terrible but temporary inconvenience that must be tolerated until it ends—in about a fortnight."

Sheila adds to her sister's description, "Mum contributes to the war effort by refusing to take part."

"Must be nice to have your mum with you," says Mia with a melancholy sigh.

Boom boom.

Thud thud.

The air shakes with the drone of planes. Little black things fall out of the sky. Every minute he is awake, Julian hears the rat-tat-tat of the anti-aircraft guns, even when they're not being fired. But the black things keep falling. White caps open over them. Parachutes. The black things drift through the air, harmless, aimless, in slow motion, until they hover above a row of terraced houses. Then they explode.

The day they explode, Julian finally learns what Frankie does for the war effort. Mute medical student Frankie sifts through the brick and glass and pulls out pieces of ripped-apart bodies. She puts them back together in her deep-freeze laboratory called the morgue. She and her team of assistants search for fragments of arms, legs, feet, bits of torso, partial skulls. They place all the remains they can find into an open wagon lined with plastic. In the hours it takes Finch to itemize lost belongings, Frankie fastidiously, slowly, patiently sifts through the dust and recovers parts of lost human beings. The medical truck leaves, the Incident Officer leaves, the refreshment truck, the fire brigade, the police, Finch and the Rescue Squad all leave, only Frankie is still there, lifting up window frames and torn apart mattresses, making sure she hasn't left a stray bone behind.

Back in the morgue, she spends days assembling. When she deems the jigsaw pieces of the body are put together with sufficient respect, then and only then does she sign off and release the body to the waiting family.

Some of them remain partials.

Frankie won't release those. Day after day, she returns to the bomb site and sifts through the mortar, poking with her spear and her spade, digging mute and unhurried until she finds the parts that are missing.

"Frankie wasn't always so quiet," Mia tells Julian. "When the war began, she smiled, sometimes even talked. But then she found a woman's arm, still in her overcoat, lying in the dirt. That arm has been torturing Frankie. She can't make peace with not finding the rest of the woman. Where did the body go? The arm has been catalogued and left in the mortuary at Royal London. Frankie checks on it every time she's there, to see if it's been claimed."

It's still unclaimed.

That's why no one has abandoned London. They are all fragments of a city. They're part of something, they belong to something whole. If they leave, pieces will go missing.

∞

Most of the days Julian has no time to think about it, but sometimes when he's walking and has time, he doubles over under the weight of London pressing down on him. The enormity of what's happening kicks him in the heart.

This can't be London!

London whose roar never stopped, not even after the Black Plague, lies deserted and silent at night. *This* black plague falling out of the sky, drifting down on white parachutes, has muted the mighty city. This London is more silent than the countryside in Clerkenwell in 1603 when the rustling of rodents and the chirping of crickets could still be heard at night. It's more silent than the dank cellar room in which Julian lay in a heroin haze, more silent than the cave with vertical ice walls hundreds of feet thick, more silent than the Southern Ocean in the ebony stillness of pack ice.

It is dead silent.

It's a black hole, except for the droning of enemy planes, except for the wailing of relentless sirens.

The Strand is burning.

Cheapside is burning.

Paternoster Row, the historic publishing street next to St. Paul's, is gone, gone like it never existed, wiped out, five million books destroyed.

Winter. Snow, then rain. The city is a muddy wreck.

Cold nights in heavy fog, visibility three feet. *Mia, Mia!*

In Battersea, no ceilings, no glass, no light.

Doors are torn off, doors they bring underground and fashion into stages.

The destruction of the doors above them means that in the caves below, they can put on a skit and dance, and maybe even laugh.

Mia, Mia.

It doesn't seem right for people to stay in a city where bombs fall daily.

And yet they stay.

It doesn't seem right to put themselves in harm's way.

And yet they do.

They are surprised in the mornings that buildings still stand like mountains. Nothing seems to be that permanent. Not the buildings, not the people.

And yet they remain.

London, the most lit up nighttime city in the world, has been plunged into darkness. The metropolis has vanished. Two thousand years thriving, and in two months it's a clutter of wattle and daub shacks, made of sticks and bricks, burning and crumbling. And they can't see any of it until the next morning when the streets are gone. Holborn, Tottenham Court Road. All the roads are misshapen. Dust, dust everywhere in the great dead city.

Parts of the city are ashes. The history of London is laid waste, made without meaning. If its tangible relics can vanish overnight, if London's physical manifest glory can disappear, what's left?

Mia, Mia.

She paints the fake buses red.

Fire engines are painted gray.

And policemen wear hats painted blue.

And yet they stay.

They get up and go to work, take buses and cabs, they walk, and the pubs are still open, and beer is terrible because sugar is rationed, but at least the terrible beer is not rationed.

And in the caves, there is life.

There's a stage and a boxing ring.

Unreality weighs upon Julian.

He wants to tell his friends, brightly colored flowers will grow in the ashes come spring. On Bread Street and Milk Street ragwort will bloom, lily of the valley, white and purple lilac, London pride. For seven hundred years, the earth near Cripplegate has been tamped down by stone. But underneath, it's still fertile soil. In it, leaps and bounds of asphodel will grow. The wounded city will see the immortal flowers return.

But not in the dead of November. In November, the kingdom will fall for a song.

Julian has picked up some new things for Mia on the black market. He got her a Brodie, a tin hat. Does she wear it? Of course not. Discarded it lies at the foot of her bunk. He bought her high heeled shoes, not patriotic wedges, bought her garters and nylon stockings, not patriotic lederhosen, acquired for her a long pink fake-fur scarf, some red lipstick, a garland for her hair, and a black velvet dress with a silk red trim.

Mia cries when he opens his hands full of offerings. "Why are you bringing me these?" she whispers so Finch doesn't hear. "These are the most wonderful things anyone's ever given me." She tries to act composed, but her eyes are wet. "Brodie's good, too, but not like this." In five minutes, she gussies herself up in velvet and fur and brushes out her hair, pulling it back from one side of her face with the floral hair clip. Twirling the ends of the fluffy scarf, Mia gets Wild to introduce her, jumps up on the door, and lustily sings and tap dances for the damp sullen people. For three minutes, she makes them happy. They cheer for an encore. She happily obliges. Four times she obliges, as if she is nothing but jaunty and carefree.

What is the song the kingdom shall fall for, and who will feel like a king with a crown? Florence Desmond's spectacular double-entendre classic, "I've Got the Deepest Shelter in Town."

Julian loves her so much and is so afraid for her, his whole body is in pain.

Mia, Mia.

12

Falling Beams

JULIAN WRAPS THE STRAPS OF HIS STILL WORKING HEADLAMP around an old bottle of gin filled with water. He points the bulb so it shines into the liquid, and the passageway fills with reflected ambient light. Everyone is impressed. Everyone but Finch who looks as if he wants to beat Julian unconscious in that ginned-up ambience.

No matter what goes on outside, the disposition of the Ten Bells gang rarely changes, but Julian's mood changes. He gets progressively less jovial, and he wasn't so jovial to begin with. They're playing the Luftwaffe roulette every night. During the day a few bombs, a few missions. At night, hundreds of bombs, dozens of missions. Some nights, fifty tons of bombs fall. Other nights, a hundred tons of bombs fall.

A hundred tons of bombs a night. Eventually one of those bombs is bound to drop on the singular spot in the city where Mia stands or rides or walks.

It's only a matter of when.

It's only a matter of time.

Outside London, nothing is any easier. Coventry gets destroyed. Half of Birmingham is destroyed, because that's where the Spitfires are made. Liverpool destroyed; that's where the American ships dock to resupply the Royal forces. And the British Rail gets hit a thousand times. Train wagons stand on the tracks by the tens of thousands, waiting, not moving. There is nowhere to go.

There is only the Underground.

Which Mia makes her life's mission to leave every day and night. She is always itching to be somewhere else. As if she doesn't even care about being safe.

"Why do you always want to go outside, Mia," Julian says, grumbling, trying to pretend he's kidding so the others don't notice. He doesn't care if she notices. "There is nowhere to go."

"Sure there is," she says. "Like the cinema or the cabaret if you were so inclined."

"A cinema, really?" a weary and skeptical Julian asks. Not another thing. Not one more thing.

"What is this, the dark ages?" Mia says. "Well, technically we are in a blackout, but—of course there's cinema! I told you, we are all going to *Gone with the Wind* next Thursday. We have to get there early, or we won't get a seat."

The girls flutter with delight. Every time they've tried to go before, it's been house full. There is only one matinee performance. No shows begin after dark. And it gets dark so early these late November days.

"Or *instead*," says Wild, "we could spend Thursday night on the lash, rolling from one West End pub to another until we are thoroughly blitzed. Oh sorry, I thought it was August, when 'blitzed' carried a whole other meaning. Swedish, you in?"

"Swedish is not in," Julian says, looking away from Wild, the days of pub crawls forever behind him. The Three Horseshoes on the Yorkshire dales has made sure of that.

"Better yet, the Windmill is still open," Duncan says with a lewd grin. "That's my kind of theatre. Who's with me, boys? Jules, you in? I walked past it the other day. Sign says, *Never closed, never clothed. Girls still naked as the bombs fall.* Is anybody's birthday coming up? Jules, yours maybe? Let's go while the girls are in Covent Garden, swooning over Clark Gable."

"You must've walked past it a while ago," Liz says. "It burned last Tuesday. No more Windmill."

"Fuck off!" Nick and Duncan and Wild cry in unison.

With the Windmill closed, the boys reluctantly agree to go with the girls to see *Gone with the Wind* except for Finch who makes a show of pretending to be excited. "It'll be almost like a romantic outing, dove," he says, taking her hand.

"Yeah, almost," says Mia.

Julian sits and twitches.

Later, Duncan and Wild mock him for his pining face, but he wants to tell them it's not just Finch and Mia that upset him. For some reason, the Germans love to fly over London on Thursday nights. The last three Thursdays, the city has been ignited by buildings turning into Swedish flames entire.

∞

On Tuesday, two days before the movie outing, there is a major attack. A hundred and fifty tons of bombs are dropped, most of them on Southbank and the Docklands.

The bombs are mixed, but most are incendiaries. London burns. The Rescue Squad must wait hours for the firemen to bring the flames under control. Wild feels powerless. Finch and Duncan sleep. Mia and Julian talk until Finch wakes just long enough to tell them to shut up.

There is injury on the streets. People are dead or badly burned. Once the worst of the flames has been put out, the squad is summoned to assist in the recovery of valuables and bodies. Are valuables first on the war list?

A one-armed Wild serves tea (slowly), while Julian is asked to shadow Duncan and Frankie in search of bodies. But he can't. Because he can't take his eyes off Mia who is searching for valuables. She's supposed to be getting out blankets and helping to bandage the wounded, but instead she is climbing into a ruined house to get something for someone. Julian can't concentrate on what's under his own feet because he is watching her so anxiously. Asking Duncan to give him five minutes, he walks over to stand behind Mia, who is balancing herself precariously on an end of a charred beam to get inside the house.

"Mia, stop."

She turns to see him behind and below her. "What are you doing here? I'm fine."

Julian blinks, the memory and the real girl colliding in his eyes. Is she Mirabelle at the peaceful Crystal Palace on a ladder? Or is she Mia in the midst of a disaster? Placing his firm hands on her slender legs, just below her hips, Julian stops her from moving. This isn't Victorian London. This is war. "I'm serious, stop," he says, giving her thighs a light squeeze. "Look." He points up at the ashy window frames above them, teetering above the ripped-out floors, at the roof breaking off in patches.

"I'll duck." She smiles.

He shakes his head.

"I've been inside a hundred houses like this," she says. "This one isn't too bad."

"It *is* bad," he says, "and your luck is going to run out."

"What, right now?"

Before Julian can nod, the beam she is standing on breaks. Gasping, she totters backwards and falls. He catches her. Like a see-saw, the half-burned crosspiece flies up and ricochets toward her. Julian has barely a picosecond to turn his shoulder to cover her before the beam smashes into his back, knocking them both to the ground, him on top of her.

Wild is the first one to run over, yelling for Finch and Duncan. "I'm fine," Julian says. "Mia, you okay?" She is still underneath him. She grunts, her mouth full of soot. Duncan moves the charred timber, and he and Wild pull Julian and Mia out, helping them to their feet. Though he said he was fine, Julian is having trouble standing. A three-inch nail got jammed in his calf when the beam fell on him. He yanks the nail out, fleetingly hoping the tetanus shot he got when he came back from Mary in 1603 is still good.

Finch looks unhappy instead of relieved. "Are you all right, dove?" he says to Mia, pulling her away from Julian. "Did he hurt you when he fell on top of you like that? You should be more careful," he says brusquely to Julian. "You could've hurt her."

"Finch, don't be an arsehole," Wild says. "Did you even see what happened? He wasn't chatting her up, he was…"

"I'm just saying," Finch says. "What's the point of hurting the people you're trying to help?"

"Don't listen to him, Jules, he's a pillock," Duncan says.

"He didn't hurt me, Finch," Mia says. "That beam would've hit me in the face if he hadn't stepped in front of me."

"I'm just saying…"

"What are you saying, Finch?"

Duncan and Wild support Julian as he limps to the HMU, his arms around their shoulders. Mia runs after them. While Sheila cleans and bandages his wound and confirms that his shoulder blade is not broken, Julian listens to Mia outside the medi truck arguing with Finch.

"Why are you standing here, dove? If you're not hurt, as you say, why don't you go…"

"I'm not going anywhere, Finch. I'm waiting for him to be done."

"Why? There's so much that still needs to be…"

"So hop to it, rabbit."

"I have other things to do, as you well know."

"So go do them."

Julian finally emerges.

"Are you okay?" Mia asks, almost timidly, stepping forward.

"I'm fine." Though Phil Cozens didn't diagnose it, Julian knows he's got a muscle tear in his calf, a common injury in contact sports. For the next few weeks, it's not going to be easy for him to walk around the bomb sites. "Are *you* okay? Was Finch right? Did I hurt you?"

"No," she says. "The beam in my face would've hurt a lot worse, so Finch was not right."

Facing each other, they stand next to the medi truck.

"I'm sorry I didn't listen to you," she says. "But it was just a freak accident."

Julian says nothing.

"Okay, how did you do that?" she says. "You came over at just the right moment, almost as if you knew it was going to happen."

"Mia, did you see what you were doing? It didn't take a genius."

"But *why* did you do that?" she says quietly.

"Do what?"

"Why did you throw yourself in front of me like that?"

"Like what?"

She can't say.

"Anyone would've done the same, believe me," Julian says.

She stares into his face a moment and doesn't say anything.

13

Gold Rings

RIGHT AFTER A BOMBING, THE SITE IS UNSTABLE IN ALL WAYS, physical and metaphysical. Fire damage, charring, demolition. Destruction of both people and property. There is bitter cold and falling rain, and wind. There is also frustration, impatience, disagreement. There are short tempers, even among the British.

The day after the beam incident, Mia gets into it with a woman who accuses Mia of stealing her jewelry. It's unusual for Mia to argue back. She is normally so placid. She keeps repeating that she did not find any jewelry in the house, but the woman doesn't believe her, so Mia keeps repeating it but louder. The woman is soon joined by her son and her uncle, both equally truculent, the uncle beefy and intimidating. All three are accusing the beset Mia of taking the woman's gold rings. Mia is too nice, even when she is arguing. She doesn't want to hurt anyone's feelings. Having listened to this from a distance, Julian is about to walk over to deal with the situation his own way, even though he knows it's not his place, but instead Finch saunters over, to deal with the situation *his* way. At first, Julian condemned Finch's response time to Mia's crisis, which, to put it politely, was somewhat dilatory. But as Julian listens in disbelief, Finch asks Mia to turn out her pockets to prove to the irate family that she took nothing from them. Before Mia can respond, the woman herself declares that turning out the pockets will prove nothing. Mia would have to strip naked, the woman says. The uncle joins in by saying even stripping naked will prove nothing because Mia could've swallowed the rings. That's when Julian has really had enough.

Ignoring Wild's admonition to stay out of it, Julian drops what he's doing, limps down from the mound of bricks, favoring his injured calf, slowly walks into the street where the quarrel is proceeding unabated, and steps between Mia and her three aggressors. He steps between them so forcefully that the teenage son loses his balance and falls. Pulling Mia behind him, Julian stands in front of her and turns to Finch. He doesn't even bother addressing the family.

"Do you know what your job is?" Julian says quietly. "Your *first* job? It's not to write down the quantity of their fucking gold rings. It's to protect your own fucking valuables. How can you be so crap at that?"

"Please step away," Finch says, all officious and prim. "You're making the situation worse, as always. I'm trying to defuse it."

"Mum, he knocked me down!" the teenager cries.

"Get up, my darling, to your feet at once! Who are *you*?" the woman barks at Julian.

The uncle joins in. "Yeah, bugger off, this don't concern you—"

Julian won't hear another word. He shoves the uncle in the chest. "Shut your fucking mouth before I shut it for you," Julian says to him before turning to the woman. "Lady, take your son, take whoever that idiot is, and get out of here. A bomb fell inside your house. You understand that, don't you, at least theoretically? The house is unstable. It can collapse any second, yet *she* still walks through it, searching for your shit while you loiter in the street drinking tea and yelling at her. Trust me, she doesn't need your gold rings. She's got forty sovereigns of her own."

The stupefied uncle scrambles forward, huffing and puffing. "I'm not afraid of you, you bloody cripple!"

"I think you are," says Julian, "and I know you should be."

"He can't talk to us like that!" the man yells to Finch.

"Yeah," Finch says to Julian. "You can't talk to them like that. This is none of your business. Maria, come here, dove, don't stand near him."

Mia doesn't move.

"Her safety is *your* business," Julian says to Finch. "You're supposed to be on *her* side. How dare you ask her to turn out her pockets? You know she didn't take their fucking rings."

"I know that!" Finch exclaims. "I know that better than you. I wanted her to prove it to them. Put this matter behind us. Not make it worse, like you just did."

"That's right!" the uncle yells, swinging at Julian, who jerks his head, pivots and punches the man with a straight left into the center of his face.

"I told you to shut your fucking mouth," Julian says. The man's nose and lip gush blood. The nose is broken. The woman shrieks, the boy shrieks. Throwing up his hands, Finch rushes off to get some rags. Oh, now he's rushing.

Taking Mia by the arm, Julian leads her away from the ruckus.

"You shouldn't have let them talk to you like that," he says. "You let it go on too long. You're too nice."

"Tempers flare," she says. "And what could I have done? I couldn't have done what you just did." She glances over Julian's shoulder. "Uh-oh," she says. "You're about to hear it from Finch."

"Can't wait," says Julian.

Before he can turn around, Mia grabs the front of Julian's coat. "Promise me you won't hurt him," she says.

"Julian!" he hears Finch call. "Look at me! I want to talk to you."

Mia holds on to Julian's coat, keeping him from facing Finch. "No, Julian, before you turn around, *promise* me you won't hurt him."

He peels her away from his lapel, squeezing her hand. "OK, fine. I promise." Then he turns around.

"Yes, Finch?" Julian says. "What would you like to discuss?"

"I don't know why trouble follows you wherever you go," Finch says, barreling forward.

Julian puts out his palm. "Don't come near me," he says. "If you really came to talk, talk, but don't come within four feet of me."

"Or what?" Finch stops.

"Or I'm going to check your distance," says Julian, clenching his fist.

"If you touch me," Finch says, "I'll have you arrested." But he doesn't come any closer.

"And what are you going to tell the police when they come? That three people were about to attack your girlfriend while you took their side against her and did fucking nothing?" Julian wishes he hadn't promised Mia to keep his hands to himself.

Duncan and Wild run up.

"That's not what I did!" Finch yells.

"That's exactly what you did."

"Maria! Tell him that's not what I did! I defended you!"

"You didn't defend me, Finch," Mia says from behind Julian, yanking on his coat to remind him not to lunge forward.

"Asking you to prove to them you didn't steal their things *is* defending you, dove!" Finch says.

"No, it isn't," Mia says.

"Yeah, Finch, it really isn't," Duncan says. "It's shite, if you ask me."

"Stay out of it, Duncan! This is between me and him."

"What's going on here?" an unfazed Wild says amiably. "I had one cigarette and suddenly it's a war zone." He turns to Julian. "War zone, Swedish, see what I did there? I made a joke, a pun. A play on words."

"I see, Wild. Step back."

But Wild doesn't step back. Just the opposite. Wild steps forward. He puts his one arm around Julian. "Swedish, I keep telling and telling you. You can't take a single thing Finch says or does personally or seriously. Why won't you listen to me?

I thought we were friends. The man is mad as a bag of ferrets. I've been drumming it into your skull from day one. He is not your problem. He is Folgate's problem. Let's you and me go have ourselves a cigarette and a stiff drink and leave the girls to sort out their own shit."

"No," Finch says. "Move away, Wild. He and I are going to solve this once and for all like men."

Wild laughs.

"When words stop working, things need to be resolved without them," Finch continues. "The way men resolve things." Dusty and panting, he throws off his coat. "I've been accused by him of sticking up for the wrong side, and I won't have it."

"Wait, Finch," Wild says, still between the two men, "but Folgate also accused you of sticking up for the wrong side. Is it her you're getting ready to brawl with? Because that would make more sense. Folgate, take off your coat. Your man is about to fight you."

"Not her—*him*," Finch says.

"A fight, Wild!" Duncan says. "Finally."

"Yes, Wild. The men are fighting." Finch puts up his fists. "What's the matter?" he asks, glancing at Julian's hands, which remain down. "Are you afraid to have a real fight? Come on. It's been a long time coming. I won't have you insulting me anymore. Let's settle this." He starts bouncing around in a boxer's dance.

"Finch, stop it," Mia says. "You're being ridiculous."

"Stay out of it, dove. This has nothing to do with you."

"Wait, what? I thought this has *everything* to do with her," says Wild. "Finch, I know you played Jack Dempsey once at the Playhouse, and I know you think you can lick Swedish…"

"Wild, stay out of this!" Duncan yells. "Let him try."

"I don't think it, I can!" Finch says, and then to Julian: "What's the matter, tough guy? Backing off? Hiding behind the skirts of a raspberry ripple?"

"Whoa," Wild says, mock offended. "Suddenly, I have a good mind to let Julian do it."

"*Do* it, Jules, *do* it!" says Duncan.

"Okay, Finch," Julian says, moving Wild away and stepping forward. Mia keeps yanking on the back of his coat. "You want to fight? Let's go. But for real stakes, not some Mickey Mouse bullshit. If I win, you're going to leave Mia alone."

"What do you mean, leave her alone?"

"You know, kind of like you just left her alone with her assailants," Julian says. "But leave her alone for good."

"No! That's rubbish! Absolutely not!"

"Why the fuss, Finch?" Wild says. "I thought you were sure you'd win?"

"It's bollocks, that's why."

"Wild, let go of me," Julian says, prying Wild's calming arm off his shoulder.

"No, Swedish," Wild says. "He's not of sound mind. It would be like fighting a baby. He's not mentally competent."

"Step back, Wild!" Finch yells. "I'm a lot more competent than you!"

"Do it, do it!" says Duncan, jumping up and down.

A small crowd has gathered around them in an excited circle. Men's raised voices often means a physical confrontation, and people always want to see that, even these people, who you'd think have seen plenty.

Unfortunately, the fight is stopped before it can begin. From down the block, the Incident Officer orders Finch to duty. A disappointed growl runs through the crowd. Picking up the coat he threw on the ground, Finch backs off, but not before saying, "This isn't over. This isn't over by a long shot."

∞

When Finch returns to Bank that evening, the first thing he says to Wild is, "Where is he? Hiding like a rabbit?"

"If you mean sleeping, Finch, then yes," Julian says, sitting up in his bunk, stretching his stiff back, flexing his injured calf.

After a long rest, he has calmed down. He was hoping Finch had also calmed down, realized perhaps how imprudent a fight would be. Julian is ready to shake hands, let bygones be bygones. They live in too close quarters to let bad blood come between them. But clearly Finch, instead of calming down, has been getting himself into even more of a lather.

"You want to forfeit?" Finch says. "Just say so. I want everyone to know what I've known all along—that you're nothing but talk. Maria, especially."

Julian sighs. "Are you sure you want to do this, Finch?"

It's not just Finch. No one is letting Julian off the hook for a fight. Who doesn't like a good fight? It's been brewing between the two of them, Duncan says, and everyone knows it. It's high time the matter was settled by combat. Julian shakes his head. It's fun and games now. Just wait until Finch gets a black eye.

Mia comes to sit by Julian. "You promised me," she says quietly.

"Mia, talk to your boyfriend," Julian says. "What do you want me to do? He wants to fight. You don't want him hurt, talk to him, not me."

You'd think the older men would be the voices of reason but no. The older men, Phil and Robbie, say the fight absolutely must proceed but needs to be done properly. It needs a ring, it needs rounds, an announcer, a bell. Nick wakes up long enough to say, "Fuck off! Just let them duke it out on the platform. Wake me when it starts," and goes back to sleep.

Mia calls everyone to her and declares there will be no fight unless it's staged as a performance in front of the Underground dwellers. With satisfaction, she glares at Julian, as if she has come up with a perfect solution for a low violence outcome— fighting in a ring in front of an audience. Does she even understand what fighting is? Julian gazes at her with amused tenderness.

"Staged?" Wild asks Mia. "So is it a real fight or fake?"

"Most definitely a real fight," says Finch.

"No, it's a fake fight," says Mia, staring down Julian. "It's for their entertainment." She points to out there.

"Those people have been baying for a fight for weeks," Duncan says. "Only real blood will quench them."

"Entertainment or not, we'll *actually* be fighting, dove," says Finch.

"No, Finch," Julian says. "We won't be."

"I don't blame you for being afraid," says Finch.

"Because that's what I am."

"You don't think I can deck you?"

Julian allows that Finch can.

"You don't think I can beat you?"

Julian doesn't reply for a moment. "Last thing I want to do is insult you, Finch," he says. "It's still on my list, though."

Wild and Duncan guffaw.

"I'm taller than you and bigger than you," Finch says loudly. "I have both my hands. I heard that a boxer needs his hands to fight, but what do I know about such things, right? Plus I'm not all lame after a little nail scratched my leg. Get in the ring, buddy. I'll kick your arse."

"Okay, Finch, let's get in the ring." Julian turns to Mia. "Even if you think the fight isn't real," he says to her, "the stakes should be real, don't you agree?" There's a twinkle in his eye. He can't help himself. If there's going to be a fight, it might as well have some positive consequences for him.

"I'm not fighting for what you said earlier," Finch says. "I'm not going to leave my girl alone."

"Wild, how about this," Julian says. "If Finch wins, I take the entire gang to the Savoy Grill for dinner."

The passageway gets quiet.

"*All* of us?" Duncan says in a thrilled gasp.

Even Nick Moore stirs. "Fuck off!" says Nick.

"Yes," says Julian. "If I lose, I will take all of you to the Savoy for a meal. Wine, cover charge, all food off ration. Anything you want. On me."

"Don't fall for it," Finch says. "I don't like it. I don't like it one bit." The young man is so gangly and earnest, and Duncan and Wild are so excited about the Savoy, that Julian almost feels bad. "What do you get if *you* win?" Finch narrows his eyes.

"If I win," Julian says, with a smile at Mia, "and if it's okay with Mia, I get to sit next to her tomorrow night at *Gone with the Wind*."

Mia beams. "Fine by me," she says.

Vehemently Finch shakes his head. "Absolutely not," he says. The gang descends on him.

"Isn't it my choice who I get to sit next to, Finch?" Mia says.

"What's wrong, Finch?" Julian asks. "I thought you were going to win?"

"Finch," Mia says, "I'm a small price to pay for a chance of a dinner at the Savoy. Tiny risk for a lot of reward."

"It's not a risk I'm prepared to take," Finch says loftily.

Duncan, Wild and Nick berate Finch. Don't be a ninny, Finch. Folgate's right. It's for a great cause.

"No," Finch says. "We don't need the Savoy. Let's just fight for the principle of it. For the satisfaction of victory."

"Oh, sod off," Wild says. "You better not frigging lose."

"Hey, buddy!" an indignant Julian says to Wild. "I thought you were in *my* corner."

Wild walks over, gives Julian a slap on the back, a manly embrace. "Swedish," he says, "we had a good run, you and I. But it's over. Our friendship against dinner at the Savoy? Like it's even a choice. Nice knowing you. Tonight, I'll be actively working against you, and I don't feel bad about it one bit. Finch, come. Dunk and I will show you how to beat the crap out of him."

"Okay," Finch says, allowing himself to be led to the empty platform, "but I don't want to fight for what he said."

"If you win, it will be the greatest day of our lives," Duncan says. "But if you lose, well, first, we'll beat the shit out of you for losing, but second, all you've given up is a few hours of sitting silently next to a chick at a theatre watching a stupid picture.

He's not asking to shag her, Finch. He's asking to sit next to her in public. It's a no brainer. Swedish is a sucker. He should've asked for more."

Finch bristles. "How dare you! Who says my Maria would agree to more?"

They turn to Maria, smoking in the passageway, watching them on the platform. She shrugs. "A girl doesn't know what she will and won't agree to until she is asked. How much more are we talking about here, Jules?" She gleams.

They turn their gazes to Julian, standing near her, hands in his pockets. "This is a gentlemen's fight," he says evenly. "We're not haggling at a wench auction. I get to take a lovely young lady to the pictures. That's it."

The young lady blooms under his watery gaze.

"It's too much," Finch says. "It's not right."

"Poor Swedish is getting the sharp end of the stick either way," says Wild.

"Shut up, Wild!" Mia exclaims. "Or I'll show you the sharp end of the stick."

"Finch, you gotta beat him," Duncan says, shaking Finch like a cotton doll. "You simply gotta. I want the Savoy so bad. Mia, go to the lobby and tell them the fight will start in an hour. It'll give us time to train your boyfriend. Come on, Finch, this is for all the marbles. Let's practice."

"Why?" Finch says. "*He's* not practicing."

"Thank Christ. You stand a chance of beating him then."

∞

"Ladies and gentlemen!" Mia yells. "What a *treat* we have for you tonight! Finally, we have a real fight for your viewing and listening pleasure! Yes, it's true! So get comfortable, get a drink, and take your seats on the luxurious concrete floor! To start, I will—" Before she can continue, Wild interrupts her by jumping on stage.

Throwing his arm around her, he yells, "Ladies and gents, usually it's either blood or beer here—but tonight, in the Underground, we're proud to offer you blood *and* beer!" The men in the audience roar. "For the main event, we have the middleweight world championship bout between Finch Smith, the undisputed champion of the world, and Julian 'The Hammer' Cruz, his challenger from Scandinavia, a Swedish lord who's come to take the crown from one of our very own! The fight will last five rounds, two minutes a round, with a two-minute rest in between. Low blows are not allowed, neither is kicking or biting. Otherwise, anything goes! It's going to be a good one. But first, some light and mostly unintentional comedy from Folgate—I mean, from Maria Delacourt." He plants a happy kiss on her cheek and jumps off to thunderous noise.

Duncan and Nick move the door and the two-by-fours off to the side. They get four chairs to make the corner posts of a large square space and tie rope around them to mark an almost regulation-size ring, while Wild lays out blankets and pillows around the perimeter.

"Is Finch going to be having a fight or taking a nap?" Julian says, watching Wild.

Wild grabs Julian by his shirt. "Go easy on that poor git, Swedish," he says. "He's not batting on a full wicket. Love has made him soft in the head."

"Not love but pride," Julian says.

"Same difference. Let him win," Wild says. "Please. For the Savoy!"

"Have faith in the boxer you trained, Wild," Julian says. "As for me, what can I say, I'd like to sit next to the girl."

"You sit next to her every frigging night in the jeep and on the rubble and around the fire! You literally can't will yourself to leave her side! No wonder Finch is incensed. You have to sit next to her in a chair, too?"

"Not a chair. In a theatre. Like on a date." Julian smiles.

"Swedish, *please*."

"Have faith in your boxer, Wild."

"Oh, fuck everything," Wild says.

∞

They don't have a bell, but they have a whistle. Mia blows it, shouts Round One, and Finch and Julian begin. They're dressed in trousers and white tank tops. Julian has taken off his crystal necklace and left his shirt close by so he can dress as soon as the fight is over. He doesn't mind Mia seeing his muscled body, but he'd prefer her not to catch sight of his armful of tattoos, not to see her own name engraved on his skin. Last time with Shae it spelled nothing but trouble.

When the men stand next to each other, it's obvious that while Finch is taller, Julian is much stronger. Finch is a stalk, and Julian is a fighter. They circle each other. Finch lunges for Julian, goes barreling forward. They dance around for a minute, with Finch flailing his fists and Julian weaving around. He doesn't want to hurt Finch.

Well, maybe he wants to hurt him a little.

He lets Finch get a couple of swings in. As in a pro wrestling match, Julian exaggerates the force of the hits, nearly falling at one point. For three rounds, he puts on a pretty good show. He feints and swerves, lets Finch shove and push him. He gets in only a few light shots, to make it seem like a real fight and not to let Finch get too close. The audience loves it. They're all on their feet, screaming. If this was a real fight, it would almost be fun.

Who is Julian kidding. It's still so much fun. There is nothing like the drama of the ring.

When one of Finch's punches connects a little too squarely with his face, Julian unleashes a flurry of jabs and crosses from left and right and knocks Finch down with a soft left hook. Of course, Finch refuses to stay down, and jumps up on seven, dazed, but with his fists raised. Julian is forced to knock him down a second time, more forcefully. It's a good thing Duncan is ready with that pillow, shoving it under Finch's head the moment his head hits the ground. The young man has a swollen eye and a cut lip, but is otherwise intact, except for his pride. He refuses to shake hands with Julian until Duncan and Wild force him.

"Good fight, Finch," Julian says smiling up at the young man.

"You got lucky," Finch says, gruffly. "We're going to have a rematch."

"Any time, my friend," says Julian. "Name the day. Except tomorrow night. Because tomorrow night, Mia and I are going to the pictures."

14

Gone with the Wind

FOUR MEN AND FOUR WOMEN—JULIAN, FINCH, WILD, Duncan, Mia, Frankie, Liz, and Shona—meet at Leicester Square in Covent Garden at one o'clock in the afternoon to line up for the four o'clock show. The queue is four blocks long, almost to the Strand. It's been cold and then it rained and now it's cold again and everything on the ground is black slush that squelches in Julian's boots as he stands next to Mia, and Finch says, "Hey, who said anything about standing next to her? That wasn't part of the deal."

Inside the enormous Empire, they find good seats right in the center. At first, Finch plants himself on the other side of Mia and acts all surprised when he gets hollered at by the boys. "What? Why can't I sit here? He's sitting next to her, as agreed."

After Duncan and Wild threaten to forcibly remove him if he doesn't remove himself, Finch sneaks off to a seat next to Frankie, a row behind. After a few minutes of Finch *literally* breathing down his neck, Julian motions for Mia to get up. They move a few rows behind Finch and Frankie. "Sorry to play musical chairs," Julian says, "but the film is four hours long. He's going to put a curse on me. Throw me off my game. What if I want to hold your hand?" He smiles. "Or kiss you?"

"Oh, I don't think he'd like that," Mia says.

"I'm not going to be kissing him, am I?"

She blushes. "Never mind him," she says. "He's just shocked he lost. That's why he's acting like this."

"Is *that* why."

"Why do you think?"

"Why do I think what? Why is he acting like an idiot or why did he lose?"

"Heh. Why did he lose?"

"He just didn't want it bad enough," Julian says.

Mia chortles. "Unlike you?"

"Yes. Unlike me."

They get comfortable in their plush red seats. Their coats stay buttoned and the gloves stay on because it's cold in the mammoth theatre. But she does take off her headscarf. She has brushed out her fine brown hair, scrubbed her face, put on mascara, a little lipstick, even some perfume. Julian can smell the floral delicate something every time she moves her head.

"How did Finch put it?" Julian says. "This is almost like a romantic outing."

"Yes, almost," she says, bubbling. "Movies are so great, aren't they? You know what must be romantic? To be in one. Oh, Miss Delacourt, Clark Gable is here to see you. Oh, Miss Delacourt, would you like your caviar and champagne now or after you have your hair done?" Mia sighs happily. "Vivien Leigh is such a star. I wonder if she and Clark Gable had a fling. Who could resist him?"

"Um, maybe someone who's married to Laurence Olivier?"

Mia looks doubtful. "The picture is supposed to be amazing. I can't wait. How long before it starts?"

"Another hour."

She tuts. "So long."

"To sit next to you for an hour? Doesn't seem long at all."

She smiles into her lap. "Want to play a game?"

"Sure, what kind of game are you thinking? Or would you like me to pick?"

"Julian!"

Finch hears their chatter, their laughter, and spins around to glare at them.

"What, Finch?" says Julian. "Are we not allowed to talk?"

"The deal was to sit next to her."

"In *silence*?"

"That was the deal."

Duncan slaps Finch upside the head, and so does Shona.

"Shut up and face front, Finch," Wild says. "You should've fought harder if you wanted to sit next to Folgate in silence. We all would be happier, frankly. We'd be at the Savoy, drinking from a champagne fountain and eating caviar out of crystal goblets."

Wild has found a seat between Finch and Liz. Mia leans to Julian. "It doesn't seem like it, watching them from behind," she says, "but this is the best day of Lizzie's life, sitting next to Wild."

"I know how she feels," says Julian.

"Why, you want to sit next to Wild, too?" Mia says, but she removes her glove, leaving her white right hand lying uncovered on the armrest, close to Julian's fully-fingered rough and square left.

It's almost time. The theatre quietens.

The red curtain opens. The lights go out. "Tara's Theme" plays. *Gone with the Wind* begins.

Right before the intermission, the air raid siren goes off. The auditorium groans in collective displeasure. The film stops playing, but no one moves. Miraculously, it's only a warning, and the all clear blares a few minutes later.

An hour before the end, the siren goes off again, and this time there is no all clear. Above the soundtrack, the drone of the German planes is heard and distant explosions. The movie stops rolling, and the PA comes on, telling everyone to head for shelter. "Walk, ladies and gentlemen, don't run, there's no need for that. Walk, don't panic. Remember, you are British."

Half the auditorium stays behind, including the Ten Bells gang, everyone but Liz. She leaves *Gone with the Wind*, leaves

Wild! and runs for shelter. "Truly, she is hopeless," Mia says. "Her last name, *Hope,* is merely ironic."

There's whistling outside. The explosions get nearer, thud thud thud. Mia chews her fingers. "Let's wait a few more minutes," she says to Julian, glancing around. "See, we're not the only fools in the theatre. But how can we leave? I *can't!* It was just getting to the good part."

"Oh?" Julian says. "And what part is that?"

"Rhett and Scarlett have been fighting and fighting," Mia says. "Which means that the scene where they make up is coming up."

"Yes, that's true, it's coming up."

"How do you know, you've read the book?"

"Something like that. If you like, I can tell you what happens. Just in case the movie doesn't restart."

Mia turns to him. She is sitting so close. Her limpid face, her huge brown eyes, her full glossy mouth is a breath away. "You want *me,*" she says incredulously, "to miss a scene where *Clark Gable* is going to make up with Vivien Leigh? You're going to *tell* me about it instead?" She boos. "Honestly, Jules. What words do you think you could ever use that would be a substitute for my own two eyes?"

While they slink down in their seats, hoping the projectionist returns to his post, Julian thinks of some words to substitute for Mia's own two eyes.

"Rhett Butler comes home late and drunk," he says, leaning to her and lowering his voice. "He's all hunky and hulky and reeking of alcohol. His hair is disheveled. His white shirt is open at the collar. Scarlett is sitting at the kitchen table, waiting for him in a little bathrobe, and underneath it she's naked."

"How do you know she's naked?"

"I just do."

"The book said?"

"Yeah. The book said."

"Okay, go on."

"Scarlett sits at the table in her red silk robe, and she's acting all mad."

"So mad," Mia says.

"She's mad, but underneath the robe, she is naked," Julian says. "And Rhett knows this."

"How does he know?"

"He's a man. Men know these things."

"All men?"

"Most men. Rhett Butler certainly."

"Okay, go on."

"Rhett is angry, too, but for different reasons. He is so tired of all this Ashley talk. So *damn* tired. Ashley is milquetoast to a *man* like Rhett Butler. He can't believe the woman he has loved all these years, the woman he has married, keeps telling him, *him*! that she loves another." Julian pauses. Mia's head is tilted so far over, it's touching his own. "Do you want me to stop using my words? Or would you like me to continue?"

"No, don't stop," she says in a breathy whisper. "Continue."

Julian takes her soft hand into his paw.

"They're in the kitchen, and Scarlett is acting *so* nonchalant, as if she doesn't even notice how hot he looks."

"Hot?"

"Hot, like superman-sexy. And Rhett is fed up with her nonsense, with her not paying attention to him. Fed up with her not wanting to be loved by him. So he spins her chair around and looms over her, and she can see him now, and smell him, and she says, you're drunk, and he says *yeah*." Julian's thumb caresses the inside of Mia's palm.

"What happens next?"

"Rhett leans down and kisses Scarlett so hard, the chair tips back and nearly falls. Scarlett's hands are up in the air like she's surrendering. And he says to her, tell me, would your *Ashley* kiss you like that? But Scarlett can't speak after being kissed so forcefully."

Julian stops talking. Mia's flushed face—her parted, barely breathing mouth, her blinkless gaze, her intense focus so she doesn't miss a word—disrupts him.

"No, no, no," she whispers, "don't stop. Please."

Julian says nothing. He is turned to her, leaning in, his head pressing against her head, his forehead touching her hair, his fingers kneading her hand. "You don't want me to stop, Mia?" His voice is low.

"I don't want you to stop. Go on. Go *on*."

Julian speaks into her ear. "Scarlett looks up at him and sees the way he's looking down at her. He's not waiting another moment, and he's not going to ask if it's okay. He is going to take what he wants. That's the drunken lusty look Rhett gives Scarlett, though he doesn't say anything. It's all in his eyes." Julian takes a breath. "Do you want to know what he actually says, Mia?"

"Oh *yes*!"

"That's *it*, Rhett says. That's *it*. And he picks up Scarlett, and in his arms carries her up their long enormous staircase to their bedroom and with his foot kickslams the door shut behind them."

Mia nearly groans. Julian leans back.

"What happens next?" she cries, raising her impassioned eyes to him.

"Well, it's a *movie*," Julian says, "made in 1939. So what happens next in the movie is morning. But would you like me to tell you what would happen next in real life?"

They stare at each other, both dilated and blinkless. *Yes*, she inaudibly whispers.

The projectionist returns. Everyone applauds.

Everyone but Mia.

15

The Great Fire

WITH THE BOMBS STILL FALLING, THE LIGHTS ARE LOWERED, and *Gone with the Wind* resumes. She sits by his side, pressed into his coat, her warm hand in his. She faces the screen, watches the love scene, and the others that follow. After it's over, on the way out of the theatre, everyone chats about the film, everyone but Mia. Finch asks her opinion, and pensively she replies that she loved it and doesn't say any more. For some reason, this makes Finch give Julian a dirty look. He tries to draw Mia away. Disengaging from Finch, she remains at Julian's elbow.

They're barely out of the theatre, having just turned the corner on the Strand when the siren sounds for the third time. Above their heads, in the illuminated clouds, Julian sees the pencil-thin fuselage and the elliptical wing silhouettes of the Spitfires, and a shadowy bulky formation of the much larger Hurricanes.

They hurry down the Strand, but they can't get to Temple fast enough. The incendiaries fall by the dozens, lighting up the thoroughfare from end to end. The gang runs for cover and disperses.

Seeing the Strand on fire, Julian knows. The world will not end in ice.

"You know I really did love the movie, even though I didn't want to talk about it," Mia says to Julian while they hide out in a doorway arch off the Strand. It was cold before and slushy, but the searing heat makes everything melt, even their faces. The hot air is heavy; the flames too near. They got separated from the others, peeled away, ran in confusion, and are now by themselves, waiting out the bombing, the gruesome noise of the enemy and RAF planes above them, the stone buildings crackling.

"I know you did," Julian says.

"But I liked your words even more." Beat. "Do you know why?"

Julian waits for her to speak. How familiar this is, their faces hot, their hearts aflame, speaking of difficult things while London burns around them. Mia, he keeps wanting to ask. Don't you remember me? Don't you know who I am?

"The scene on the screen ended so quickly," she continues, quietly adding, "even the real thing ends rather quickly, to be perfectly honest."

"Sorry to hear that," says Julian.

"But your words I will relive over and over. Every time I hear them, I will feel what you made me feel in that theatre."

"And what was that?"

"I don't know if I can explain," Mia says. "Alive? Or maybe that I wished I were Scarlett."

Julian says nothing.

"Or maybe," she says, "that I wished it was me."

His eyes pour himself into her eyes.

Looking away, as if she can't take the way he's staring at her, Mia pulls out her pack of cigarettes and tries to light one, but her hands are trembling. "Can I ask you a question? The first time we met and you...you know, you..."

"I what?" says Julian. "What did I do?"

"Well, you know."

"I kissed you?"

"Yes." Her eyes shy away.

"What's your question?"

She cocks her head. "That thing you described between Rhett and Scarlett, that wasn't what was in your kiss."

"No?" He shifts from foot to foot, glancing out onto the Strand. How are they going to get out of here before they burn?

Are they going to get out?

"Something else was in yours," she says.

"Like what?"

"I don't know how to describe it."

"Try. Use your words, Mia." He takes a step toward her in the small space. "What was in my kiss?"

"It was…" She can't look at him. "Like it wasn't about *that*. Oh, some of that was in there, too, for sure, but mostly it was other things. It wasn't a first kiss is what I'm saying." Mia inhales, exhales. "It wasn't tentative and it wasn't questioning, and it wasn't purely amorous."

Julian is silent.

"Are you not going to help me?"

"You're using your words quite nicely," he says. "Keep going."

"But do you know what I mean?"

"Keep going."

"It was an open kiss of a mighty and well-worn heart," Mia says. "It wasn't the kiss of love…"

"Mine wasn't the kiss of love?"

Mia doesn't know where to look. "What I mean is—it was how Rhett might've kissed Scarlett if she hadn't been pretending that she loved dumb Ashley."

Or dumb Finch.

"If they had stayed together for years, and he went off to war, and when he came back, their house had burned down, and she was gone, and he searched for her across the scorched South, and when he finally found her, he took her in his arms and pressed her to his lips." Mia's face is aglow, breathless, shimmering, as if she is imagining real love instead of Rhett's love. "And he said to her, Scarlett, I have searched for you for a thousand years."

"He might say, I have searched behind the sun for you, at the bottom of the earth for you," says Julian, taking her into his arms, one arm over her shoulder, one through her waist. "He might say, my *love*, I found you again."

"Yes, something like that…"

Bending his head, he kisses her, first softly, then openly, his arms wrapped around her coat, a papa bear embracing his mama bear.

"And there it is again," whispers Mia.

∞

When Mia and Julian return to Bank, they overhear the Ten Bells gang ladling out to Finch some deeply unwanted advice.

"Break it off with her, Finch. It's inevitable."

"I don't want to break it off with her!"

"Do you know what the word *inevitable* means?" Wild says. "You can't stop it. Don't take it so personally."

"Don't take another guy making a play for my girl personally?"

"That's right, Finch," says Duncan. "This shit happens."

"I'm not going to let it happen."

"Come now, mate. You can't stop the real thing when it comes."

"What real thing? Only yesterday you told me it was nothing but acting!"

"That was yesterday."

"So what changed?"

"Well, today came, for one."

"She promised she'd marry me. *Me!*"

"Don't feel bad," Wild says. "Nick ended it with his girl."

"Fuck off!" says Nick.

"Sheila ended it with her fella."

"He ended it with me, you mean," says Sheila.

"And Frankie over there told me last week she liked you. Didn't you, Frankie?"

"Yeah," Frankie says, busy with her jigsaw puzzle. "I like you, Finch."

"Frankie, do you like Duncan, too?" Finch asks.

"Yeah, I like him."

"What about Wild?"

"Yeah, him, too."

"What about Kate?"

"Yeah, I like her."

"I don't know what your point is, Finch," Duncan says, "but *my* point is that there are other fish in the sea."

"I don't want other fish," says Finch. "I want the fish that was promised me."

"Yeah, but, mate, your fish has found another fish to swim with."

"And soon there will be a school of them." Wild grins.

"Where are they? He doesn't know this town, doesn't know which way to go. He took her the wrong way, straight down the burning Strand, they probably ran right into an incendiary," Finch says.

"Are you hoping for that, mate?"

"We're all right, Finch." Mia steps into the passageway, letting go of Julian's hand. "No incendiaries."

Finch jumps up. "It's not true what they're saying, dove. Tell me it's not true!"

"I'm very sorry, Finch. It's true." She tries to touch him. "Let's go talk over there. Just you and me."

He recoils. "No! How can you do that? We're engaged!"

"Well, okay, engaged, but I don't see a ring on my finger."

"Is that what it's all about? I said I'd get you one for Christmas."

"Now you don't have to."

Finch swirls to his friends, laid out on the blanketed concrete and the bunks, looking up at him with sympathy and affection. "I told you *Gone with the Wind* was a terrible idea," he shouts. "You mocked me when I said it's not just sitting next to her. Well, who's laughing now?"

"Not me."

"Not me."

"Not me," Frankie says. She never laughs.

"And it doesn't look like you either, Finch," says Wild.

"Oh, you taunted me, come on, Finch, don't be such a ninny, Finch, it's just a movie, Finch."

"Come on, Finch," Wild says.

"Don't be such a ninny, Finch," Nick says.

"It's just a movie, Finch," Shona says.

"Don't you want her to be happy, Finch?" Duncan says. "We're at war. We could die tomorrow."

"Oh, sure, hope for that." Finch swirls to Julian standing silently by Mia's side. "What, cat got your tongue?" he says in a bark.

"Don't you want her to be happy, Finch?" says Julian. *We could die tomorrow.*

"You're saying she won't be happy with me?" Finch clenches his fists, squares off, then backs off. Julian doesn't even take his fists out of his pockets. He has pity for Finch, but he's also relieved he can finally stop pretending.

It's Liz who comes to the rescue. Putting her arm around Finch, she leads him away to the pile of their stashed whisky hidden under coats and sweaters. "Look at it this way," Liz says, pouring him a large mug, "your life is too precious, especially nowadays, to waste on someone who doesn't feel about you the way you feel about her."

"Oh, isn't that rich, you of all people saying that!"

"Shut up, Finch," says Liz.

"Hey, he never gave me a ring!" Mia calls after them indignantly.

And then deep night comes, and the siren goes. They hoped because there had been so many raids that day, that they'd be spared another one in the middle of the night. But no such luck.

Exhausted, still half in their cups, they stagger upstairs to the jeep parked on Lothbury, switch it on, turn to Mia, like a sleepwalking drill, and in the dark ask where to.

Leman Road in Whitechapel, she says, half-asleep.

And Whitechapel gets ignited that night.

The Germans come for Whitechapel.

The road Finch usually takes is blocked off by fallen burning buildings. He takes them another way through an alley. Mia tells him not to because the alley is narrow. Two cars can't pass each other, and a car can't turn around if it needs to. But Finch says it's the quickest way to Leman.

Julian hears the words *narrow* and *alley*, hears *two cars can't pass each other*, and says Finch please don't go that way, *please*. Find another route. I have a bad feeling.

But Finch is mad and defiant. He goes that way.

There is no other car, no head-on collision, no oak tree. There is a bomb that falls through the narrow buildings, cascades, and explodes, cratering the earth thirty feet in front of their vehicle. Julian has just enough time to push Mia down. The force of the blast propels the truck half a block in reverse and shatters the windshield, which sails through the interior of the jeep like hail.

16

Finch and Frankie

JULIAN IS SPARED THE WORST OF THE GLASS, BUT A PIECE OF concrete hits him in the face and breaks open the skin above his brow. It's not a life-threatening wound but a profusely bleeding one. He can't see, and he can't find Mia.

Mia, Mia.

He hears Wild's voice, *Swedish, can you help.*

He hears Mia's voice, *Jules, my God.*

He presses his palm against his eye, tries to orient himself. Mia presses her hat into his gushing wound.

Mia, you okay?

I'm okay, but Finch is not okay.

Swedish, can you help Finch?

Finch is slumped over the wheel. Duncan has crawled out into the street.

Dripping blood, Julian helps Wild drag Finch from the truck. They lay him on the ground next to Duncan. An enemy incendiary has dropped into one of the nearby houses to let there be light. As the alley burns, Julian pulls shard after shard out of Finch's face and neck. Wild lies on top of Duncan to stop his convulsions. Mia keeps pressing her soaked wool hat and then her headscarf against Julian's forehead as he continues to work on Finch. Julian's coagulating blood drips thickly onto Finch's head and into Mia's hands.

From the back of the jeep, Wild gets what bandages they have while they wait for Phil to arrive in the HMU. Mia wraps the gauze around Julian's head. *Tighter, Mia, tighter.*

I don't want to hurt you.

You want me to stop bleeding, don't you? Tighter.

Duncan is moaning. He has stopped shaking, which is a good sign. But the HMU isn't coming, and they can't hear the siren of the fire brigade or the police, only the siren of the enemy.

That's a good sign, too, says Mia. That means someone out there needs Phil more than us.

Julian doesn't know if that's true. Finch's neck just above the collarbone has been opened by a piece of glass. It didn't hit his carotid, or he'd be dead, but it must have nicked the external jugular vein. Julian is having a hard time stopping the bleeding.

Maybe we can try to get him back into the jeep and find a Fixed Unit, says Mia.

He needs the hospital, Julian says. He knows the portent of the word "hospital." He wouldn't say it if he didn't mean it.

Mia, Wild, and Duncan gasp. Everyone knows most injuries are dealt with at the HMU, all suturing, splinting, cleaning, bandaging, tracheotomies, even some amputations, are dealt with right on the field. The Fixed Medical Unit takes care of the larger abdominal and head wounds, open fractures, blood transfusions, people unconscious for more than fifteen minutes. There's a surgeon on staff at the Fixed Unit. But the hospital? The hospital is where you go when there is almost no hope.

Mia's right, let's get him back in the jeep, Wild says. Maybe you can drive it to Royal London, Swedish.

The Rescue Squad needs a rescue.

But before they move him, the Heavy Mobile Unit finally arrives. Phil, Shona, Sheila, and Frankie jump out.

I guess we needed help after all, says a flattened Mia.

Phil and Sheila attend to Finch. Everyone else tensely watches. They manage to compress his neck wound to slow the blood loss. They lift him into the truck.

"You need the hospital, too, Duncan," Phil says, and everyone shudders.

"Fuck no," Duncan says. "I'm not going to the hospital. I'm fine."

"You're not fine. After Shona drops off Finch, she'll take you to the Fixed Unit if you really insist."

"I'm fine, I said."

Duncan is not fine. He is walking funny. Phil says he may have a cracked vertebra. One of his legs is dragging; it's a tell-tale sign. The big man doesn't want to hear it. The squad needs him. Plus, he's got to be at the Docklands by one.

"Dunk, don't be daft," Shona says. "What Docklands? Phil's right. You can't walk, how are you going to lift things?" The worry for him on her face surpasses professional interest.

"Well, you know what they say," Duncan says, "don't lift with your back."

Shona gets him to put his arm around her as he stumbles around, trying to get his legs to cooperate. "Come on, Dunk, you mule, come with me and Finch," she says, looking up at him. "Not the hospital, just the Fixed Unit. Let them X-ray you. Please." She looks relieved when he agrees. Seconds later, she's off with both Duncan and Finch in her truck.

While the fire brigade works on putting out the flames, Phil sutures Julian's brow, and Sheila wraps his head, expertly, tightly, and without fear of hurting him—either without fear or without care.

Julian didn't think anyone could walk away from a head-on collision with a bomb, but he, Mia, and Wild walk away on their own two feet. Wild is dizzy and wobbles as he walks. He might have whiplash or a concussion. And Mia limps and can't flex her left elbow. Phil has wrapped her ankle which might be sprained or broken and put her arm in a sling. Julian's eye socket is turning black and blue. The eye has swollen almost completely shut. Of course the injury is over his good right eye. *Of course.*

Tonight the Rescue Squad can't help the displaced families locate and tag their valuables or to put out small fires in their kitchens. Tonight all the fires are enormous, and the squad can barely help themselves.

With difficulty, Julian drives the jeep. He doesn't want to confess to Mia and Wild how poorly he can see. What a black irony it will be if he crashes. Burning London, with its pockets of intense heat between strips of frigid night air, looks and feels even more unreal through the Gaussian blur of Julian's long-damaged left eye. The jeep is also not doing great. He almost couldn't get it started. It's sputtering. He can't get it into gear. He drives the whole way in first and second.

"Finch will kill you, Swedish," Wild says. "Not only did you take his girl, but you wrecked the transmission in his truck. Frankly, I don't know which is worse."

∞

By the time they return to Bank, it's after seven in the morning and everyone else has gone to work, except for Lucinda who wakes up long enough to take a look at them, not acknowledging their injuries in any way, ask if they've seen Phil and Sheila, and after determining that her husband and daughter are okay, to turn back to the wall. Wild climbs into his bed and is asleep or passed out in seconds. Julian and Mia stare at the empty bunks, at each other. They're covered in blood and grime and dust.

"The laundry truck is coming at nine," she says, uselessly patting the dust off Julian's coat. "We can wash our clothes then."

"We need a human laundry."

"That's at ten. Let's sleep for a few hours. Then we'll get up and take care of other things."

"How can we sleep? We'll get everything bloody. Look at us."

"So?" Mia says. "We'll wash the sheets and blankets, too. But I can't climb into the top bunk. Let me lie down with you."

On his side he lies down in the bottom bunk, and she fits in front of him, propping her injured arm with a pillow. He pulls up the blanket to cover them and carefully lays his arm over her. Mia, it's *us*, he whispers. *The way it's always been.*

"What I wouldn't give for a bath and a proper bed," Mia whispers back, as if she didn't hear him.

"After we wake up, let's go," Julian says. "Let's go to the Savoy."

Thinly she laughs.

"I'm serious," he says. "We'll eat at the Grill and get one of their rooms. We'll have a real bath."

"Are we listing our dreams?" she murmurs, sounding almost asleep. "Because I've got a few of my own. On whose largesse are we going to do this?"

"Yours."

"With what, the forty sovereigns you told the old bag were mine?"

"Precisely." Julian feels in his pants' leg for the pouch with the coins in it. Less than forty coins now. He sewed the pocket closed a few weeks ago after the purse had nearly fallen out during a tumble in a bombed-out house. Her money isn't safe. She is not safe.

"I won't lie, tonight was a little bit frightening," she whispers. "Being enclosed by fire like that with no way out."

Saying nothing, he presses himself to her, his face at the back of her head.

"Can I tell you something?" Mia says. "I had the strangest sensation when we were there. I can't even describe it. It was almost like a memory. I'm breathing the hottest air I've ever been in. My throat is bloodied, and I'm about to hit the ground, and the bottoms of my feet are melting. I put my hand out and pray *please don't let us die like this.* But it felt like I was the one on the ground not Finch, and you were leaning over me. It was so damn peculiar. I've never felt anything like it. I couldn't tell if I was living it or *re*living it."

Peculiar indeed, Julian whispers.

Don't take your arm away from me, Mia says. It's not too heavy.

Wasn't going to, he says.

They sleep through the laundry truck and the human laundry. They sleep until Wild wakes them at nearly five in the evening. He gives them an update on Duncan and Finch. Duncan's X-rays were inconclusive, and the giant took that as good news and went to work, even though he could barely stand. "He told Shona he preferred being in a horizontal position anyway," Wild says, grinning. Finch is still at Royal London. He needed a blood transfusion. Frankie gave two pints of blood to Finch. "Now when Finch wakes up, he's going to start making puzzles, too," Wild says.

Wild makes a Swedish flame, just like Julian taught him, and Mia and Julian warm up a pot of water and clean their faces and hands. Mia's elbow feels better, she says, though Julian doesn't believe her, since she's not moving her arm. Phil and his daughters are not back yet, so Wild and Mia together perform emergency medical services on Julian's head wound. Mia cleans it, and Wild wraps it, and she re-wraps it because Wild can't tie the gauze with one hand. For dinner, they go to a cafeteria near Monument, and when they return to Bank, everyone's back. "Frankie, you're a hero, you gave two pints of your blood to Finch?" Mia says.

"Yeah, by the time it was all said and done," says Frankie. "You want *more* blood? I said. I didn't know I had any left."

Struggling up on a bench, Mia whistles to get the Ten Bells' attention. She's always up on a stage. "Listen, squad, and listen good," says Mia. "We know that the Savoy Hotel has been hit seven times. But despite that, the Grill remains open for business. That's how we need to look at life. Hit seven times, yet still open for business."

"Are you open for business?" Duncan shouts.

Shona smacks him. Wild yells at him. Mia continues.

"The food there continues to be excellent, despite the rationing and the mortar dust. And rooms are available, rooms that have their own private baths and showers! The reason I'm telling you this is because as a Christmas gift to us, Julian is taking us all to the Savoy! Yes, it's true. So cheer up, mates. Cheer up, Frankie. Let's get cleaned up. Dresses for the ladies, lounge suits and bowler hats for the gents. We are going to the Savoy!"

She beams at Julian. He fakely beams back. Hadn't he suggested just the two of them going? He doesn't remember inviting the entire Ten Bells gang into his reverie.

"Swedish," Wild says, "you're a gem."

"Yeah, well."

Liz jostles Nick. "Did you hear? Julian's taking us to the Savoy."

"Fuck off!" says Nick.

"After afterward, he's getting us a room and we can sleep in a bed and take baths."

"Fuck off!"

"Are we all going to sleep in a Savoy bed?" Duncan asks, red with insinuation.

"Duncan!" Shona yells. "One more remark like that, and you're not going."

"Mia's right, though," Julian says. "We need clothes that are less dusty and torn. We need to look less…"

"Less *what*? Less like we're in a war?"

"Yes."

"Fuck off," says Nick.

"Let's go to Oxford Street," says Mia. "We'll meet up tomorrow evening and find something to wear, and the next day we'll go to the Savoy. It'll be a Friday, so no work on Saturday. It'll be perfect."

"Are we really going to stay overnight?" Duncan says, unable to wipe the smile off his face.

"Why not?" says Julian.

"All of us?"

With a slight headshake at Mia, Julian nods at Duncan. "Sure, why not."

They become immeasurably excited, even Peter Roberts, who cautiously says, "Are you sure about this, young man? That's going to be very expensive."

"Robbie," Wild exclaims, "good God, what are you doing? Don't talk him out of it!"

Frankie is subdued. "Poor Finch. He would've liked to go to the Savoy, too."

"If you want, we can wait until he's released," Julian says. Everyone turns to Phil Cozens and his daughters the nurses for their prognosis. And they turn to Frankie who was last to see him.

Smiling a pasted-on smile, Frankie shakes her head. "We shouldn't wait," she says. "He isn't doing great. He is still losing blood. The doctor thinks he might have a small piece of glass traveling through his body ripping up his veins."

"Fuck off..." says Nick.

"Poor Finch."

They agree to go to the Savoy without Finch. They make Julian promise that when Finch is released, they'll go again to have dinner at the Grill.

They plan to meet on Oxford Street the following evening at six o'clock, hoping there will be no bombing. Last Thursday, when they were at *Gone with the Wind*, bombs fell on Tottenham Court Road at seven. The Germans are not waiting until late night anymore. Their attacks have become more indiscriminate, more random, and therefore more vicious. Because you can't prepare for them.

On Thursday evening the siren goes off at five. Julian is still walking up from Holborn. Before the Ten Bells can shop and dine, the planes fly and the bombs fall. One drops near Holborn, one on Chancery Lane, and one on Oxford Street. As a limping Julian run-and-guns, he opens and closes his hands. Are they tingling? Or is Mia still alive?

She is still alive. She was late getting out from Lebus and missed the worst.

An entire black cab got blown into a shop window.

One woman's torso couldn't be found.

Another woman, waiting on Oxford Street with her husband, was found hours later on the next block still holding her husband's arm. Only his arm.

That man was Phil Cozens.

And the woman was his wife Lucinda.

The evening at the Savoy gets postponed.

On Friday morning, Oxford Street is mobbed. Despite the massive post-bombing clean-up, Londoners scour the stores, hunting for bargains, getting ahead on their Christmas shopping before the real crunch in mid-December, and all the while Frankie sifts through the rubble and dust. Julian, Mia, and Nick help her. Days later, when Frankie's work on Phil and Lucinda is complete, they're released to their daughters, and Kate and Sheila can bury their mother and father.

Afterward, Frankie travels to Royal London with what's left of the gang, and those who can donate three more pints of blood to Finch.

17

Ghost Bride and
Johnny Blaze

TO CHEER THEMSELVES UP, THE TEN BELLS PUT UP A SMALL
Christmas tree outside their passageway. They trim it with some
garland, Mia's Brodie for a topper, and a red ball. Julian and Nick
go together to pick up some more things from the lorries behind
Smithfield. Duncan is nursing his sore back, and Wild is up in
North Camden, visiting his parents. Julian likes Nick. He doesn't
say much, but what he says is choice. To every black-market price
he hears, his reaction is the same. "Fuck off!" says Nick. "It's a
steak and kidney pie, not fucking caviar!"

"Who said anything about *steak*?" the seller says. "I'm not
guaranteeing what meat's in that pie. Could be horse. Could
be possum. Could be anything. You want it or not? Look at the
queue behind ya."

Back at Bank, they have a wake for Phil and Lucinda. They
eat black-market meat and kidney pies, they drink good whisky,
have chocolate, they smoke. Julian makes a Swedish flame, and
in thanks, Kate changes the dressings on his head wound. Their
jeep has died. It won't start at all. It's parked on Lothbury, nothing
but a giant paperweight on the street. Soon it will be impounded.
Everyone wonders how Finch will take it when he finds out.

"I went to visit him again today," says Mia. "He squeezed
my hand but didn't open his eyes."

"Poor Finch."

"Poor Phil," says Robbie. He and Phil were the same age, were good friends. They'd known each other forty years, since the turn of the century.

Everyone raises a glass to Finch and Phil and Lucinda.

Mia questions all her choices. If only they hadn't gone to Oxford Street to buy new clothes to go to the Savoy without Finch.

The gang mocks her. Doesn't she know that bombs fall anywhere? Or does she think it's karma? That the Germans are singling her out for mutilation because she dared to want to buy herself a dress?

"Mock if you will," Mia says, "but the council keeps telling us that overindulging is unpatriotic. And doesn't it feel like the Krauts are getting closer and closer?"

"It certainly must feel that way to Phil and Lucinda," says Robbie.

Boom boom.

Thud thud.

They drink to Phil and Lucinda, and they sing.

Weigh-HEY, up she rises
Weigh-HEY, up she rises
Weigh-HEY, up she rises
Earlye in the morning…

At first they talk about the dead, but the more they drink, the more they talk about the living.

The single girls lament spending their nights underground, waiting for their lives to begin.

"There's *plenty* of stuff we can do down here, ladies," Duncan says, liberated by the absence of censorious parents. "Do you want me to show you?"

"Duncan is terrible but right," Julian says. "This isn't waiting. This isn't limbo or the in-between. This is your life. The trenches are your life. The temporary thing, the impermanent thing, the chaotic thing, the impossible thing. This is it. It's all you've got."

He won't look at Mia, and she won't look at him.

They drink some more, hoping it will make them less maudlin.

We're not going to die. Dying is for old people.

"The old people don't want to die either," Robbie says.

Shona walks over and hugs him. "We know, darling. We're sorry."

There's too many things we haven't done.

They entertain themselves by listing some of the things they haven't done.

"I haven't been with two women," Duncan announces in a tone of someone who fully expects the women around him to do something about it.

The girls throw newspapers at him, towels, empty bags. Shut up, Duncan. Enough out of you, Duncan. Now that poor Phil and Lucinda are gone, you think you can say things like this, Duncan?

"I didn't say I necessarily wanted it to be you girls, my dear sisters of mercy," Duncan says to Sheila and Kate. "I mean like in general." He glances at Shona and then away.

Shona doesn't seem like the kind of gal who would put up with that kind of nonsense, and yet she does. "So what if you haven't been with two women?" Shona says. "What man here can lay claim to such a thing? Nick, can you?"

"Fuck off!" says Nick.

"Robbie, can you?"

"I'm not even going to respond," Peter Roberts says.

"Wild's not here. I bet you he has," says Duncan. "Lucky bastard. He's done it all."

They turn to Julian. "You've told us some crazy stories, Jules," Duncan says. "Dungeons, corpses, bloodshed. Perhaps you've got a naughtier story? Now's the perfect time for it."

"Now is most certainly *not* the perfect time for it, and if I did have that kind of story, you think I'd tell *you*?" Julian winks at Mia, and she laughs.

"I haven't danced a jitterbug," says Kate. "Me and Bobby were going to go, and then the dance club was bombed, and the following week he died."

"I've never received a telegram," Liz says.

"*That's* on your wishlist?" says Nick Moore. "Receiving a telegram? Fuck off."

"I'm just saying. I thought we were listing things we haven't done."

"Like a litany of everything?" Nick says. "We ain't got that kind of time, Lizzie. We're at war. Give us your top ten. Telegram is first, we got that. Then what?"

"I never had a standing ovation in a large theatre," Mia says. "Sure, people clap in the Underground. I think sometimes they stand up because they're stretching their legs. Also," she adds, "I'd like to walk down the aisle. In a white dress."

"Hey, why do you get two?" Liz says.

"We're still waiting for what comes after the telegram, Lizzie," Nick says.

"In a *white* dress, Folgate?" Duncan says. "Really?"

To which Julian says *hey*.

"We're all friends here, Swedish," Duncan says. "Mia's not fooling anybody. She knows that God knows the truth no matter what color dress she puts on."

To which Julian says *HEY*.

They laugh, they drink.

Frankie speaks! "I had a fellow propose to me once," Frankie says. "He got me to put down my jigsaw and everything."

They ooh and ahh.

"He seduced me," she says, "by telling me we might die tomorrow. That was some powerful aphrodisiac. I fell for it."

"I must try that," Duncan mutters.

What happened to him?

"He died."

"I'd like to have a baby someday," Mia says.

"That's number three for you," Liz says. "Pipe down!"

"Liz, we're still waiting," Nick says. "Don't be shy. Jump right in. Telegram and then what?"

Everyone knows what it is. Everyone knows how Liz feels about Wild.

"I can't believe I envy my mum," Mia says. "I've never envied her about anything. I thought I was so smart. And now look at me. I lie here in a stinking passageway in bitter envy because she got to be a mum and I haven't."

"There's still time," Frankie says. "It's not too late."

They drink.

"I'd like to have somebody look at me," Liz says unbidden, "just once in my life, the way he looks at her every minute of every day." She points at Julian. "Like she's all he wants."

Mia blushes. Julian looks away.

"Is that before or after you receive the telegram?" Nick asks. "What guy wouldn't ogle you while you're reading *that*. Telegrams are *so* sexy. Or is 'telegram' slang for something else, and I'm not aware?"

"Yes, it's slang for you're a wanker."

"Fuck off," says Nick.

"At my wedding, I want to use my own words for my vows," Mia says.

Liz complains. "Why does she get five things, including Julian's glad eye, and the rest of us get nothing?"

"No one recites their own vows," Duncan says. "That's idiotic. How would that even go?"

Inebriated and determined, the crew springs to drunken action. They have an idea for their next skit. They will stage a wedding! Julian will marry Mia. It'll cheer up the glum folks.

Yeah, glum folks like us.

"It's not great tonight, I admit," Mia says. "Tomorrow will be better. But tonight we all could use a little bit of joy. Jules, are you in?"

"I'm in."

"You have to find a tie and wear your posh three-piece suit. And what are you going to do about the bandage on your head? That's not very matrimonial. We'll leave it, I suppose."

"What are you going to do about the sling over your arm?" Julian says. "You're going to be a bride with a sling?"

Mia slips the sling over her head and lets it drop to the ground. "Can you do the same with your head wrap? I didn't think so. You'll look like Frankenstein. Now, who wants to be the minister?" She turns to Peter Roberts, sitting by himself in the corner. "Robbie, would you like to serve as a fake minister at our fake wedding?"

"You're asking me to take part in one of your stories?"

"Yes! Please."

Robbie gets up. "I thought you'd never ask."

Mia embraces him. "Do you need me to find you some words to say?"

"No. I got this." He straightens out his suit jacket and adjusts his bowtie.

"Tie is straight, Robbie," Duncan says. "Your tie is like a level. Shelves can be put up off your tie."

"Thank you," Robbie says. "It's hard to keep it straight with Wild around. He's always fooling with me."

"I hope Wild forgives me for having a fake wedding without him," Julian says. "I told him he could be my best man."

"Serves you right to make promises you can't keep," Duncan says. "You'll have to make do with the rest of us. Now…where are we going to find a white wedding dress for our virginal bride?" He winks at Mia. "We might just have to suspend our disbelief and imagine her brown skirt is white."

Mia slaps him and after some rummaging produces an off-white sheet. "Kate, can you make arm holes in it with your father's scalpel so I can wear it like a cloak? Who's got a belt? I will be Ghost Bride." She claps. "Perfect! That's what we're going to call our play. The War Wedding of Ghost Bride and…Jules, what should we call you? Swedish Fjord?"

"Johnny Blaze," says Julian.

"Who is Johnny Blaze?"

"He is Ghost Rider."

"Oh my word," Duncan exclaims, "is our straight-laced Julian being naughty? Ghost Rider indeed. Delicious! Watch out, Mia."

Julian shakes his head. Duncan is incorrigible.

Mia leans to his ear. "It'd be okay with me if you were being a little bit naughty," she whispers, and then louder, "Robbie, you'll introduce us. The War Wedding of Ghost Bride and Johnny Blaze. Will you remember?"

"No," replies Peter Roberts dryly.

"Because 60-year-olds are incapable of recalling nine words strung together," says Julian.

"Exactly, my boy!"

Liz remembers they have no rings.

"We don't need rings," says Mia, writing in her small notebook. "Julian, we'll do some bits from Shaw toward the end, but to begin, do you know a serious poem? You'll need to be straight man to my comedy. I'll be the funny one, okay? I'll make a joke, I'll say, why do couples hold hands before their wedding? Because it's a formality, like two boxers shaking hands before the fight begins." She chuckles. "Funny, right?"

"I guess," Julian says. "What kind of a poem? Something from Kipling? *Then come, my brethren, and prepare the candlesticks and bells, the scarlet, brass, and badger's hair wherein our Honor dwells.*"

"Hmm, no, more like, shall I compare thee to a summer's day."

"So you get to be funny, and I get to be maudlin and sentimental?"

"That's right," Mia says. "Because you're a Gloomy Gus, especially tonight. I will make them laugh. See if you can make them cry."

"How is that a fair deal? Who wants to cry at a time like this?"

"You should've thought of that before you had that face on."

Julian is not the only one grumbling. "You sure are quick to jump into marriage without any frills," Frankie says to Mia, her tone accusatory. "You didn't marry Finch because he didn't give you a ring."

Julian interjects. "A ring is hardly a frill, and that's not the only reason Mia didn't marry Finch."

"Poor Finch," says Frankie. "Maybe he didn't give you a ring, Maria, because he knew you wouldn't give him any of your blood."

"I couldn't, Frankie! I'm AB positive and he's a B."

"Well, isn't that convenient," Frankie says. "You're the universal receiver? Why am I not surprised?"

"Come on, Frankie," says Julian. "We're trying to lighten up here."

"Frankie is right about one thing," Mia says. "We do need a ring. Liz, go get some tin foil. Twist it up and make two rings out of it."

"And where am I going to get this tin foil from, pray tell?" Liz says. "We can postpone the wedding till tomorrow, and I'll try to get some."

"No," Mia says. "Look at them out there. They need it now. And what if there won't be a tomorrow? Look what happened to our plans for the Savoy."

"We'll go to the Savoy," Julian says. "Now we must go. Where else are we going to celebrate our fake wedding? And also—I have the rings." He slips the rawhide rope off his neck. They gather around him like birds.

"What's that, Jules?" Mia asks, pointing to the crystal quartz.

"Is that a diamond?" says Duncan. "Because if it is, we could stay at the Savoy until the war is over."

"It's not a diamond," replies Julian.

"What's the red thing tied up?"

Julian unlaces the leather strings, unfurls the beret, smooths it out, shows them.

"It's a beret!" Liz exclaims. "Mia, look at that. Not only does Julian have a ring for you, but he's got a spiffy head covering as well. It's not a veil, and it's red, but it'll do."

Mia puts it on her head. It's dim in the tunnel; the kerosene lamps don't give off enough light to see the old faded blood stains.

There's hearty approval of the beret, of the gold bands, of Julian in general.

"Where did you get the rings?" Duncan asks with envy.

"Are they real gold?" Nick asks and before Julian can answer follows up with "Fuck off!"

"I had a gold coin melted down into two rings," Julian says.

"Are these the coins you keep talking about?" says Mia, tilting her red-beret-clad head. "I really thought you were joking." She stares at him uncertainly. "Were you married before, Jules? Is this not your first fake wedding?"

"Don't worry." Julian smiles into her questioning, fascinated face, leans over and kisses her cheek. "I came close to a fake wedding once. Real close. Never quite got there."

"You won't get there tonight either," Frankie says, suddenly a stickler for propriety. "You haven't asked Mia to marry you."

"Calm down. He's already asked me," Mia says. "On stage. When I was Cecily, and he was Algernon. But if you insist, he can ask me again tonight. Right, Jules?"

"Whatever you want, Mia."

She slips the smaller ring over her finger. "It fits perfectly," she says with amazement.

"What a shock," says Liz.

"Go us, right?" says Julian.

"Go us," echoes Mia.

"Somebody help Jules with his tie. Somebody shine his boots. Hurry up. The gallery is getting restless. Who can sing 'Ave Maria'? For me." Mia smiles. "Because I'm Maria."

"I can," Shona says timidly.

"You can sing?"

"A little. Driving is not the only thing I do."

"Oh, yeah?" Duncan says, instantly towering over her, his grin wide. "What else do you do, darling, besides sing and drive?"

Shona slaps his chest. Not, get away from me, Duncan, but, aren't you so funny, Duncan.

Liz remembers they have no flowers.

"Damn it," Duncan says. "What kind of a fake wedding would it be without flowers?"

"Girls, go find a towel," Julian says, "white preferably. Pleat it loosely on top and tie it at the bottom so it looks like a bouquet."

Shona and Liz run off, find a towel, follow Julian's instructions. It looks pretty good.

Already on the stage, Peter Roberts motions for Julian to stand with him as they wait for Mia. The door wobbles. They shift their positions.

"The stage is not fixed," Peter Roberts says. "It's alive like us, unstable like us. It buckles and bends under the weight of our bodies."

Julian nods. "It changes its shape under the movement of our feet. And its new form in turn affects and alters our own motion."

With a nod and a smile, they shake hands.

It begins.

"Dearly beloved," says Peter Roberts, facing the audience. "We are gathered here for your evening's entertainment to act out for you the love story of Ghost Bride and Johnny Blaze, ending in their matrimony which they do not enter into lightly or wantonly but reverently, with hope and with purpose."

"Ending in their matrimony or their weddin' night?" someone from the back yells, not Duncan. "Now *that* would be a show."

"Lords and Commoners of England!" Robbie sternly rejoins. "In the words of John Milton, consider what nation it is whereof ye are, and whereof ye are governors. Behave yourselves. You want that kind of play, wait for the Windmill to reopen. Is everyone ready? Birdie, hit it."

Shona sings Schubert's *Ave Mariiiia.* To everyone's astonishment, Shona has an operatic soprano. *Ave Maria, gratia plena...Maria gratia plena...* The concrete walls of the station amplify and echo her voice, and even without a microphone she sounds as if she's performing for the King at the Royal Albert Hall. Shona sings so expressively, she makes everyone tear up, even Duncan. Especially Duncan.

While Shona sings, a gleaming Mia, dressed in a white sheet and carrying the white towel bouquet, glides through the rows of people, taking her time, smiling left and right. She looks like an otherworldly specter. She said she wanted to walk down the aisle, and she's savoring the opportunity.

Julian gives her his hand to help her up. She balances out the rocky door with her weight as they bob and sway toward each other as if on deck of a ship.

"Ever since they met, on top of this rickety door masquerading as a stage, Bride and Johnny have had quite a tumultuous time together," Peter Roberts says. "Love being a majestic bird, they fell in love deep inside a cave, while outside and above, they've been baptized by fire. Tonight, they have returned to the cave to unite themselves in holy matrimony, because they know it is in the cave that the life of the world began, the old world and the new. They will be together until death do them part," Robbie says.

"Not even then," whispers Julian and Mia says, "What?"

"To commemorate this joyous occasion, they're going to speak at their own nuptials. Yes, ladies and gentlemen, you heard correctly. Who goest first?"

"I do," Mia says. "Every love affair should begin and end with a joke or a poem. I have the joke. And Johnny Blaze has the poem." She stands half facing him, half facing the audience.

"What is the *Ideal Man*?" says Mia. "The *Ideal Man* should *lavishly* praise us for all the qualities he knows we haven't got!

But he should be quite *pitiless* in reproaching us for any virtues we never cared to have in the first place. The *Ideal Man* should *worship* us when we are alone." Coquettishly raising her brows, she bares her white neck to Julian, which he obliges by kissing. The audience hoots and whistles. After a few soaked moments, a flushed Mia steps away, clearing the thickness from her throat. "*Worship* us, yes," she says, "yet he should be always ready to have a perfectly terrible scene—in public or private—whenever we want one. And after a dreadful week of fighting he should, if necessary, admit that he has been *entirely* in the wrong, and then be willing to do it all over again—from the beginning, with variations. Are you that *Ideal Man*, Johnny Blaze?"

"Without a doubt," Julian replies.

Chortling with joy, she offers him her hand to kiss. "O, Johnny, do you have a poem to make them cry?"

"I do." He takes a breath. "What is your substance, whereof are you made," he says, taking both her hands in his, "that millions of strange shadows on you tend? Since everyone has, every one, *one* shade, and you, but one, can every shadow lend. Speak of the spring and autumn of the year, the spring does shadow of your beauty show, the autumn as your bounty does appear—*in you is every shape I know*. In all external grace you have some part, but you like none, none you, for constant heart." Julian's eye throbs. Pressing his palm into his brow, he looks away from her emotional face and into the clapping audience.

"We will now recite for you a short dialogue from George Bernard Shaw," Mia says. "Are you ready?"

"Always, Ghost Bride."

"On your knees. If you can," she adds, a gentle reference to his torn-up calf.

He descends to his knees, wincing slightly. Her soft hand remains in his.

"A man cannot die for just a story and a dream," Mia says. "I know that now. I've been standing here with death coming nearer and nearer, and reality coming realer and realer, and all my stories and all my dreams are quickly fading away into nothing."

"Are you going to die for nothing, then?" Julian says.

"No," says Mia. "I have no doubt that if I must die, I will die for something bigger than dreams or stories."

"Like what, Ghost Bride?"

"I do not know," Mia replies. "If it were for anything small enough to know, it would be too small to die for. What about you, Johnny Blaze?" She gazes down at him. "Will you be ready to die for something other than a dream or a story?"

"No," Julian says. "You are my dream. You are my story. I will die for you." He gazes up at her. "I am your soldier, and you are my country. But first, will you please come down to earth, Ghost Bride? Come down from your cloud of dandelion, and marry me in the asphodel, please, will you marry me in London pride?"

She bends to him, he lifts his head to her, and they kiss.

They kiss and kiss.

"Well done," Mia whispers into his ear, embracing him. "They're all bloody weeping."

"So I win, right?" With effort, he rises to his feet.

Robbie takes the job of fake minister as seriously as he takes learning French. He stands pin straight and instructs them to put the rings on their fingers. Then he speaks in deep and sonorous British. "Ghost Bride and Johnny Blaze, we sit around the fire and tell each other stories in order to live. This is the start of your story." (If only. Julian squeezes Mia's hand to keep his own from trembling.) "You are here to make a new life. And your marriage is not a declaration, just once, at the beginning. As a boxer, Johnny, you don't say, I fought one fight and thus I'm always winning. Your marriage is a choice every day. You choose to love one another, to honor your friends, to play it for a new crowd. Your life is your ever-changing stage. Bring it every night, and leave nothing in the wings. Do not say, once upon a time in December, I was in a war wedding. Say it eight times a week, fifty-two weeks a year. To be faithful, you must first have faith—in the whole dang thing. That's what love is. So go forth, and live your story, Ghost Bride and Johnny Blaze."

After it's over, Mia takes off her ring and returns it to Julian. She asks if she can keep the beret. Why not, he says. He lets her have it. After all, he is not going to need it anymore.

"Are you sure you don't want to keep the ring, too?" he asks.

She laughs as if he is the funniest man in the Underground.

For his performance, Robbie gets more handshakes and compliments than either the fake bride or the fake groom. Two days later, a red double-decker bus gets caught in a bomb blast and stands motionless in the middle of Cannon Street with its passengers dead in their seats. One of those passengers is Peter Roberts, who was on his way to Victoria to take a train to Sussex to be reunited with his wife. He is found upright, open eyes staring ahead, the bowtie under his chin perfectly straight.

18

Deepest Shelter in Town

AFTER THEY LOSE ROBBIE, WILD SAYS TO HELL WITH IT. "Swedish, I will never forgive you and Folgate for getting fake married without me, but I'm not missing your wedding reception at the Savoy because of the fucking Krauts. Let's go. No Oxford Street, no new clothes. Men, clean the damn suits you've got, ladies, shine your shoes, a little lipstick, a little perfume. Tomorrow is Friday. A great day for a celebration. Things can only improve."

Mia puts on her Florence Desmond black velvet dress with red trim, in which she sang "The Deepest Shelter in Town." She has two other dresses, she says, but she liked the way Julian ogled her when she danced in that one. They clean their faces, change their dressings, shave, and brush their hair. Mia takes her arm out of the sling. Julian tries not to limp. His brow is healing, the swelling has gone down, the black eye is yellow and purple. Phil was supposed to take out the stitches, but then he died. Julian pulls them out himself, probably a few days too soon. Duncan tries to walk like his back isn't killing him. They all do their best to look worthy of the Savoy dining room. Unfortunately Nick has gone back to Dagenham; he heard that the Ford plant was reopening.

Julian makes a dining reservation for nine of them: himself, Mia, Wild, Liz, Duncan, Shona, Sheila and Kate, and Frankie. It is an understatement to say that the three boys are delighted to be outnumbered by the six girls. "This way, 'tis heaven," Duncan says.

"Imagine the hell if 'tis was the other way," Wild says. Liz does not look thrilled with the current arrangement. She would prefer Duncan take four women on himself so she could have Wild all to herself. By Duncan's expression, that's what he wishes for also. "And technically, Swedish is taken up by Folgate," Wild adds, "this being their fake wedding reception and all, so it's even better for us, Dunk. Two real men against five fine women."

"I'm not a real man?" says Julian.

"And why only *technically* taken up?" Mia says. "You think my fake husband is about to bolt now that he spies the bounty out there?" She takes Julian's arm as they enter the Savoy, like they're a gentleman and a lady, or maybe a husband and wife.

The porters hold open the heavy doors, and in their lounge suits and bowler hats and dresses, the Ten Bells stroll in as if they belong at a place like the Savoy. No one looks twice at their stitched-up and bandaged faces.

A concierge approaches them to ask if they know where they're going.

"Tell him, Mia," Julian says, "tell him, do any of us really know where we're going, C.J.?"

"How do you know the concierge's name?" Mia whispers.

"To the Grill," Julian tells the man. He's eaten there a few times. Many times, he and Ashton had gone to the art-deco American Bar for drinks. They'd gone to the Grill with Riley for Julian's birthday in March, and for Ashton's in August. Riley loved the place. And later on, so did Zakiyyah. Julian had even taken Devi and Ava there once, though Devi partook of the French-English cuisine like it was rookery gruel.

"Very well, sir," the concierge says. "But you're headed in the wrong direction. The Grill is not to the left of the lobby. That's where our jewelry store is. The Grill is at the back of the hotel, overlooking the Thames." He coughs. "Though, of course, no river view tonight. The curtains are drawn."

"Of course," Julian says. "And thank you." He forgot the hotel had been renovated recently and the restaurants rearranged.

As they walk through the reception hall, Wild asks Julian if he's still thinking of getting a room after dinner.

"Indubitably," Julian replies. "After all, it's our wedding night."

Mia rolls her eyes. "He's kidding. It's our fake wedding night."

"What about the rest of us?" Wild asks.

"You're *definitely* not going to be in the room with us," says Julian.

"He's kidding." Mia shakes her head.

"I'll get you your own room," Julian says to Wild.

Duncan and Wild look doubtful. "Are you sure you have enough money for such an extravaganza, Jules?" asks Duncan.

"I hope to soon be too drunk to care, so yes."

They are placed at a large round table in the middle of the dining room underneath a crystal chandelier. Everyone tries to contain their glee as the menus are brought. They order the Savoy specialty—Pink Gin cocktails—discover they are teeth-rattlingly strong, and gasp at the prices on the menu.

"No one eat a thing," says Duncan. "Not even a piece of bread. Or Jules won't be able to afford the rooms he's been promising. What would you rather have, ladies, caviar or a bath with me? It's either steak or Duncan, girls," he adds as a variation of the Minister of Food's justification for the rationing at restaurants: "*It's either steak or ships, citizens of London.*"

"Most definitely steak, Duncan," Kate says.

To calm Duncan down, Julian slaps a twenty-pound note on the table. "Dunk, eat, drink, be merry, don't worry about a thing."

Duncan relaxes. After two Pink Gins, everyone relaxes. Plymouth gin, a dash or two of angostura bitters and a splash of soda, though for the second one, Julian asks the barman to add some tonic water, or they'll all be under the table by the time the main course is served.

"Chaps," Mia says, "did you know that the Savoy Hotel and Theatre, and my favorite Palace Theatre on Cambridge Circus, were all built by the same man?"

"Richard D'Oyly Carte, right?" says Julian with a twinkle. "With his profits from *The Pirates of Penzance*." Julian smiles as he recalls the depth of his long ago bedazzlement high in the ancient mountains of Santa Monica when she was still Josephine, waxing poetic about a man who loved a woman so much he built her a theatre.

But tonight it is Mia who looks bedazzled. "I still don't know how you know that," she says, "but yes, he built the Palace as a labour of love, but my point is that it was art that made real life possible—that imaginary, make-believe things came first, and they helped build real historic places."

"And please real women," Julian adds.

Mia becomes flustered by his expression, and he by hers.

"We heard the Savoy rooms have steam heat and soundproof walls and windows," Shona says, refocusing the conversation on where it needs to be.

"Do you *need* soundproof windows, dear Shona?" Duncan asks, grinning like a clown.

"I'm done with you, Duncan," she says in the liquid tone of someone for whom the opposite is true.

They order grilled chicken and roast potatoes, foie gras and caviar, steak, bouillabaisse, and bangers and mash. They eat family style, a little of everything. It's all delicious.

"Eating out is a morale booster," Wild says.

"So is sex," says Duncan.

"Duncan!" the girls yell.

"There's help for people like you, Duncan," Wild says, swallowing a tablespoon of caviar without any bread or butter. "In Piccadilly. Sure, Eros has been evacuated, but even in the blackout, the Piccadilly Commandos walk back and forth in the darkness, carrying torches so you can easily find them. Go, Dunk. They're waiting for you. But remember, don't ask for any extra. No use getting fancy. There's a war on, as the council keeps telling us. Luxuries in sex are unpatriotic."

"Everything is either unpatriotic or compulsory," Duncan says. "What we eat. How much we eat. What we wear. What we wash our hair with. How we file our war damage claims, where we sleep. Why can't they make sex patriotic *and* compulsory? Like every day, to do your part for the war effort, you must have a minimum of this. You can have more. But *this* must be the absolute minimum."

"Duncan," says Frankie, "is it possible for you to talk about anything else? Have you got anything else in that head of yours?"

"Trust me, Frankie," Duncan says, "it's not my head I'm thinking with. Besides, these are modern times. You girls keep saying you want to work like men, dress like men, live like men. Well, this is how men talk. Get used to it. This is what sexual equality means."

"Sexual equality, you don't say," Liz intones slowly—nearly the first thing she has said all evening. "Sexual equality would be if after each act of love, both parties were uncertain as to which of them would conceive the child. Now *that* would be true equality. Until such time, shut up, Duncan, and act like a gentleman. Look, Julian and Wild are behaving themselves." Her voice melts when she speaks the name Wild, though she doesn't dare raise her eyes.

"Wild has never behaved himself in his life, Lizzie," Duncan says. "And have you forgotten how Julian mauled another man's girl the second he laid eyes on her?"

"Excuse me," Julian says. "I did not maul. Right, Mia?"

"Why ever not?" Mia says, raising her glass. "To Finch!" They have another boisterous Pink Gin round.

They've decided that Pink Gin is supremely patriotic. Wild raises his glass and says it's his privilege to do his small bit to hold up Hitler's plans. He downs the cocktail in one gulp. Wild can really hold his liquor.

"Yes, it's miserable now," Julian says, offering words of encouragement, "but it will get better, I promise you."

"It's not so miserable now." Duncan smiles, looking around the glorious room, happily smoking.

"Sure, Swedish, *eventually* it'll get better," Wild says. "Either the Germans will run out of planes, or we'll run out of people."

"Oh, we'll definitely run out of people first," Duncan says. "How can we not? No one's shagging, no one's bonking. Truly the world is about to come to an end."

"The world *is* coming to an end," Shona says. "Did you hear that Peckham was destroyed two days ago?"

"Do you know why?" says Duncan. "Because everything is worse south of the river, even the bombing."

"Oh, I don't wish that even on poor Peckham."

"Let's pray for Peckham."

"Yes, let's raise a glass to Peckham."

They drink again.

"My auntie lived next to a paint factory," Shona tells Duncan, leaning into him. The drunker those two get, the chummier they become. "You can imagine how that burned, all those chemicals, all that turpentine. Oh, it burned magnificently, in all the colors of the rainbow. If you weren't so terrified, you had to admit it was very beautiful."

"But then you died from the poison fumes," says Wild.

"Yeah, but while you lived you saw beauty, not a bloody tunnel in a bloody tube station."

"The Bank is home, Shona," Wild says solemnly. "Don't judge. Everything can't be the Savoy. We need the contrast."

"Between the ditch and the Savoy?" Shona smirks.

"Yes," says Wild. "The ditch became Tower Street became Eastcheap became Cannon Street became Ludgate Hill became Fleet Street became the Strand became the Mall became Buckingham Palace."

"Wild, you're a boy after my own heart," Julian says, raising his glass. "But speaking of Buckingham Palace, I don't know why the King and Queen have not evacuated. They'd be so much safer in Canada." In 1666, Charles II fled during the Black Plague, as Baroness Tilly had informed him. What's happening now is worse than the plague.

"How would it look, the King said, if we left our people and ran for the hills?" says Mia. "What kind of an example would that set? The King's exact words were: How can we look the East End in the face?" She shrugs. "Good old George needn't have worried. Soon there'll be no face left in the East End to look into."

"At least Buckingham Palace hasn't been hit," Julian says.

"Oh, it has," Mia says. "Fourteen times. Once again, where have you been that you don't know that?"

"Hand on heart 153 Great Eastern Road," Julian says. "And Greenwich."

"The King is right to stay," Duncan says. "The very awareness of our impermanence is what gives our lives meaning."

"You're less impermanent than you think, my friend," says Julian.

The radio picks that moment to start playing "The Land of Hope and Glory," and the genteel patrons of the Grill, who've all had a bit to drink, let their guard down for a few minutes and sing along, none more raucously than Julian's gang. *"God who made thee mighty, make thee mightier yet!"* they bellow, their arms around each other. By the end of the song, their rousing drunken voices drown out Vera Lynn's on the speakers.

"Getting together with friends and holding court over a meal is one of the great joys in life," a smiling Julian says when the song is finished. A great actor, Robert Duvall, will say that one day.

Hear, hear, his new friends yell. We told you things must improve and have they ever.

What a thing it is to have friends again, Julian thinks, taking Mia's hand under the table.

For dessert they have chocolate bread-and-butter pudding with vanilla bourbon sauce. They wash it down with cognac, listening to the slow intoxicating beats of "When the Lights Go On Again," watching a tall, elegant woman in trousers dance with her gentleman.

"Englishmen are unhappy at the sight of women in trousers," Duncan proclaims—too loudly. He's had an inordinate amount to drink. "A woman in trousers is considered fast." He burps. "What I would give for a fast woman. The faster, the better. Who's got time for a slow woman? Not me."

"Not me either," says Wild. Both men bob their heads and grin at Julian. "What about you, Swedish? You got time for a slow woman?"

"He most certainly does not," says Mia, standing up and extending her hand. "Would you like to dance, my fake husband?"

Wild asks Liz to dance. Liz physically swoons as she rises from the table. Duncan asks Shona *and* Sheila. They both say yes. He asks Frankie and Kate, and they also say yes, though Julian senses that if it were allowed, Frankie and Kate would like to dance together. There is something in the look they give each other as they stand up. Liz dances with Wild, and Shona with Duncan and then Duncan switches four times, and dances with each of the girls, at one point, the changeover coming so slowly that he seems to be dancing with all four at once. Julian and Mia laugh as they watch the intoxicated giant with his tie askew, two-stepping under the dimmed down lights, his big arms around the ladies, looking as if he's already in heaven.

Julian holds Mia lightly around her waist as they waltz while "There'll be Bluebirds over the White Cliffs of Dover," plays on the turned-up radio, and Mia sings along, her gin-spiked breath near Julian's mouth. *Just you wait and see*, she murmurs, and he replies with, *but tomorrow, right, and not tonight?*

"Don't be afraid," she says. "There will be a tomorrow."

He is glad she is sure. "How's your arm? How's your ankle?"

"They're fine," says Mia. "What kind of Brit would I be if I complained about a sore ankle? How's your back?"

"All better."

"Your head better, too? Because it still looks…"

"Yup, it's good," he says.

"Your leg? You're dancing but when you walked, you limped."

"Can't feel a thing."

They smile. She sways a little closer. Her breasts press against his chest. Liz leans over to them on the dance floor and says, "Hey, leave a little space between you two for Jesus."

"We're united in *holy* matrimony, Liz," Mia says. "It's not only allowed, it's expected." Her arms go around Julian, the injured left arm gingerly. "Right?"

He kisses her as they dance. "More than expected," he says. "It's encouraged. The natural instincts and affections imparted to us by God are hallowed and directed aright in marriage."

She smiles into his face. "Julian Cruz, do you have some natural affections that you might like to direct at me?"

"Direct at you aright," he says. His hands tighten around her waist. "Perhaps we should go see if they have any rooms available."

"Yes," Mia says. "It would be a shame if they were all booked up."

"Such a shame."

"Duncan is looking forward to being upstairs," she says. "And do you hear Wild over there, drunkenly trying to persuade Liz to give him her virtue because who knows what tomorrow will bring? I can't believe him. He's trying to seduce her!"

"Does he really need to try?" Julian says, and into her tut, adds, "Mia, Wild knows how Liz feels about him. He doesn't need to say anything. He knows she will give it to him without any words."

Mia steps back and studies Julian. "So why is he talking to her like that then? What kind of a farce is this?"

"Not a farce." Julian pulls her back to him. "He does it because he knows that's what she wants. He tells her what she wants to hear to please her. She wants to hear him want her with his words, even if they're drunk words."

"Hmm," says Mia, shimmying against him. "If that's the case, how come you're not trying to seduce *me*?"

"Who says? What do you think all that Pink Gin was for? Are you dancing with me? Letting me maul you? Did you kiss me, go to the movies with me, fake marry me? What won't you do with me?"

"Julian!"

"Yes, Mia?"

"Let's go get that room."

Julian pays the check, and the nine of them amble over to the pristine and elegant reception area. The only indication inside the marble and granite lobby that there's a war on is the three men by the open doors sweeping glass and dust into bins, the glass and dust that's been dragged into the reception hall from the Strand. One of the jobs of a grand hotel in a grand city is to shield its guests from the world outside its doors. And if ever there was a time to be shielded from that world, it's today.

"We'd like a room, please," Julian says to the tall, sharply attired front desk manager who scornfully scans their ragged inebriated ranks.

"Who is *we*?" he asks. "You and Mrs…"

"All of us," says Julian.

"You can't, sir. Maximum occupancy per room is four. It's a fire hazard otherwise." The officious man says this with a straight face, even as the fire brigade douses a flame on Waterloo Bridge just behind the hotel, even as another fire brigade douses a fire on Exeter Street, across the Strand.

"It's okay, Swedish," Wild says, pulling on his sleeve.

"No, it's not," says Julian. "How many rooms would we need?" he asks the clerk. "There are nine of us."

"Well, then, you would need a minimum of three rooms, sir." The man smirks.

"Very well," Julian says. "We will take four rooms. Preferably adjoining. Any with connecting doors?"

"We don't have four rooms tonight. The house is full. We have two rooms. We also have a two-bedroom suite."

"We'll take it," says Julian.

"Uh-huh," says the clerk. "That will be ten pounds per room, or twenty pounds for the suite, sir." Self-satisfied, the smug man snaps closed the reservation book.

"We'll take the rooms and the suite."

"That would be forty pounds."

From the jacket pocket, Julian takes out his cash. He counts off forty pounds, and another forty—and another forty.

"Here's one hundred and twenty pounds," he says. "Paid in full for the entire weekend." He gives the stunned man another five. "Please bring extra robes, towels, pillows, blankets, extra soap and shampoo, toiletries for the ladies, and for the men razors and shaving foam." He gives the man another ten. "And also ten bottles of champagne, a bottle of your finest gin, a small bottle of angostura bitters, and some tonic water. Oh, and a tray of light sandwiches and scones with jam, in case we get hungry. You know what, make it two trays."

The clerk stands with his mouth open.

"The keys please," Julian says, extending his hand.

The gang maintains their British exterior until they get inside the suite, and then it's pandemonium. They really test the limits of the soundproof walls. Wild hugs Julian so hard he reopens the cut above Julian's eye. They scramble for the white towels to clean him up with while they continue to cheer.

"Nick will piss himself when he finds out he's missing this, the poor bastard," Duncan says.

The suite is large, warm, clean, well-lit, and has two baths. The blackout curtains have been drawn by the turndown maids. They peek outside. There is no river, no Big Ben, no Westminster Palace, no Southbank. There is nothing. What a mistake it was to look, they say, swishing the drapes shut. Let's not do *that* again.

They turn their backs on the reality outside and turn their faces to the revelry inside.

"We are five-star refugees," Wild says. "We are going to get blitzed, as in the old days, and every glass we raise, we will raise to Swedish. I don't think I've ever been happier in my life. Jules, can I call you my best friend?"

"No," says Mia. "He is *my* best friend."

"Just because you have boobs, Folgate, doesn't make you his best friend," Wild says. "Swedish and I are brothers. We have lost our appendages. We have lost our brothers. Jules, who's your best friend?"

"Why do I have to choose?" Julian says.

Duncan comes to the rescue. "Who do you want to sleep with, Jules? That's your answer."

"Duncan, if that was the answer," Shona says, "you'd be calling a hundred women from Wapping to East Ham your best friends."

"My God, where *are* these hundred women?" mutters Duncan.

"Where did you get the money for all this, Jules?" Shona asks. "The black-market runs, the dinner tonight, the suite. That's a lot of cash."

"Remember my story about a murder in a brothel? The Master of the Mint died, and left all his precious coin behind in the floorboards."

"That was during the Great Fire. I'm talking about now."

"Are we not living through the Great Fire?" Julian says. "A fire that's going to last nearly five more years?"

"Fuck off, as Nick would say," says Duncan. "This bloody war is *not* going to last five more fucking years. Shoot me if that's true. But not tonight." He grins. "Shoot me tomorrow."

"Did you spend every last penny on us, Jules, or is there more?" Shona asks.

"Why, Shona, do you want to kill him for it, too?" Duncan says. "Or do you just want to stay here with me for five more years?"

"Yes," says Shona.

Frankie, true to herself, takes out a small bag from her purse, spills out her puzzle pieces on the table by the blacked-out window, mixes them up, and begins to put them together. She is impervious to mockery, even Wild's mockery. "Why even bother to trade the Underground for the Savoy if you're just going to do the same bloody thing?" he says. Kate perches across the table from Frankie and asks her if she needs help. Frankie doesn't say no.

Wild turns up the radio. They drink champagne, argue who is getting which room, and who's staying in the suite, and who will use the bath first. They draw straws, curse, disappear behind closed doors. They dance and fall on beds and take off their dirty suits and dresses and put on fresh robes and slippers. They call housekeeping and ask for their clothes to be laundered and returned to them in the morning, all except Julian, who keeps his suit on because that's where his money is. Mia curls up on the couch and drifts off. "I think I've had too much seduction in the form of Pink Gin," she mutters when Julian wakes her by softly kissing her face. He helps her up as they begin to make their escape to their own room down the hall.

I will sleep with you, Julian overhears Liz say to Wild, *if* you agree to marry me.

Julian and Duncan exchange an incredulous stare, as in, *poor fucking Wild*. Duncan laughs. "How I wish our Nick could hear this," he says. "Shona, Sheila, what do you say, my beauties? Will you sleep with me if I agree to marry you? Because I'm nicer than Wild. I'm taller. I'm much bigger"—Duncan horselaughs—"and I've got two of my arms."

"If you think what you need is two arms," Wild says, "I pity your women."

A few doors down the hall, Julian and Mia's room is positively a tomb compared to the revelry in the suite. Mia disappears into the bathroom. Julian takes off his tie and vest, unbuttons his shirt, loosens his belt and lies down on the bed to wait for her. She draws a bath that seems to last hours. He may have fallen asleep. "Are you okay in there?" he calls through the closed door, too tired to get up. "Come on out. You're going to dissolve in that water."

"Like a sugar cube," she says in a purring voice. "Jules, it's so nice. It's *so* nice. I haven't had a bath in months. Why don't you come in here with me? *Walk in, my lord, walk in,*" she burbles. "It's from *Troilus and Cressida*, in case you were wondering."

"I wasn't wondering, Miri," says Julian. "I know."

As he is about to come in, there's a knock on the door. It's Liz. She doesn't even notice that Julian is half dressed, his shirt unbuttoned, his chest bare. She looks panicked.

"Uh-oh," Julian says, off the expression on her face.

"I need to ask Maria a question."

Julian points to the bathroom.

Liz wants to know if she should take Wild up on his offer even though she knows he will not marry her, even though she knows he doesn't really love her and will not stay with her. And if she does take him up on it, which room should they use? She asks Mia for other advice, too, advice that is too hushed for Julian to eavesdrop on.

There's giggling, intermittent exclamations, a "*What?*" and an "Oh, my goodness, I can't do *that!*"

There's another knock on the door. It's Shona and Sheila. This time, the women have come to Julian for advice. Duncan has made them an offer—to love them both—and they don't know if they should accept. "At the same time!" says Sheila.

"Not in tandem, but at the same time, Julian!" says Shona.

"Yes, um, I got that," Julian says.

"What do you think?"

He looks over the women's glistening faces, their beguiled expressions.

"I think it would be extremely patriotic of you," he says. "You will be going above and beyond your call of duty for the war effort. Just think about how happy you're going to make that man. Trust me"—Julian smiles—"Dunk is going to have a smile on his face for a month. He needs that to work the bomb sites every night."

They're excited, but they want a second opinion. Julian points them to the bathroom.

There's another knock. It's Frankie. With all the potential debauchery about to go down on the fifth floor, Frankie wants to know which room she and Kate can sleep in, because they're tired and have had too much to drink. Julian gives her the key to the second room. Wild and Duncan can divide the suite bedrooms between them as they see fit.

He barely has time to let Frankie out before Duncan and Wild crowd the doorway. "Has the party moved in here? Where did our dates go? Only Kate was left in the suite, and she looked so terrified of us, we had to scram before she called for security."

Behind the bathroom door there's mad exalted giggling.

"What are they yakking about?"

"Take a guess," Julian says.

There's a pause. "How long is *that* going to take?" Duncan says.

"I guarantee, longer than the act itself," says Wild.

"Yeah, if you're crap at it," says Duncan.

"Shut up."

"You shut up."

"Swedish, when are they coming out?"

Julian knocks on the bathroom door. "Mia?"

"Don't come in," she says. "We've run Liz a bath." There are peals of laughter.

"Liz has her own bathroom, you know," Julian says. "We don't all have to live in one room like communists."

There is no answer, only hilarity.

Duncan and Wild stretch out on their backs on the bed, while Julian sinks into the armchair.

By the time the girls finish talking and bathing, dry off, and leave with the boys, it's nearly two in the morning.

Julian finishes with his bath in five minutes, but it's five minutes too long. Still damp, wrapped in her robe, Mia is unconscious on top of the covers. He rolls her inside the bed, climbs in himself, and is asleep before his hand can find her.

Some time later he's awoken by her feline voice.

"Jules," she's whispering. "Jules!"

He bolts straight up like he's in the army. "What? What's wrong?"

"Nothing. But…you're *naked*."

He falls back on the pillow. "You woke me up to tell me that? I know I'm naked. What time is it?"

"Nine in the morning."

"Ugh."

"Why are you naked?"

"You and your friends took all the robes."

"Oh."

He uses the bathroom, brushes his teeth, swills his mouth out with gin, takes a swig from the bottle, and climbs back under the covers.

It's dark in the room. The heavy curtains block out the morning. He closes his eyes and when he opens them, she's still staring at him.

"That damn Wild." She touches his brow. "Your cut is bleeding."

"It's fine."

"Do you want me to change the dressing?"

"I'm okay for now."

She is silent. "Did you think it was going to go differently last night? I'm sorry I fell asleep."

"It's okay."

"And took so long in the bath."

"That's okay."

"You're not upset with me?"

"No, Mia."

"Then why are you staring at me like that?"

Julian shuts his eyes. He doesn't mind her seeing the love, but he doesn't want her to see the seeping sadness he feels even during happy moments like this. He doesn't want her to see his fear. The fear of the broken clock, of the dying days, of the limitless horrors perpetrated on him and her. *Look down on us and this holy house with pity, O Lord.* He takes a deep breath, composes himself, opens his eyes, and smiles.

"A better question is, why are you staring at *me*?" he says, his full eyes twinkling.

In the dark, her pupils are dilated. "I'm not staring. But, um, why are you so muscled?"

"I'm not really."

"You are. Very."

"I train."

"For what?"

"To fight, I guess. To endure." He smiles. "You think it's easy being in the line of fire with you? You think it's easy walking through ice caves?"

"That story you told us about the ship and the fight on deck, and the knife that took half your hand and nearly your life, that wasn't true, was it?"

"What do *you* think?"

"I thought you were embellishing things. But seeing you right now, I'm afraid it might be true." But she doesn't look afraid. She looks tantalized.

"What, Mia?"

"I don't know," she whispers. "Do you always sleep… naked?"

"When I'm next to sleeping beauty, yes," he says, reaching for her. They thread their hands together. Turning her onto her back, he leans over her. She has taken off her robe. She is also naked. "You are beautiful when you are happy."

"Then I'm beautiful all the time," she says, stroking his arms and shoulders, "because I'm almost always happy." Her breath quickens. "Jules, you are so…*awake*."

"Yes, *my flesh rises with your name*." Julian opens her mouth with his kiss.

Moaning, she reaches for him. Oh my word, Julian. She squeezes him, strokes him, tugs on him to beckon him on top of her. Come here. Honest, I can't wait another second.

You can't wait another second?

There's a knock on the door.

"Go away!" Julian yells.

The knock gets louder.

"Jules! It's us! It's Wild and Dunk!"

"I know who you are! Go. Away."

There's another knock. "Jules, it's Shona."

And another. "And Sheila!"

"We're starved, Jules."

Me too, he says to Mia, his body over hers.

Me too, Mia says into his collarbone.

The knocking persists.

They groan. Mia hides in the bathroom, while Julian throws on a pair of trousers and grabs some pound notes from his pocket. He unlocks the door, opening it two inches and keeping the chain on. "Go away!" Julian says into Wild's laughing face.

"Swedish, the morning is no time for what you're about to do. It's disgraceful. It is, however, time for breakfast. Let us in."

"Go back to your suite or I'll have you arrested. Here—take my money. Order room service, get whatever you want. We'll be there shortly."

"Not too shortly, I hope?" Mia whispers from behind.

Wild and Dunk crack up. "Chop, chop, Swedish," Wild says, real fondness, real affection in his eyes and voice, "or there won't be any scones left."

After they leave, and he bolts the door, Julian sits on the bed and stands Mia naked in front of him, between his legs. Holding her hips, he pulls her close and presses his face between her weighty breasts. Sometimes they fit into his hands and sometimes like now they spill out. Either way, it's all good. He fondles her, plays with her, kisses her nipples gently, kisses them until her head tips back and her body arches forward. *I don't need it, Jules,* she whispers, *honest.*

But I like it, he says, running his hands over her rounded hips.

Me, too.

When he sees how softened she is and how weakened, he lays her down on the bed. She opens her arms. "Come lie on top of me. If I told you how long it's been since anyone's been on top of me, you would cry."

"Why would I cry? I'd prefer it if no one had been on top of you."

"I misspoke," Mia says. "I meant me. *I* would cry. I don't want anything else for now but you inside me. Come. It's all I want."

When his weight presses her into the bed, belly to belly, chest to breast, she does cry. She turns her head, maybe hoping he won't see it. He is careful at first and slow. She moans as if she is being hurt. He holds himself up with his arms, with his knees. Her body is bruised at the ribs, she has cuts on her stomach and neck and legs. She is a bright angel with black wounds. She sears his eyes.

"On this earth, under all the stars in the sky," he whispers, "there is a country, and in this country, a mighty unbreakable city, and in this city a mighty unbreakable girl, and in the girl a soul, and in the soul a heart."

"That's yours. Have you come to take it?" she murmurs and curves into him. "Go ahead, then. Let nothing stop you." She pulls on his arms, pleads with him to forget her pain, to lower himself on her, to flatten her, to hold himself up only a little bit, and to not stop moving.

Eventually the moving is going to cause me to stop moving, Julian says. The consequences of every act are included in the act itself. She moans in dissent, in assent, in delirium. Her eyes are closed, but toward the end, she opens them, puts her hands on his chest, and asks him to wait, wait.

Julian almost can't wait.

Wait, wait. Crawling out from underneath him, she hops off the bed, pulls off the quilt and throws it on the floor.

What are you doing?

I'm shameful, I know, she says, lying down in front of the full-length wardrobe mirror and beckoning him to her. But just once, I want to feel it *and* see it. I want to see what it looks like to be loved by you.

He is happy to oblige. He holds up her legs, one palm on the back of her raised thigh. He wants to give her what she wants. Trouble is, he's almost done.

A little longer, Jules. Please. A little longer. Pressing his face to her face, he kisses her perspiring cheek and watches her stare into the mirror—at his body pulsing over hers, a piston in motion. He watches her watch him through the mirror, watching her as he comes.

∞

"I don't want to leave here," she says, nestled into him. "I'm not hungry for food. I'm not thirsty for coffee. I just want you. How long until the next round?"

"Five minutes," he replies. "But I've got fourteen more rounds in me, and yet they're out there, waiting for us."

"After fifteen rounds," Mia says in an electrified whisper, raising her eyes, "I might not walk out of the ring on my own two feet."

"Oh, for sure you won't," he says, kissing her upturned face.

"Come on, just once more?" she says.

"The next time will go on too long," he says, and in response to her moan adds, "*Shh*. I promise you'll have it. We have the room for the weekend. We'll have plenty of time, for everything."

"For everything?"

"Anything you want."

Reluctantly she gets out of bed and looks for her robe. "I'm warning you, though, no Wild tonight, no Duncan, no Liz. No one. Just me and you."

"You don't have to tell *me* about it."

Before they leave the room, she embraces him. "Out there, you're going to be all proper with me, as always, but I want you to know how I feel."

"I know how you feel." Julian strokes her face.

"But how do *you* feel?" she asks in a trembling, uncertain whisper.

"You don't know how I feel, Mia?" Almost everything he feels, he puts into his eyes. "I am yours. I belong to you."

What he tries to conceal:

And at the bar, a tune is playing, a plaintive male voice complaining: his girl has found another boy another love, while the twirling ballerina round and round and round keeps spinning and then she stops, the Cheapside girl in silk and gold receding.

19

A House on Grimsby Street

IN THE SUITE, THE REST ARE ALMOST DONE EATING. THE curtains are open, and the winter Thames flows below their windows. There may not be much traffic over the bridges, but Julian has never seen the river so jammed with boats and ships. It's become the primary mode of delivery in and out of London. The Allies and the Londoners are supplied through its waters. No wonder the Germans are hell-bent on blowing up everything on its banks.

The mood of the other seven people in the suite resembles Julian's and Mia's. Every person around the living area, eating bacon and fried tomatoes and eggs, devouring bread with jam and butter, drinking tomato juice and tea, has a smile from ear to ear. Some, like Liz and Kate, are trying to hide it. "Liz won't look at me," a grinning Wild says. "Perhaps I've disappointed her." He takes her hand. Sitting by his side, beet red, her smile enormous, Liz can't look at him even more. Frankie is at the little table by the window, doing her jigsaw. But she's smiling down into her puzzle.

Duncan is completely unsuppressed. He is the most outwardly elated of them all. There are no shadows on his joy, no pretense that he feels anything other than what he's feeling. Both Shona and Sheila are embarrassed by his open adulation. They tell him that if he makes one remark about last night, ever, in daylight, evening light, in front of other people, any time at all, they will strangle him with their own hands.

"Strangling implies you will touch me again. So it'll be worth it," Duncan says. "You can do anything you want to me after last night. Anything."

"Duncan!"

He opens his arms. "Come here, my beauties, strangle me."

Julian and Wild grin at each other. Mia, standing over a sitting Julian, throws her arms around his neck, bends to him and whispers, "Are you jealous of Duncan, Jules?"

"No," Julian says, kissing her forearm.

"Why not?"

"Been there, done that," he says, pinching her skin lightly, and smiling up at her. "You mean you don't remember? You were there, too."

They take their time with breakfast as they wait for their clothes to be returned. They wonder if the famed bomb shelter at the Savoy is all it's cracked up to be. They endeavor never to find out.

In the afternoon, dressed and washed and shaved and full, utterly sated in their bodies and souls, the nine of them strut out of the hotel, arm in arm, walk up Savoy Place and stand at the Strand, gazing left and right at their dominion, like conquerors. They hail two black cabs and make their rowdy way to Royal London Hospital to visit Finch. They go bearing gifts, bringing him scones from the Savoy, bacon rashers, some pre-made Pink Gin in Duncan's flask, and even a blooming lily.

At the hospital, they learn that Finch died the night before, from internal hemorrhage. While they were drinking and dancing and carousing, having a joyous time, the best time they've had, possibly ever, Finch was dying.

"I feel so guilty," Mia says. She can't stop crying. "Poor Finch. But we didn't do anything wrong. Happiness is not wrong."

The air raid siren goes off while they're still at the hospital. Sheila stays to work the emergency shift. Frankie and Kate drive off with Shona and a new doctor in an HMU. Julian, Mia, Duncan and Wild are loaned a medical jeep, this one with a plastic windshield, and Julian drives them just north of the hospital into their last fray.

That Saturday, the Germans bomb London four times. Over three hundred tons of bombs are dropped on the city. At night the moon is full again, and even the blackout and the decoy buses don't help. At night new London is lit up like the London of old, but with enemy fire and a bright round moon.

For seven hours that night the city shakes in the earthquake of hundreds of bombs falling so close together there seems to be hardly a pause between them.

That night Kate Cozens dies, and Shona loses her leg. A bomb falls on the HMU truck while Kate and Shona are amputating a man's mangled arm to save his life. The man dies, too.

Frankie will spend days putting together Kate's body, so she can release it whole to her sister, Sheila.

They don't return to the Savoy.

∞

The acrid air is thick with smoke. There's a prolonged rumbling sound, followed by thunder. There is unholy crashing all around them.

Grimsby Street, close to the railroad in Bethnal Green, has been almost entirely destroyed as the Germans bombed the dozen lines of tracks heading out of east London. Grimsby is opened up. What was down is now up, and what was up is now down. Houses burn out of control, many have crumbled.

But from one, awful sounds come, the sounds of live female human beings trapped under the weight of looming death.

We have to wait for the fire brigade, Duncan says. We can't go in there. We have no hoses, no water, our truck has no sandbags or buckets. How can we help?

Duncan, listen!

We need to wait.

Duncan! Listen!

We need to wait!

Julian doesn't disagree with Duncan.

Wild doesn't disagree with Duncan.

Neither does Mia. But all four of them hear the unbearable sound of a young woman's voice crying, *Michael, Michael.*

Wild is distraught, but he doesn't move.

We gotta help her, Dunk, Mia says.

The fire truck will be here soon. They'll help her.

I hate to agree with Duncan, Wild says, but it's a bad idea to go in there.

But we're the first ones here!

Is it our fault that Jules got here so quick? Jules, stop driving so fucking fast.

Michael, Michael…

It's one thing to put out a kitchen flare-up, but Wild can't go inside a fully burning house; everyone who knows his story knows that. No one is asking him to. Mia can't go inside because she is terrified of fire for reasons no one but Julian understands.

Michael!

Men! Mia yells. Are you going to make me go in there on my own?

The three of them, with Wild far behind, make their careful way through the cratered rubble up to the house.

There is trouble in that house. The second floor has fallen and collapsed into the first, and all the bedrooms and furniture that were up are now down.

Two women are trapped under a bed. They must have hidden under it, and then the bed fell through the ceiling, and a dresser and part of the roof fell on top of them. One woman is badly injured because she's not speaking, but the other one wails agonizingly, trying to point, crying *Michael! It's all right, darling, it's all right.*

When she sees the three men and a woman making their way toward her, she yells, "Not me, not me! Please—save my baby. Look. Save my baby."

Sure enough, there's an intact crib nearby, standing upright in the wreckage. It too must have fallen through the ceiling. Inside it, a child, caked in mortar dust, sits tangled in the cords of the fallen curtains. If he's making any sounds, Julian can't hear, because the air raid siren is at full throttle. It's been twenty minutes, and the siren still shrieks, like the baby might shriek if his throat weren't glued together with wet dust.

"Get him, please," the mother trapped under the bedframe and the wardrobe begs. "Forget me, just get my baby."

Every beam in the crumpling house is unstable, and the fire is raging.

Julian turns to Mia. "I'll help her," he says, "but you go back to the street. Don't come in with us, it's too dangerous. I can't worry about you when I'm trying to help her. Please. Just turn around and get away from this. No, Wild—you stay."

Mia returns to the street. Duncan and Julian try to lift the wardrobe off the woman. Wild stands back.

"My baby, my baby," the woman keeps saying. "Just get my baby. Look, he's scared. He's stuck. It's all right, darling! It's all right, son, Mummy's here. Please! Have him pull out my baby!" She motions to motionless Wild.

"Wild!" Julian yells. "Go get the kid!"

Wild shakes his head. "He's stuck," Wild says. "He can't stand up." He keeps shaking his head. "I can't."

"Wild! Go! Use the knife I gave you."

"I can't get him out with one arm." What he doesn't say is his brother was trapped like this, and Wild couldn't save him even with two arms.

Julian can't deal with Wild because he and Duncan are having zero luck budging the wardrobe. Above them, the house is burning and pieces of debris keep falling on top of them, on top of the wardrobe, onto the woman. The other woman has stopped moving or blinking. They can't look into that face. They're still trying to save the living.

A chunk of burning wood falls inside the crib.

The mother screams. Mia screams. Julian screams for Wild.

Finally, Wild moves. Taking out his knife, he makes his way to the crib. He loosens and cuts the drapery cords trapping the baby and frees the boy. Dropping the knife, he manages to pick up the infant like a puppy, by the scruff of his pajama suit. The boy, maybe six months old, grabs on to Wild's neck. Holding him with one arm, Wild carries him from the burning crib, out of the house, and into the street where Mia stands with her arms out. While Wild holds him, she sticks her finger inside the baby's mouth to clear his throat, pulling out a piece of wet wallpaper, a piece of plaster. The baby cries. He cries so heartily, he drowns out the wailing siren.

When the mother hears that sound, she calms down, stops being frantic and lies silently, watching Julian and Duncan struggle to move the wardrobe. "His name is Michael," she says to them.

"We'll get you out," Duncan says. "You can call him by his name yourself."

What's left of the house is crackling, the fragile frame turning to tinder.

"Get out of there!" Wild calls from the street. "Get out! Duncan! Julian!" He points to the quivering roof.

"Let's try one more time, Dunk," Julian says. "You lift the cabinet just a few inches, and I'll try to drag her out." With a grunt, red from exertion, Duncan raises the wardrobe. Julian grabs the woman under her arms. He is able to move her half a foot. She is stuck somewhere he can't see. "Just a little more," Julian says. "You're doing great." He pulls the woman halfway out. "Almost there."

From behind him, he hears both Mia and Wild scream. *"Julian!" screams Shae. "Watch out!"* A flaming crossbeam breaks and falls. It lands on top of Duncan and splits in two. It hits Julian across the shoulders and the woman across the face.

The woman stops moving. Duncan stops moving.

Wild is next to them. "Jules, can you get up? Dunk, can you get up?" Duncan can't. He is breathing, but can't stand up. One of Julian's shoulders is dislocated. Wild helps him to his feet. With barely two working arms between them, he and Wild grab Duncan and drag him over the burning rubble into the street, and lay him down on the pavement next to Mia who's trying to soothe the crying child in her arms. Now that she's cleared the boy's air pipe, he turns out to have quite a set of lungs on him. Wild takes the boy from her. He even lifts his stump to steady him. "Why are you shrieking, kid?" he says. "What do *you* have to worry about? Look around you. Shh."

Mia is on the ground, touching Duncan's face. "You okay, Dunk? What hurts?"

"Nothing," he says. "But I can't move my legs."

The all clear sounds. The fire truck arrives. So does the HMU.

It's obvious to everyone that Duncan requires the hospital, everyone, that is, except Duncan. He cannot feel his lower body. "What's wrong with my legs?" he keeps asking. "Have they fallen asleep? Why can't I feel them? Did I break my back? Fuck, tell me I didn't break my back. Where is Shona? Shona! Tell me I didn't break my back..."

No one wants to remind Duncan that Shona lost her leg and is in the dreaded hospital. Duncan keeps trying to grab the hem of Wild's coat. "Wild, tell them to take me to Fixed Unit. I'll be fine, but don't let them take me to the hospital. Please, Wild, don't let them take me to the hospital."

"I'll go with you," Wild says, still holding the child. He explains to the new doctor how Duncan feels about hospitals.

"Where did you get the kid from?" the doctor asks Wild. "Did you pull him out of the fire?"

"Yes."

"Where's his family?"

Mia tells the doctor the boy was the son of the woman in the burning house, but they couldn't get her out. And the other woman, perhaps her sister, is also dead.

"So he's an orphan? There's a whole procedure for orphaned children," the doctor says, reaching for the baby. "Give it here. We keep them at the hospital until either a member of the family comes forward, or we find a placement. The orphanage is on the fourth floor of Royal London. Lots like him there."

Instead of handing the baby over, Wild asks the doctor to look at Julian's shoulder. Julian is in considerable pain, and in the havoc only Wild sees it. The shoulder needs to be reset. While Julian bites down on Mia's scarf, the doctor yanks his arm back into joint. Julian doesn't know how he doesn't pass out. He feels better, but not much.

"Chaps, I'm going to ride to Royal London with Duncan," Wild tells Julian and Mia. "Dunk needs me, and I might as well get this thing to the fourth floor, like the doc said. When you're done here, pick me up from the hospital. Jules, can you come with me to the jeep for a second, help me out with something?"

At the truck, Wild asks Julian to take some rope and attach the boy to his body in a protective sling. "The HMU jostles on the road, and I don't want to drop him when we hit a pothole. He'll be more secure this way." Wild holds the infant to his chest, and Julian fashions a harness around the boy, tying him snugly to Wild. For extra warmth, they hide him inside Wild's coat, the coat Julian bought for him. After Julian buttons it, you almost can't see there's a baby inside. To protect the boy's exposed, nearly bald head, Mia fixes him with the red beret Julian gave her. "That's okay, Jules, right? I don't have anything else. You ruined my wool hat with your blood. The beret will keep him a little warmer. And Wild will bring it back in a few hours."

"You're talking about the beret, right?" Julian says.

The plump shivering mass that is baby Michael has quieted down inside Wild's coat, stopped crying, stopped moving. Only his alert eyes with huge black pupils are open. His ear is pressed to Wild's chest. He looks up at Wild and smiles toothlessly.

"What is he doing?" Wild says in a panic. "What does he want?"

"He's just smiling at you, Wild," says Mia.

"Why?"

Down the street and affixed to the stretcher, Duncan is howling, afraid they will cart him away to the hospital without Wild.

"Listen, never mind the hospital. Just head back to Bank, you two," Wild says. "I don't know how long I'll be. Look at Dunk, that poor bastard. I may be in for a long day. I'll come back when I'm done. Jules, I know there are some black-market lorries near Brick Lane. Want me to pick up a few things?"

Julian reaches into his trouser pocket. He gives Wild what's left from the sale of one of his coins, over a hundred pounds. A hundred pounds in 1940 is five thousand pounds today. "Get whatever you think we need."

"That's a lot of whisky, mate," Wild says. "But we're going to need it. A wake for everyone."

"A wake for everyone," Julian says.

"What do babies eat anyway? Can they have whisky?"

"If it's laced with milk, absolutely." Julian and Wild smile at each other.

"Wild," Duncan calls from his stretcher. "Wild…"

"Pipe down, woman! Honestly, he cries more than the baby. I'll be right there!" Wild rolls his eyes. "All right, I'm off. I'll see you, Swedish."

"I'll see you, Wild."

Julian doesn't know why he feels such a stinging ache watching Wild and Duncan drive away in the medi truck.

"Do you know the names of the women who lived in that house?" the Incident Officer asks Mia. "I need to record it into my log book. Where is Finch? He knows everything. I can't do this job without him. Is he not better yet?"

"Finch died," Mia says.

The Incident Officer, who's been everywhere and seen it all, does an unprecedented thing. He bursts into tears.

20

Lunch at the Ten Bells

WILD DOESN'T RETURN TO BANK.

And then there were four.

Only Julian, Mia, Liz, and Frankie are left in the passageway.

On Monday morning when Julian and Mia arrive at Royal London to visit Duncan, they learn that Wild left on Sunday afternoon for the black market and did not come back. Duncan is in bad shape. He did break his back. Now he's paralyzed from the waist down. Julian and Mia sit with Duncan into the evening. When the big man finally falls asleep, they leave. They go upstairs to the fourth-floor orphanage to check on the little boy. The nurse administrator shows them the three male babies under a year old that have been brought to the hospital in the last 24 hours. They all look about right, and yet not right.

They don't know what to think.

Sheila Cozens, on her third straight shift, is angry, exhausted, and has no answers. Yesterday afternoon, Wild asked Sheila for some milk for the baby. He said the child seemed hungry. Sheila got upset with Wild, too. "Where do you think I'm going to get milk from, I said to him." She told him to go to the fourth floor. The orphanage would know what to feed a baby. He said he would, said goodbye to Duncan and Sheila, and left. That was it. Sheila storms away as if Mia and Julian are strangers.

"She is not very nice today," Mia says.

"We won't hold the war against Sheila." Julian presses his lips against Mia's head. "Not everyone can be good and kind like you. She lost her parents and her sister, and Duncan is hurt bad. We won't hold the war against anyone. Except the Germans."

Mia knows where Wild's parents moved to after their house burned down: north of Paddington. "Maybe he went to visit them?"

They don't have the parents' phone number. They're stymied. If they go knocking on Barbara Wilder's door, asking if she's seen her one remaining son, what happens if the answer is no? Are they going to panic the mother, too? Isn't there enough frenzy to go around?

∞

A week later, on a Saturday afternoon in early December, Julian, Mia, Liz, and Frankie drive to Ten Bells for lunch. Julian picks it. It's Wild's favorite, and he likes the witty sign on the call board outside. "IN THE EVENT OF AN INVASION, WE SHALL CLOSE FOR A HALF-HOUR."

After burying her sister, Sheila moved back into her family home in north Islington. Shona is in a rehab unit on the fifth floor of Royal London, learning how to function with one and a half legs. A paraplegic Duncan is there, too. No one knows when or how he'll be getting out. Shona hobbles on crutches to sit with him every day. Sometimes she stays until after blackout and sleeps in the chair next to his bed.

Yes, our ranks have been depleted, Mia says, raising a mug of beer, but we push on. Like Wild said, things can only improve.

London has suffered before, Liz says. We'll pull through this, too. We can take it. I just wish Wild would come back.

Hear, hear.

The women speak differently to each other, more formally, as if realizing they too might soon be separated. Julian barely speaks at all. "There has never been any drama in London to compare to the drama of the Battle of Britain—" he starts to say and breaks off, watching helplessly as Liz weeps and says she would take the bombing for five more years if only they could find Wild.

She says it like it's even a choice.

Craters in the street, cellars open to the air, crumbling walls, gas mains in flames, water pipes burst, pavements crunching with broken glass. Dust everywhere. Glass powder, plaster. Gray ash cinders. London like Pompeii after Vesuvius.

Wild is gone. They've checked all the hospitals, Great Ormond, St. Bart's, St. Mary's. They even checked St. Thomas across the river. At first they didn't want to worry his mother, but Duncan gave them her number, and Mia called Barbara Wilder, casual as all that. Oh, hello, just trying to get in touch with Wild, have you seen him? She hadn't seen him. He missed his weekly visit last Wednesday. She wasn't too concerned. Sometimes he misses a Wednesday, she said.

After Mia hung up, it was the only time they saw Frankie cry. Frankie! She cried for Wild.

"Oh, guess what?" Liz says at the Ten Bells. "I got a telegram!" She waves it around for emphasis.

Liz got a telegram!

"Congratulations, Liz!" says Mia. "What does it say?"

They wait for her to open it.

It's from her mother in Birmingham. It says: *Do not come home STOP Not even for Christmas STOP Brum bombed STOP Our house gone STOP Shelter in London STOP Be safe STOP Love Mum*

Commiserating they pat her back.

That's okay, Liz says, wiping away her tears. I got a telegram.

Mia tells the girls that Julian keeps trying to persuade her to leave London and travel to Blackpool where her own mum is. She says it in a tone of someone who's tattletaling on another someone and not even feeling ashamed about it.

"I want you to be with your mother on Christmas," Julian says. "Why does that make me the bad guy?"

"He's been trying to get me to leave London since he got here," Mia says.

"After everything that's happened, do you feel this is irrational?" Julian says.

"He's right, Maria," says Frankie. "You should go."

"But if Birmingham isn't safe, how is Blackpool safe?" asks Liz. "Blackpool is much farther away, and the railroad keeps getting bombed."

"Exactly!" says Mia. "Nowhere is safe."

"Blackpool is safe," Julian says.

"But we still have to get there," Mia says. "And my job is here, and my friends…"

"Fewer and fewer," Julian says.

"Okay, Mr. Brightside," says Mia, opening the menu, "do you know what you want? Because I'm starving."

Five minutes after they've ordered, there is no siren, but there's a rumble of plane engines. They groan. A crunching explosion rattles their beers. They hear commotion in the back of the pub. They wait. They don't know whether to leave and try somewhere else, or to stay put. The Germans were on their way to elsewhere. ("Maybe Blackpool?") They dropped a stray bomb on the Ten Bells just to fuck with them.

"We're never letting Julian choose where we eat again," Frankie says.

"Good call," Mia says. "Jules is a bomb magnet."

They've already ordered so they decide to wait a bit longer.

Ten minutes later, the pale but composed waitress appears with their food.

"Sorry the lunch is a bit dusty, mates," she says, primly setting down the tray with the plates. "The ceiling's down in the kitchen."

After she leaves, they have a laugh and raise a glass to the steadfast British woman, not easily rattled. "Nothing can replace the grace of London town," Julian says.

"Sometimes when things look bleak," says Mia, "and we feel a little down, we might say what's the use? What's the use of anything, we wail. But those with whom you share your pot and your bed and your bread will not say that. Those with whom you share your days will never say that. And that is worth a great deal."

"Because what matters most is how you walk through the fire," says Julian.

Hear, hear. Julian, Mia, Liz, and Frankie raise their pints to London.

And then, another stray bomb falls outside the Ten Bells windows.

21

Empty Igloo

WHEN THEY LAY UNDER THE RUBBLE, BLOWING DUST OUT OF their mouths, feeling for each other's bodies, feeling for each other's faces, when he held his palm to Mia's bleeding head, Julian said in a moment of overpowering weakness for which he was sorry, *we're not going to make it, are we, you and me.*

"If you're speaking, and I can hear you," Mia said, "then we already made it. We just have to get out of here."

But that was then, in the heat of battle. Now that it's three days later, and she's left the hospital, and he reminds her of her words, she denies ever uttering them. She tells him he misunderstood. She meant get out from under the rubble, not get out for good.

"Maria."

"What did you call me?" she says. "Are you using my full name in anger, my holy name that's a prayer?"

"No. But—"

"What's the rush, Jules? Where's the fire?" Mia laughs. "See what I did there?"

"Yes. Very good. Don't you want to see your mom for Christmas?"

"*Mom?* What are you, a Yank? And what do you care if I see my mum for Christmas? If we leave for Blackpool, what about Liz? What's she going to do?"

Julian hasn't thought about Liz. He is thinking only about Mia. He's thinking about time. It's December 11, 1940. He's been with her 34 days. Yes, it's 240 miles to Blackpool. In the present day, they could get there in an afternoon. But this isn't the present day. The present is a shadow. The past is what's alive. And in December 1940, the distance between London and Blackpool through the bomb corridor of central England might as well be 240 parsecs through a time warp.

Besides the brevity of minutes, they have another problem. All travel to Blackpool has been cancelled. Julian found this out when he went to Euston to get some information or, even better, two tickets. Between London and Blackpool lie Birmingham and Coventry, lie Liverpool and Manchester, and those cities and the trains to them are getting swallowed up almost as bad as London, which is to say irrevocably.

Irrevocably, like Julian and Mia have been swallowed up. All his boxing, his fencing, his fighting, his Krav Maga is nothing to him now. It has no meaning against the current enemy. The strong as well as the weak are laid waste in front of its black lair.

Mia was injured in the Ten Bells bombing. She hit her head when she was thrown from her chair. She has a hole in her upper chest where a piece of shrapnel entered and broke her right collarbone. A few inches higher, and it would've shredded her carotid. A few inches lower, and it would've collapsed her lung. Ten inches to the left, and it would've nicked her heart. She has a wound at the back of her head that bled like Julian's brow had bled a few weeks earlier. She is weak from blood loss and concussed, showing mild disorientation and lightheadedness. Her head has been shaved on one side and is wrapped in white. Her customary headscarf has been replaced with a field dressing. The doctors told her to take it easy, not to lift things, not to bend, not to sneeze. They're worried about blood clots and burst veins. She's been in the hospital for three days, and they want to keep her longer, but Julian knows Mia has no time for hospitals or blood clots. Blackpool is a galaxy of peace away.

"Is it possible to get to Blackpool some other way?" Julian asks the British Rail ticket seller.

"Possible?" the ticket woman says. "Yes. Wise? No. Fast? Definitely not. Easy? Pfft."

"But not impossible?" He is encouraged. Julian is the prince of all nigh-impossible things.

"You're better off staying here," the woman says, as if Julian has asked for her opinion.

They can get to Blackpool by traveling north to Leeds, where they can go to Leeds Cathedral and pray for a couple of trains due west. It's the longest way but the safest, safest if you don't count Sheffield, which lies between London and Leeds. Sheffield is a major steel producer, and if there's anything the Germans want to hobble more, besides Liverpool's ports and Birmingham's Spitfires and Julian's girl, it's Britain's steel factories. "Don't wait too long," the ticket seller says. "The closer you get to Christmas, the fewer civilian trains there will be. The servicemen are coming home. They get priority on the tracks. Even now there's only one civilian train a day."

"There's a number less than one?" Julian says.

"Yes," the woman says, her voice dripping with disdain. "Zero."

Julian is not in great shape himself. He needed forty stitches from the top of his trapezoid to the middle of his back. It's so hard to move his right arm that he suspects that underneath the sliced-up muscle, his shoulder blade may have a fracture. His right forearm is almost certainly broken, but he refuses to put his arm into a full cast. He can't protect Mia with one arm immobilized. To move a broken arm through pain is one thing. Not to be able to move it at all is another. The doctor fitted him with a field splint and a sling. At least two of Julian's right ribs are broken. A piece of glass has pierced his cheek. It's been sewn up, but the bone underneath is swollen and aching. The injury makes it difficult and unpleasant to eat. The Frankenstein gash above his eye is healing poorly. He had pulled out the stitches too soon, and any new trauma to the body opens up the old wound. And his right knee got twisted. He may have an anterior ligament tear. The torn left calf muscle is going to take another month to fully heal. Favoring his right side where most of his upper body injuries are, Julian hobbles like an old man, slightly stooped, limping on both legs.

But despite this, or maybe because of this, he is determined to get Mia out of London. It's hard not to take the bombing personally. Frankie died in the explosion at the Ten Bells. Liz didn't die, but she was badly burned. He doesn't want to point out to Mia the brutal reality, hoping she can see it herself, but there's no one left to piece together the jigsaw that is Mia if the puzzle maker herself is dead. Most certainly Julian can't tell Mia the unspeakable truth. If he dies before she does in one of these attacks, there is no chance for her. This struck him as he lay bleeding in the dust of Ten Bells. Their days are like grass. She will vanish as Wild has vanished, a dandelion fuzz in the passing wind, a lover like a flower. If Julian dies, he will never know what happens to her.

As he tries to persuade her with fake persuasion, Mia uses on him the unassailable logic of those whose knowledge of the future is woefully and blessedly nil. "Trains are bombed, too, Jules," she says. "And what about the cities the trains pass through? Everything's bombed. Coventry's been leveled. The entire cathedral is gone!"

"We're not going to Coventry," Julian says. "We're traveling north to Leeds. From there we'll make a sharp left to Blackpool."

"Soon Blackpool will be leveled same as the others," she says. "We have a better chance in London. It's bigger. More places to hide."

"Where has our hiding gotten us?"

"Are you here? Am I here? I'd say pretty far."

"What if I told you," Julian says, "that Blackpool will never come under direct attack?"

Mia is quiet. "What do you mean, never? You mean, not yet?"

"I guess."

"Then I'm right, and there's no reason it won't be bombed tomorrow or the next day."

"It won't be bombed tomorrow or the next day."

"How do you know?"

"I just do."

"How?"

"I just know."

"How sure are you?"

"One hundred percent."

She mulls. "You don't think it will *ever* be bombed?"

He shakes his head.

"Oh, yeah? Where's Wild, then?"

"That I don't know." He may never learn of Wild's fate. It cuts him up to think this, to say this. It's an open wound.

∞

And then there were three.

Julian, Mia and Liz return to Bank. Liz has nasty burns on her legs that need to be cleaned three times a day.

In the passageway that's been Mia's home since September, a dozen new people lie in their bunks. One exquisitely far-sighted young bloke with a pair of magnifying lenses for glasses, one lens cracked, says, "Sorry, mates, we in your spot? It was empty for days, the warden said we could…"

Liz asks if anyone has seen a blond man without an arm. He's easy to recognize. No one speaks up. "Let's go sleep somewhere else," Liz says to Julian and Mia after she collects her few things that have been thrown in the corner with the rest of the trash. "I have to go to work in the morning. The *Evening Standard* still needs me to proofread."

Challengingly, Mia stares down Julian, as if she believes Julian is too nice a guy to tell Liz they're about to abandon her and run for the hills. Julian is about to open his mouth to prove to

Mia just how wrong she is when he hears a familiar voice calling for them from the top of the station, coming down the escalator. The speed with which all three of them spin around would make a stone weep if a stone was watching them, and could weep.

But it's not Wild.

It's Nick Moore, unharmed and joyously ignorant.

"What happened to your head, Ghost Bride?" he says, all chipper and jokey. "It's a good look for you. Did you miss me, kids? I've been at the Ford plant!" he announces, as if it's the most exciting news. "Well, it *is* exciting. We're bombed every fugging day, yet look at me, not a scratch. Well, that's not true." He pulls up his pant leg to show them a cut on his shin. "A scratch." He laughs. "I gotta show Dunk. Where is everybody?" He glances inside their passageway and frowns in disgust. "Fuck off, who are *they*?"

"Javert told them they could bunk there," Liz says.

"Fuck off, why would he do that?" Nick still has a smile on. "Where's our crew?"

Mia shakes her head.

Nick is still smiling but frozen. Like his mouth can't catch up with what his brain is processing. "What, no one?"

Mia shakes her head. "Sheila might be okay."

"Fuck off, I don't believe you. Duncan?"

"He broke his back. He's at Royal London."

"Fuck off!" says Nick. The smile is gone. "Fuck off! Robbie? Kate? Frankie? Doc Cozens? *Wild*?"

Mia shakes her head. Liz looks away.

Nick stops saying anything else, just keeps repeating his two worn-out words over and over. A few minutes later he spins and leaves. They watch him stumbling up the motionless escalator, crying, "Fuck off! Fuck off! Fuck off!"

Julian gets an idea. He tells Mia. They ask Liz to wait and run up the escalator after Nick. "Nick! Wait! Nick!"

"Fuck off!" sobs Nick.

∞

"Fuck off!" Nick says when Julian tells him of his plan.

"Come on," Julian says. "Liz can't go to Birmingham. Her mother told her so. And we're leaving for Blackpool..."

"Jules insists." Mia rolls her eyes.

"We'll leave today if you take her," Julian says. "There's no one to look after her here."

"So take her with *you*."

"Nick, Dagenham is five miles away," Julian says. "Blackpool is half a country away. She is not safe with us. In the spring, the British Museum will reopen. She has a job. She'll move back to London. It's just for a little while."

"Well, *I* can't look after her! Are you daft? Fuck off!"

"Come on, mate," Julian says. "Just take her with you."

"And where will she live, may I ask?"

"You must have an aunt, a grandma, a spinster cousin she can bunk with, no?"

"Fuck off," says Nick, but quieter.

"And Duncan still needs you to visit. Shona, too. And maybe when spring comes and London gets quieter, you and Liz can look for Wild."

"Fuck off," whispers Nick.

Only once Nick agrees, does Julian give Nick a gold sovereign to help with Liz's expenses. He didn't want to offer it until he knew for sure Nick would take her. Because otherwise, what would happen to Liz when the money ran out?

They return to the platforms below, sit Liz down in a chair near the makeshift stage by the escalator where Mia had put on so many shows, where Julian and Mia entertained the troops, where Julian and Finch fought to the death, and talk to her about their plan. Go, Liz. It's only for a little while, until things get better. Be safe. *Safer*. Go with Nick.

Liz cries. She wants to hug Mia, but Mia's broken collarbone prevents physical displays of farewell. "Will you come back?" she asks.

"Of course," Mia replies. "After the holidays. Maybe in March when the weather gets better. I promise."

Julian says nothing. The 49th day is like the 49th parallel. Either the victorious armies push through, or they're vanquished. And the 49th day is 14 days away.

All four walk up the long escalator, three of them painfully slowly. Before they leave Bank for good, Julian turns and casts one last look below, catching a sideways glimpse of the tunnels where he and the Ten Bells crew lived and slept and sang and drank, casts one last look on their igloo and remembers the words Edgar Evans said to him about his own confinement on Inexpressible Island. *"There was no light in the sky. And yet every night when we made it through another day alive, we felt so happy. We drank, and read aloud to one another, we mocked each other, told jokes, sang songs. I got closer to those men than I ever got to anyone. Because we weren't alone. We were in it together."*

Julian and Mia walk Nick and Liz to Liverpool Street, and by the old Great Eastern Hotel watch them take the stairs down to the trains. Liz carries her purse, her Bible, and her mother's favorite blanket, the only things she cared to salvage from her life in London.

"I got my first telegram, Nick," Liz says to him tearfully.

"Fuck off. How was it? Was it everything you dreamed of?"

"Yes. It was a life and death thing."

"This way, Lizzie, and mind the gap." Nick puts his arm on her back. "You don't want to trip." Turning around, he looks up and waves goodbye to Julian and Mia, mouthing to them, "Fuck off."

22

A Girl Named Maria

AND THEN THERE WERE TWO.

Before they go to King's Cross and leave London, Julian asks the cab driver to take them to Baker Street. Julian wants to show Mia a café. Of course, it's not warm; it's terrible out, there's snow on the ground, and she's not wearing a summer dress, and the red beret is gone, gone, gone, but there's a café on Baker Street that looks…well, if not quite right, it looks familiar. He wants to show it to Mia, to see if it jogs her memory. To see if her standing on that street nudges something well-known in his own heart. He wants to see if there's a small glimpse of the fading dream he can catch with her in their all too real life.

The café is shuttered. The golden awning is pulled up. The large glass window has been blown out and plywood is nailed in its place. The sidewalk is mush and black mud and ice. Mortar dust melts into the water, covering their boots and the hems of their coats in granite glue.

"*This* is what you wanted to show me?" Mia says.

"I had a dream that I waited for you at a table outside a café like this one," Julian says. "Not quite like this."

"I should hope not. This is the pits."

"There was sun, and a bus, and cabs. Does it look familiar?" He hangs his head. It's unrecognizable even to him.

"It doesn't and let's go," she says, taking his good arm. It's hard for her to stand, to walk. "I don't want to miss the train because we're gawping at some non-existent thing."

"It's not non-existent," Julian mutters inaudibly. "It's just invisible to the naked eye. Like *time*."

At King's Cross, there's one train headed to Leeds. It's not a direct train, there are several stops and a change in Sheffield. Great, Julian thinks. Sheffield comes under heavy attack sometime in December 1940. He wishes he could remember the day. But if it hasn't happened already, they're fast running out of December days. Which means it's still up ahead. No one can say for sure how long it will take to get to Leeds. No one can even say how long it will take to get to Sheffield, a hundred and seventy miles away. The civilian train must stop and wait for the military trains to pass before proceeding. No trains run past eight p.m., not even military. It's not safe. They stop on the tracks to wait out the darkness in case of an attack. If there is bombing and the tracks get broken, they need to be fixed before travel can resume. Track engineers are few and far between.

When Mia hears the litany of assault on British Rail, she stares at Julian interminably, as if something is happening here that she doesn't understand and is afraid to ask about. Why would you be taking me into the war zone, the mute question in her eyes reads. Why would you think this is a good idea? He doesn't return her gaze.

It's three in the afternoon by the time the train pulls out of King's Cross, traveling slow. There is no first class or coach. There is only train. She sits on his left by the window, looking desperately forlorn. Julian wants to put his arm around her, but they're both so injured.

Be careful with your body. Flesh is mortal. It can and will perish.

"It's been so blitzy the last few weeks, hasn't it?" Mia says, as if reading his mind.

"It has." Julian helps her light a cigarette with the lighter that says *sad girls smoke a lot*.

"I'm a little bit down today," she says, her eyes welling up. "I'm not as beautiful when I'm not happy, right?"

"Still more beautiful than anyone," he says, stroking her bandaged head. "The sadness levels the playing field slightly."

"Is there any food?"

They didn't bring much. They can't carry much. Julian has a bottle of whiskey in his coat, cigarettes for her, old bread, and a bar of chocolate. She eats the bar of chocolate by the time they stop for the night, somewhere near Stevenage. They're barely out of London.

She closes her eyes. He watches over her. God above, *help her.* Mia, once I saw you holding a baby. All of it a mirage. The sight, the baby, you. Do you remember? We sat in Grey Gardens and held baby Jacob on our laps and pretended he was ours. It was summer. We were warm, you made jokes. We thought the worst thing that could happen to us was those hateful Pye women trailing us through the halcyon London streets.

∞

Early the next morning, the train resumes its sclerotic pace across the wintry British countryside. They're traveling north to Sheffield by taking the more easterly route through Cambridge, to get as far as possible from the continuously assaulted Coventry. From the restaurant car, Julian gets them some fresh bread, hot tea, a pat of rationed butter, and some rationed cheese, and he and Mia pass the time, reading the names of the towns outside their windows and imagining living in them.

They manage to get past Cambridge and then stop for nearly half a day. The tracks have been blown up. While they wait for them to be fixed, the conductor turns off the engine because it's unpatriotic to waste coal, even though human beings might freeze. The train stands forsaken between a field and a forest, somewhere between Biggleswade and Bulby. Mia says she'd like to live in Bulby. Julian prefers Biggleswade.

Hours later, the tracks are fixed, and the train moves on, traveling barely twenty miles before darkness falls. But this time they're between two open fields and no cover. The engineer comes through and tells everyone to disembark for their own safety. If the Germans fly overhead and see the train laid out and exposed on the main tracks, it will be the first thing they'll bomb. The conductor recommends finding shelter in the woods, half a mile away, or three miles down the road in a town called Over. Maybe they could find some shelter there, but they must be back at the train by seven a.m. tomorrow...

It snowed, and a white film covers the earth. The temperature dipped right before freezing, and the film has turned to ice. The train turns off its lights. No one leaves. Staying on the train may be more dangerous, but it's blackout in the countryside, and the train is still a few degrees warmer than out there.

Julian asks the conductor for some blankets. The man doesn't have enough blankets for everyone and can't be seen favoring Julian. He'll have a mutiny on his hands. But for ten pounds, the conductor takes pity on them, and allows them to sneak into the luggage car, away from prying eyes. He brings them some blankets, a candle, and even some bandages. "Her head gash needs to be cleaned," the conductor says, handing them a bucket of snow. "I'll lock you in here but don't get so drunk that you burn the place down."

"We make no promises," says Mia.

Julian washes out Mia's scalp wound with the melted snow water and whiskey and then rebandages her. He takes off his coat and vest and shirt, and shivers in the cold while she cleans his back and rebandages him with the gauze that's left.

"Look at us fussing over each other like monkeys at Regent's Zoo," she says. "And we're locked in a cage like monkeys, too."

Before she helps him put on his shirt, she holds out his left arm and studies the tattoos upside down. She sits next to him on a steamer trunk and reads the inky names to herself, running her finger over each one, from his wrist to the crook of his elbow, as her mouth forms the words.

"How have I not noticed these before?" she says.

"How hard were you looking?"

"At the Savoy I didn't see them."

"How hard were you looking at the Savoy?"

They glance at each other ruefully. "Time for a drink," she says, helping him with his shirt and vest.

"Just one?"

They drink; they count their days. It's the 14th of December. What should we drink to?

They're not for want of things to drink to. Soon they'll be for want of drink.

To London!

To Blackpool!

To Churchill!

To Christmas!

To Bank!

To the stage!

To Finch!

To their friends!

God bless them, Mia says. Finch was a good guy. You would've liked him.

I already liked him, Julian says. He was funny.

Not on purpose, Mia says.

That's why he was funny.

They drink to their wounds, she drinks to his missing fingers. She kisses the nubs, one, two, three, and drinks to them again. This is how you know we can't get married for real, she says. You're missing your ring finger.

He raises his left hand—with all the fingers.

Oh, yeah. She giggles.

They wonder if they've had enough to drink.

Heartily they conclude they haven't.

Because they forgot to sing.

They sing, "God Save the King." Julian keeps singing "God Save the Queen" instead. His daughter is going to be queen when he dies, he explains.

Yes, all sorts of things will happen in the far-away future, Mia says. But the King is still a young man. Victoria lived until she was ninety.

And because he's had too much to drink, Julian says, the King won't live until ninety. He smokes too much. He's going to get lung cancer.

Mia puts down her shaky cigarette. You can be a real pill sometimes, she says.

I said the King, not you. Julian flinches from his own words. *Terrible ignorance is better than terrible knowledge. Yet no one can protect us if we are not ready. Sometimes they can't protect us even when we are. Not because they won't. Because they can't. I carry oil in my lamp. And yet the day of your death is near. I am your grave. As you are mine. You are my grace. But am I yours?*

What else, weepy Nostradamus? What else do you know, Mr. Seer of Seers, Mr. Smarty Pants? Will Hitler win?

No.

Will he invade England?

No.

Will the bombing stop?

Yes. In the spring.

Really, spring? The war will be over in the spring?

No. Only the bombing. Will pause, not end.

Where is Wild?

I don't know.

What's going to happen to you and me?

I don't know.

Will Liz and Nick make it?

I don't know.

So, when *will* the war be over?

I told you. 1945.

But you know nothing personal that could help us?

Yes, I know nothing that can help us, Julian says. I'm a font of useless information no good to fucking anyone. Let's drink and sing.

They sing "I Vow to Thee, My Country." Except Julian sings it with garbled lyrics Mia says she's never heard. *Her sword is girded on her side, the helmet on her head, and all around her are lying the dying and the dead.*

Either I've had too much to drink or you are crap at knowing things, Mia says.

It's both, Julian says.

They sing the Drunken Sailor song, to which they can't remember the words, even though they had just sung it at Bank. *What do you do with a drunken sailor* is all they know.

And *weigh-HEY up she rises*

Weigh-HEY up she rises...

They stand, they sit, they slouch, they slump, finally they slide to the floor and lie on their backs, covered by the nastiest scratchiest blankets, and slur their dreams to the ceiling. They wish they could see the stars. They wish the bloody blankets were better. Americans gave us these blankets, Mia says. Would it have killed them to make them softer? It's like covering ourselves with sandpaper.

They wish it weren't so cold.

She wishes she had the magic power to not need food. He wishes he had the power of two extra arms, and she says if you're going to be asking for extra anything, are you sure you want it to be arms, and with a small smile he says yes because elsewhere he already has the superpower, and with her own small smile she says she wishes she could know it again.

They wish their bodies weren't all busted up. They ooze blood out of their wounds and live inside their regret.

She wishes she could reverse time.

Trust me, he says, reversing time is not all it's cracked up to be.

She wishes they didn't only live once.

Trust me, he says, living more than once is not all it's cracked up to be.

Rolling up his sleeve, Mia touches the tattoos on the inside of his arm, touches her own name in a small script right at his wrist, whispers it in a drunken purr. *Mia, Mia…*

Are these the girls you've loved before?

Yes, he slurs back. These are the girls I've loved before.

She giggles, like she thought of something incredible. Jules, have you noticed how all of them are a devi—deri—devivative—derirative—devirative of my own name, of Maria?

What do you know, Julian says. I hadn't noticed that until you pointed it out just now.

I want me to be there, too, she says. But as Maria.

The name of a fervent prayer, he says.

That's right.

I loved a girl named Maria, he sings, and smiles.

That's right! I want to be above Shae and ASH. But in big letters. Huge. Like this MIRABELLE.

Okay, he says. You will be. He closes his eyes.

Shae is not Maria.

It is. It was Mary-Margaret.

ASH is not Maria.

No. ASH is Ashton. He was my friend.

Must've been a good friend to end up on your arm, all ridged and raised like that.

He was. He was my brother. He died.

Don't cry, Jules. Can you sit up and cheer up? Let's have another round. Drink and sing to me about the girls you've loved before.

They can't sit up or cheer up. They're drowning in whiskey.

What are the dots for? She runs her finger over one set of columns, then the other, touches the dots by MIRABELLE's name. He doesn't answer her, and she doesn't follow up.

Which one of them killed a man in cold blood, she asks. No, don't tell me that either. I don't want to know. Rather…how do you atone for something like that? *Do* you atone for it?

You do, he says. Your body is the price. Your soul is the price.

Mia is quiet. Did she atone for it? she asks haltingly.

I think she did, yes.

Tell me about the first, tell me about this other Mia. Was she nicer than me?

It's not another Mia, he wants to say. *There is only one.* She was not nicer than you. Sometimes she went by a fake name, Julian says. By Josephine. Josephine Collins.

Oh, I quite like that name, Mia says.

I liked it, too.

But Mia is better, right? She smiles.

Of course.

Bloody right. Where did you meet her?

She was up on a stage.

Like me?

Just like you.

Did she love you?

I don't know, he replies. I thought she did. But she didn't love me true. She wasn't true to me. She kept secrets, Julian says. I could taste them on her lips. But I didn't want to see.

How about a poem for Josephine? A short one, like a haiku.

I will forgive you
If you don't love me enough
But not for dying.

Dying or lying? asks Mia.

Dying, Julian replies, looking away.

What about Mary?

We bickered and joked
dreamed of Italy and babies, not
his hands on your throat.

Mallory?

The world ends in fire
We run and run and run and
But the world still ends.

And Miri?

On Gin Alley, we
drink and make wishes while thieves
pitch rocks at your tears.

Mia kisses the tattooed names on his arm after each one. Funny, because you and I are drinking and wishing, too. And MIRABELLE, all capital letters?

MIRABELLE, my love
Cholera prevails and war.
But you and I more.

This Shae character, what about her?

You flense seals, carve up
My dreams. I thought you chose ice
But you chose me.

What will you say about me, Mia whispers. What will you say about our brief but perfect love affair?

We rode horses to
Where the bombs still flew, dreaming
Of a dream machine.

Not horses but trains, she says, and he says, same difference.

I used to work a Dream Machine, she says, on the boardwalk in Blackpool. Did I tell you that? Is that how you know?

I don't think you told me that.

The girls you loved, what happened to them?

They died.

All of them?

He pauses. Yes.

Wow. That's unlucky.

Yes.

But to love is lucky, she says.

That is true, I suppose.

You don't think to love is lucky? Did you love them all?

I loved them all.

Me too? she whispers.

I love you most of all.

I bet you say that to all your girls, she slurs. Their whiskey gone, she falls asleep, but not before she says, will I die, too?

I'm asleep, Julian says, I can't hear you. I'll tell you one thing, though. I definitely don't want to live in a town called Over.

23

Two Prayers

THE NEXT DAY, BOY ARE THEY SORRY THEY HAD SO MUCH TO drink. Their sore heads lowered, they repent and beg forgiveness with their parched dry mouths. They drink the rest of the melted snow water out of the bucket and bang on the door for the conductor to let them out.

Mia is lightheaded. She can't orient herself for a few moments. She has not recovered from her concussion. They scrounge in the food car for something to eat, but other people without hangovers got there first, and all the food is gone until the next stop. They find an old dry scone on the floor. They break the bread. It's delicious.

The train doesn't move. Five miles ahead, the tracks are still being repaired.

They bundle up and go out into the fields for a walk in the frigid air to clear their heavy heads. The ground is white except for the black grass.

Maybe we'll have a white Christmas, Mia says, as they look for something in the fields to eat. They find a potato! They break it in half and eat it raw. It's delicious.

They stumble on a pond blanketed with crystal snow.

They slide on the ice. They can't run, and they can't jump, but they slide to see who can go the farthest. She wins. They pretend to skate, trying not to bend their swollen knees, holding hands and gliding in their wet boots. For a few moments he takes her gingerly into his arms, and they waltz on the ice, until they hear the whistle of the train. They hurry as best they can, limping through sheets of snow, yelling, don't leave without us, don't leave without us.

Back in their seats, their flushed faces red, they hold hands, his left, her right. She is pressed against the cold window and he is pressed against her. She tells him about the Blackpool boardwalk, how much fun she had there in the summers with her friends. She wonders if the Ferris wheel is running in December, if the amusements are open. You were right about leaving London, she says. I'm sorry I didn't want to listen. My mum will be so happy to see me for Christmas.

Let me out. Don't leave me. Let me out. Don't leave me.

Mia, Mia. Mia, Mia.

Free me.

Don't leave me.

Bristol, Birmingham, Portsmouth and Hull, Belfast, Coventry, Glasgow and Liverpool, Cardiff, Manchester, Plymouth, and Cornwall. London.

Not Blackpool.

But everything else is bombed.

Including Sheffield. Oh, how Sheffield is bombed the night of December 15, as their train stands abandoned and out in the open. They're evacuated a quarter mile into the cold woods, where they huddle under fallen trees and watch as their train blows up and burns.

Covering her with his body, to protect her, to comfort her, Julian whispers to her of happier times in the unknowable future.

Don't worry. I will never leave you or forsake you. We are co-stars. We'll always be co-stars.

We're bomb magnets, she says.

No, we are train jockeys, he says. Riding companions. Camping buddies. Lovers. Adventure seekers.

She smiles. How do you do that, Jules, make even a wartime bombing sound romantic?

His lips are against her cold cheek. We'll go roughing, you and I, another day when we are healed, Julian whispers. In the summer when it's warm, we'll set up a lean-to in the field. No light, no water, no heat. Just us under a trench coat tied between two trees on the side of a meadow. It will pour with rain for days. It won't matter. We'll be together.

What are we going to do under a trench coat for days? she says.

I will show you.

Mia is skeptical. Can you imagine *me*, getting down in a tent, she says.

Oh, you'll get down in a tent, all right, Julian says.

And she laughs.

∞

They survive Sheffield, with new small wounds, new cuts, new burns, their old wounds seeping fresh blood. Several hundred of them were in the woods. Eight have died. The rest get slowly transported by buses and trucks twenty miles east to Doncaster, where they wait another day for a train to take them forty miles north to Leeds.

Did you catch the names of the towns we passed, she asks. Dinnington, Doddington, and Diddington. Which one for you?

I'd like to live here, in Loversall, Julian says, pointing to a few glum shacks in the middle of the desolate flatness.

In Leeds, there are no civilian trains on the docket. They have the rest of the day free to find the Leeds Cathedral on Cookridge Street, a half-mile from the station. The church is unharmed and quiet. To their surprise it's also Catholic! This does not distress Mia. She tells him her family is Catholic.

"Mine, too," says Julian.

They're both pleased. "I can't believe it, Jules. Both of us Catholics, on top of everything else. It's like we're meant to be."

"You think?"

They sit inside the cathedral the rest of the afternoon, waiting for the five o'clock Mass to begin.

"I feel bad that so much of the time we live as if there's never been a cave in Bethlehem or a cross on Calvary." Mia sighs. "But inside we all want to believe so much, don't we? Believe that there is light eternal somewhere over yonder."

"There is," Julian says. "I know there is."

"Oh, *that* you know."

"I know it!"

They fall asleep in the pews until a deacon wakes them, sternly saying there is no sleeping inside the church. He softens when he sees their battered bodies.

"Did you pray?" Mia whispers to Julian.

"Of course." *God on high, hear my prayer. Help her—please.*

"What did you pray for?" she asks.

"What did *you* pray for?"

"My priest once told me besides the sacramental prayers and the Jesus prayer, there are only two personal prayers ever worth bothering God for. One of them is help me. And the other is thank you. Which was it for you?"

He smirks. "Mine is almost always help me," he says. "You?"

"Mine is almost always thank you," Mia replies. "Because what have you got, really, that you have not received?"

24

Mytholmroyd

Two evenings later, after finally catching a train out of Leeds, they stop twenty miles east in a picturesque upland town called Mytholmroyd, high in the Yorkshire moorlands. They're ordered off the train, which has been requisitioned for the military. They're told the next civilian train won't be until the day after tomorrow. They have just sixty miles to go until Blackpool, yet can't seem to get there.

Christmas is six days away.

And Boxing Day is seven.

Julian is distraught, but Mia is enchanted. "There's a town right below Mytholmroyd called Hoo Hole," she exclaims, studying the map at the station. It's not even four in the afternoon, yet the sun has already gone down. "I want to live in Hoo Hole, Jules! If not live, I want us to find an inn there."

He doesn't want to travel too far from the station in case there's an earlier train. "Look," he says, pointing across the road. "There's a perfectly good inn right here called Shoulder of Mutton. What's wrong with that? It's on a brook."

"Shoulder of Mutton! What happened to the romantic in you?"

"It's on a burbling brook!"

At the Shoulder of Mutton, all the rooms but one have been taken by travelers without leg injuries and broken clavicles who didn't take so long to peruse maps and dream of Hoo Hole. Their room is in the dormered attic up on the third floor. It takes them a while to climb the steep narrow stairs. The room is nice. It has a bathtub and a small standing balcony between the dormers.

"Mia, look," he says, "a view. Overlooking the brook perhaps." It's hard to tell because it's blackout, and all the lights are off for the war, even at the foot of the hilly Pennines.

She is not impressed. "That's not a balcony," she says. "You can barely fit two people on it."

"Actually, it is," he says. "It's a Juliet balcony." His voice almost doesn't break.

She softens. "Named after Juliet?"

"Yes."

"Well, I suppose that's a little romantic." She softens some more. "Can you help me out of these clothes," she says, "and maybe you can recite some Romeo to me."

It takes them a long time to undress, to have their shallow baths, to be mindful of the wounds they can't get wet. He dries her and changes her dressings, and then she changes his, as best she can, because her broken clavicle makes it painful for her to move her arm. They are bandaged, but they leave themselves naked, they allow themselves the small indulgence, a hat-tip to better times—for Julian in remembrance of the days gone by, for Mia, in hopes of the days to come.

Alas, that my love so tender should be so tyrannous and impolite, Julian whispers.

Finally I get my Romeo.

And I my Juliet.

Where is this tyrannous and impolite love? she says. Alas, indeed! When did we get so old, Jules?

He helps her into bed, covers her, and carefully lies down facing her under the heavy quilts.

The splint for his fractured forearm is inadequate. He must lie on his left side, but he can't raise his right arm to touch her. His shoulder, shoulder blade, and the ragged, stitched-up back wound are on fire. With his index finger he caresses her skin below her bandaged chest. Even her breasts are bandaged, her nipples.

Are you sleepy? she asks.

Not really.

Do you feel like talking? They lie on their sides, face to face.

Sure. What do you want to talk about?

I want to ask you about something you said to Duncan at Bank, and to me at the Savoy.

Uh-oh.

When Dunk asked if you've ever had a thing with two girls you said it wasn't the time for that kind of story, and you wouldn't tell him even if it were.

Julian twinkles at her.

She twinkles back.

Is now a good time for that kind of story?

As good a time as any.

Well…did you?

Did I what? If you want to know, you might as well say the words.

Were you ever with two girls at once?

Yes.

She snaps to attention. Really?

Really.

She tries to scoot closer to him and hurts herself. Oh, no, she says. Oh God, I can't move, I'm so sore. Don't do this to me.

What am I doing? I'm barely even touching you. His index finger continues to draw small circles on her stomach. He can't extend his arm, can't lower it to seek out paradise.

You scintillated me into moving, she says.

Don't ask questions if my answers distress you.

Wait. Let me get comfortable before you tell me more.

You want to get *comfortable* for this story?

Yes, I can't have my body agitated by you. You're going to pop all my bandages.

Is *that* what you call it?

Ha. Okay, I'm better now. Where were we?

Lying on his side, he gazes at her, his pupils amused and dilated, his body stirring. I'm still in love with you, he whispers. I'm so in love with you.

Still? I should hope so. You've known me barely five minutes.

He smiles, even though his cheek hurts. You want to hear a story or no?

Yes, I'm quite curious to hear this one. Were they the girls tattooed on your arm?

One of them was. Every story I have, Julian says, is about the girl on my arm.

The girl? You mean *a* girl. When he doesn't reply, Mia asks to guess which one it was. Not MIRABELLE, she says. You're too fairytaley and soppy about her.

Is that what I am?

Yes, and not Shae because—I don't know—she seems kind of the opposite to me. Opposite of a fairytale.

Like a horror story maybe?

Kind of. I think either Miri or Mallory. They seem like the type to go for that sort of thing. If I had to pick, I'd say Mallory.

Very good. It was Mallory.

Tell me more. Who was the other one?

A girl named Margrave.

Were they both pretty?

Of course.

And naked?

Of course.

And you? Were you naked, too? Don't tell me—of course!

He laughs, and it hurts his face and back and ribs.

How should we do this, she says.

Do what, Mia, says Julian. What would you like to do?

Don't be naughty. Do you want me to interview you, like before? There's no stage anymore. No audience.

You're my audience. So, whatever you want.

Look at you acting all accommodating. I suppose you'd have

to be, being with two girls. Okay, I'll ask you questions. That way you can tell me only the parts I want to hear. But will you promise to tell me the truth?

If that's what you want, yes.

No matter what I ask?

If that's what you want.

How did you get two girls to agree to that sort of thing, anyway?

They needed almost no persuasion.

This is girls we're talking about, right? Okay, set the scene for me, she says, failing to keep the breathy excitement out of her voice.

There was a dormered room, a little like this one, but much larger, with nothing in it but a bed. A fireplace. A table with candles on it. On the bed was a silk sheet and two naked women. The bed was a four poster so the girls could grab on to the headboard or the posts if they needed to.

Mia breathes shallowly. Did they *need* to grab on to the headboard or the posts?

Sometimes.

She exhales in a long breath full of unquiet imagination. Did you kiss them?

Yes, I kissed them.

Did you kiss them...everywhere?

Yes, I kissed them everywhere.

Both of them?

Yes.

Did you use your mouth *and* your hands? She tries to keep calm.

I used everything at my disposal.

Oh my goodness, Jules...

Yes, Mia?

She falls silent, as if she can't breathe and ask questions at the same time. They lie wordlessly but not quietly. When she can't formulate her next question, Julian volunteers by whispering to her of soft breasts and the shimmering fire, of the summer night air unable to cool their bodies, and the cries of pleasure from a trio of impassioned throats.

The things you did with your mouth, did you like doing that to them?

Yes. Very much.

Did they kiss you all over, too?

Yes.

I suppose you liked that.

I suppose I did.

Did they touch each other?

Yes.

With their mouths and their hands?

Yes.

Did you like watching that?

That was one of my favorite things, Julian says, inching closer. With effort, he lifts his broken arm and drapes it over her. At one point, one of them was on her hands and knees between the legs of the other and I was behind her, doing my thing, and watching them both.

She moans from the pain of inflating her lungs. How could you focus on the job at hand?

With some difficulty. Another time, one of them kneeled over my mouth—grabbing on to the headboard—and the other used her mouth on me.

Wait, *wait*, Mia says, stop, I can't take it…

Julian waits. He can't take it either.

I wish I could do that, Mia whispers.

Which part?

All of it. Kneel over your mouth. Use my mouth on you.

Yes, me, too.

Here's the part I don't get, she says, resuming after a few minutes. Right now, we're just talking about it. We are not the man and woman in that bed…

Are we not?

No. We're in this bed. And though we're doing nothing but talking, I can feel you. She curves her lower stomach into him, with a groan of pain tries to lower her trembling arm to touch him, and fails. Despite all your injuries, *this* still happens?

What does one have to do with the other? That's like saying if you're hungry it can't happen.

But you're all busted up.

So?

If you're this excited when we're just talking about it, says Mia, how did you manage to last through the actual thing itself?

Who says I did? The second time was better. After that it got easier.

After that?

It's not often you get to drink from that cup, Julian says with a smile. You want to make sure you get to every last drop.

Mia scoots forward and kisses him. They kiss with their heads not leaving the pillows, their mouths barely touching. Remember what I told you about the Ideal Man, she whispers. Whatever we ask of him, his answer should always be about us.

Then I have fulfilled my obligations admirably, Julian says, pressing her to him with his field-splinted arm, trying not to groan. He doesn't want her to think it hurts to touch her. Though in every way it hurts to touch her.

What did the girls like best? she asks.

He doesn't reply right away. There had been so much joy that hot night at the Silver Cross, so much unbridled uncontained happiness.

I know what *I* would like, she says. Of course I'd like your mouth, your hands. But most of all, I'd like the thing I glimpsed at the Savoy, the thing you promised me I would have again, the abundant thing Rhett gave Scarlett.

You mean the abundant thing Rhett took from Scarlett.

Oh, Julian.

Oh, Mia.

She lies, breathing heavily. You are a bad man, she says.

No, I'm so good.

You know what you did.

I have never been this polite, he says. I've done nothing but lie here chastely and answer your questions.

Chaste is the problem.

I agree with you there.

Did you know you'd get us this excited?

Um, did you *not* know?

No! I thought we were just talking.

Naked in bed at night, face to face, talking about men and women getting it on?

Naked yes, but bandaged and injured, too. What's your plan now, smart guy?

Who said anything about smart?

Ah. Her dilated dark eyes burn. But you have a plan?

About this sort of thing? Always.

They kiss and mill and groan from the pain, from the wounds, from the pulsing ache at the core of their bodies.

I can't take it, she says.

Me neither. Lie on your back.

And then what?

And I will lie on my back.

Um…

Mia. Just…lie on your back.

Carefully she turns onto her back. He turns onto his, even though his shoulder blade is killing him, and with his freed and functioning lowered left hand, he caresses her until the only sound from her is an aspirated *oh*.

And now what? she says, panting, turning her full-up gaze to him. Her own hand lowers to take hold of him. She moans; he moans. What I want is you. She strokes him. I want what I've had the least of in my life. Isn't it always the way?

It sure is, he says.

You can't lie on top of me, she says. I can't get on top of you. Your knees are torn up, so you can't get behind me. Is there something I'm missing?

And when infirmities thicken upon us, Julian whispers, *and old age comes, and we can do little else but lie still, still we persevere.*

You think we can overcome it?

Yes, my darling Mia. We may be broken. But we are not hopeless. Slowly he gets off the bed. We will overcome it by patience. He helps her off the bed, too.

Are we going to make love like salmon, standing? Are you going to lift me up?

In another life perhaps, he says. In this one, we will overcome it by faith. Sit on the bed, and lie back. Carefully he helps her lower herself onto her back, and prods open her legs. Her hips are at the edge of the bed.

We will overcome it by hope, he continues, stepping between her legs.

She moans. You think this is going to work?

Yes. Let me show you.

He kisses her. Holding open her legs, he lowers his head between her thighs like he is doubling over, trying not to groan from his broken ribs, from his broken heart, and rubs his mouth softly against her softness. She moans, trying not to move. Her legs quiver. His ribs are throbbing. But he doesn't want to straighten out until he brings her a little bit of happiness.

And now? she whispers, her hand running through his hair.

We will overcome it by love.

That wasn't love?

It was. He steps in, to meet her at the bed's edge, and guides himself, searching for her. But you asked me for something else.

God, yes. She groans. Something less polite.

As you wish, Mia.

They fuse together. She cries out. His palms press down on the backs of her thighs. His fractured forearm pulses pain with every beat of his quickened heart. In this position, the love is efficient and effective. The stress on her body is great. Soon she is overcome.

It's too intense for her, Julian can see it, he can feel it. Her tumultuous moaning borders on suffering cries. She can't take it light or heavy. Supporting himself by his one functioning arm, he leans over her for a moment, and kisses her lips. She moans and pleads for something he can't decipher and then cries through it. Not after; during. She moans and cries and cries. He asks if he's hurting her, and she says no. He asks if she wants him to finish, and she says *NO*.

She loved him. And he loved her.

He wants to lie on top of her so much, thread his arms under her, press his weight onto her, kiss her lips again. But he can't.

He moves slow and deep. He wishes not to move at all. Intermittently he speeds up, to bring her agony and relief, and then slows down once more.

Julian doesn't want the future to come, the war of the world to intrude, the briefness of their minutes to be upon them.

The little room is heavy with their cries. Their sobs disturb the curtains.

But his groans sound as if he's fallen into a tiger trap and now casts forward dragging the trap behind him still attached to his smashed-up body.

Mia, *please* don't cry. Why does love feel so much like pain.

It's *so* sweet she whispers, her body shuddering, tears trickling down her face. This love of yours is sweeter than any words I've ever known, and I desperately don't want it to be over.

25

Land of Hope and Glory

BUT THAT'S IN MYTHOLMROYD, AMID THE HILLSIDES AND slopes and steep-sided valleys of the British moorlands, amid a rolling landscape in the open country, near woodlands and country houses, above the waterlogged soil that has frozen in the winter. Julian sleeps and dreams of purple summer heather blanketing the uplands for stretched-out scenic miles.

In the morning, they sit downstairs with a small breakfast and a hot tea, and afterward she walks to buy the paper while he waits for her by the river. He watches her limp downhill to him, lit up by the sun, her shining face beaming at him from across the street. He can't help it. He smiles back. And then on the train, he sits with his eyes closed, trying to imprint the image of her full of hope and happiness onto the wretched lens with which he sees the known world.

Before they get to Blackpool, there is Blackburn, and in Blackburn there is a parachute mine that had fallen some time ago and burrowed, and which detonates in the rumble of the passing locomotive, breaking the tracks and derailing the front of the train. The train, traveling slow, skids in the snow. The engine and the first two cars tip over. The rest of the train pops off the tracks and pitches against the trees and the snow banks. Julian and Mia, sitting close to the front, suffer primary blast injuries. Her ear drum bursts. She bleeds from her ears and nose. A sandbag rips open, and the sand flies through the air and lodges in Julian's eyes.

"What did you say to me in the rubble at the Ten Bells?" the irrepressible Mia asks him, swaying and bumping him in the medical van, having lost with the burst drum not only all sense of how loudly she is speaking but her balance, too. Despite the injuries, her tone is peppy.

"I don't remember." Julian can't see.

"You said we're not going to make it, are we, you and me. Well, aren't you sheepish now, mister, to see how wrong you were."

He can't see her, but he sure can hear her.

"We made it pretty far since then, haven't we?" Mia says, kissing his head, ruffling his hair. "It's been almost three weeks since you were Mr. Gloomy Gloomerpants. And look at us."

"I would," Julian says. "But I can't see."

"You'll be fine," she says at top volume, rubbing his stubbled cheek. "I'll be right back. Don't go anywhere. That was a joke. I'm going to find something I can shave you with. You've got a 5 p.m. shadow that's weeks old." She nuzzles his cheek, kisses his face. "That was also funny, Jules. I was funny there."

"Ha."

A sliver of metal got stuck in the cornea of Julian's bad eye, and though the medic pulled it out, it nicked his pupil and now he can't see. The sand grit has scraped the sclera and cornea and irises in both eyes. He hopes *that* will at least be temporary and his right eye will regain some vision. For now he's bandaged around both eyes and is blind.

Mia shaves him, and feeds him, and reads to him, and brings him drink. She remains by his side for two dark days in a room at a small tavern near the station in Blackburn until the scratched cornea heals and he can dimly see out of one eye. Once again, they walk away from the blast on their own two feet. Julian's left eye remains patched and sightless. Mia makes a substantial number of jokes at his expense. "What did the one-eyed pirate say to his fake wife? 'I have no eye dear.'"

"Always be yourself," Julian says in return. "Unless you can be a pirate. Then always be a pirate."

They manage to get on a packed-to-the-gills daily train from Blackburn to Preston. Mia is excited when they arrive at Preston, and why not? Only twenty more miles until Blackpool! But in Preston they learn there are no more civilian trains. It's too close to Christmas, there are not enough engineers, and the military trains get priority. "Maybe in 1941, there'll be a train for you," says the station master in Preston. "Come back then. Happy New Year."

"Come on, Jules, we can walk twenty miles, what do you say?"

With his one eye he appraises her, her still-bandaged head wound, busted ankle, swollen knees, cracked clavicle. He doesn't bother to appraise himself, his injuries too numerous to count.

"Don't give me your evil eye, Long John Silver." She smiles. "It will take us three days. Four if we dog it."

"Christmas Eve is tomorrow," Julian says. What he doesn't add is, *it's the 47th day*. He tries not to even think it. Whether or not he thinks it, the fact of it doesn't change. Tomorrow is the 47th day.

"I know. Do you have a better plan? Or are your plans only about fooling around with susceptible women?" She is always smiling.

He stares at her, at his own reflection in the station window, chews his lip. He is about to go talk to the station agent, to beg him for mercy. He is about to offer the man what he offers everyone who has something he wants. A barter. An Elizabethan coin that will feed the man's family for a year in exchange for opening the doors of a cargo hold on a military train. But before he can do that, Mia nods to someone behind him. It's the station agent.

"There's a train coming through on its way to Blackpool North in about an hour," the man says. "If you're quiet, and ready, and standing where I tell you, I will open the hold. The train will be at the station for ten minutes. So if you're not on the platform, you aren't getting on."

"*Thank* you," Mia says, because all other words are inadequate.

Julian asks her to wait and follows the agent.

"What?" the man snaps, grim and overworked.

"I want to give you something," Julian says. In the palm of his left hand, he holds out one of the gold coins.

"What's this?" the agent says with suspicion.

"It's a present for your family," Julian says. "Don't lose it. Find a coin dealer as soon as you can and sell it. Don't accept anything less than four hundred pounds. Shop around. Auction it if you have to. If you're patient, you may be able to get six hundred for it."

"How much did you say?"

"You heard me."

The station agent looks disbelievingly at the coin in his hand. "Well, crikey, thanks a million," he says gruffly. "It's really not necessary."

"I know."

"Not necessary," the agent adds with the body tremor of a man having encountered a miracle, "but *deeply* appreciated."

"Merry Christmas."

"Yes, Happy Christmas to you, too."

The agent opens the hold for them, gives them two blankets, half a bottle of cheap whiskey and a Brodie hat full of bread and potato stew. "Left over from me dinner earlier," he says. "The wife made it. Cooking is not her strong suit, but the hungrier you are, the better it'll taste."

It tastes like bouillabaisse at the Savoy. By the time the train terminates at Blackpool North an hour later, Julian and Mia have never been so full or so drunk.

It's still three miles to her house.

They stumble in the dark like vagrants, their arms around their sore bodies, holding each other up, hobbling down the streets, slurring the words to "The Land of Hope and Glory."

God who made thee mighty, make thee mightier yet!

"We ain't so mighty," Julian says.

"Are you joking?" she says. "Half-blind, you brought me home for Christmas. With two working arms between us, one working leg, three ears and three eyes, we traveled across a war-torn country and lived to tell about it. We are invisible, Jules. Alone, not so great maybe, but together, we're fucking invisible."

"You mean invincible?"

"That's what I said. Invisible."

He wishes he could marry her and carry her in his arms.

26

Dream Machine

THE HOUSE IS A PINK-PAINTED, TINY, SEMI-DETACHED COTTAGE with an iron gate and a narrow walk. It stands on a street called Babbacombe, near Pleasure Beach. "How can you not love that," Mia says. "Babbacombe, near Pleasure Beach."

"There's no way I can *not* love it," says Julian. "It's a pink palace. But I thought you grew up in London?"

"I did. We lived here when I was young. We keep it as a summer place. Wilma and her family stay in the other half."

Doesn't look as if anyone's there now, the day before Christmas Eve. The house is locked up and dark. The street is treeless. The few bare bushes and the road are covered with ice and mud and old snow.

To get in, Mia finds a key under one of the plant pots in the front yard. Inside there's no light. The electricity has been turned off for the winter. No one thought they'd be coming back to Blackpool until June. Julian and Mia blunder around the kitchen until they find matches and some candles.

There's a note for Mia on the table. It's from her mother. Mia reads it out loud.

> *Mia, my love, my dearest darling! Nothing would make your mum happier to know you read these words, because that would mean you were all right and safe. I haven't heard from you in over a month. Last I heard you met a new fella. The news*

*from London has been so bad that your silence is crushing me. I
am sick with worry. We went with Wilma to Morecambe Bay to
her father-in-law's to spend Christmas and New Year's.*

*If you come home for Christmas, and you get this in time,
please take a train if they're still running to Morecambe and
walk 4 miles to Danvers Lane. Send word to the Morecambe
telegraph office to let me know you're all right. I go every
day to check for news from you. If I don't hear from you by
New Year's, I'm returning to London. I can't take your silence
anymore. I left you some of my ration tins in our secret
cupboard in the pantry off the kitchen, you remember where.
So many empty houses have been burgled. There's Spam,
tinned peaches, milk, tomatoes. There's even a tinned pudding.
I know how you like those. I luv ya, my angel, God be with
you, kia ora, have life, be well, and Happy Christmas.*

Your Mum.

Julian frowns. "Why did your mom say *kia ora*? How does she
know the Maori greeting?"

"I was born in New Zealand," Mia says. "How do *you*
know it?"

"You were?" He is drunk but astonished.

"Yes, in McKenzie county, north of Dunedin. We returned to
Blackpool when I was a baby, so I don't remember any of it. My
mum's family is from here."

"What year were you born?"

"1912."

He stares at her deeply, deeply, deeply. Shae died at the end
of 1911.

"What's your mum's name?"

"Abigail. Abby. Why?"

It doesn't ring a bell. But there are no coincidences. If he has a
chance to meet her mother, he can ask Abigail if she's ever heard of
Agnes or Kiritopa or the Yarrow Tavern in Invercargill. "What do
you think? Can we get to Morecambe in time for Christmas Eve?"

Mia shakes her head. "I can't," she says. "I'm tired. I don't feel well." It's the first time since they've met that Julian has heard her admit that. "I'll walk with you to the sea tomorrow, but that's about it. There's no direct train to Morecambe from here, anyway. We'd have to return to Preston."

"No," Julian says. "We are not going to do that." He has brought her home. And look what it took. They're not going anywhere.

"Right. Everything closes early tomorrow, and stays closed for Christmas and Boxing Day." She steps closer to him. "If I tell her I'm here, she's going to try to take the first train down. And then we won't be alone anymore." She doesn't lift her arms, but she presses her face against his coat. "I want to feel a little better so I can be with you again, before they descend on us. My family is like locusts. There are so many of them, and they never stop chirping."

The house is cold. They decide not to sleep upstairs. Their legs can't carry them up and down. Julian builds a fire, goes up once to bring down some blankets and pillows and makes a bed for them on the floor in the parlor room in front of the fire. Together they lie down, though neither knows how they're going to get to their feet tomorrow.

"I long for fish and chips, for biscuits and tea," Mia says like she's already dreaming. "What about you?"

"Palm trees and highways, the ocean, and music in the lit-up mountains."

"Where is this magical place," she murmurs before falling asleep, her forehead at his arm.

The next morning she wants to go to the boardwalk.

Looking her over, Julian says maybe they've done enough walking for 1940.

Her ankle is puffy and swollen and bruised. She won't let him touch it. How does she think she can walk on it? And his knee looks like her ankle.

"You've never seen Blackpool," Mia says. "You told me you wanted to."

"What's the hurry?" says he, *he*! "Let's go after Christmas. We'll go when you feel better."

"I feel okay now, let's go." She is determined not to let the day pass by.

They limp in the freezing foggy rain to the empty boardwalk. Holding on to his good arm, she tells him of summer days when the Ferris wheel spun and the music played. She tells him of Belle Vue Gardens and Fairgrounds, of the Captive Flying Machine, of Pleasure Beach and the plunge pool.

She worked at Fun Palace, she tells him, and always dreamed of going out to sea. They spot a rowboat below the boardwalk, moored in the wet sand. Taking the stairs (what a bad idea *that* is), they walk out to the shoreline and clamber into the boat. The tide's coming in. "I loved spending my summers here," Mia says. "I ran the Ferris wheel and the little go-carts, but my favorite was the Dream Machine."

"Why?"

"You wrote a poem about it, you should know."

"Which poem? Oh, yeah. *Dreaming of the dream machine.* I was making stuff up."

"Well, it's a real thing. It's a wheel and you give me money and ask it a question, and then I spin it, and when it stops, you have your answer."

"What kind of question?"

"That's the part I liked best," Mia says. "Hearing what people asked the machine."

"They didn't ask silently?"

"Not always. They asked if they would get married, or have a baby, or have another baby, or if he loved her, or if he *really* loved her, or if he liked her long hair, or if he thought she was too skinny." Mia laughs. "For some reason the answer to that one was always yes! He always thought she was too skinny."

"What about the men?" Julian asks. "They had no questions?"

"They did. Usually, they were quieter. One man's wife was sick. He asked if she would get better and broke down before the wheel stopped spinning. And the wheel's answer was, *not in the way you want*. That was awful. Some other ones, too. Will she still love me even if I never make more money? She said she could never marry a plumber, should I apprentice at the masonry guild instead? I did a terrible thing, will my best friend ever forgive me?"

Julian lowers his head. "What was the answer to that one?" he says. "Or do you only remember the questions?"

Mia admits she mostly remembers the questions. "And their faces as they walked away. They were either hopeful or crushed."

"Okay," Julian says, giving her his hand and struggling up. "The tide is high. Let's go find this Dream Machine of yours."

It's Christmas Eve, 1940. There is not a soul around up and down the long wide boardwalk. It's gray and misty, it's about three in the afternoon. The sun is getting ready to set, the sky is heavy and darkening. The Irish Sea is black. The wind whitens the small angry waves as they break against the rocks and the wet pier.

They hobble to the amusement arcade at Fun Palace. The Dream Machine is usually wheeled out onto the promenade, Mia says. Not today. They find it in the back of the arcade, behind the billiards, looming like a huge roulette wheel, lonely against the back wall.

Julian stares at the possibilities.

Signs point to YES.
It's time to settle your debts.
You may rely on it.
Don't count on it.
Cannot predict now.
Better not tell you now.
Only if it will make you happy
Try again, outlook hazy.
Not in the way you want.
Follow your heart.
There's nothing to worry about.
Nothing is impossible with God.

Julian stares at the last one the longest. It's in the narrowest groove. The tongue of the wheel barely has width to lodge in it.

From his pocket he produces a Fabian coin and hands it to her.

"What's that?" she says.

"A gold sovereign."

Frowning a little, she stares at it in the palm of her hand, looking troubled. "It's *weird*," she says, "but why does it look so familiar to me? I must have seen it in a book or something."

"Or something," he says.

"It's so shiny. How much do you think it's worth?"

He shrugs. "Six hundred pounds."

She laughs. "You are a real comedian. Why can't you ever be straight with me?"

"I'm telling you nothing but the truth. Are you going to spin?"

"Are you going to ask a question?" She groans as she lifts her arm to grab the lever.

"I've asked it."

"You're not going to tell me what it is?"

"Will this time be different?"

"That's your question? *Will this time be different?*"

"Yes."

"Okay. But if you don't like the answer, and you want me to spin again, you'll have to give me another coin." She grins.

"Okay."

"How many times can we spin?"

"Thirty-six." He has used four coins in London for the black market, the Savoy, Wild, and the one he gave to Nick. That's a lot. Plus a fifth one to the station agent yesterday. "Are you going to spin or not?"

She pulls the lever. There's a grinding sound of the gears ripping. The wheel spins and spins and spins and spins. They watch it for a long time until it finally stops moving.

Try again, outlook hazy, the groove marker says.

She sticks out her hand. "Another coin, please. It says try again."

Julian produces another coin. She goes to pull the lever, but it won't catch on a gear and won't spin. "Oh, no," she says. "We broke the Dream Machine."

He stands, looking at it grimly.

She hands the coins back. He gives her his good arm. "Let's go home. You look exhausted. I'll go back out by myself to get our Christmas rations. I'll get everything today so we'll have enough for the holiday. I'll get eggs. Is there some whisky in the house?"

"Eggs and Scotch, what a combination. Maybe we can make Scotch eggs, hardy-har-har."

"Hardy-har-har," he echoes, his arm around her, leading her away. "Did you ever ask the Dream Machine anything?"

"Never," Mia replies. "I never wanted to know my future."

"You wanted to once." *Have the smell of death be built in, like a death hack. That way, everybody would know right away what was coming.*

You'd want that?

To know exactly when you were going to die? Absolutely, Josephine said. Who wouldn't?

"No, not me," Mia says. "It must've been one of your other girls. It's easy to get confused, you've had so many." She smiles. "What if the machine told me something I didn't want to hear? I saw the faces of the people who asked it questions. The faces of those who received the right answer never looked as bright as the black expressions of those who got the wrong one." Holding on to him for support, she falls quiet as they walk. "Kind of the way you just looked," she says, "when you asked your seemingly innocuous question. What did you mean, will this time be any different? Will what be different?"

"Nothing," says Julian.

Mutely she stares at him. Something pulls and tears behind her eyes, some alteration laced with the inexpressible truth.

27

Cargo Cult

When he comes back later that night on Christmas Eve, after getting the rations, Mia stands with her hand on her hip, thrusting her little notebook at him, open to the back page, where he had scribbled some words and forgot.

> *Welcome, you said, in any language*
> *smiling at me from your metal hedges*
> *And I said*
> *I want out.*
> *The dream machine is broken.*
> *The box in which I live with you*
> *Is nothing but*
> *A cargo cult.*
> *On the edges flowers, true,*
> *But inside hollow.*
> *I ask you please*
> *I beg you please—*
> *just let me out.*

"Did you write this?"

He puts the bags down.

"Did you write it for me?" She tuts in disgust. "Like a *love* poem?"

"Well, it is a poem," Julian says. "And it's about love."

"*This* is about love? About a love that's run out?"

"Not run out." Running out.

"Is this what you think of me? That I'm a hollow box?"

"No," he says.

She jabs the paper with her angry finger. "It says so right here."

"Can I explain?" But he can't explain. *Look for me in the box with you,* says Mark Antony to his dead Cleopatra. *That's where I will be.*

"Why do you say the Dream Machine is broken?"

"I didn't write that today."

"It reads like some final thing."

"It's just a poem."

"About real things!" She's yelling. Mia is yelling at him. They stand in the cold kitchen. She starts to cry. "Why—*why* did you get me away from London if all you wanted was out? You could've left me there, where I belonged, and been out!"

"I didn't say I didn't want to be with you, Mia."

"What did you mean, then?"

Clutching his busted forearm, he stands with his head deeply bowed. "I just wanted you to be with your mom on Christmas. We can come back to London in the new year if you want." He starts to walk over to the hearth. "It's so cold. Let me build a fire."

She hobbles after him. She grabs his shirt, turns him around to her. "Why do you want *out*?" she cries.

"I have a sickness in my veins." He tries to put a calming arm around her, but she won't have it.

"What sickness?"

"The Epiphany of ruthless math, the Advent of despair," he says.

"What are you talking about?"

"Like when you're counting the days and realize you're a life short."

"You're foul," she says to him. "Can't you just speak plain? Tell me what you mean."

"Don't yell."

"Tell me straight," she keeps repeating. She pushes him, she shakes him, she shoves him, hits him, she cries.

"I love you," he says, his arms going around her.

"You love a hollow box?"

There is terror on his face.

And when she sees it, there is terror on hers. Her soul is laid bare. She pushes him away.

"Oh my God, it's because you think I'm going to die," she says, her breaking voice full of fear and trembling. "You may not know where Wild is, but somehow you think you know this, like about Blackpool not being bombed. You *know* it! Who *are* you? You've known it from the very beginning. That's why your hands are always out to catch me." She is shaking. "Will this time be any different? you asked. And the Dream Machine said no and broke. Why else would you look so shattered? I know that look. That's how the old man looked when he asked about his wife who was dying."

No, Julian says and even he can't hear his own voice in the screaming silence.

"I'm the one, aren't I?"

"Yes," he says. "You're the one."

"Let me finish. I'm the one who dies. The girl on your arm, the one you keep searching for."

His head remains like he's praying.

Not even old rusty water drips from the tap. Nothing moves except the wind outside.

Eventually they retreat into opposite corners. He builds the fire, she makes some eggs. With one candle burning between them, they eat in silence in the small old kitchen, they drink in silence, clean up in silence. They couldn't turn on the radio if they wanted to. There's no electricity. In silence they change each other's dressings. Mia finds some clean gauze and iodine. When they're done, they lie down together under the scratchy blankets and wait for the fire to go out.

Mia speaks first.

"Tell me the truth," she says. "You promised to be true to me, so be true. Did you bring me here for my mother? So that when I died she could find me?"

The house is dark and cold. "Yes," Julian says. "I brought you here for your mother." So when you died, she would find you. "So you could spend Christmas together."

They can't touch each other. Their chests rising and falling, they lie staring at the ceiling, trying to breathe through their broken bones, their seeping wounds.

"Drop by drop," he whispers, "my love falls upon your heart."

"That's not bad," she says in reply. "Why couldn't you have written down *those* words instead? I'd be a lot less upset."

Minutes tick by. Sideways she leans her head to him. They can't get any peace to fall asleep.

"Where did we go wrong?" she says. "Did I not give you myself?"

"You did. Of course you did."

"Then why?"

"What can I tell you that you don't already know?" Julian says. "I've told you so many stories. I know nothing about why. I only know about you. You were beautiful at every age. You always loved the stage. You embraced your vice like virtue." Things he doesn't say: You didn't want babies. You killed a man. You robbed men. You were an angel. You tried to kill me. "You loved me. And I loved you." He presses his palm into the black wound that is his sightless eye. His voice almost doesn't break.

∞

On Christmas, Mia sleeps till noon. Their holiday feast is a quiet Spam and eggs and tinned pudding affair, cooked on a gas stove, washed down with some milk and sweet tea and whisky. He doesn't leave her side, trailing her around the house. Let me open the cans, the edges are sharp. Let me boil the pudding, the water is hot. I will get the peaches in the pantry. I will light the candles and change your dressings.

"What is *wrong* with you today?" she says. "You're worse than at the bomb sites."

She shows him her childhood bedroom upstairs where it's too cold to stay for long. The room is full of books and scarves and stacked-heel shoes and pictures of Clark Gable and Carole Lombard. "She was the love of Gable's life. They were such a great couple once," Julian says without thinking, and twitches with regret when she clams up and storms downstairs, him hurrying behind her. It's only 1940. He forgot that Lombard died in 1942. Using the correct tense is so important in time travel. He never learns.

Downstairs, she complains they can't hear the King's Christmas radio broadcast, and Julian, who's read up on many things, recites some of it from memory. "'War brings, among other sorrows, the sadness of separation.' To all his people, the King wishes every happiness that Christmas can bring. 'I can say to them all on our dear island that they may be justly proud of their race and nation.'" And off her expression, says, "This is what the King *might* say. It's just conjecture."

"Sure it is," she says.

From when she first woke up, they have barely three hours of daylight. By the time Julian performs for her the fragments of the King's speech, it's already dark. They have some bacon rashers and the rest of the eggs and sugar with their tea. Unhappy with him and quarrelsome, she tries to pick an argument, about the dumb things he says, has said, might say. It's a one-sided business. He wants no part in it. That only makes her more bad-tempered.

"Mia, why would I fight with you on Christmas?" he says.

"It's always something with you," she says. "Christmas, a little bombing. Next thing I know, you'll be telling me we're not allowed to argue on Boxing Day."

"No, we can have a good and proper fight on Boxing Day, if that's what you want."

In the firelight, they take turns reading from one of the plays they found in her room, William Saroyan's *The Time of Your Life*, and when the fire goes out, they recite parts of the plays they know from memory. *Earnest. Midsummer Night. Othello.*

"This is our first Christmas together," he says when it's late, and they've run out of other people's words.

He regrets it instantly when she says, "Is that so? And how can it be any other way, dare I ask? We only met in November."

In the dark they lie on their backs.

"Tell me, Julian, is tomorrow going to be our first Boxing Day?"

"Yes," he says.

"And in a week, our first New Year's?"

"Yes."

"And in March, our first birthday celebration together?"

"Yes."

"So, you were just stating the obvious?"

"Yes."

She grinds her teeth. "Why are you holding your breath?"

"I'm not." He makes a show of breathing.

"Tell me, is this our first war together?"

"Yes."

"Is this our first fight?"

"No. It's our second. The first one was yesterday."

"Oh, you think you're so clever. You think you're Mr. Know-it-All."

To cheer her up, he sings her a war song, hoping she'll join in. Marlene Dietrich's "Lili Marlene." He wishes he had thought of something more chipper. *I'll always keep you in my heart, with me, Lili Marlene.*

"War song, you say? Never heard of it."

He doesn't reply. Is 1940 too early for *waiting for you the whole night through, for you, Lili Marlene?*

"Tomorrow," says Mia, "I'm going to walk to the pier and buy a newspaper and read the text of George's holiday message to his Commonwealth. All I can say is, heaven help you if there is a single word in the actual speech the same as what you told me earlier."

"What, not even Christmas?" says Julian.

"That's right," Mia retorts. "Not even Christmas."

∞

Early on Boxing Day morning when he comes back from getting her the newspaper and more eggs from the woman down the road with chickens in her yard, he finds Mia standing by the sink in the kitchen. Her back is to him.

Are you okay? he says. Here's your newspaper.

Leave it on the table. I'll look at it in a minute.

I have the eggs, too. Four of them.

That is egg-citing, she says. She doesn't turn around.

What's the matter?

Nothing, she says. I'm dizzy. I have a bad headache.

So sit down. You need food.

She turns around to face him. She is pale gray.

And he turns pale gray, too.

He pulls out a chair from the kitchen table and eases her into it. "What happened while I was out?" He was gone for barely twenty minutes! "What did you do?"

"Nothing. I bent to rebandage my ankle, and I sneezed. Does that count as doing something?"

"Well, sure," he says. "If you do it right."

Weakly she smiles.

He stands, still in his boots and coat, staring at her, and then into his tingling hands.

"What's the matter?" she asks. "Are *you* all right?"

"Of course," he says. "But I just realized I must have dropped one of the eggs in the snow."

"Was it a penguin egg? An emperor penguin maybe?"

He stands.

"I'm yoking," she says. "You're not the only one who can crack yolks. Go find your egg."

He steps outside the pink country house. Snow is falling. There is ice on the path to the gate. He stands looking at Babbacombe Road, at the other houses. One or two have smoke in their chimneys. The invisible stars have dropped their deception. All pretense is gone. The waters froze, the skies opened up and rained ice for months, the wind wasn't the cave, it was the whole world.

She has gotten herself so far. So far, and no farther.

Limping, he makes his way to the gate and grabs on to the iron finial. He holds on to it like a lifeline and stands motionless. The cold freezes his throat. He crosses his wrists, presses his splinted arm into his stomach. His mouth opens in an agonized silent scream.

He hears Mia's voice from behind him. "Jules?"

He doubles over. After a moment, he forces his fists to unclench. His arm falls to his side. He breathes in the icy air, once, twice, begs for mercy, for some self-control. Slowly he straightens out, turns around to her, and smiles.

"I couldn't find it." He returns to the house. She follows.

A few minutes later she is whisking the eggs at the counter when she sways. He is right there to catch her.

"I don't know what's wrong with me," she says. "One second I'm fine and the next so dizzy."

"Let's sit."

"Okay, but just for a minute. I really want the scrambled eggs."

Julian needs to sit down himself. His legs are having trouble holding him.

"Why are you looking at me like that?"

"Like what?" Julian says, barely audible. "Rest. I'll finish breakfast."

He begins to get up, but she stops him.

"Wait. My headache is so bad. Maybe you're right; maybe

it's because I haven't eaten. But my ears are ringing. I'll be fine, but—Jules...I think I need to lie down for a minute."

He lays her down on the blankets by the fire and stands over her.

"A minute ago everything was all right," Mia says, looking up at him apologetically. "I'm sorry, Julian."

"Don't be sorry. It's just a headache." He struggles not to avert his gaze. She could've had a slow subdural bleed for weeks, since the Ten Bells bomb. She could've burst a vein in her injured brain when she sneezed. It could be cholera. It could be the pillory.

"Do you want to know why I'm sorry?"

"No."

"I'm sorry," Mia says, "that I couldn't make this time be different."

"I don't know what you're talking about." Julian is nearly unable to stand. He must hurry. Turning his back to her and reaching into his trousers, he pulls out the brown pouch, loosening the silk ribbons, glancing at the gold coins. Slipping the rawhide rope over his head, he clutches the crystal and the wedding rings in his numb hands.

"Jules, what are you doing?"

"Just a sec."

"Why are you taking it off?" she asks. "I thought you said it never comes off?"

Julian didn't say it to her this time around. He said it to her in 1603 when she was Mary. "I won't need it anymore."

He takes one last look at the quartz in its silver holster and drops it with the rings inside the leather satchel.

He gathers her little notebook, where she wrote down her wedding vows and the names of his girls, and lies down awkwardly next to her, almost like falling. He leaves the notebook near her head and places the leather purse into the palm of her hand.

"What's this?"

"Your bag full of sovereigns."

She sticks her hand inside the pouch. He hears her sifting around, jingling the coins. She smiles. "Finally you're giving them back to me," she says.

"Yes."

"It feels like a lot less than there was."

Does she know that, too? "Yes. We lived."

They turn to each other, lie face to face.

Her body jerks.

He holds her against his chest. "It's going to be okay, Mia," he says. "Everything's going to be all right."

Her clouding eyes beseech him, yearning for life. She wheezes erratically into his collarbone. With her breath, she makes his throat warm, then moist, then warm again. It feels as if his throat is crying.

"You're shaking, Jules. Convulsing."

"I'm cold," he says.

"Me, too. Maybe you can cover us with another blanket? No, no, don't move, don't get up. Everything hurts so bad."

"Yes." He presses his cold lips to her warm forehead. He is losing his partial sight.

"I'm the Cheapside girl in silk and gold receding," she whispers.

"No."

"It can't be me," she says. "I've never worn any finery. Except that once. At the ball."

"You've always been that great girl," Julian says. "Clothed in purple and scarlet, decked in gold and precious stones and pearls."

Drip, drip, tick, tock. The wind howls outside. Sounds like a blizzard is coming.

"I'm going to close my eyes for a minute," she says. "I need a short sleep. Yes, a brief rest and then I'll wake, and make you eggs."

"Okay, Mia. You sleep if you need to." His head glides over to hers, and his lips press softly against her lips.

"What are you doing?"

"Nothing." *I'm kissing you the last time I see you.*

Seconds fly by.

Suddenly, she opens her eyes and stares intensely into his face. "Julian!" She is gasping. Her expression is one of profound, crystal-clear recognition. "I know who you are," she says in a rupturing voice. "My God, I know who you are! It's you, Julian. O my soul, it's *you*."

"It's me." At the end of your days, the immortal secrets of all hearts are disclosed.

"Oh, my love," she echoes hoarsely, in red remembrance of things past. "Oh, my *love*."

I tried not to walk through life with a downcast face, Mia. Because of you.

Despite our troubles, there was glory in the uplands over the moors. There was ecstasy. There was paradise.

I searched for you. You gave me shelter.

I may have taught you how to run in the rain, but you taught me how to live forever.

They stare at each other, all their memories entwined.

"You gave yourself to me," she whispers wrenchingly. "You blessed me with your life."

He smiles at her, into the face that knows him. "A bomb goes off inside the pub," Julian says, with supreme effort raising his limp arm and cupping her cheek into his mutilated hand. "They sit and they wait. Ten minutes later, the waitress appears with their food."

"I'm sorry the lunch is a bit dusty, my *love*," says Mia, her voice fading. "The ceiling's down in the kitchen."

Part Two

Trace Decay

And soon, too soon, we part with pain,
To sail o'er silent seas again.

Sir Thomas Moore

28

Morecambe Bay

WHAT WAS JULIAN?

Was he his injured legs, his blind eyes, his missing fingers?

No.

Was he his scarred head?

No.

Was he his empty gut, his grieving heart?

No, none of these things.

Was he his body?

Also no. When the breath would leave it, no one would look at his body and say it was him. They would say the body had belonged to him. It was Julian's body, his property, but it wasn't *him*. Like his house wasn't him, or his Volvo, or his clothes.

Not his body, not his head, not his heart, not even his feelings were him. The feelings were what the thing that was him felt. They weren't the man.

So who was it that the body belonged to?

Who was it who felt?

Who was it who mourned, who loved, who *was*?

Before everything else was his soul.

And what could a man give in exchange for his soul?

∞

Not his body. Because the body was like London after the war. There wasn't much left. The body had suffered primary, secondary, and tertiary blast injuries. It had lost half its hearing, half its sight. It needed to be patched and grafted and sewn up. It needed to be surgically renovated. Julian lost the ability to walk unaided and without pain. Most of the bones in his feet had developed hairline fractures. His body was covered head to toe in irregular Lichtenberg flowers, a sure sign of getting struck by lightning. He had scars on his face, on his back, on his arms, on his legs. His body needed intravenous antibiotics and a number of surgeries. Plastic surgery on his face to fix the scar on his cheek and above his eye. Surgery to repair the improperly set forearm, which, instead of healing straight, had hooked toward his body. Surgery for the anterior and posterior cruciate ligament tears that required a knee replacement. The surgery on his left eye that did not return his sight to him. There was light but no detail.

Tama the Maori warrior was wrong. Julian's body could tell some story.

Too bad the storyteller was mute, on a morphine drip the first six weeks at Queen Elizabeth, and mute for weeks afterward at the Hampstead Heath convalescent home.

Franco and Ricks, his sparring buddies from the gym, visited him once when he was still in the hospital.

"Whoa, man, that was some nasty ass fight you been in," said Franco. "Who was it with this time?"

"Junkers Ju 88 combat aircraft," Julian said. "But not one. Thousands of them."

They didn't understand. They mock-sparred in front of him, jabbing into the air, wanting to know when he would come back to them.

Instead, Julian retreated to Hampstead Heath and fell into the routine of a place where silence and tranquility were designed to bring about healing. He would sit with Ava in the garden if the weather allowed, or in the common room by the windows. Like him, Ava didn't speak. It had only been a few months since her stroke. But unlike him, she wanted to. When she first saw him, she cried. She knew he had failed, and this time for good. Her shaking hand reached for him. Often when they sat in their chairs, she held his hand.

In June, he was still at Hampstead Heath. He thought he was getting better, ready to leave maybe, but one afternoon when he was out in the garden, he fell as if cut down and couldn't get up. An X-ray showed he had fractured his pelvis. No one could figure out why. He didn't trip, hadn't been pushed, hadn't been blasted out of his seat by a sonic wave of a nearby bomb. The bone just crumbled.

"We see this injury in very old people," the flummoxed doctor said. "Their bones disintegrate. I've never seen it in a young man like yourself."

Julian wanted to tell the doc he wasn't so young.

He received a hip replacement, like many of the old folks in the home. Painful rehab took him through August.

Now when he walked he walked with a cane.

Devi visited both Julian and Ava.

Julian didn't speak to him. He had nothing to say.

And then, one September night, when the moon was new, he dreamed of Josephine again. The golden awning was above him, the metal table stood on the familiar sidewalk. The umbrella swung side to side in her hands. The red beret was on her head.

He screamed when he woke up. He thrashed in his bed. No, he begged. No.

But she was smiling! Smiling, strolling down the street with a spring in her step, as if everything was never better.

The devil was mocking Julian. Now he knew: ridicule is what he'd been given in exchange for his soul. Julian could hear the diabolical cackle all the way from the underworld.

After dreaming of her, he decided to leave Hampstead Heath. But he couldn't leave without talking to Ava first.

"Ava," he said, pulling up a chair by the window where she sat. "Look at me, please. Blink if you can hear me. I need to ask you something. Years ago in L.A., Josephine—I mean Mia—told me you couldn't make it to our wedding because you were out of the country visiting relatives. I know that was a lie, but what she said was: you were visiting relatives in *Morecambe Bay*."

Ava nodded. The stroke had ruined her speech and disabled her ability to write or spell or remember the order of words, but she could still understand. The doctors thought she might get better with time, but she wasn't better yet.

"Is that where your family is from?"

Ava nodded.

Silently Julian watched her. "What about a pink house on Babbacombe Road in Blackpool? Do you know it?"

With a baffled frown, she shook her head.

"A woman named Abigail Delacourt lived in that house. Did you ever hear of her? Or her sister Wilma?"

Grabbing his hand, Ava tried to form words, first with her mouth and then on a legal pad. Julian couldn't make sense of her markings. For a long while she drew nothing but manic circles.

Julian wasn't getting anywhere.

"Who was Abigail?" he said.

Vehemently she shook her head.

"Who was Wilma?"

She nodded.

"Can you write and tell me? Who was she?"

On a fresh sheet of paper, with her weak left hand, Ava slowly scratched out a stick figure. It was an O with two criss-crossing lines underneath it, forming a t. She drew another figure and below that a third. With a pencil she kept tapping at the third stick figure, tapping so hard she made a hole in the paper.

It was a game of Pictionary between a woman who couldn't draw and a man dense like a wood plank.

On a new sheet of paper, Ava drew the three stick figures again, this time in a vertical line, one above the other, and then a connecting line from the bottom figure to the middle and from the middle figure to the top. She tapped the top figure with her finger.

"The top one is Wilma?"

Fervently Ava nodded. She tapped the bottom stick figure and then herself on the chest.

Julian opened his mouth. "Wilma is your *grandmother*?"

Ava cried.

He sat stunned. "Wilma had three daughters," he said in a disbelieving voice. "Which one was your mother?"

Ava lowered her hand below the arm of the chair.

"The youngest? Kara?"

Ava nodded.

Julian took Ava's frail hand. "Kara was your mother? Oh, Ava. What year were you born? I can't believe I don't know this."

Through headshakes and nods, he learned that the year was 1945.

"Ava, what did you know about your great aunt Abigail? She had a daughter named Maria. She was your mother's cousin. She died five years before you were born."

Pressing an arthritic fist deep into her heart, Ava's eyes glistened with anguish.

"Ava," Julian whispered, "did you name your daughter Mia after Abigail's daughter?"

Her eyes spilling over, Ava nodded.

"How did you and your family get from Morecambe Bay to Brooklyn?" Julian asked.

Ava found the first scrap of paper she had drawn on. Holding the index finger of Julian's maimed hand, she guided him over the series of circles, one after the other. With his pointer, she tapped on one, then the next, and the next. Julian stared at the circles, at Ava, outside into the garden. He counted the circles, but it was unnecessary. He knew the answer already.

36.

Thirty-six Fabian coins he had left with Mia in the pink house on Babbacombe Road.

29

Junk Shop

THE DOORBELL RANG OVERHEAD AS JULIAN OPENED Quatrang's door. Devi came out from the back, wiping his hands. "Look who's finally here," he said. "Would you like some lunch?"

"No," Julian said. "I'm not staying. I came to ask you a question."

Devi put down the dishtowel and stood small and straight by the counter.

"Are you telling me the truth?" Julian said. "Is there really no way to go back?"

"There is really no way to go back."

"Then why did I dream of her again?"

"I don't know," Devi said. "Grief?"

"No."

"Take a walk around London, Julian."

"I would but—" Julian waved his umbrella that doubled as a walking stick.

"You should've been more attentive when it was easier," Devi said. "You've been walking, but you haven't *seen*. Otherwise you might've learned something."

"Do I look to you as if I haven't learned enough?"

"Every soul out there is dreaming and searching for something they loved and lost," Devi said. "Every one of them is seeking the unattainable thing. On the streets of London is the answer to why you dream. It's the human condition. Watch the men and women when they're by themselves. They're all searching. For faded beauty, for old love, for a new career, for warmer climes, for health, for their dead mothers. For their lost s-sons." Devi's voice almost didn't stammer. "We're all like you."

"That's not what I'm asking."

"Of course not. You refuse to get it. *Everyone* sees the faces they love in their dreams!" Devi rocked backward, unsteady on his feet. "But you had the real thing. You *had* it. I told you what it would cost you. And now you're upset you had to pay the price? Looking for another miracle, are you? Well, I'm all out, Julian."

"You call what you gave me a miracle?" Julian said through his teeth.

"Oh, you ingrate," the Hmong cook said, his own teeth clenched. "Do you know what I would give to see my son again?" Devi's stiff hands gripped the counter. "*Everything.* I would give everything I had, everything I would ever have, every single thing under the sun, and everything else in the universe. Ashton was right about me. If the devil had asked me for your soul in return for my boy, I would've betrayed you like *that*." Devi snapped his fingers. "I would've handed you over."

"You did hand me over."

"Then I was duped because I got nothing in return."

Julian's heart was black as it flew over emptiness.

Nothing was stronger than death.

Not even him.

Not even her.

And while he was busy feeling sorry for himself, time carried the marrow of his life away.

He was quiet. Great Eastern Road was quiet.

"You destroyed my life," Julian said. "Yes, I was a husk before I met you, but you ruined me for good." His shoulders quaked. Without saying another word, he turned around, took his umbrella, and limped out of Quatrang, the doorbell ringing behind him.

Devi followed Julian down the street.

"Julian, please come back. Let me help you."

"You can't help me. You said so yourself."

"Where are you going?"

"Nowhere. You've made sure of that."

"You're not being fair. You have been too long with your pain, and it has brought corruption to your life. Come back. Let me heal you."

"No. You're all out. And I'm out, too. As Kiritopa told me, I'm bowed in the middle where everything that gave me life used to be." Julian continued down the street, leaning on his umbrella. "Soon I'll fall to the ground."

"Please, Julian."

"Leave me alone, Devi." Let me fall.

Julian ended the lease on his Notting Hill apartment and sold or gave away most of his things. He kept a few clothes, a photo of him and Ashton, the Bob Marley poster, Josephine's books, his old multi-tool, his journals, and the loose, chipped-off shards of what was left of Mia's crystal in a small glass jar. Basically he took what was on top of his nightstand. The 37th gold coin that he had brought back with him years earlier from the Great Fire he returned to Ava. She shook her head, but he insisted. It was never his to begin with.

He turned off his cell service, threw away his phone, and left no forwarding mailing address. He moved to Greenwich, where he found a room for rent above the Junk Shop on the High Road, a full circle from Mrs. Pallaver's on Hermit Street all those years ago, another tiny space with a twin bed.

Every single day without fail from October to the end of February, Julian had lunch at the Rose and Crown, where the barkeep would ask him what he was having today, and then hobbled through the park up the steep hill to the Royal Observatory and stood at the black Transit Circle with the crystal shards in his palm, waiting for the midday sun to give him a sign.

Every day Julian waited for the portal below to open to him again.

And every day it did not, as if it had never opened, as if it didn't exist.

30

The One-Eyed King

In early March, there was a knock on his door.

It was Mark, the owner of the Junk Shop.

"Someone's here to see you," Mark said.

Devi stood on the landing.

Julian didn't tell him to come in. He came in anyway. "How did you find me?"

"How difficult do you think it was? Were you hiding? How do you think you found this place? You don't remember I told you my good friend Mark sold all kinds of junk out of his yard?"

"No."

They stood.

"How have you been?"

"Great."

"You know who I keep seeing in church almost every Sunday?" Devi said. "Ashton's father. He comes, brings flowers to the graveyard. Brings lots of flowers. Almost looks like two bouquets."

"Did you come to tell me about Ashton's father's weekend schedule?" Julian said. "What do you want?"

"What are you doing with yourself these days?"

"What do you care?" Julian grabbed his keys, his umbrella, the jar of her crystal pieces, the signed playbill from *The Invention of Love*, the books she had held in her hands, and pushed past Devi.

The cook followed him down the stairs and to the street. "You haven't been to the gym. Franco and Ricks are upset."

"They'll manage."

"Why haven't you gone back?"

"I've been busy."

Julian had been going to a gym in Greenwich, but he'd be damned before he told Devi that. He turned off the High Road to the Royal Park, trying to be brisk about it. Devi was surprisingly spry. Or was it Julian who was surprisingly slow? Nowadays he struggled to walk without limping, and he could no longer sustain the feats of endurance that used to cast him for miles around London. He still looked for the café with the golden awning, but only in Greenwich, and sometimes he looked for it in Sydenham, where Mirabelle used to live, but he stopped his excursions across the river.

"Please don't make me walk up the hill to the Observatory with you," Devi said.

"I'm literally trying to get away from you. You going with me is the last thing I want."

"Slow down. Let's have a drink first, let's talk."

"I have nothing to say to you."

"Julian, please."

Even a hobbled Julian managed to leave the elderly Hmong man behind.

Devi found him inside the Transit Room, standing in front of the telescope, palm out, shards in his hands. "Julian." Devi was panting. He held on to the black railing to steady himself. He wouldn't look at the deep dark well at the foot of the telescope— as if he was afraid it would swallow him if he so much as glanced at it. "Explain to me what you're doing."

Julian didn't reply. He glanced at his watch. It was only 11:30. He couldn't take another half hour of this.

"It won't open," Devi said.

"Maybe it won't. And maybe it will. Maybe it opens every new moon, or every full moon. Or randomly. Or on every other solstice or every other equinox, or on the first and last day of every month, or only on the 29th of February. Maybe it opens when someone wishes it real hard. You have no idea. But one of these days, it *will* open," Julian said. "And I will be here when it does."

"Okay, say it does. Then what?"

Julian whirled to Devi. He knew he must have looked manic, palsied, desperate and enslaved, but he didn't care. "It took me eight years to understand a central fact of my life," Julian said. "I have been lost, reformed, made smaller, weaker, sicker. In some ways larger, yes, but not the important ways. For many years I lived with no comprehension of the most vital thing open to me, yet with a total indifference to everything else that mattered. The more filled with mystery my life became, the more frantic I grew, and the more determined to fail at everything else, as long as I succeeded in my one imperative—to save her. In other words, to do the one thing that I could not do, that made the least sense, yet somehow was the sanest thing in my life."

"You're upset with me—"

"Oh, we're way past that. I'm furious. With myself, too, for allowing you to do this to me. I've been pissed off for years. Silly me, I thought if I did everything right, if I lived right and leaped by faith and learned to fence and fight, to ride horses, to plant, to make candles and love, to write her poetry and keep evil men away from her, that it wouldn't all be a pantomime, it wouldn't all be the dumbest fucking dumbshow on this earth. The idiot that I was," Julian said through gritted teeth, "I thought that through the sheer immovable force of my effort and hope, I'd pull off the *impossible* and make her possible, that I would change her fate and give her back her life, the life she had never finished living, the life she had barely begun to live when we met."

"How can you give her back what you didn't give her in the first place?" Devi asked quietly.

"Because I'd been given a miracle! You said so yourself! I'd been given a second chance, and I *refused* to believe it was for nothing. And here's the thing," Julian said, leaning forward. "I *still* refuse to believe it."

"Yes, you're the master of not facing facts." Devi waited. "But now what? All these self-discoveries, encouraging though they are, don't explain what you're doing here."

"I've been looking at everything all wrong, thanks to you."

"I knew it had to be my fault somehow."

"The Dream Machine said *outlook hazy. Try again.* So that's what I'm doing."

"What is this Dream Machine?"

"A large roulette wheel on a boardwalk that spins and tells you things."

"So a Magic 8-Ball?" Devi said. "You're making your life decisions based on a plastic cube inside some water? Do you think perhaps this holy oracle had simply meant *spin again*?"

"No," Julian said. "And you know who told me that? *You.* When you quoted C.S. Lewis to me. Very often what God helps us toward is just this power of *trying again*, you said."

"So now the Almighty is communicating with you through an amusement park fortune wheel?"

"It said *try again.* I will find a way."

"No, you won't."

"That's what you're afraid of, isn't it? You're afraid that the portal will open. Once again, you're trying to talk me out of it."

"That's not what I'm doing."

Julian glanced at his watch. "Stop talking. It's almost noon."

"So what?"

"Be quiet! I need to focus."

Noon came.

Noon went.

Nothing happened.

Julian lowered his hand with the crystal chips that looked a lot like glass shards in the blown-apart jeep in wartime London. Carefully he returned the slivers into the jar and tightened the lid.

"Are you done?" Devi said.

"Until tomorrow."

"Julian…"

Julian stormed off.

Devi hurried down the hill behind him, all the way to the High Road. "I'm going back to Quatrang," he called out. "Are you sure you don't want to come for lunch? Now would be a good time."

Julian didn't reply, walking away as fast as his fake hip and fake knee could carry him.

∞

A week later on March 15, Julian spent his birthday utterly alone, almost as if he hadn't turned forty.

Five days later, on the March equinox, Devi was back at Mark's.

"Come to say goodbye?" Julian said.

"Why, where are you going?" Devi said.

Julian clearly thought he was going somewhere. He was more prepared than he'd been the past few times. Weaker, but more prepared. He was bringing a headlamp, extra bulbs, another two flashlights, hooks, a knife, weatherproof gloves. Under his clothes, he had donned a wetsuit again. He had placed her books in sealed plastic bags to keep them from getting wet. He brought a chest pack. He brought everything he could think of.

Devi watched him, his usually impassive face bearing traces of anxiety and incomprehension. "If only you knew how worrying your parade of delusion is to a casual observer."

"Funny that, you calling yourself a casual observer."

"Don't you see what's happening? The thing you've been obsessing over has finally driven you insane."

"After noon today neither you nor I will have to worry about it."

"Are you sure about that?"

Julian allowed himself a thin smile. "*You* certainly think so."

"No," Devi said. "I really don't. You know how you know? Because I'm going with you. If I really thought the portal would open, I wouldn't be here."

Together they walked through the park, up the hill, side by side, not saying much. In the Transit Room, a few minutes before noon, Julian commented on Devi's uncommon agitation. "What are you so stressed about, shaman?"

"In the kingdom of the blind, the one-eyed man is king," Devi said by way of reply.

"You think you're mocking me?" Julian pointed to his seeing eye. "I'm not blind. I'm the one-eyed king."

And then Devi said something even more incomprehensible. He said, "I *know*."

As noon approached, Julian's heart pounded as it always did before he flew into the void. Like war drums.

But noon came and went on this March 20 without a glimmer of blue hope, without a yawning, without a maw. It just came and went like all the noons had been coming and going—uneventfully. Julian kept his palm out for a few minutes, refusing to accept it.

"It said *try again*," he muttered in confusion. "How can this be?" He wouldn't look at Devi.

Outside, Julian stood in the courtyard. Devi pointed to the observation plaza, and Julian felt so exhausted, he followed the cook to a bench, where they sat high above the banks of the winding Thames and gazed silently over the scenic vista of London spread out before them for miles in the hazy sunshine.

"Today wasn't the day, that's all," Julian said.

"Clearly."

"But tomorrow might be. One of these days, I will find a way."

"But why?" Devi said. "Everything you already know, you know. Everything you could do, you've done. What would be the point?"

Julian stood from the bench and faced Devi. The small man didn't look up, continuing to stare at his feet.

"Devi."

"What."

"Look at me."

"I'm tired of looking at you."

"Look at me."

Devi raised his black weary eyes. "Even if there was somewhere for you to go, and there isn't, you can't save her. You *know* this!"

"Here's what I *do* know." Julian spoke with the determination of a man possessed. "Even though it's *hopeless*, and I'm fuck out of luck and out of chances, and out of time, and my body is a fucking disaster, and even though she's probably still going to leave me, not on *my* time, not on *her* time, but on some random nonsense fucked-up time for no reason and no rhyme, even though I know this, I will still try again. Do you know why?"

"Yes," Devi said, a tear rolling down his face. "Because that's what you do. You don't give up. Even when you know it's hopeless."

"That's right," Julian said. "You perform an angioplasty on a 98-year-old man—to save one life. You move your alcoholic wife into a dry county and put a lock on her steering wheel—to save one life. You poison the body with Cisplatin, drive it for miles to hospitals and meeting halls on ocean beaches, you talk of rehab and operations, Antabuse and amputations. You run into a burning house and rip a child from the hands of death—to save one life. You went into the cave of Red Faith, even though you knew your son's soul was new, and there was no point. My mother still called every oncologist in the country begging for a different prognosis for my father, still drove him to radiation even though she knew that the demon mass that attacked his lungs had no intention of ever leaving. You sacrifice a lung, then part of another, you forsake your business, your friends, your girls, and move to another continent to live with a depressed deranged fool—to save one life. You empty the vodka bottles and refill them with water, you stop drinking yourself, hoping it will make your friend drink less—to save one life. You do what you can, even when you fear it's hopeless. You will probably fail, yes, but you don't give up. That's what love is. That's what faith is. You suffer to live, you struggle to help them. *You never surrender.* That's the part I didn't understand until now—that *that* was the only true thing that had ever been offered me, the only true thing I had to give her, from the very beginning. Nothing else. Just myself at her feet." Julian took a breath. "God gave me the power to try again, and that's what I'm going to do. Besides," he said, "the Dream Machine didn't say there was no hope. It said *outlook hazy.*"

"Well, if Zoltan the Magnificent has spoken." Shaking his head, Devi sat as if his heart weighed him down. "Imagine the million atoms that make up the smallest thing in the galaxy and that would still be a trillion times larger than every single thing you know and will ever know." He extended his arm to Julian and supported by him stood up. "Come with me, tiger catcher," he said with fond and broken resignation. "Stop wasting your precious time on nonsense."

"Where are we going?"

"Back to Quatrang."

"Why?" Julian said. "Because as I suspected—there is a way?"

"There *is* a way," Devi said. "But you're not going to like it."

31

Dark Equinox

"It's a terrible thing for a man to find out that all his life he has been speaking nothing but the truth," Devi said, quoting Oscar Wilde. "But it's even worse when no one hears him."

"Oh, I hear you," Julian said. "I'm just not listening."

Devi helped Julian pack up his meager belongings. They said goodbye to Mark at the Junk Shop and returned to Quatrang together.

There had to be ritual before true words could be spoken and listened to: a liturgy of tiger water, of sake, of prayer, of garlic shrimp and kimchi. There was communion: with her books, her playbill, the slivers of her crystal.

"You're not going to be happy with me," Devi said, his hands gliding over the artifacts, his mouth moving with inaudible words.

"What else is new," Julian said. "I've hated almost everything you've ever said to me."

"There's no way out of this without you having to make some hard choices."

"You mean some *more* hard choices?" Mutely he and Devi regarded one another. How glib Julian had been once, how careless and cavalier. Uncertainly, he waited.

Devi inhaled. "I don't know what's beyond the world I barely understand. I myself did not succeed in what I'm about to offer you—obviously—since I'm still here. But the only way you could even *try* to return to her and your old self in L.A.," he said, "is if you leave your body behind."

Julian zeroed in on Devi's words.

"You travel back in time with your *soul only*," the shaman said.

Julian exhaled. "Leave it behind where?"

"In the river. Ghost rider becomes a black rider. Black rider becomes ghost."

"Leave it behind," Julian slowly repeated. "You mean...*die*?"

"Yes." Devi did not equivocate.

Julian fell silent. Is that why the river was black? Because the hollowed-out bodies after the souls had fled were buried in it? All that relentless gnashing and screaming. It wasn't imagined. It was real.

"To find her again, I must die?"

Devi did not look happy when he said, "L.A. is her last time on earth, and you are already there with her. If you insist on searching for her again, yes, you will have to find her with nothing but your soul."

Julian's breathing was shallow, his thoughts smashing against one another. *To have something you've never had, you must do something you've never done.* "How do I do it," he said. Not how *would* I do it. But how *do* I do it.

Devi's shoulders turned in, as if he'd been hoping Julian would call him crazy and storm out. "You go in through the dark equinox. In September."

"Damn, so Cleon *was* right! There *is* a foot tunnel under the Thames. It's nearly impossible to find, he said. I knew it!"

"Well, you are Mr. Know-it-All," Devi said. "It *is* nearly impossible to find. For one, the moon must be new."

"Why?" *Only sorcery opens it,* Cleon said. *Nothing on that footpath but battle and torment.*

"Because the moon is inconstant, always waxing and waning. It lacks fortitude. It lacks devotion. Nothing new can be done under a fickle moon."

"What else?"

"The tide must be at its lowest point. And you don't go in at noon," Devi said. "You need a time when the sun is directly over the equator, and the earth is tilted neither toward nor away. You go in at the exact moment the center of the earth intersects with the center of the sun. The opening on the meridian lasts less than a minute and falls at varying times. Some years, it happens at night, others, early in the morning. And some years, it doesn't open at all, like when the tide is high and the moon is full. But your bad luck is with you, because this coming September the equinox and solar noon both fall at 12:07 p.m. The moon will be new. The tide will be low. You will have those things to help you. And you'll need all the help you can get."

"Once I go in, then what? Is there still a leap, a moongate?"

"There's a river," Devi said. "You'll be on it a very long time. It will feel as if there's no way out. You'll panic. It might feel like you're suffocating."

How could he leave his body? What did it mean to be on a river with no way out?

"I don't recommend this course of action," Devi said, seeing Julian's raging doubt. "You have another choice. You can make peace with what you've got left."

"And what would that be, Devi?" Julian said. "Please—do tell me."

"Yes, you never thought you had anything."

"And eventually I was proven correct." As soon as Julian said it, he sighed with shame. What a pill he was, always barreling forth with the bitter words of the dying.

He knew Devi so well, he could tell the cook was keeping something from him. "Anything else?"

"Still not enough for you?" Devi twisted his finger nubs.

"Are you going to tell me or am I going to have to guess?"

"Where the chasm is, the breach is," Devi said cryptically. "It's the song of the earth, it's what your soul leaps over. That's the only way you can climb inside your own life."

"She is the breach in my life. That's how I've always gotten in, that's how I'll get in again. Why the hand-wringing?"

Devi pressed his mangled fingers to his healthy ones. "I told you, you won't be climbing into her life. You'll be climbing into yours."

"What's the difference?"

"Not much," Devi said. "Just the difference between lightning and a lightning bug."

"Maybe because I enter differently, things might turn out differently," said Julian, sounding almost hopeful, almost optimistic—until he saw the miserable expression on Devi's face.

"Devi! What?"

"Nothing." Devi didn't look at Julian. "There is another thing you must know. Before you make the choice whether or not to go."

"Is it even a choice?"

"Yes, Julian, it most certainly is," Devi said. "And you must make it in the here and now. What do you want to be? A happy pig or an unhappy Socrates? That's your choice. Because after this, there are no more do-overs."

Julian rocked back. "Sounds like a false choice to me."

"Memory is retained by the body," Devi said. "Not by the soul. And only your soul can make it out of the cave." He took a breath. "Do you understand what I'm telling you?"

"No."

"If your soul manages to make it out, and there are no guarantees, there is a good chance your memory will be wiped clean."

"Wiped clean of what?" Suddenly Julian had a hard time inhaling. "What, like everything? Like...*her*?"

"Maybe." Devi didn't meet Julian's eye.

Adamantly Julian shook his head. "No. Absolutely not. That *won't* happen."

"Okay."

"I will never let that happen."

"Like you have a choice."

"You just said I did. Literally just now."

"Okay. So you've answered one crucial question. You'd rather be an unhappy Socrates."

"That's right. One hundred percent."

They let it go and did not talk about it again for days.

Julian was the one who brought it up after one exquisitely long acupuncture session when he thought he was sufficiently calmed to resume the crazy conversation.

"How would you even know something like that?" He swung his legs from the table to sit up, not wanting to be lying down when contemplating his own extinction. "You said yourself you failed to do it right."

"That's not what I said, but there are many reasons I know it." Devi remained on his little stool in the corner of the small room in the back of Quatrang. "And I'm not the only one who knows about memory. You know who else knows it, even better than me? You."

"What are you talking about? I *don't* know it."

"No? You've seen her soul, Julian. You've found her half a dozen times. One soul, different bodies. Did she know you?"

"That's not the same thing!"

"No?" Devi said it so quietly.

"And she did know me. The last time she actually knew me."

"Yes, at the very end, the veil between life and death had lifted, and her soul saw you clearly for a briefest moment."

"Exactly."

Devi took the stubborn silence that followed as an opening. He looked up; he raised his voice. "It wouldn't be so bad. Yes, you might forget her name, her face, the days of your love. But you'd also forget her death and your grief. All of it would take on a patina of a dream. The details will grow blurred."

"Without detail nothing can be known, not the flower or the woman," Julian said.

"It's true, you might not know the woman. It doesn't sound ideal. But think!"—Devi leaned forward, his eyes glistening—"What you've been through will fade from you, as time makes all things fade. There's hope in that, don't you think? Because if you forget," the cook said, "you might live again."

Julian jumped down from the table. "No," he said hoarsely. "No. I don't want to live again. Memory is all I have, Devi. The time I spent with her, what she and I have been through together. It's all I've got."

Devi started to say something, began to point, but Julian cut him off with, "I don't want to talk about it anymore," and went upstairs, to the empty rooms where Devi's mother once lived.

An hour later, he stormed back downstairs like a rain cloud. Devi was out front, slicing up cabbage and onions for tomorrow's lunch.

"Devi," Julian said, stopping the cook from his task. "Don't you see how impossible it is what you're saying?" His hand was on his chest. "If I go back without my memories, then how will I know it's her when I see her again?"

"You might not," Devi said. He pointed outside Quatrang, to Great Eastern Road. "*There's* London. Go live with your memories."

Julian was shaking. No, no, no, no.

Devi put down his cleaver and wiped his hands on his apron. "All right, so you won't know the hour of her death. Why does that make you so upset? All that means is that you will once again live like the rest of us. Like you did the first time with her in Los Angeles. Do you remember yourself? I know it must feel as if a different man had lived that life, but do you remember how happy you were? Why would you not want that? To live and not suffocate under the weight of your useless knowledge?"

But Julian was suffocating now. How could Devi not see it?

"It's *mercy*, Julian!" Devi said. "Nothing but mercy. Recall what you've been through, how you have suffered. You haven't forgotten *that* yet, have you? To live joyfully is better than to remember everything, yet live not at all. How could you of all people not agree? To not know the future—it's God's gift to us. Your life returned to you. Your free will returned to you."

Julian's throat was constricted, his heart was erratic. "Will she still die?"

"As we all must," Devi said, "but with any luck you won't know about it. The times you've gone back to her, you knew she would die, yet you still went back. Isn't that what you just told me? No matter how hopeless, you tried again. And how did that work out?"

"Devi," Julian said, unwillingly creeping up to something so painful, he didn't want to give voice to it. "But if I won't know the outcome, how will I save her?"

"How did you save her when you knew the outcome?"

Julian put his hand on his throat. He wanted to rip open his windpipe. He couldn't breathe. "But if I meet her, and she still dies, what will be different about it?"

Devi sat motionless. "Who said anything would be different?"

"And after she dies, will I move to London again? Will I seek you out again, find a way to travel back in time again? Will I make the same choices? Will I lose everything—again?" Julian made a wretched sound of an animal in agony. "Without memory, will I just keep circling the same drain over and over, again and again and again?" He crossed his hands over his chest. "Oh my *God*," he gasped. "Is this even my first time around?" In horror he stood frozen. "I just realized. *This may not be my first time around*."

He slept twenty hours each day to fast forward his life one year when there would be light again for 49 days and then darkness. He slept inside his wound, he lived inside her death, while on the outside other men laughed in bars.

What will you be having today?

How are you today?

But now the counter was empty, and the guy who cleaned the glasses and the guy who poured his whisky to the one refused to serve him anymore. Because they knew that he had been there, he'd sat there and cried there, he'd drunk, died, and despaired there all before.

Julian doubled over.

It was some time before he could straighten out, even longer before he could speak.

Devi's stony face confirmed or denied nothing.

"I don't want to believe we are in an endless loop with no way out," Devi finally said. "That to me is the definition of hell. Even if I knew it to be true, I would still refuse to believe it. Which is why, like you, I kept hope alive during your travels. But I have no answer about how to break out of the vicious circle."

"By making different choices, I reckon," Julian whispered.

He crept to a stool, sank down on it. "Don't you see, I *can't* not know who she is," he said in a guttural voice, slumped over the counter. It was dark in Quatrang, the lights dimmed, the clocks whirring. "How could I help her, then? And what if I walk by her? What if I miss her? I go to *La Traviata* instead of *The Invention of Love*. I meet her at the grocery store, my old lover, now a stranger, and pass by her as if she is nothing to me."

Devi didn't say okay. What he said was, "So stay. Stay here. That would be quite novel."

Julian didn't want to stay, to go, to think, to feel. He didn't want anything. He wished he had never asked for Devi's help, never returned to Great Eastern Road.

"You say you can't bear to not know who she is," Devi said. "But how did you, knowing everything, endure your limited days with her?" It took Devi a few moments to collect himself, and when he spoke, he stuttered. "If I knew for certain that all I would have with my son is two months, and that no matter what I did, he would still die, I would go mad. And you are not as sane as I am."

"You are literally describing to me my life," Julian said. That's how he had just lived with Mia through their last underground days, their moorlands sojourn, through bombs and mines and blindness and Pink Gin love. Like he would go mad.

"I know." Devi curved inward. "I don't know how you did it. It nearly killed me just the once. I have not been whole since, and never will be."

That's what death did. It fractured the living. Through centuries of torment, Julian had been flopping around like an electric wire, begging her soul to love the manic him, the desperate him, the terrified him. He had all knowledge and all prophecy, and where did it get him?

And yet...Julian couldn't bear to forget who she was and what she meant to him.

He thought back to L.A., faded so far into the past, it felt like someone else's life.

Julian thought about his emptiness, the crater he lived in. If he remained in London, she would stay by his side, at least for a while, be alive in his memory, the way Devi's son was alive.

But the thought of his days stretching out before him with everything and everyone he once loved fading into nothingness filled Julian with a sorrow too deep for words.

He groaned, his life emptied from his lungs. "I don't want to live my life without love," he whispered, his body coiled into itself. "I don't want to be a happy pig. Yes, there is suffering. But there is *love*. Even in her absence, like now, I still remember how I loved her." Julian sat up a little straighter, getting at something, reaching for something. "More than remember. I *still* love her."

"Now we're getting somewhere," Devi said.

But Julian was trying to grasp at something else, at an answer to a vague question of profound faith. He was trying to grasp at revelation. "Devi, do you know what trace decay is? Multiple studies in neuroscience have shown that memories leave an actual physical and chemical change in the brain. Forgetting occurs when this trace fades, or decays."

Devi nodded. "That would explain why memory might stay behind with the body when the soul leaves."

"Yes, but listen," Julian said. "What if love is the memory of the soul? What if *love* has left a trace of her inside *me?* Inside the me that's not my body." He jumped off the stool. He was filled with grim agitation. "What if an imprint of the people you love is carved into your soul like into walls of a cave? Like the negative of a photograph, it might fade, but it never disappears. Like your son from you. Like Ashton from me. Like Mia."

Devi bowed his head in acceptance of this possibility.

"Maybe that's why some people look more familiar than others," Julian said. "Because in one form or another, we knew them. We loved them."

"Does that comfort you?"

"Doesn't it comfort you?"

"Sometimes I wish I could forget," Devi said.

"You don't mean that."

Minutes drifted by, the clocks ticking ticking ticking.

When Julian spoke again, he was calmer, determined, resigned. "You've been wrong about so much. You said I would never return. You said I could never go again. You said she wouldn't know me. You told me Cleon was a fool, not the smartest man in the sewers. You're wrong about this, too. I'll remember. I know I will." His voice broke.

"You'll remember it like a fairytale from childhood, my son," Devi said with deep tenderness. "Like a long-ago dream not lived."

32

Fathers and Sons

FOR THE LAST SIX MONTHS OF JULIAN'S LIFE, HE AND DEVI lived side by side. They ate sesame noodles and cabbage salad, made kimchi and sliced calamari, grated ginger and ground garlic paste. Julian learned how to cook. He went with Devi to the market to buy squid and octopus and shrimp, and to the shanty town in Hoxton where the hippies grew the sweetest, juiciest tomatoes and cucumbers so sweet they tasted as if they had no skins.

Every Sunday after church, they took the tube to Hampstead Heath and spent the afternoon with Ava. She was doing better. The therapist kept working on her speech, and little by little she relearned how to write with her dominant hand. The first thing she wrote in a childlike scrawl and showed to Julian was her name.

Ava Maria Delacourt McKenzie, she wrote.

And the second thing she wrote was to Devi.

I think I love you.

"You *think*?" Devi said.

She held their hands as they sat by her side, read the paper to her, and Julian told her jokes and stories of a Mia Delacourt of Morecambe Bay and Babbacombe Road.

∞

"By the way," Julian said to Devi inside St. Monica's, waiting for Mass to begin, "don't think I forgot how you told me Ashton's father comes almost every Sunday to pay his son a visit. Funny how I haven't seen him for sixteen Sundays in a row. I knew you were making it up just to get a rise out of me."

"Why would I need to work that hard to get a rise out of you?" Devi said calmly. "You are on a hair trigger every day. But ironic you should mention him, because he was here two weeks ago. I thought you ignored him deliberately."

"Why would I ignore him? Clearly I didn't see him."

"Now's your chance to prove me wrong," Devi said. "Because he is here today."

Julian spun around. In one of the pews in the back, the older Bennett sat, glum and gray.

"He looks so old," Julian whispered, facing front.

"He's probably a few years older than me and Ava. Are we old?"

"I take the fifth," said Julian.

"Which one of us walks to the market with an umbrella he's too vain to admit is a cane, you or me?" Devi said. "I rest my case."

"It actually is an umbrella," Julian said. "You never know when it's going to rain."

"Yes, because you need a three-foot umbrella. Now *shh*."

After the service, Julian got up to look for the man, but he had already slipped out.

"He's probably at the graveyard," Devi said, holding a small bouquet of lilies he had brought for Ashton.

"I really don't want to confront him at the grave of his son," Julian said.

"Confront him? Why are you always in beast mode? Why not say, hello, Mr. Bennett, nice to see you again, Mr. Bennett. How have you been? Thank you for giving me a job, sir, and keeping me on even when I was derelict in my duties. Why not try something like that?"

"I don't want to talk to you anymore." Slowly they moved toward the exit doors. "He's just going to cry," Julian said.

"You sure you're talking about him?"

"I *really* don't want to speak to you."

In the small, tree-covered cemetery on the side of the church, Julian and Devi made their quiet way to Ashton's grave. Ashton's father wasn't there. His bouquet of flowers was left propped against the black granite. "Where is he?" Julian whispered, looking around, as Devi laid his lilies down.

On the far side of the cemetery, in a secluded corner under a tall oak, Michael Bennett stood with his wife at another gravesite.

"There's someone else here he visits?"

"You never listen to me. I told you it looked as if he brings two bouquets," Devi said. "Maybe someone on his fifth wife's side?"

"Yeah, maybe."

"Are you going to go say hello?"

"I don't know, should I?" Julian watched the stooped man put down the flowers, leaning on his walker, supported by his wife.

"Of course you should. I'll wait here. The grave needs weeding anyway. You're a terrible executor."

"Yeah, yeah."

Julian walked slowly, reluctantly, through the tombstones, supporting himself with the umbrella. He didn't want to fall on the uneven ground and break his other hip. The wife meanwhile had left, and Bennett lingered alone under the trees.

Quietly Julian came up behind the old man and stood back at a respectful distance. After a few seconds, he took a tentative step forward, clearing his throat. "Hello, Mr. Bennett. I don't want to startle you. It's me, Julian."

The old man turned and glanced at Julian as if he didn't recognize him.

"Julian Cruz, your son's friend, remember? I worked for you for seven years?"

"Yes, of course. How are you, Julian?"

"Fine, sir, how are you?"

Michael Bennett blinked once, his mouth moved, and he said nothing. His gaze returned to the grave marker. Julian's gaze followed to read the name on the old stone.

FREDERICK THOMAS WILDER

BELOVED "WILD"

1910—1952

Julian reeled. For a moment, to steady himself, he clutched Bennett's walker with his fingerless hand.

"What's the matter with you?" Bennett said.

Julian stood without words.

Wild lived. He didn't die. He lived.

"You knew Wild?" Julian said hoarsely. "How?"

"What could you possibly know about anything," Bennett said, just as hoarsely.

Julian's heart thumped heavy and full. "How did you know Wild?" he whispered. "Oh my God!" He gaped at the man. "You're *Michael*. You're *that* Michael."

"He raised me," Michael Bennett said. "He saved me and raised me."

Julian shook. He turned his head away.

"What's *wrong* with you?" the old man said.

"Where did he go?" Julian asked, wiping his face. "We looked for him everywhere."

"Who is we? Who are you talking about?"

"Sit down with me for a minute," Julian said, placing his hand on the man's back. "It'll be easier for both of us." Certainly it would be easier for him. He led Bennett to a stone bench under the trees and collapsed on it.

"Did my son tell you about Wild?" Bennett asked.

"No." Julian didn't want to reveal to the broken man sitting next to him that Ashton was so disgusted with the way he had been cast off by both his parents that he never spoke about anything having to do with his family unless he was forced to, pretending for all concerned that he had sprung from a cabbage leaf. It was years before Julian found out that Ashton's father was British, years more before he knew the father was still alive, multiply re-married, and running a successful business. Julian had never heard a word about the war, the Blitz, London, or a man named Wild.

"Who is Bennett?" Julian asked. "Why weren't you Michael Wilder?" His friend could've been Ashton Wilder. Then Julian would've known. He would've known as soon as he met Wild.

"Bennett was my family name. Wild looked them up after the war. He refused to return me to my one surviving aunt, but out of respect for my mother, he left my father's name on me. He hoped I'd have a son to pass my own name to, and my son would have a son, and so on."

"Yes, and so on," Julian said, willing his mind a blank, trying to erase every single thing about the dead end of that shabby dream.

"I can't believe you forgot Ashton's stories," Bennett said. "How could you? The stuff about Wild was the stuff of legend. Ashton grew up on tales about Wild. I don't know, maybe he forgot, too. He was so young when I left. How Wild and his friend Swedish found me in a fiery blaze that took my mum and my aunt." Michael Bennett smiled, his eyes wet. "It always seemed so implausible, like Wild had made the whole thing up. He said I fell out of the sky while the house burst into flames around me. There wasn't a scratch on me. He said I fell with grace from God into his one arm. My mother died, but he pulled me out. He told me I changed his life. He was supposed to deliver me to an orphanage. But he said he would kill anyone who tried to separate me from him. He asked Swedish to tie me to him with ropes so he wouldn't lose me; he hid me in his coat and fled London. It seems so far-fetched. I was an infant, and he had one arm and had never even touched a baby."

Julian couldn't speak. There was silence in the cemetery on a balmy Sunday afternoon.

"Where did he take you?"

"Somewhere in Wales," Ashton's father said, "to a tiny village in the middle of some unknown forest. He said Swedish had told him about such a place. Away from coal mines, trains, anything that could be bombed."

"What happened to him? 1952, he was still so young…" About the age Julian was now.

"Lung cancer. Like the King. He died a month after George, in March." Bennett's eyes welled up. "When God couldn't save the King, I knew he'd never be able to save my Wild. Why are you staring at me like that? What did Ashton tell you?" Bennett studied Julian with suspicion and misgiving. "I don't know why you're so interested in Wild. What's he to you?"

"Ashton was in my life because Wild had saved you. So, everything."

"I suppose." The man sighed.

"You two returned to London after the war?"

Bennett nodded. "Wild's mother wasn't well. We lived with her up in Camden and when she died, moved down here. Not far from this church actually, a few blocks away, on Folgate. The area was rebuilt after the war. For the first few years we searched for Wild's friends, especially for Swedish, and then gave up. When Wild died, I became a ward of the council. They found my aunt, eventually. I lived with her for a while."

Julian forced himself to stop shivering. When Ashton's mother died, he, too, became a ward of the council. He, too, was twelve. Except Ashton still had a father.

"The name Ashton was Wild's idea," Michael Bennett said. "If he ever had another boy, he always wanted to name him Ashton."

"But he died before he got a chance to," Julian said. "So you did." He took a breath. "How did Ashton end up with the red beret?"

Bennett considered Julian with anxiety and unhappiness. "What could you possibly know about that? I left it with him when his mother and I split up, if you really must know. What happened to it, I have no idea."

"He gave it to me," Julian said.

"What did you do with it?"

"And I gave it to you. Folgate and I put it on your head."

The old man whirled to Julian. "What did you say?" he croaked. "How did you know what he called that girl…"

Julian put his palm on his heart. "Because I'm Swedish," he whispered.

Terror and disbelief was on the old man's face.

But more of the former than the latter.

Bennett's wife came rushing back. "Oh, you've upset him!" she said, glaring at Julian. "Look at the state he is in. He's cold and sweating. Well done." She gave Bennett her arm to lift him off the bench. "Come on, luv, let's go home. No use hanging around here. I'll make you lunch and a nice cup of tea. You can sit in the garden."

Julian tried to help. The wife would have none of it. "Haven't you done enough?"

Before he left, Bennett turned to Julian. His lip trembled. "I wish my son could've known Wild. He was a remarkable man."

Julian shook his head. "Do you know who else was a remarkable man? Your son."

"I know that," Michael Bennett said, crying, his head low. "I learned it too late." Leaning heavily on his walker, he shuffled away.

33

Silver Angel

JULIAN AND DEVI LIVED SO LONG IN STEADY, HUMMING, comforting, regimented proximity that Julian lost track of time. He jumped up in the middle of one night, not knowing where he was, or when he was, terrified that three equinoxes had passed, or twenty.

It was the middle of September. Devi didn't say which September.

On their last night together, Julian took Devi to Chinatown for dinner at Tao Tao Ju on Lisle Street, just off Leicester Square. Eating food with Devi that was cooked by other men was a two-hour stand-up act. Julian didn't know Devi could be so petty. It was hilarious. Nothing was to his liking. The fish was too salty, the dough too stale, and the sake not strong enough. They dared bring him low-salt soy sauce and overcooked his garlic brisket.

"What's Lahpet?" Julian asked.

"Pickled tea leaves served in a salad. But they didn't prepare it correctly," Devi said with scorn. "They didn't add enough vinegar. It's not pickled, it's watered." They had pork buns with mango. They drank a white palm toddy or coconut wine, a fermented cloudy sap. "It contains many nutrients," Devi said, "including potash, which you could add to your suet if you wanted to make candles."

Julian chuckled. "There are some things I don't regret having behind me," he said. "That's at the top of the list."

"Nah, I bet it doesn't even make the top five," Devi said, both of them mutely acknowledging some of the greater horrors. "Did you know," Devi said to change the subject, "that longer fermentation produces vinegar, not stronger wine?"

Julian smiled. "Yes, Devi," he said, "I did know that."

"I forgot I was talking to the King of Vinegar," Devi said.

Afterward, the cook said he had a good time. "Maybe when Ava is discharged, I can bring her here for a celebration."

"I don't know. She's not thrilled with *your* food. You want to take the chance she'll like someone else's?"

"Maybe I'll take her to the Savoy, then," Devi said. "I seem to remember she enjoyed it that one time you took us."

"*You* didn't," Julian said. Devi had derided the French cuisine at the Savoy almost as strongly as he derided the food at Tao Tao Ju tonight.

"Like you, I'm capable of making small sacrifices," said Devi with a straight face.

They took the long way back to Quatrang, the really long way back. They meandered through the lit-up dusky Soho and Covent Garden. It was a Sunday night, there was street music everywhere, the city was pulsing with people, with laughter. The Festival of Lights re-formed some of the roads into a kaleidoscope of color. Buildings, statues, awnings were dressed up in red and gold. It was like fireworks on every street from Carnaby to Seven Dials.

Like fireworks on every street.

And the Spitfires and the Hurricanes weren't in the clouds overhead and the air wasn't pierced by a wrenching up and down wail.

They walked down St. Martin's Lane and sat on the steps in front of the National Gallery, watching the happy people and the hungry pigeons wage battle for domination of Trafalgar Square, listening to a choir sing Allegri's "Miserere," the sentimental harmonies mournfully carrying through the open doors of St. Martin-in-the-Fields.

"I'm going to miss London," Julian said. It was a warm windless September evening, loud and crowded and sublime. "How do you figure I could ever forget this? You haven't forgotten Kolka Mountain."

His head lowered, Devi stammered when he replied. "That's true. But that's how I continue to carry his soul with me—by not forgetting. I don't have his earthly life to look forward to. I'm not as lucky as you."

"Devi, Mr. Lucky is leaving tomorrow. And we've known each other many years."

"What of it?"

"There is hardly a thing you don't know about me. Tell me about your son." Julian put his arm around the sturdy little man. "Come on. Look what we've got. Our bellies are full after a farewell supper. We're a little tipsy on sake…"

"Speak for yourself."

"We have a view, a camaraderie, a breathtaking choir. Now is the time we sit around the fire and tell stories."

Devi sighed. "I suspect that Tama's love of storytelling around the fire is the least important thing you took from that experience. But fine. What would you like to know?"

Julian shook his head. "Nope, no Socratic method this time. You tell me a real story, and I will sit and listen."

"He went missing on the September equinox," Devi said. "Four years and eight equinoxes later, I went into the Q'an Doh cave to find him. I was willing to give up everything for a chance to make different choices that might lead to a different result. My mother begged me not to go. She said the breach in my life was his death, and by that time it would be too late to do anything to stop it. But I was obstinate, foolhardy, broken by grief. Sound familiar? A snowslide had formed a gravity current, carrying massive forces at astonishing speeds. Ice, rocks, trees compressed as if down a funnel. But despite the destruction, when I arrived in Karmadon, the villagers swore they'd seen my son alive near the gorge. And why shouldn't I have believed them? I kept seeing him myself. Why are you back, I kept repeating to him. I thought you were shooting through October? I stayed for two years, searching for him. He was so real, I refused to believe he was dead."

"Like Ava with Mia," Julian said.

"Not just *Ava* with Mia."

Julian hung his head.

"The mystery of my son's death," Devi said, "is contained in the millions of cubic yards of stone and ice. He vanished without a trace, except for the trace he left in me."

"Did you ever stop seeing him?" Julian had not stopped seeing Mia. He still dreamed of her walking in the wet sunshine.

"No." Devi made a sound with his mouth, a cross between a click and a groan. "I should've listened to my mother—a good lesson for us all. She warned me there was nowhere for my soul to go except into his death. He was brand new. There was no past, no other body, no possibilities. But I went in anyway. Because I thought I knew best. Like you, I was arrogant enough to believe that my love could save him. I was convinced he wasn't dead. He keeps appearing to me alive, I told my mother. Why would he do that if he weren't?"

Julian, Devi, and Ava all shared one grief.

"I told myself that as long as the portal opened, I stood a chance," Devi continued. "A portal to *where*, my mother said. You better pray it doesn't open, she said, because it will either kill you or show you things that will make you wish you were dead. But I didn't care. I didn't know then that there's another reason no one goes into the meridian caves in September. Because that's when the bats return to hibernate for the winter. Ten million of them, twenty million. I don't know. Infinite million."

"I don't like bats," Julian said.

"You know my answer to that," Devi said. "Don't go. I nearly died from a nasty fungal infection I got as a result of touching bat guano, unavoidable really at that time of year. I had a heart attack. They had to revive me." He sighed.

"The bats and the precipice nearly killed me, and past the moongate there was nothing but ice. Ice under my feet. Ice in the walls. Ice above me. I was forever in that cave." Devi sunk inward. "I'm still there."

Julian well remembered the Mount of Terror that formed into a frozen river that led him down and away from the black ditch atop Crag Hill in York, to the *Hinewai* in the Southern Ocean.

"The cave didn't take me across time," Devi said. "But it did take me across space, all the way to Asia, to the Kolka Mountain. The cave of Red Faith didn't let me save him or see him alive," Devi said. "But it did let me find him. After a long time of meandering through the frozen tunnels, I looked up, and there he was. He hung above me suspended in the glacier cave ceiling. Frozen below the collapsed mountain, in a block of ice four hundred feet deep. You asked me what I see. That is what. Every day of my life, I see my son's floating body, a dragonfly in crystal, trapped for eternity in the icy depths above my head."

Staring at their crippled hands, the two men sat, their heads low. "How did you get out?" Julian asked.

"The same way you get out," Devi replied. "I found light, a fissure, an opening. The dark equinox left me half dead and with half my soul. It brought me out into a geographical place called Karmadon, the divide that split my life into before and after. It was as if you had climbed out to Normandie Avenue and saw Josephine on the sidewalk."

"How many years has it been?"

"Twenty-four. Twenty since the cave. I go back every other year. I'm still waiting for the ice to melt so I can bury him. The geologists say any time now. They've been saying it for two decades."

"Oh, Devi."

"He was engaged to be married, like you. His soon-to-be wife married another. She has three grown children now."

"So—not quite like me. What was his name?"

"S-s-s-s-samang. Sam. It means lucky in my language. Lucky in life."

Julian was afraid to touch Devi, afraid the stony man would fly apart like glass in a car crash. Julian's body bowed forward as it always did when it remembered car crashes and all lost things. He listed sideways, toward the Vietnamese man.

"What does *your* name mean?"

"Devi? It means angel."

"Not devil?" Julian almost smiled. "And Prak?"

"Silver."

"Aha. So you're the Silver Angel."

"I can't help what my parents called me. Just like Sam couldn't help what I called him."

"It's not his fault he wasn't lucky." Julian put his arm around Devi, comforting him. "It's not your fault either."

"Whose fault is it?"

"Nobody's. It's nobody's fault."

"And finally at the eleventh hour, we're getting somewhere, ladies and gentlemen." Devi did not move away from Julian's arm.

"Devi," Julian said, "I'm really sorry I couldn't help you."

"Don't be sorry," Devi said. "Do you know when I realized you might show me something I've never seen? Long ago, when you told me you were a boxer. Rather, when you told me that a boxer was all you ever wanted to be. Do you know why? Because to be a good boxer, you must train harder than at anything else. You must have discipline over yourself as over nothing else. You must be an ascetic, a monk. You must know how to break your own will. Coordination, limited rest, masochism, superhuman endurance. You must first become grit before you can build your body up from nothing to be a silent killing machine—and the only thing that can direct that is your soul. That's how I knew. You are brave and strong, Julian. You have the perseverance of the saints. You have kept your faith even when you were greatly afflicted. In many ways, you have surprised me over the years. Don't ever be sorry. My friendship with you has been the best of my life."

∞

On September 22, a reluctant Devi nonetheless accompanied Julian to the Greenwich Observatory.

Julian brought nothing with him except his old multi-tool, a few slivers of her crystal and his headlamp.

They left in plenty of time for noon. They walked slow, because they had time.

"Yesterday was a good day," Julian said.

"Yes, it wasn't a bad day for a last day."

"Right. There was church, a stroll through a legendary city, a dinner, some drink, a conversation, even a few laughs."

"Very few," said Devi.

Julian laughed.

"Now a few more." Devi smiled.

They walked on.

"Do you know what's inexplicable?" Julian said. "I never did find that café with the golden awning. I had been so sure I would. I'm beginning to think it was never here. Who knows, maybe I did just dream it." He shrugged away his disappointment. "I've walked through London as one walks through the desert. I've lifted every grain of sand. I've lived through centuries of fruitless searching. It must have been a mirage."

"Not fruitless."

"But where is it?" They were in the Royal Park, in the gallery under the trees. It was eleven, another hour to go.

It was a while before Devi answered. "It's still out there somewhere."

"That means she's still out there somewhere."

"You know she is. Where are you headed to, if not her?"

They continued their slow walk under the canopied trees. Julian wasn't used to Greenwich being warm like this. The equinox in March was always so rainy and windy.

"You don't have to leave, you know," Devi said. "You could wait."

"For what?"

"Next year. You could continue looking for the café. You could stay. Help me shred and grill." He looked up at Julian, knocking into him lightly. "We could go to the market together, to church. I bought a French pastry book. Ava keeps teasing me, so I'm thinking of learning how to bake." Even as he was saying it, Devi smiled ruefully, as if he knew that it would never be.

They bought their tickets for the Observatory and wandered around the leafy grounds, not speaking.

At 11:49 they made their way into the Transit Room. The roof had been retracted. The bright sun streamed through the open slats. The Transit Circle stood enormous and shiny black, exactly as it was in 1854 when Julian first set eyes on the wonder that was Mirabelle.

At 11:55, he lay the fragments of her crystal in the palm of his hand and gave the glass jar to Devi. Julian didn't want to admit it, but he was so afraid. "Devi," he mouthed, nearly inaudibly. He couldn't give voice to his terror. He didn't want to die! He didn't want to die...

"I know," Devi said, as if he really did know.

"I won't go until you bless me," said Julian, tilting toward him.

"Be, and be not afraid," Devi said. "Remember the one who is always with you."

Noon came and went. Julian reflexively held out his hand. "Just in case," he said.

"Good thing it didn't open," Devi said. "Then where would you be?"

12:03.

12:05.

"This is it, Julian."

"This is it, Devi. One more time—for her. *Once more into the breach, or we can close the walls up with our English dead.*"

"Remember, go with your gut on things," Devi said, fixing the zipper on Julian's jacket. "Trust yourself. If you feel something's right for reasons you can't explain, go with that. There's a reason for your intuition: this life and your suffering."

"All right. But...I'm going to try hard to actually remember."

Devi allowed that Julian might remember some things.

"Devi...will I remember *you*?"

The two men stood wordlessly.

12:06.

"I don't know, Julian," Devi said. "But I'll remember you."

Julian climbed over the railing. The chasm was about to open for the beggar again. The earth was full of his cries. Just before the sun moved into the crosshairs of the equinox, Julian turned around, leaned forward and pressed his head to Devi's head. They were already ringed in the shimmering blue halo. "Goodbye, my friend."

12:07.

"Goodbye, my friend," Devi whispered into the dark empty footwell.

34

Seven Stars

JULIAN HAD NEVER BEEN ON THE RIVER SO LONG. AND THE river was unlike any he'd been on. It was narrow, languid, and deeply meandering, still waters zigzagging their way through the steepest cave mountains. He stumbled on an abandoned old boat without oars, and in it he floated, shining his headlamp at the cave walls. When he got thirsty, he drank from the river and smiled when he thought it might be the River Lethe, the mythical river of forgetfulness, and when he drank from it, he'd forget.

Then he became afraid it wasn't a metaphor, and he really was on the river of forgetting. He stopped drinking and stayed thirsty instead, standing in the rowboat like a wherryman and counting off one by one the names of the places he had been with her. Collins Lane, Whitehall, Silver Cross, Drury Lane, Seven Dials, Holborn, Monmouth, Gin Lane. Taylor Lane, Crystal Palace, Langton Lane, Grey Gardens, Clyde and Dee, Bluff, Ross Sea. Grimsby, Bank, the Strand, St. Martin's Lane, Savoy Place. Mytholmroyd...Loversall, Blackpool, Babbacombe... Yes, everything was all right. He was still with his memories, the water wasn't a potion, his mind was intact. Devi was wrong.

When he got thirsty, he drank, and to test himself he recited again and again the names of places, and then, the names of the faces.

Aurora, Cornelius, Cedric. Baroness Tilly, Margrave, Fabian. He would never forget Fabian; how could he. Agatha, Cleon,

Fulko, Little Legs, there was a lot to remember from that life. George Airy, Spurgeon, Aubrey, Coventry Patmore. Kiritopa, Edgar Evans. The Maori and the Welshman were the only two Julian wanted to remember from New Zealand, banishing the names of all others from his memory.

Liz Hope, Nick Moore, Peter Roberts, Phil Cozens, Sheila, Shona, Frankie.

Duncan and Wild.

Wild.

He wouldn't forget any of them, ever.

Wild most of all.

He got thirsty and drank again.

The light in Julian's headlamp dimmed. A sudden swirl of icy wind knocked it off his head. In the dark his hand clasped around the shards of her crystal. God forbid he should lose them. Yes, Devi said Julian was his own totem, yes, Devi said Julian's soul would find the breach in his own body, he was his own holy relic, but without the bits of crystals, how would he find *her*?

After a while, when he recounted the names of the places, he could no longer recall the name of the town in his first trip back, or Mary's last name, or the given name of her mother. He remembered Cedric the hostler. And then not even him. The names of the madam and the poisoned whore faded from him, the names of the sewer hunter and the hanged man slipped from him, the faces of Spurgeon and Airy grew blurred. Kiritopa remained tall and Edgar Evans sat strong in the boat.

And then, not even them.

Goodbye, Swedish, a man kept saying with a smile, walking away, holding a baby in one arm, a baby wearing Julian's precious red beret. I'll see you, Swedish.

I'll see you, Wild.

He was okay. He remembered the important things. But what Julian really wanted was for the river to come to an end. His body was sore, hurting, empty, misbegotten, blackened, burdened, hollowed out.

When will it end?

When will it end.

As his boat floated, his exhausted eyes blinking open and closed, he held the crystal slivers up to the cave, perhaps to bounce off something, to give him a little light. He was so tired of the darkness. While his pleading hand was stretched out, there was a flare, and in the brief reflection, he saw the river up ahead. He was headed into a junction. Julian stood at attention peering into the darkness, holding the tiny slivers up, again, again, *please!* trying to catch a glimpse of the tributaries.

And there they were.

To the right, in a spacious cave, the river flowed straight and swift. He saw it clearly. There was current and welcome movement. He thought he almost saw, almost! the crystal sliver reflect off something in the distance. Was light filtering in through a crack somewhere? Squeezing his hand shut, he stared intensely into the darkness. Look how fast the river was moving. He had no oars, but he could paddle with his hands to catch the current. He could be at the breach in a few minutes. He would climb out. He would find her. This would all be over. Maybe Cherry Lane, maybe Book Soup, maybe the crest of the Santa Monica Mountains. He still remembered her so well. *Mia, Mia.*

To the left flowed the same winding, barely rippling, unhurried river he had been on for an eternity, disappearing around the bend between the steep ragged cliffs.

Julian didn't want to be on the river another second. It had already been too long without her. It was time to see her face. Julian reached into the water with his strong left hand and started paddling, turning the boat into the current.

Oh, no—her crystal! Gasping, he jerked his hand out of the water and stared desperately into his empty palm. He had forgotten that he had clenched his fingers around the shards, and when he opened his hand to paddle, they had fallen out. They were gone, all gone. How could he have been so careless. He just forgot.

Nothing to do about it now. He had to get into the current. He didn't need the crystal anymore. He knew what she looked like in Los Angeles. Cherry Lane, Normandie, Book Soup. He'd find her.

At first he paddled frantically, and then slower and slower.

Soon he stopped altogether.

His mind kept catching on something it didn't want to catch on.

The river was at a junction.

That meant there was a choice to make.

Both ways might lead him to her.

But what if only one did?

The short, straight way was better. Because he still remembered! He wanted so desperately not to forget. He thought he wanted that most of all. But what did Devi tell him, what were the terrible words Devi had spoken that Julian barely heard then and wished to God he wasn't remembering now?

In seven short weeks, in forty-nine days, seven times seven, she will be gone from you again. You know how this story ends, Julian. It's a loop with a noose.

In seven short weeks she will be gone from you again.

Can you bear it?

Which way the river? Which way her life?

He had tried it already every which way. Every approach, every angle. He tried to warn her, to stay away, to be slow, to be fast, he tried friendship and romance, reserve and abandon, to look far ahead, and to live day by day.

And now another unfathomable choice was rising up in front of him.

When you didn't know what to do, how did you decide which path to take with the future unknowable and one way infinitely preferable?

Julian knew. The thing you didn't want to do was nearly always the right choice. You did the thing you didn't want to do. Did you tell the truth, did you give your love, were you free, did you leave, did you dream, did you work? Did you go to York when your closest friend begged you to go with him, or did you bow out? Did you run into a burning house? Did you hear a baby cry?

Julian was so bone tired.

What if that was the choice he must make—to remain on the river until the end?

But what if it wasn't?

So many unanswered questions.

He tried to argue himself out of it. He couldn't see around the bend. Both streams could converge in the same place, probably did converge in the same place, so what was the difference? It was the stupid thing to do, not the right thing. And no one should do the stupid thing. That was his other life hack: don't be an idiot. Sometimes you needed to use the shortest route between warehouse and shop. Wasn't this the ideal time to heed *that* advice?

Julian slumped in the boat, his head hanging.

He recalled something unwanted about Lethe, the river of oblivion.

Only when the dead have their memories erased can they be truly restored. Only after life was pronounced extinct on the streets, the names of which he was so desperately trying to hold on to, could he live again.

Switching arms and lowering his deformed claw into the water, he began to slowly rake with his index and thumb, angling the boat away from the bold current.

With deep regret, Julian raised his mutilated hand and waved goodbye. He couldn't see a way out. But maybe, just maybe, if one thing was different…

Maybe she would live. Live how she wanted, with hope and bright lights, with her dreams and the stage. Live without him, if that's what it took. Just live. That's all Johnny Blaze wanted for his rollerblading Gotham Girl, for his ephemeral Ghost Bride. No tunnels of love. Just to live. *I vow to thee, my country, all earthly things above*, he whispered. Take my life, Mia. Take my life.

The port side hit the dividing crag, the boat lurched and shifted into the meandering stream, and continued to glide forward without a care.

He stood for as long as he could, but eventually he sat down.

And eventually he lay down. Sometimes it felt as if the dinghy was moving so fast that it wasn't moving at all but standing still, rocking in the cold river. Julian wanted to raise his head and look around, but he was so tired.

And then he didn't want to get up anymore. He was all right with that. He lay face up, not moving, his eyes open, trying to find light in the blackened cave, find anything that could signal the end of the line.

And when Julian couldn't remember much else, he lay in the boat, remembering her.

Mia, Mia, the soul of my soul.

They lived.

They dived under the waves of the Pacific. They had picnics under the trees in Fynnesbyrie Field. Walking arm in arm, they saw elephants in St. James's Park. They danced drunk on the tables in the cellars of St. Giles. They laughed in Grey Gardens and strolled across Waterloo Bridge. They huddled under elk skins in the polar ice. He lay on top of her body, hiding her from Hitler, hiding her from Hades.

They lived. During their brief bright days, he thought they didn't have time, didn't have much, there was always regret for the litany of things they hadn't done. They never bought a house, never traveled, never got married, never had kids, never grew old.

But they had these things. They lived in brothels and mansions, in shelters, and up near the sky. They rode horses, and trains, and ships. They slept out in the open fields and in soft beds.

They lived through all kinds of weather.

They got fake married, put real rings on their fingers, spoke true vows, they kissed and danced and sang in revelry. They held babies, helped save babies. Once they talked of babies.

They were young, hungry, lustful, joyful. They were angry, bitter, fighting, hurting. Their bodies flexed like they were gymnasts; their bodies broke like they were old. They lived in peace and in terror. They lived like they were going to live forever. They lived when death was raining down upon them, and when the night was young.

Together they walked through fire. Together they walked through ice.

The whole world and all that was in it was their Inexpressible Island.

They lived. They lived.

Josephine, Mary, Mallory, Miri, MIRABELLE, Shae, Maria!

You have my faithful heart. You will always have it.

I may forget you, but my love for you is carved into the walls of my soul.

Something will always remain.

∞

The wind had died down. It wasn't cold anymore. It wasn't hot. Julian could almost see the outlines of the stalactites above his head, the etchings on the cave walls of twisting human shapes knotted in love and struggle.

Who holds the keys of hell and death?

Where is Ashton, my lost brother, my companion in trial and tribulation? It has been an eternity without him by my side.

Whose voice is the sound of many waters?

Whose passion is astride this wind?

The sound of gnarling metal sorrow, bending the embittered human will to another's, who did that?

You have been graced with seven golden candlesticks, the healer told him. Whether you light them, whether you even can, is up to you.

Seven times, seven weeks, seven swords, seven hearts, seven stars.

Who knows my grief, my misfortune, my poverty, who knows I'm blind and a beggar and says it's all right?

Who knows my alms, my gifts, my offerings, who knows my love, who knows my heart?

Julian was in agony, the lungs trying to expand, hot needles burning his veins, his body melting.

Who searches my soul for my hidden burdens and my sleeve for the sins I wear?

Who will lend me his ear and give me a morning star?

Who will take the iniquities from my hands and from my overflowing cloak? My sins fall out behind me as I walk. I've forgotten my friends, my family, my mother, forgotten those who cared for me. I've turned away from joy, thus I've turned away from life. Lost in my suffering, I was bound in chains, and I crumbled before what I have not seen. Who has set before me an open door anyway, even though I'm not strong but weak, I'm not rich but wretched, not a prince but a pauper?

Who knows that I'm not the one who needs nothing? My need is so great, my will so small, my misery and nakedness so blinding. Who knows this about me without any need for words from me, and is all right with it?

The winged beasts fly past blaring their trumpets. I say to the mountain and the rocks, hide me, hide me, please hide me from my life.

In supplication Julian raised his arms.

He thought he wanted to check if the charred flowers had formed on his skin, to see her name blazing on his forearm, to feel the scars of their days. It was dark, and he couldn't see.

Nothing hurt anymore, because thank God, there was no more pain.

35

Perennial Live-Forevers

THE NOSE OF THE BOAT SCRAPED THROUGH THE SAND, BUMPED
and stopped moving.

Finally!

Julian jumped out into the shallow water. His hiking boots
were soaked and filled with grit. He was confined in a small
space, and it was hard to move his arms to get to his multi-tool—
though to be fair, it was also hard to see how a multi-tool would
help him. In his current predicament, what he needed was an
earth-mover.

The ceiling was low; it was not so much a cave as a space
between boulders, a space large enough for just him. Light filtered
through a break somewhere up above, a glimmer between loose
and heavy rocks. He climbed to it, but the rocks crumbled under
his feet, and he lost his footing and slid, and the rocks slid with
him, packing on top of him. He tried again. Why hadn't he put
crampons on his boots to help him climb?

The rocks were heavy. He couldn't move them. After many
attempts to free himself, Julian panicked. It felt as if he'd been
under a long time. He took deep breaths to make sure his lungs
were still working, and then searched through his pockets
again, one by one. In one of the deep pockets of his cargo pants,
he finally found his multi-tool. It was better than nothing. With
the end of the needle-nosed pliers, he frantically stabbed around
the packed-in dirt, chiseling away at some of the crushed stones.

He was always chiseling away at something or other, trying to make openings in stones. He was determined to forge through this damn rock. He couldn't die down here when he was so close to getting out.

Blinding sunlight streaked through the cracks above him. If only he could get the opening big enough to fit his arm through, he would wiggle out. The cook was wrong, that funny little guy. Julian was okay. His body felt okay. His head really hurt, though.

The crack became a crevice, then a hole, and finally, after some increasingly desperate hacking, a bright opening big enough for his arm, his shoulder, his aching head. He shoved one boulder after another out of the way, and crawled out.

For many minutes, he lay on his back in the dirt, his eyes closed, panting, sucking in the hot air, trying to catch his breath. He was out! That was the most important thing. It had been scary for a while. It was silly to admit it now, but there were intervals when he felt he might never climb out.

The sunlight blinded him, literally blanched his pupils, and it took him a while to adjust to the daylight. Even when he could see, he couldn't focus well, especially out of his left eye. Things were murky and blurry. Well, sure, didn't he get blinded in that eye?

No, what was he talking about? When would he get blinded? Julian sat up, hugging his knees. He was so happy to be out of the cave. He was never going into a cave again, he pledged with solemn honor.

He didn't feel strong enough to stand up yet. He looked around. He didn't know where he was. Nothing looked familiar, and it was very hot. There were no rolling hills, no hawthorn hedges, no buildings, no pubs, no rookeries, no observatories, no antipodean flatlands, no collapsing streets. He was in the highlands this time, in the dust of pampas grass. It wasn't recognizable. But it wasn't unrecognizable either.

He stared at his forearms, looking for damage, for the tell-tale signs of injuries, old or new. The arms were smeared with mud and dust. With his right hand he rubbed the dirt off his left arm to see the marks but couldn't find any. Was it his imagination, or were there supposed to be marks? Wasn't one of his arms engraved with lines, dots, symbols, a map of where he had been and where he was going? He stared into his hands. He clenched and unclenched his fists. His hands were sore, his right hand especially from digging so long with a multi-tool not made for digging, but otherwise they weren't too bad. No broken bones, thank God.

The top of his head hurt. When he touched it, it *really* hurt. His fingers came back bloody. The back of his neck was sticky with blood, the back of his shirt. Ah, so he had a cut on his head. No wonder he wasn't feeling great. The hot sun that was nice a minute ago after being in darkness for what felt like forever was now making everything worse. Julian was fruitless and weary.

When he thought he could bear the pain, he felt around the top of his scalp again. Under the swelling, he found a groove under his fingers, a compound depression in his head. Oh, no—he had an open head wound! He had to cover it with something quick—before dust and dirt got in. He didn't want to take off his shirt in the sun, so he searched his pockets for anything else, and that's when he realized he had dropped his multi-tool. Probably when he was moving rocks with both hands to get himself out. No, no. He must find it. It was a Leatherman tool and expensive; it had been a birthday gift from Ashton, the first thing Ashton ever gave him, or as Ashton put it, "the first thing he'd ever given anybody." Julian didn't want to lose it. Look how it helped him just now. On his knees, with his bare hands, he plowed through the excavated sand, searching for it. He glimpsed something faintly red in the dust and rocks. He brushed the dirt away, flung away the pebbles that covered it, pulled it out of the earth, flattened it out.

It was the red beret.

He couldn't believe he had brought it with him. What luck. He must have stuffed it into his pants' pocket at the last minute, and it had fallen out. The beret was dusty but otherwise in pretty good shape. The leather was soft. Carefully, Julian fit it over his head.

And there was the multi-tool in the sand close by! Oh, thank God.

It was time to stand up, get going. Wobbling slightly, he got to his feet. He was so hot.

Okay. Now what?

For a long time, Julian wandered through the desert wilderness, the untrammeled rattlesnake weed and poison hemlock, through the low-lying, burned-out coyote bush. He was desperately thirsty. He should've drunk from the river when he'd had the chance. He stopped walking.

What river?

He peered into the hazy distance for a few minutes. He must have imagined it when he was trapped under the rocks, a mirage of water for men lost in the desert. He distinctly remembered dipping his feet into a stream, but his socks and boots weren't wet. They weren't even damp.

Julian kept circling what looked like the same pair of cacti, the same eucalyptus, kept doubling back, tripling back, over this hill and the next, toward the sun, away from the sun. Nothing made any difference. In every direction, it was the same sparse foliage, the same low shrubland. He found a spray of pink live-forevers, a wildflower weed. It had succulent stems. In seconds he sucked out all the liquid inside them. It wasn't nearly enough. He searched for more, but there weren't any.

He found a rotting sheep carcass. He stuck his multi-tool inside and maggots exploded out. He thought blood would drain from his body through the hole in his head. Revulsed, he vomited up the bile in his gut. His head wound bled anew.

His mind wasn't focusing on the terrain because it was anxiously trying to remember something. Something about ice or mountains or both or death. Was it ice *and* death? He was supposed to know something, maybe about a coming avalanche? Tell someone something.

He sucked the salt from his dirty hands, and then looked at his right hand and thought, wait, I have all my fingers?

It must be heat stroke. Under the brutal sun, for a moment Julian thought he wasn't supposed to have all his fingers.

He was dying of thirst. Literally dying.

Julian tried to hold on to the tenuous thread of landslide memory, he really tried. But life took over.

As he wandered in the heat and dust, he forgot the ice and the mountains; he forgot about someone else's death, because his own was looming so near.

And soon Julian couldn't even remember that he was supposed to remember.

He was having another problem, one that needed to be addressed immediately, or soon it would become his only problem, and then he wouldn't have any. His head was hurting so bad, it was making him blind. The blood had dried but the skull felt so tender and swollen that Julian had a flashing worry that maybe it was more than just a cut, that maybe it was a more serious head injury. Like a fractured skull. He dismissed the thought. He couldn't afford a more serious injury out here by himself in the open country.

Disoriented, he sat out his confusion on a boulder and played with the multi-tool, opening and closing all its instruments, trying to think. A straight-edge knife, a serrated blade, a saw, wire cutters, a bottle opener, a pair of scissors, a flathead, a Phillips, a flashlight, a pen, a titanium toothpick, a sewing needle. Thinking was difficult, the brain like midday concrete. To cool himself down, Julian cut off the legs of his pants and then flensed the cotton twill into long strips, tying the ends together to create one long rope. Did he need a rope? What if the head was throbbing because the brain was swelling? Could he have some intra-cranial bleeding, a hematoma maybe? If the pressure from the hemorrhage got to be too much, he would pass out. Maybe he could use the titanium toothpick to find his dura mater through the opening in his cracked skull, puncture the membrane, release some of the pressure on his brain.

Oh, God, he *was* having a sun stroke. To think he could perform brain surgery on himself.

Yet he had to do something.

His ears were ringing, his eye movement impaired. He couldn't count down from a hundred and didn't know not only where he was but where he was supposed to be. The rocks bashed his head in good. He couldn't stand up. He tried to motivate himself with quotes from Muhammad Ali. The boxer hated every minute of training. But he forced himself not to quit. *Suffer now,* Ali said, *and live the rest of your life as a champion.*

And: *To become a champion, fight one more round.*

Julian suspected he didn't have much time to keep mulling boxing wisdoms. With intense effort he fought the most overpowering urge of all—to lie down in the sand and go to sleep.

But maybe it was like Ali said: *Suffer now and live the rest of your life.*

He dragged himself to his feet and hunted through the dry chaparral until he spotted the lilac flowers and ashy green leaves of sacred sage. Nearby some common yarrow grew, with its clusters of white buds and pungently sweet scent. Sage was an analgesic, and yarrow stanched blood flow. Sometimes sage was called soldier's woundwort. Julian pulled off several handfuls of leaves, chopped them up roughly with the knife and used sweat and spit to moisten them. He rubbed the plants between his hands to bring out their strong-smelling natural oils. Carefully he pressed the damp leaves into his head and then fit the beret over it to keep them in place. He took off his T-shirt and wrapped it around the beret. He fixed the contraption in place with the rope he had made. Better a blister burn on his bare back than to pass out alone in the desert.

He found a stick to help him walk and got going again. Walking while leaning on a stick seemed weirdly familiar—and easier. Why didn't he think of it sooner?

After stumbling through another plain of dying witch grass that like him was being singed into tumbleweed, Julian found a paved road. Valhalla! The place where kings and heroes were received. But this Valhalla was empty and in the middle of nowhere. There were no houses or fences or lights in either direction. But at least it was a road, and it was divided by a yellow line. It ran east–west. He decided to head toward the sun, for in his experience, a path heading west often ended in a large body of water. He would drink salt water now, if he could get to it.

A truck up ahead barreled toward him at rocket speed. Julian couldn't judge how fast it was traveling and didn't want to get run over. Tottering he backed off into the sagebrush shoulder, watching the truck slow down, its horn blasting full volume. It whizzed by, knocking him back with a gale of hot air. The driver turned his head to stare at him before stepping on the gas. After the vehicle disappeared from view, Julian got back on the road and resumed his sclerotic pace.

It wasn't long before he heard a high-pitched siren behind him. Or it could've been hours. Julian couldn't tell. In the distance he saw flashing lights zooming toward him, heard the pitch of another siren, and another. A posse of red and blue lights screamed so loud, he became afraid.

He hated the sound of sirens.

Plus, in their haste to get to wherever they were going, they could run him over and not even know it. He stepped off the road to give them a wide berth and then thought, what if they were coming for him? Hadn't he killed a man with his bare hands, fought and killed others? Hadn't he conspired to dispose of a man's murdered body and stolen a dead man's gold? Julian had never accounted for his crimes.

In slow motion, he staggered away into the bush.

What was happening? Was the dehydration breaking down his body, his mind? What men did he kill, where?

He was angry he was being forced back into the scrubland after it had taken him so long to find a road. He didn't want to return to the grasses. But he remembered a dark-haired man telling him to follow his gut, so that's what Julian did. What *was* that little man's name? It was on the tip of his tongue. It would come to him, he was sure of it, come to him when he wasn't so hot and anxious. He would hide now, Julian decided, but get back on the road as soon as the cops left. Surely there would be regular cars driving by. He would flag one down.

He wondered if the present commotion was the truck's doing. Could the driver have called Julian in? Sometimes the trucks and the cops were connected by special-frequency wideband radios. Julian should've hidden from the truck, not the police. He regretted getting caught off guard, cursed his sugar-deprived, swollen, leaking, non-reactive brain.

He stumbled into the dusty plain to let the insistent cars pass. His shins were bleeding. He thought a bone in his foot might be broken, because it hurt to scramble back into the desert. After he'd gone a fair distance and couldn't hear the sirens anymore, Julian glanced back, to make sure they had passed him, and it was safe again.

But no.

It was the opposite of safe again.

All the lights in the kaleidoscope of his failing vision were pinholed at the place in the road where he had just been, colors spinning like a silent carousel. They were all stopped—as if they had stopped for him. There was even an ambulance. As Julian watched, a civilian car screeched to a stop, the driver door opened, and a man jumped out. A police officer pointed in Julian's direction. Leaving his car door flung open, the man started running toward Julian.

Was that right, or was it another illusion?

Julian's one eye had crusted over and the other was filled with dirt and swollen with poison ivy. The one eye that could still see was playing tricks on him. Through his blurred myopic haze, Julian could almost swear the running man was getting closer to him in the dried-out skeleton grass. And his ears were deceiving him. He thought he heard a voice calling his name in the wilderness.

Julian...!

The man kept tripping on the rough ground full of ditches and rocks and poverty weed, falling, getting up, running, shouting his name. *Julian! Julian...*

The man was coming toward him clumsily, frantically—or was it frantically and clumsily? Consequences were important. Causes and effects were important. Was the man clumsy because he was frantically trying to get to him?

Julian wavered, fearfully watching the blur come into focus. His head hurt. But his heart hurt more.

Maybe it was being too long without water in the pitiless desert, but for a moment, the mirage in front of Julian glimmered like a ghost of the most familiar shape of all. Ashton.

Except this yelling running ghost was calling out his name.

Instead of taking another step away, like he thought he wanted to, Julian took a step forward, whispering a parched prayer through a throat that couldn't make a sound. *Oh God, please PLEASE let it be Ashton.*

Dimly he recalled the lies he had told himself in some flat subarctic city where he searched not for one lost soul but two, peering into the faces of faceless men the way hopeless people do when they've lost everything, when every back, every jacket, every hearty laugh looked and sounded like a beloved someone forever gone. But this mirage wore no jacket and wasn't laughing and yet looked and sounded like his vanished friend.

Julian took another step forward.

A few feet away from him, the panting man stopped running. His hands fell to his sides. Gasping, he crossed his arms over his stomach and doubled over. When he straightened out, he spoke. "*Julian,*" the mirage said, the eyes welling up, the voice breaking.

Ashton.

Julian dropped his stick, walked toward him, threw his arms around him.

Ashton threw his arms around Julian. The two men stood, gripped in a deadlock.

Julian was dry heaving.

Ashton clasped him around his back. "It's all right. It's all right," he said, holding Julian up. "You're okay. You'll be okay. Can you walk? Holy shit, dude. Can you walk? What the fuck happened to you, Jules? We thought you were dead."

Me, too. Julian tried to speak, but no sound came out. He grabbed Ashton's shirt. His mouth opened. Ashton waved to the cars in the road. "It's him! It's him," he yelled.

With Ashton's arm around his neck, a barely upright Julian limped through the grass, was almost dragged through it. It's all right, dude, it's all right, Ashton kept repeating. Then Julian couldn't walk anymore. Ashton yelled for help, but Julian was falling. Before the paramedics could get into the bush with the stretcher, Ashton carried Julian to the stretcher himself.

Julian heard anxious rapid-fire conversation over his head, as if he wasn't there, as if he couldn't hear. "White male, twenty-two years old, IDd by his friend Ashton Bennett as Julian Osment Cruz. Found in Topanga Canyon, severely injured, bleeding from his nose and ears, presenting with a compound skull fracture, likely cerebral hemorrhage, vocal cord paralysis, risk of infection, loss of blood, one eye shut, the open pupil not responding to light, concussion certain, sun stroke definite, visible spider bites, possibly a snake bite, poison ivy, body swollen from burn blisters, dehydration, and bee stings."

Bee stings? Julian thought. Aren't bee stings good?

Someone covered him with a blanket. Someone put a wet cloth over his face so he couldn't see even out of his one bad eye. He managed to lift his hand, yank the cloth off his face and stuff it in his mouth, trying to suck the water out of it. Did it not occur to a single medical professional that he might need water? Did that really need to be explained? Yes, he couldn't speak the word, but did he *have* to speak it? They pried the cloth from his clenched teeth.

"Why can't we give him some water?" Ashton said loudly. "Look at him."

"We're starting an IV on him now. Don't worry, he'll get his fluids through a vein. He can rupture his stomach if he drinks too fast. He's in trouble. It's a hundred degrees out and he is not sweating. His temperature is 104. Pulse 180. Look how shallow he's breathing. He's about to crash. We need to get him to the hospital stat."

Ashton leaned over Julian. "I'm going to call your family. I hope the nurses will clean you up, so your mother doesn't have a heart attack when she sees you. Behave yourself when the nurses fuss over you, cleaning you up, oh, nurse, how much do you charge for genitalia, same as I do for Jews, Mr. Gideon..."

"Mr. Bennett, excuse us, please..."

Ashton ignored them. "Hang in there, brother," he said.

Don't leave me, Ashton. Please. Don't leave me again. How clearly Julian remembered Ashton gone from his life. The man was wrong. Look how much Julian remembered. Too bad he couldn't recall the man's name. All in good time.

The EMT was pushing Ashton away, but he kept leaning over the stretcher. "Dude, I wish you knew what you've put us through. Do you have any idea how long we've been searching for you, how long you've been missing?"

No. Tell me. How long.

"There's been an APB out on you for seven days, Jules. *Seven* fucking days. Where have you been? You vanished off the earth. And not for nothing, but you popped up nearly fifty miles from where you and I were camping at Mugu Point. All this time we were looking for you in the wrong place. How the hell did you get *here*?"

Julian blinked with his one open eye.

"Mr. Bennett! You're preventing us from doing our job. You know he can't speak to you. He doesn't even know who you are."

"He knows who I am," Ashton said. "Don't you, Jules?"

Motionlessly, Julian stared at Ashton.

"Exactly! He can't answer a single basic question. Does traumatic brain injury mean anything to you? Do you want him to die? Move away from the patient. Go visit him at UCLA Medical Center. He'll be the one in the critical unit."

Ashton didn't move. "Don't worry, bro, I'm not leaving you. I'm never leaving you again. I'm driving to the hospital right behind you." He patted Julian's chest.

Julian kept mouthing, kept trying to form a word.

"Look, he is trying to say something," Ashton said to the paramedic.

"He's probably trying to say *water*, Mr. Bennett."

"Or my name." Ashton mined Julian's face. "Jules...?"

Julian looked up at the sky, hazy in the heat. A tear rolled down his temple. What was the name of the girl he had loved so much? Did he dream her, the mystical girl that changed shape and size, changed his life, changed the shade of her auburn hair, the cream color of her eyes? Was she myth? Did she exist?

With great effort Julian lifted his arm from under the blanket and pressed his palm against his friend's unshaven, relieved, scared, familiar face, as familiar to him as his own. Summoning his breath before he passed out, from a dry desert throat he eked out what was to him a shout but to everyone else barely heard.

"*Ashton*," said Julian.

Part Three

Future Imperfect

When a man is tired of London, he is tired of life,
for there is in London all that life can afford.

Samuel Johnson

36

Phantasmagoria in Two, Take 2

JULIAN STOOD IN FRONT OF HIS BEDROOM MIRROR AND loosened the knot in his tie. For some reason it felt too tight. It kept pressing on his Adam's apple. He would've left the tie off, but he didn't like to go into studio meetings without one. Everyone took him more seriously with it on.

He drove to Coffee Plus Food to get a drink before his trip down to Fox. While in line, he caught a girl's eye. It pleased him to catch it. He was glad he'd worn his good tie. She was in front of him, long-haired and slim, though not too slim. The Timberland boots made her appear taller than she actually was. She wore a denim mini skirt and a sheer blue blouse. He liked the backs of her slender legs and the roundness of her hips. Her waist was tiny. She turned around, glanced at him. He affected a neutral face and stared intently at the specials board.

"So what's good," she said.

"The buns are pretty good," he said. "The morning buns, I mean."

She faced front. A few moments later, she turned around again.

She had a soft voice and a large shy smile. She wore feather earrings, thick black mascara, red lip gloss. She was a glowing bohemian rhapsody.

"So, what *else* is good?" she said, looking up at him.

∞

@survivalchick21 1:32 p.m.
What a difference a day makes. I am watching a
completely mismatched man and woman fall in love before
my very eyes at a coffee joint on Melrose and Gower.
When my day began, it sucked. And now it doesn't.
#CoffeePlusFood
#love

@survivalchick21 1:33 p.m.
He is an immaculately groomed Mr. Arms with deep-set
eyes and designer stubble in a custom-made suit. She is
a hippie chick in a tiny skirt. The only hippie thing about
him is his wavy hair, down to his neck, slicked back behind
his ears and partly tied in a hot little bun.

@survivalchick21 1:35 p.m.
He is prim and she is improper. He is tightly wound and
she is all flowy.

@survivalchick21 1:36 p.m.
I don't know how they started talking. I wasn't paying
attention. I think she started it. He doesn't seem like the
forward type. He doesn't need to be, does he.

@survivalchick21 1:38 p.m.
Suddenly she's telling him she's an actress and used to
work at some joint on Coney Island, and on and on. I don't
know what he does. She won't let him get a word in.

@survivalchick21 1:41 p.m.
Next thing I know they're off about boxing, and he's staring
at her like he can't believe the words pouring out of her.
#dying

@survivalchick21 1:44 p.m.
Every syllable out of her mouth he receives as a
gift. She doesn't even see it, she's so worried as
soon as she stops talking, he'll lose interest. She talks,
and he grunts mostly yes. When she smiles, he instantly
smiles back like they're the same star reflecting in one
mirror.

@survivalchick21 1:47 p.m.
I thought they just met, but I heard her say O my God
I know you! They gape at each other like Meredith and
Christina on #GreysAnatomy. You're my person!
#prayingforlinetogoslower

@survivalchick21 1:49 p.m.
He took off his tie and stuffed it in his pocket. Like he
couldn't breathe!

@survivalchick21 1:50 p.m.
She tells him 49 is her magic number. He says he never
cared for it himself, plus it's rather high. His is 7. She
smiles and says that's rather low. She asks if 7 has any
special significance and he TURNS RED! But recovers in
time to smile and say no.
#!!!!!!!!!!
#RIPme

@survivalchick21 1:54 p.m.
I can't. She just asked him to give her a ride, and they left
together. Am I allowed to follow them to find out how it
turns out?
#restrainingorderanyone?

@survivalchick21 11:30 p.m.
I can't stop thinking about them. It's a cynical world out
there, I know, but I'm telling you, it happened in front
of me. This morning I was flatlining, and this afternoon
everything had changed.

∞

She kept turning around and staring at him. He kept smiling
politely.

"Sorry, but didn't you come to my play a few weeks ago?"
she asked.

"I don't think so."

"New York? Cherry Lane Theatre?" Theatrically she
spread out her arms and said in a British accent, "*I'm dead then.
Good.*"

"Definitely not. Sorry." The British accent stirred him up a
bit.

"Huh. I could've sworn it was you."

"Wasn't me." She had a breathy soprano that sounded oddly
familiar. Yet he had never heard such a combination of sexy and
innocent in a woman's voice.

"You sat in the third row between your date and your friend.
You were all pretty wrecked by the end. I don't blame you. I was
excellent, if I do say so myself."

"I'm sure. But it wasn't me."

"*The Invention of Love*? I played A.E. Housman. I was Nicole
Kidman's understudy. *Love is ice in the hands of children.*"

"Sounds good, but I haven't been to New York in years."

"Incredible."

It sure was. A squinting Julian studied the specials board
again. He had that specials board memorized.

She faced front for barely a second. "I just had an audition
for a Mountain Dew commercial," she said, turning around.

"Oh, yeah?"

"I was also in *Six Characters in Search of an Author*. I was one of the six characters. And I was in *Top Girls*."

"Were you one of the top girls?"

"How did you know? Actually, I wasn't, so—ha. I was one of the second-tier girls. You're not a producer by any chance, are you?" She appraised his suit. "Maybe I could audition for you."

He demurred. "The kind of producer I am you don't want to audition for."

"Why?" She batted her eyes. "Are you in…naughty films?"

"No." He lowered his gaze, took a step back. "I sponsor and train some fighters at a gym near here."

"Oh my God, really? I love boxing!"

"You do?" He tried to remain impassive.

"Oh, sure." She put up her fists. "Hey, can you train me, too?"

It was hard to stay impassive. "I don't train girls, sorry."

"Why not? That's sexist. Girls can fight."

"They sure can. I just can't train them. I'd be like, don't get hit, duck, move away, run."

"So maybe somebody should train *you* to be a trainer of girls."

"Yeah. Maybe."

She kept looking him up and down, reviewing the shine on his shoes, the cut of his jacket. She roamed his face, from his forehead to his chin, peered into his eyes, studied his full mouth, his twice-busted nose, stared at his Adam's apple above the open top button of his shirt. He had taken the tie off. He had to. "This is how you dress for fight training?"

"No, suit is for a meeting," he said. "The boxing's usually first thing."

"What kind of meeting? I didn't know there was a gym around here."

"Freddie Roach's place, just up on Vine."

"Yeah, I know it. The Chiquis Taco food truck in the parking lot is pretty good."

"I prefer the Han Tai Vietnamese truck next to it."

"Oh yeah? I've never had Vietnamese food." She waited.

"Oh yeah?" Was she expecting him to say something else, like invite her out? "You should try it. It's very good."

"I bet. Did you know I used to run the Gotham Girls Roller Derby rink?"

"I don't think I knew that, no. But it doesn't surprise me."

"I did. On Coney Island. That's me, I'm a Gotham Girl. I bet I roller blade better than you box." She smiled.

"I bet I roller blade better than you box, too." He smiled.

She laughed and edged half a foot closer. "Have you ever been to Coney Island?"

He stayed put. "I haven't, no." There was nowhere for him to go; the small place was packed.

"It's awesome. We have a boxing gym there, too. Plus a Ferris wheel and amusements. We have fortune-tellers and a kiss me quick promenade"—she grinned—"and we had Sideshows by the Seashore where I used to work with my dad. I was the emcee, an amazing emcee, by the way, I was a carnival performer, did a little of everything, including juggling knives while riding a unicycle."

"That sounds pretty great."

"Oh, it was incredible. But we closed unfortunately. Coney Island still has a world-famous roller coaster, the Cyclone, and a boardwalk, and the best pizza joint in the entire world."

"Thank you." He couldn't help smiling. "I know what Coney Island *is*."

"Oh!" She almost blushed, but quickly regrouped. "So what do you do, Mr. Boxing Guy? Do you just train others, or do you box yourself? Oh, you box, too, really? Maybe I can come to one of your fights. What do you mean, not professionally? But you used to? Wow. Were you any good? You were? Why'd you quit? Oh no!—that sounds terrible. Head injuries are the *worst*. No, I never had one myself, knock wood"—she rapped on her own head—"but I knew a guy who dived into the shallow end of the pool, and he was never the same after. Mind you, he probably

wasn't all there to begin with, to dive into the shallow end.
I really do like boxing, you know. I'm not just saying that."

"Why would I think you were just saying that?"

"Like to try to impress you or something."

"Why would I think you were trying to impress me?" He
twinkled at her.

She twinkled back at him. "I used to follow this blog online,"
she said. "Then I got busy, I don't know if I mentioned it, but I'm
in both film *and* theatre…"

"Yes, you mentioned it."

"Well, I have *no* spare time is what I'm saying. But I found
time to follow this dude's blog. He was a former boxer, like you,
but he was also a Mr. Know-it-All, and he ran an awesome boxing-
slash-survival-slash-life hacks-slash-lonely hearts website."

There was a pause. "The lonely hearts part wasn't
intentional," he said. "Everyone kept asking all kinds of personal
questions, even though it was supposed to be just life hacks."

"Oh, you know the blog, too?"

"I do," said Julian. "It's mine."

"No, the guy was an *actual* boxer, plus he also knew a ton
of survival stuff. Not that I needed it, but it was so much fun to
read."

"I'm that guy."

There was a second or two of processing silence. "Shut up—
you're *not* Julian Cruz!"

"Um…"

Her smile, wide before, became Hawaii-wide. She stuck out
her hand. "Well, well, Mr. Julian Cruz, we meet at last. I'm Mia.
Actually, Mirabelle, but most of my friends call me Mia. But you
can call me Mirabelle or Mia, or whatever you want."

Her soft slender hand remained in his. Julian let go first.
That didn't happen. The girl was usually the one to pull away.

"What's your stage name?" he said. "I'll look you up on
IMDb."

"You're going to look me up, are you?" Irrepressibly grinning.

Now he was at a loss for words.

"I'm kidding. It's Mirabelle McKenzie."

"That's a good name."

"I like it. For a while I wanted to change it to Josephine Collins. I saw it written out in an old diary and liked the ring of it, and how it looked on the page. It sounded so historical and posh, like British aristocracy, Josephine Collins, a Shakespearean star of film and stage! But my mother said she would kill me."

"Mirabelle McKenzie is better."

"I told my mom if she kept making me mad I'd change it to Mystique McKenzie. Moms was *not* amused. She doesn't even know who Mystique is."

"Do *you*?"

"Oh, yeah, baby." She clicked her tongue. "I know everything. I'm like Miss Know-it-All. You said the morning bun?" It was her turn at the counter. "What else?"

"The sausage rolls are good. Australians run this place. They know their coffee and sausage rolls."

"So you come here a lot?"

"Yes, semi-regularly."

"Like around lunchtime?"

"Uh, no, different times. Depending on the day."

She ordered, paid, and barely waited for him to order his own coffee before resuming. "I have an audition coming up for a London play," she said. As if London and Australia were interchangeable. "The director is flying in all the way from London, casting for a revival of *Medea* at the Riverside Theatre. It's right on the banks of the Thames. My life's dream is to live in London and be on stage there, ideally at the Palace Theatre, which is my favorite. Have you heard of it—the play, I mean? *Medea*, the woman who kills her children to avenge her betrayal. *Dress up murder in handsome words, why don't you.*"

"Well, kids can be such a handful," Julian said dryly. "I hope you get the part. London sounds fun. Though I hear the weather's not great. Five months of drizzle followed by a day of sun."

She laughed. "Clearly you've been to London."

"No. Always wanted to go, though."

"Me, too. Did you know that if you laid all the streets of London end to end, they would reach from New York to L.A.?"

"Yeah, but who'd want to?"

"Well, there's that. I really hope I get the part. It'd be like a year commitment, though." She blinked at him, as if inviting him to follow up with…

"But what an opportunity," he said. "And you'll get used to the rain."

"How do you know?"

"Because people can get used to anything," he said.

They waited for their food and drinks in the mobbed place. She got hers first, but wouldn't leave, kept talking to him.

"Well, best of luck to you," Julian said, when he got his coffee. "Break a leg."

She was chewing her lip, her eyes darting up and down.

He turned to walk out.

"Jules, wait!"

37

Paradiso and Purgatorio

THEY HURRIED DOWN THE STREET.

"I hope it's not a terrible inconvenience," she said. "I know the Greek Theatre is out of the way."

"It's not a problem. Don't worry about it. I'm right here." Julian pointed to his black Mercedes AMG two-seater with its top down, parked just around the corner on Larchmont.

"Oh, swerve! Look at your car," she said, impressed. He held the door open for her, closed it behind her, walked around. "Must be smoking fast out in the desert."

"It's smoking fast everywhere," Julian said, "and the City of Beverly Hills never lets me forget it. They haul my ass into court every few months." Slowly he drove up Gower, debating whether or not to take Fountain. "Are you visiting from New York?"

"Me? No. I live here now. A transplant. I moved out west a few years ago. Why do you ask? Oh, because of *Invention of Love*? I couldn't pass up the part. Marty told me it could be a career break. Marty's my agent. I was there for two months. But when my contract ended, I came back. That was less than a week ago. But I think I have a good shot at the Mountain Dew commercial and now this *Paradise in the Park* thing at the Greek. Plus a horror movie I'm auditioning for on Thursday..."

"You live in L.A. but don't drive? How do you get around?"

"My roommate drives me, or I take the bus, or a cab, or I walk. I walk everywhere. My *female* roommate," Mia added.

"Her name is Zakiyyah. She's my oldest friend. We grew up together."

"Is that safe, walking everywhere?"

"It's fine. I keep meaning to get a car, but I can't afford the payments yet. Soon. Maybe if I get this Dante gig and I don't go to London. I know it seems crazy to an Angeleno, but in New York I never needed a car."

"But you're not in New York," he said.

"Old habits die hard," Mirabelle said. "Did you know that Ray Bradbury lived his whole life in L.A. and never got a car? He took the bus everywhere."

He drove, and she didn't stop talking. "Where do you live, Julian?"

"I'm up in the hills."

"That's pretty swanky," she said dreamily. "I like going up in the hills. I have a place I sometimes hike to…which way do you face?"

"Every which way. We're on a mesa that we've cleared on all four sides. Plus we have a roof deck."

"Ah, a roof deck," she said, suddenly subdued. Her mouth tightened. "Who's we, your fam, your wife?"

"No. Me and my friend Ashton."

She continued to look disappointed; at first he couldn't figure out why. "I mean, my actual friend Ashton," Julian said, getting it eventually. "It's not a euphemism."

"Are you over thirty?"

"Yes, just—why?"

"You're not allowed to have a roommate if you're over thirty."

"Says who? And didn't you just say *you* had a roommate?"

"I'm not over thirty, so there."

"Technically, Ashton and I are not roommates," Julian said. "We bought two adjoining lots and built two houses, connecting them by a pool and a common patio. So, together but apart."

"I know what you mean," Mirabelle said. "When we lived in New York, me and Z shared a studio not much bigger than your car. Our two twin beds were separated by a privacy curtain, so we too were like together, but apart. And I guarantee, we paid more in rent than you pay for your spread. But then again, we were in the best location, Theatre District, 46th Street between Broadway and Eighth. What does Ashton do, is he a boxer like you? What's the Treasure Box? You have a prop store, too? You're a busy guy, aren't you? That sounds like amazing fun though, running a prop store. Nothing but joy every day."

"Ashton is a lucky guy," Julian said. "He only likes to do what he loves."

"Welcome to the human race," Mia said. "I must check it out. I like haunted houses. I used to love your blog, you know." There was hardly a pause between sentences.

"Thanks, but why past tense?"

"Well, like I said, I got busy, plus you went dark a while back. What did you do, write a book?"

"Actually, yeah," Julian said. "I kind of did."

"Did you really!"

"That's why the blog's been quiet." The book had been on the bestseller list in the self-help section for the past seventy-two weeks. Because of that, he now taught a survival course at the community college, traveled sporadically around the country giving motivational speeches, and offered consulting services on movie sets needing survival experts. He had almost no time for boxing, which is why he got up at dawn every day.

"I've never met a published writer before, wow," she said, assessing him in cheery wonder. "What's the book called? *Cruz's Compendium of Clever Creations?*"

"Cute—but no. *Tips from a Boxer and a Know-it-All.*"

"That's good, too. I actually wrote to you a few times. I was one of the lonely hearts." She hadn't put on her seat belt. It kept beeping every 15 seconds, to which she was utterly oblivious. "Don't tell me you don't remember me?" She didn't stop smiling. Or looking at him.

"Sorry. Did you sign as yourself or use some other name? Most people use…"

"I signed as Gotham Girl." Her body was turned all the way to him in the passenger seat.

He kept his eyes on the road. Her laser focused attention was slightly disorienting. "Did I ever write back?" He didn't remember a Gotham Girl. But so many people wrote to him.

"You sure did! We went back and forth. I heartily disagreed with your assessment of my personal situation."

"What did you ask me?"

"One was why, if I was so talented and so gifted and was doing what I was meant to do, blah-di-blah, was I always so flipping broke."

"And I said…"

"You quoted Marlon Brando. *Never confuse the size of your paycheck with the size of your talent.*"

Julian nodded in understated self-approval. "And the second?"

"I asked how a girl could tell if a guy had a thing for her."

"To which I…"

"Told me to run." She laughed. "You actually said that. You said if you have to ask, he doesn't."

"Ouch."

"You're telling me. Then you asked if he'd seen my favorite movie."

"And?"

"That's it. I really took that apart. And you kept writing back, repeating, but has he seen it? You were very annoying."

Julian vaguely recalled that exchange. The girl had been insistent, writing to him several times a day, presenting bags of evidence, but refused to answer his basic question and one day went radio silent. "Well?" he said. "I never did get an answer from you. *Had* he seen your favorite movie?"

She threw up her hands. "Do you see now why I stopped writing to you?"

"Why, because you don't like answering questions?"

With the top down, the wind blew about her hair. Julian pulled over to the curb. She looked worried for some reason, like he was going to throw her out of the car or something. He nearly reached out and stroked her flushed cheek to reassure her. "I want to put the top up," he said. "You don't want to be a wild Beatrice for your audition, do you? Probably best not to be too disheveled."

Her face melted at him, confounding him.

At the Greek Theatre in Griffith Park, she asked him to come in with her instead of waiting in the car. He checked his watch, texted Ashton to take the Fox meeting without him, and followed her into the amphitheatre.

With a spring in her step she hopped up onto the stage when her turn came, waited for her cue from a man with the clipboard, nodded to Julian, and began. She was well prepared. She was phenomenal.

After his eyes had sought the starry guide,
they turned again into the light.
"Tell me who you are," he cried.
And thus I answered:
"A while ago the world possessed me.
Had my time been longer,
Much evil that would come,
Had never chanced upon me
Because you loved me well, and had good cause:
For had my sojourn
Been longer on this earth,
The love I bore you in return
Would've put forth
more than blossoms."

The producer sat mutely, like Julian, but less open-mouthed. Then he said, "Miss McKenzie, what *was* that? Was that Dante? Because I cannot find it in my book."

"It was from memory, sir," she said. "I rewrote it a little. Condensed some lines."

Silence from the front row. "You *rewrote* Dante?"

"Yes, sir. I wanted to do my best."

"Thank you, Miss McKenzie. We'll be in touch. Next!"

"That was excellent, Mirabelle," Julian said as they walked to his car across the street. "Really. If it was my play, I would've given you the part on the spot."

"You would have given me a part in your play?" Her whole face lit up, even her little nose. "Like a walk-on? Or a lead role?" She laughed when he could find no response. "I'm just teasing you."

"I know," he said.

"And would I first need to tell heaven from hell?"

"No, just a smile from a veil," he said.

She high fived him for the musical wordplay. "The being-prepared, I learned that from your blog, you know," she said. "You can't over-prepare, you wrote. You said always do your best but learn to accept that it is probably not going to be enough."

"I sound like a real pill. Did I ever say anything remotely cheery?"

"So many wonderful things. Lessee, you said to always go out into the world dressed like you were about to meet the love of your life."

"That's not too bad, I suppose." They squinted at each other, him in his suit, her in her mini skirt. "Can I give you a ride somewhere, Mirabelle?"

"Like where? Maybe the Vietnamese food truck by Freddie Roach's?" She smiled.

"You're funny. Right now, I'm afraid I have to run." It would take him a while to drive home in rush hour. And Ashton commanded him under penalty of death not to be late. Riley and Gwen were coming over for dinner. They had announced they needed to talk to the men about their relationship status. Julian was forbidden to leave Ashton high and dry.

Mirabelle gave him her address, and Julian drove her home. She kept talking, telling him about the other auditions she had lined up, and how after New York she couldn't get used to L.A. weather, always so sunny and mild, but her friend Zakiyyah took to L.A. like fish to water, but on the other hand had terrible taste in men (Julian was going to ask Mirabelle if she too had terrible taste in men but couldn't find a spot to interject), always picking the *worst* guys, "like she's sort of seeing this guy now named Trevor, and if his name isn't bad enough, we went out the other night and he orders a Sloe Gin Fizz! I said to her, Z, your new boyfriend drinks Sloe Gin Fizzes? Does he wear flip flops, too? This is who's going to be your rock in times of trouble? Is he going to put down his green drink before he sandal straps your assailant—"

Abruptly Mirabelle stopped talking.

Julian had been driving, catching the breath of her words, until there was nothing to catch. "Please continue," he said. "I'm fascinated by Zakiyyah's romantic travails."

Mirabelle was staring at him with a peculiar expression. Like troubled disbelief. "Julian...why did you bring me here?"

Blinking, coming to, he looked around. "This isn't where you live?"

"No, I told you, I live off East Hollywood, on Lyman."

"Sorry," he said, putting the car into reverse. "I must've misheard."

"Julian, wait." She reached over and touched the top of his hand. An electrical charge went through him. His fingers, gripping the gearshift stick in the middle of the console, twitched. "Why did you bring me *here*?"

He wasn't sure where here was. The Hollywood Freeway was on the next block, but he'd never driven down this street before.

"I brought you to the wrong side of the 101," he said. "Sorry."

"That's not what I mean. You brought me to *Normandie Avenue*. Why?"

He looked around. "I don't know. You don't live here?"

"No!"

"Weird." He couldn't get off the road fast enough.

"That's not the weird part," she said. "The weird part is that Z and I *used* to live here. You pulled up to our old house. The neighborhood was so bad, somebody was always getting whacked, so we moved."

"See, so you did live there." Julian didn't wait for the light to change before he made a right on Melrose and sped away under the 101. If his hands were clenched any tighter around the wheel, one or the other would break. He tried to be casual but couldn't turn his head into her flummoxed gaze. With tremendous effort he straightened his tense fingers, took one hand off the wheel— the left one—and drove on.

"I did live here," Mirabelle said, "but how could *you* have known that?"

Julian could not explain it. "You must've given me the old address by mistake and not realized it." But he didn't remember her saying *Normandie*. She had said *Lyman*. He was sure of it. And she shook her head like she was sure of it, too.

Baffled, incredulous, she stared at him for a few more moments. Julian kept his eyes on the road. Something inside him started to hurt, and he didn't know what it was.

They dropped it, because what else could they do? But the conversation, so delightfully free-flowing a minute earlier, ground to a halt.

It took him ten silent minutes to drive down East Hollywood. Lyman Place was sleepy and gum-lined. The girls were renting the top half of a small two-story blue stucco house, covered by overgrown foliage. "Well, here we are," Julian said fake-brightly. "Is this the right place?"

"Yes," she said. "Would you like to walk me to the door?"

Hers was a private entrance off to the side. On the upstairs patio bloomed some well-tended yellow petunias in two large plant pots. She pulled out her keys. "Do you want to come in for a minute? Z is not home from work yet."

He shook his head. "I can't. I'm already late."

"For a very important date?" She smiled, but there was tension in her previously carefree grin, a new puzzled concentrated intensity. "Are you sure? I can make you something to eat. I'm not the best cook, but I can…"

"I really can't. Thanks, though."

They stood awkwardly.

"You said to always end on a joke," she said.

"Okay, let's hear it."

"What do you call a pile of kittens?" She paused. "A meowntain!"

When he laughed, she extended her hand. "Well, nice to meet you, Julian Cruz."

And he, without thinking, brought her soft hand to his lips and kissed it. Afterward he became even more awkward.

"They teach you that in boxing school?" she said breathily.

He couldn't return her warm liquid gaze. He stumbled back on the steps.

"You sure you don't want to come in?"

"Another time perhaps," Julian said.

"Okay, when?" Mirabelle said. "Or were you just being polite?"

38

Hollywood Hills

"I DON'T WANT TO SPEAK TO YOU," ASHTON SAID WHEN Julian ran into the house at nearly eight.

"Traffic was a motherfucker. Sorry." He threw down his keys on Ashton's front hall table, right below the Bob Marley poster.

"Pick those up. You can throw the keys around at your own place. The girls will be here in ten minutes, and you've left me to do fucking everything. You didn't even set the table. I had to do it." The table was set out on the pool patio.

"Sorry, man. I'll make it up to you."

"What am I, Gwen?" Ashton said. "You're going to make it up to me? Buy me flowers, take me to dinner?" They stood. The smoke from the grill wafted inside the house. It smelled good. Ashton loved to grill.

On the way to his own house, Julian sank into a chair by the blue pool. Ashton had turned on the LED lights, lighting up the palms and the ficus trees in shimmering aqua.

"Dude, are you *insane*?" Ashton stood over him. "They'll be here any minute. What's the matter with you? Go get changed."

"I will. I need a minute."

"Time for sitting is over. You had a whole lengthy car ride from wherever you were to sit. No more sitting."

"Ashton, five minutes, and then I'm yours. Five."

"Fuck, Jules."

"Five minutes without you speaking."

After five minutes, Julian got up, his body like concrete.

The traffic was bad on Benedict Canyon. It was a bitch driving up the mountains at rush hour. Gwen and Riley were running late, too. But the girls being late gave the men a chance to calm down. Julian changed, got the music ready, made an extra large pitcher of margaritas. He and Ashton opened two beers, sat by the pool and chatted about the Fox meeting, the inventory at the store, about Buster "The Executioner" Barkley's fight coming up in Vegas next month, and about Riley.

"Last Sunday she told me I wasn't meeting her emotional needs," Ashton said. "She said that after three years I was still nothing but potential."

"So, like a parent–teacher conference?"

Ashton laughed. "I said, Riles, I've been the same the whole time you've known me. She said that was one hundred percent her problem with me. I never changed."

"Did you ask her why she went out with you in the first place if she wanted you to change?"

"I did! She said she went out with me because she had hoped I would. She said I was too wild. Like I was an untrained poodle or something. I'm not wild!"

"Sometimes you are."

"You're not helping. Don't say that in front of her. Call me domesticated and house-broken. Next time you buy coconut water at Whole Foods, talk to her, put in a good word for me. I really don't want to have another fight. I'm beat."

"Me, too."

"You too what? You love fighting."

Julian took a breath. "I think I met a girl," he said.

Ashton downed his beer, laughed, and sat up straight. "Which part are you not sure about? Whether or not you met her, or whether or not she is a girl?"

"Oh, she is most definitely a girl."

"Really? Dude!" Ashton grinned. "What did she look like?"

Julian was quiet a moment. "Bliss," he said.

"Dude!"

The doorbell rang. Gwen and Riley were here.

"Whose idea was it to build a place on Mulholland?" Riley said, striding into Ashton's house, holding what looked like a bakery box. Despite the long ride, she looked as effortlessly creaseless as ever. "It took us an hour and a half to go eleven miles."

"Definitely Julian's," Ashton said, cheerfully throwing his friend under the bus.

Julian took the bakery box from Riley. "What's this, Riles? Don't tell me—bean sprout cookies?"

"Yes! Wait—are you mocking me? Ugh. You two are impossible. Not everything has to be a joke. These are very good. They're made with honey."

Julian turned on the music too loud, deliberately, so no one would feel any need for real conversation. He drank the margaritas liberally, but had no appetite, making the odds of success for any later, more serious conversation negligible. He didn't want to talk to Gwen because he had nothing specific to say. His feelings were a jumble. He couldn't talk to Gwen about every girl he casually chatted with. And when Julian had nothing specific to say, he always preferred to shut the hell up.

Unfortunately it was taciturn Julian's very nature that Gwen wanted to address. The couples ate, swam in the pool, lounged in the Jacuzzi, sat on the upstairs deck, drinking and chatting about nothing, and then retreated to their respective homes.

Gwen was all set to have a long discussion about the state of things between them. After a pitcher of tequila, Julian was less inclined to do so. She said his brooding nature was getting under her skin. He wanted to tell her he wasn't brooding, he just had a lot on his mind, but didn't want to detail exactly what it was he had on his mind and didn't want to lie. So he said nothing, trying to smooth things over between them with his silence, which was precisely the wrong thing to smooth over the problem of his silence with—more silence. Gwen continued to bristle, and Julian continued to respond in monosyllables. She suggested taking a break, and instead of the requisite protest, he gave her no argument. He said—because he wanted to be agreeable—if you think that's what you need, that's fine. I want you to be happy.

Clearly, what would've made her happy was a fight. As if she didn't know him, as if she didn't know he didn't like fighting with girls. She announced she was going home, which was difficult since she had come in Riley's car. Julian offered to drive her. "Are you insane?" Gwen said. "What kind of a storming out is it if you drive me home?" She called a taxi, shouting at Julian before it came, shouting and shouting, and then stormed out.

Afterward Julian sat a long time in the silence by the lit-up nighttime pool trying to hack through the jungle inside him. That night he dreamed the brown-haired girl was on top of him, completely naked, her hips gripped in his hands, while he was fully clothed, wearing his suit and tie and even his shoes, sexy, yes, but also as if to protect himself from her. When he woke up, he thought, yeah, right, no confusion there.

39

A Dress for Beatrice

In the early morning, after Riley left, Julian dragged Ashton to the gym with him. They sparred, talked about Gwen, used the speedbag, the weights, then Ashton hung out and watched Julian fight Lopez, his former trainer's son and his boxing buddy since UCLA. They were showered, dressed, at HomeState for breakfast tacos by eight and at the Treasure Box by eight-thirty.

The store was not even open when the front door bell trilled, a few minutes before nine. Julian was in the back on the computer, doing the books. Ashton went out to see who it was.

"Jules," he heard Ashton call. "Come out here. Someone's here for you."

It was Mirabelle.

She wasn't alone. Next to her stood a striking, serious, black woman, dressed business-plain, with wild curly hair more or less tied up.

Mirabelle was breathy. Her boots were black and slick today, not brown and coarse, and her denim skirt was even shorter than yesterday, though that didn't seem possible, and her coral blouse was even more see-through, though that also didn't seem possible, and her slim bare legs were even more smooth and shiny, though that didn't seem possible either. The tank underneath didn't cover her belly button. There was light makeup on her face and gloss on her lips and the loose bun piled on top of her head looked designer messy, not rolled out of bed messy. She looked casual but *top to bottom* put together, not thrown together. She wore hoop earrings and bangles on her wrists.

"Hey, Julian."

"Hey, Mirabelle." They stood wordlessly for a moment until they remembered their manners.

"Z, *this* is Julian." The way Mirabelle emphasized *this* made Julian feel awkward. Had they been talking about him?

Ashton coughed. Zakiyyah coughed.

"Sorry," Julian said. "Ashton, Mirabelle. Mirabelle, Ashton."

"Yes, sorry," Mia said. "Ashton, Zakiyyah. Zakiyyah, Ashton. But, Ashton, you can call me Mia. My friends do." She smiled. "And you can call her Z."

"Zakiyyah will be fine," said Zakiyyah.

Mutely Ashton studied Mirabelle, and then Julian. He said nothing. He turned to Zakiyyah. "Zakiyyah," Ashton said. "Like Obadiah?"

"What?"

"Hey ya, hey ya," Ashton said.

She looked annoyed. "What is *that*?" she said.

"Um—a song? By Obadiah Parker?"

"Never heard of it. What's it called?"

Ashton spoke real slow. "'Hey Ya.'" He gave Julian a you've-*got*-to-be-kidding-me look.

Meanwhile, Mirabelle was looking around the chock-a-block prop store, her jaw open.

Among other things, Ashton had a display shelf of tin Brodie helmets and gas masks. "Why do you have those?"

"Productions like to rent them," he said. "Plus my old man was born in London during the war, so it's a hat-tip to him. Not that he's ever been here to see it."

Ashton had an *I Dream of Jeannie* bottle, a perfect replica of the original.

"Where did you get that?" Mirabelle asked in fascination, as Zakiyyah stood with her arms crossed, saying nothing, and not looking around.

"I ask the top Jeannie bottle guy in the country to make them," Ashton said. "One at a time."

"And the guy makes them for you to order?" She smiled.

"Sure, he does. Because I ask nicely." Ashton beamed his full-teeth smile back at her.

"You can get a lot, asking nicely."

"You sure can."

An unsmiling Zakiyyah rolled her eyes. "Mia, I gotta go, I'm going to be late. Can we hurry it up?"

"Oh, yeah. Actually, I came to ask Julian a favor—asking nicely." Mirabelle beamed a full-teeth smile at Julian, who tried to maintain a poker face. "I have a callback for that *Paradise in the Park* audition at the Greek you drove me to yesterday. Thanks for that, by the way."

"You're welcome."

"Sorry it ran so late. Did you get to your dinner on time?"

"No," Ashton said. "He was unforgivably late. But is that why he was late? Because he was at auditions with you?"

"Uh…" Mia said.

"Ashton," Julian said.

"Mia," Zakiyyah said.

"Oh, yeah, sorry, Z. Anyway, they want me to play Beatrice, isn't that great?"

"Yes," said Julian.

"Mia," repeated Zakiyyah.

"I remembered that you told me you two had a prop store, and I was wondering if you might have some kind of a glittery snazzy dress I could borrow for like a day. But something spectacular. I need to look like the kind of girl Dante would go all the way to hell for."

"That's a lot to ask of a dress," Ashton said.

Hitting Ashton on the back with his fist, Julian said they might have something and motioned Mirabelle to follow him to the gown room, leaving Ashton and Zakiyyah alone.

40

Free Licks

THEY STOOD. WITH HER GLARE, ZAKIYYAH QUESTIONED Ashton's choice of attire. Ashton was wearing his favorite faded vintage T-shirt that said Free Licks. Zakiyyah was having none of it.

"What?" Ashton glanced at his chest, not one to let anything go. "You don't like my shirt?"

"Did I say anything? I'm just standing here, minding my own business. But now that you ask—who would?"

"It's a name of a band. I take it you're not up on indie rock? Shame. They're very good."

"Uh-huh."

"Perhaps you should get your mind out of the gutter. Unless"—and here Ashton raised his eyebrows and razzledazzle smiled—"you prefer it there. In which case..." He opened his arms.

Zakiyyah did a double-take. "Are you kidding me? Are. You. Kidding. Me?"

"I'm making a joke. Can't a man joke?" Lowering his arms, he stepped away.

"What about that did you think was funny?" said Zakiyyah.

"I'm not going to explain what a joke is," Ashton said. "That's like explaining tennis to a Doberman."

"So now you're comparing me to a vicious dog?"

"Oh my God. I can't."

"No—you can't," said Zakiyyah.

Ashton studied his phone for the time.

Zakiyyah studied her watch. "Mia! Can we please hurry it up! I gotta go!"

"Great!" Ashton muttered.

They were still scowling when Mia emerged, wearing a thousand-watt stage smile and a gorgeous billowing ankle-length purple taffeta gown, Julian walking dazed behind her.

"I take it back," Ashton said. "You found the dress Dante would go to hell for. Good job, Jules."

Julian mumbled something, averting his eyes from her.

"Yeah, Mia, that'll work," Zakiyyah said brusquely. "Can we leave? Some of us work in the mornings."

"Like *us*," Ashton said.

Zakiyyah suppressed a scoff. "Did you ask him how much the rental is going to cost you?"

Julian waved her off. "It's on us."

"No, no," Zakiyyah said. "We want to rent it, like everybody else. Right, Mia? We don't want any favors."

"But, Z…" Mia began.

"Zakiyyah is right. Let her rent it, Jules," Ashton said, turning to Mia. "That'll be a hundred bucks a day."

"Z!"

"That's fine," Zakiyyah said. "Whatever it costs. Full price. No discounts."

Julian glared at Ashton.

Mia glared at Zakiyyah.

Ashton rolled his eyes.

Zakiyyah took out her wallet.

"When's the audition?" Julian asked Mirabelle.

"Ten-thirty."

"I need to drop you off like right now and jet," said Zakiyyah. "I'm going to be late."

"Mia, if you want," Julian said carefully, "I could take you. So your friend could get to work on time. And then you can return the dress to me right after, so it won't cost you anything."

"Absolutely not," Zakiyyah began to say, but Mirabelle cut her off.

"Yes, please, Julian," she said, beaming. "If it's not too much trouble."

"It's no trouble," said Julian.

Zakiyyah rolled her eyes. "Mia, *no!*" she whispered.

"It's fine, Z," Mia said, and louder to the two men, "maybe I can help out, to return the favor. Is there anything I can do for you around here, work the register, sweep the floor?"

"Mia, we talked about this! It's not…"

"It's fine, Z!"

Zakiyyah could not leave fast enough, slamming the door on her way out.

"She's really nice," Mirabelle said to Julian and Ashton, standing by the counter, watching one woman storm out, one woman stay behind. "She's just worried about me, that's all. She's like a mommy hen."

"Yes, she seems *super* sweet," Ashton said. "Friendly, too."

"What the hell did you do to that poor girl?" Julian said to Ashton when Mirabelle was out of earshot.

"Nothing! I was an angel like always. She might not have approved of my attire."

Julian grinned. "Good thing you didn't wear your Thunderpussy shirt," he said, looking Ashton over. "Or she might have killed you."

41

Crystal of Souls

After he dropped off Mirabelle at the Greek, Julian waited for her in the parking lot. The callbacks were closed set.

She was gone only a few minutes. When she came out, she looked dejected, though stunning in that violet gown—like he couldn't take a deep breath stunning. The girl was making him inarticulate.

"Don't give up," he said. "They have to think about it."

"They thought about it," she said. "Told me on the spot I wouldn't make a good Beatrice. Too something or other. I stopped listening when I realized I wasn't getting the part."

"Oh, shame. What about the narrator?"

"They have someone for that already." She shrugged. "*C'est la vie.* I didn't want this stupid part anyway. I have more auditions tomorrow. Plus, like I said, Abigail Jenkins is flying in from London next week. That's the gig I really want. Medea. I'm going to London, I feel it."

It was a warm sunny late summer morning.

Julian had Buster Barkley to train before his meeting in Century City with a former propmaster from the *Scream* movies. "Can I take you home?" He smiled lightly. "To your actual home this time. Because I've got a full day…"

"There's something beautiful in those hills," Mirabelle blurted, pointing up to the eucalyptus lining the desert mountain. "It's like a rainbow wishing well. Do you want to come see it with me? We can only catch it at noon, and only for a few seconds. I think you'd like it. I hardly ever get to go up there. I want to make a wish for London. I need all the good karma I can get."

What could Julian say but yes to a violet girl asking him to follow her to a wishing well atop a mountain? Where had he seen a girl in a flowing purple dress like this before? For the life of him, he couldn't remember. She was like a painting.

A painting of a memory.

His palm opened up, as if he could almost feel placing his hand on that dress, on the girl's back. Quickly he clenched the hand into a fist, hoping she didn't notice. "You're going to hike in a dress and high heels?"

"I'll be careful. But you're right, the heels are a bit impractical." Half a minute later, below layers of purple silk, she had her black boots on and laced up. "I'm ready."

"Lead the way," he said, taking a swig from his Japanese thermos filled with lemon ice water and offering her some. He took off his jacket and rolled up his shirt sleeves. He knew he'd get too warm after hiking up a mountain.

They began to climb through the bush, keeping to the narrow sandy path. After a few minutes she commended his speed. "You're keeping up nicely."

"You mean *you're* keeping up nicely." He raced ahead of her.

"Hey, you can't be ahead of me!" She tried to catch up. "You don't know where you're going."

"Do any of us really know where we're going, Mia? To the top of the mountain? How hard can that be to find? I go up, right? I stop when I can't go any farther? Come on, slow poke. I haven't got all day."

By the time they reached the crest, she was flushed. Julian had barely begun to perspire.

"Not bad," Mirabelle said, panting. "I didn't know boxers could fight *and* hike."

"Boxers can do a lot."

"Oh, yeah?" She squinted.

He squinted right back.

"I like your spunk, Julian." She had the most inviting, genial face. It was a face in a permanent state of smile. "You don't run in vain, nor labor in vain."

"I try. All anyone can do, really."

"Yoda says do or do not. There is no try."

"Yoda is wrong. He doesn't know everything."

"Oh, yeah? Does Mr. Know-it-All know there's magic in these hills?"

"Mr. Know-it-All knows there's magic everywhere."

But when they reached where they were going, and up ahead he saw the stone enclosure on a flat mesa overlooking the valley and the city and the ocean—Julian stopped walking.

Mirabelle called for him. "A little farther, Jules. Over here."

It wasn't that he couldn't walk.

He couldn't walk because suddenly he found it hard to breathe.

"I know, it's the oxygen," she said, coming back and taking his hand shyly. "It's thin up here. Harder to fill your lungs."

He pulled his hand away from her. He didn't think that was it. Words for some reason became inadequate. Doggedly he followed her into the center of the stony circle.

"We're going to catch us some wishes, Jules." From her bag she retrieved a jagged crystal on a long leather rope. "Are you ready?"

The sight of the crystal had a peculiar effect on Julian. He started to shake. Seeing it, seeing her standing in the sun, holding the quartz in her hands, triggered the heaviest sensation in his chest. He became freezing cold. He had not experienced anything like it, except ten years earlier when he was dying in the desert and saw a mirage named Ashton.

Burning soot filled his throat. *She let go of his hand and disappeared into the smoke.*

"Please, *no*," he whispered. "Don't go into the fire."

"What fire? Don't be scared. Watch and see. Prepare to be amazed."

"*Josephine, no,*" he whispered. "*Please, Josephine…*"

"I'm not Josephine, remember?" she said with good humor. "I'm Mirabelle. Mia."

Dumbfounded he stared at the inside of his bare left forearm, as if the hieroglyphs to explain what was happening to him could be found there.

She positioned herself in front of him, so close she was almost touching him, the stone in her open palm. Julian did not look at her and could not look at her. He did not feel well.

"You look pale. You okay? Don't look so glum. What time is it?"

He showed her. 11:59.

"Excellent. Almost time. Don't forget to make a wish." Her face was enchanted, enchanting, smiling. "At noon, for a brief moment, the stars and the earth and all of creation will be so perfectly aligned that any wish asked for in faith can be granted."

He wished he had something to hold on to.

"Place your hands under my hands," she said. "That's it, like that, like Red Hands. Don't shake. Is the boxer scared of heights? The boxer should've told me."

"*Your heart is a refuge of coiners and thieves,*" Julian said. "*But I'm the one who has come to steal your life.*"

"What?"

His heart grew numb, awash with terrible suffering and blinding fear. When the aurora flash of noon light hit her crystal, bouncing off the quartz stones around them and dispersing into a carousel of color, Julian started to choke. His hands fell from her hands and rose to his throat. He felt old love, and pain that swallowed him whole. His lungs were paralyzed. She stood in front of him smiling, and he was crying. He forgot to breathe. His heart forgot to beat.

She vanished for a moment inside the light, and as she vanished, ugly things reared up to replace her, crowding with

Julian inside their intimate seclusion. He fell to his knees, scraping the ground, his palms slamming into the dust to stop himself from plunging face first into the sand.

Blind and deaf, he swallowed fire and then was under ice. Death was falling out of the sky. Sound was everywhere, life was elsewhere. And then sound was nowhere. He was drowning in a vast ocean of want, of impossible struggle, of bottomless sorrow. Was that him who felt these things for her, getting iced in the liquid grief for all she wanted to be and would never be?

Julian, he heard dimly. Julian, what's the matter?

The bright light receded. His senses came back. He was in the dirt, on his knees, shivering, and she was in front of him holding on to his hands. She wasn't smiling anymore. She looked very concerned. "I'm so sorry. Are you okay?"

He stared into her face. She was blue, and she was dying. And as she was dying, she said, *come then, take the last warmth from my lips.*

Julian groaned.

"Anyone can stop a woman's life," he said, *"but no one her death: a thousand doors open onto it."* He clutched his throbbing right hand to his chest. It felt like blood was pouring out of his missing fingers. Oh my God. What was happening to him?

"What are you talking about, what doors?" Mirabelle said. "Everything's okay. It's just a trick of the light. When the sun is at zenith over the meridian, it sometimes does that, disperses in a kind of rainbow. It's just a pretty earth science thing. There's nothing to it."

She tried to help him up, but he lurched from her. Grabbing onto the stones, he pulled himself up and without dusting off, still clutching his hooked right hand to his chest, said, "Let's go."

In utter silence he staggered downhill. He didn't even brush the dust off his knees before climbing inside his spotless car.

"You want to go grab some lunch?" she said. "I'm starved. My treat."

"I can't. I got…things."

"You sure? You were so good to me today. I want to return the favor."

And for some reason he said, "*Today*?"

"What do you mean?" she said. "As opposed to another day?"

"I don't know what I mean," Julian said. He drove her to her house on Lyman.

"Are you really okay?" said Mirabelle. "You are still so pale. What happened to you up there?"

"I'm fine. Probably just oxygen deprivation. Not used to it. Well, here we are."

"The right place this time, thank goodness," she said. "One of these days, you'll have to tell me how you knew about Normandie." She saw him sitting with the car still in drive, the foot slammed against the brake, his hands on the wheel. "You're not even going to put the car into park?"

Reluctantly he shifted gears.

"Come in for a minute. I have to give you your dress back anyway. Come on, I'll make you a cup of coffee. You look like you need it."

"I'll wait here, if you don't mind. I have some calls to make."

She came back a few minutes later carrying the dress and laid it carefully in the back seat.

Julian didn't look at her. She began to say something, but he cut her off. "Well, so long," he said. "You're welcome," and peeled away before she could open her mouth to respond.

42

Inferno

"Jules?"

Julian opened his eyes. He was on the floor, in the corner of Ashton's bedroom, by the sliding glass doors leading to the pool. Ashton was sitting up in bed, having just woken up, staring at Julian.

Julian's body was stiff from sleeping coiled on the hard wood. Next time he might consider a pillow and a sleeping bag.

Next time? Next time he was going to have a nasty piece-of-shit dream and get so shook that he'd have to walk to Ashton's house, break into his friend's bedroom and sleep on the floor like a dog?

"Had a bad dream." Julian struggled to his feet.

Ashton appraised him. "Bad enough for you to sneak into my bedroom in the middle of the night?"

"Worse than that."

"Have you considered upping your dosage?"

"Go to hell."

"What was the dream about?"

Julian waved him off, made a joke, refused to say. But the dream was so awful that before he lay in the corner, he leaned over Ashton's bed, and pressed his hand against his friend's sleeping head to make sure it was still warm.

He creeps on black ice, slipping and falling and crawling, trying desperately to get to something in the frozen grass. With his hands numb from the cold, he digs through the hard blades and when he looks at his hands he is missing all of his fingers and black blood is pouring out onto the ice. With the mutilated nubs of what's left he scratches through the grass to get to the ditch underneath. In the trench, dozens of pale babies, sculptures made of ice, crawl on their cracking and breaking limbs. Julian's blood drips onto their snowy backs. And underneath their crystal knees lies a dead and mangled Ashton.

∞

Mirabelle sauntered into his gym a day later while Julian was training Buster. She was fresh and dewy, wearing a strapless, casual, pull-on milk-chocolate sundress. Her hair was styled half-up, half-down in meticulous cascading waves, and she wore open-toe platform sandals, not boots, and lots of bangles on her wrists, bangles that jingled with her every bouncy step. And that wasn't the only thing that was bouncy. She wasn't wearing a bra, her perky breasts bobbing as she sashayed toward him, the nipples eye-popping through the thin cotton fabric.

When Julian saw her, he forgot to duck and got walloped by the guy getting ready for a title fight.

"See, this is why you should switch to tennis," Mirabelle said, coming close to the apron of the ring and peering at him through the ropes as he lay on the floor. "If you screw up in tennis, it's 15-love. If you screw up in boxing, it's your ass."

"I didn't screw up," he said, pulling himself up and moving his sore jaw around. "You distracted me."

She smiled like that was the best thing she'd heard all week, that she distracted him. He didn't smile back. He didn't, because he couldn't.

He leaned over the ropes looking down at her gazing up at him. "What are you doing here?" A boxing gym was no place for beguiling gleaming girls.

From her bag Mirabelle pulled out his book. "I went to Book Soup last night and picked up a copy. Boy, do they love you there.

You have a whole display. Book's amazing, by the way. I finished it in one sitting."

"It's not exactly *The Brothers Karamazov*."

"It's much more readable. First of all, it's in English." She kept on smiling. "I want more. When's the sequel coming out? Can you sign it for me?" She took out a Sharpie, like he had come off the stage, and she was waiting for him at the barricades, waving her playbill around.

He was sweaty, dressed in a black tank and boxing shorts, in other words barely dressed. She had her eye trained solely on him, while every guy at the gym was focused only on her. Except for Julian. He could barely look at her. He told her he'd meet her outside in fifteen, then realized he'd just asked a girl to wait out in the parking lot for him, knowing she didn't have a car. Real classy, Jules. He gave her the keys to his Mercedes. "Turn on the AC if you want. I'll be right out."

She was sitting on top of his hood with her legs crossed humming to herself when he walked out, showered and dressed for the day: jeans, a collared shirt, a thin black leather jacket.

"I don't know how men do that, get ready so quick," Mirabelle said, hopping off and smiling. "It took me two hours to put myself together this morning."

Julian said nothing. Two hours and she forgot to put on a bra.

"Can you sign my book?" She handed him a pen.

To Mirabelle, he wrote, *may you never get sucker punched, but if you do, know how to take it. Best, Julian.*

They stood in the morning California sun, she twinkling at him, he like a gloomy Sunday. She tried again. "I learned a boxing joke," she said. "Want to hear? Why don't boxers have sex before a fight? Because they don't fancy each other."

"Ha." Julian said ha. He didn't actually *do* ha.

"Are you hungry?" she said. "There's a place called HomeState around the corner from me. They make great breakfast tacos with spicy chorizo."

He knew the place well. Many mornings he and Ashton ate there before Treasure Box. "I can't, I've got stuff."

"Always with the stuff. Even busy people make time for breakfast. It's the most important meal of the day, you know."

"How did you get here?" He looked around the lot.

"Z dropped me off. She'll be in Sacramento the rest of the week. So the apartment's all mine for a change." A beat. "There's no one home."

"Ah," Julian said, not meeting her eye. "Well, do you want me to drop you off at home or at HomeState?"

There was another brief breathy silence. "Why don't you come over? I'll make you breakfast."

"I can't, I've got a meeting at CBS and…"

"What about after CBS? How about dinner? I'll cook. What do you like to eat? I'll make whatever you want. Burgers? Steak? I can make roast potatoes and Yorkshire pudding. My mom taught me. I bake mean chocolate chip cookies. You like those, don't you?"

"Yes, but I can't tonight."

"So when's good? Any night this week is okay."

His head was swimming. There was nowhere to look. At the ground were her long bare legs and red-painted toenails. If he looked up, there were her glossy smiling red lips and her Bambi eyes. And in between were her eager standout nipples. What was that easy-on, easy-off dress even held up by? There were no straps, no sleeves, barely any elastic. One deep breath, one tug and—

Julian pulled out his phone. "How about I call you." He couldn't look into her bright beaming face. She read off her number to him, he punched it into his phone, and she stood next to him, looking over his hand, telling him to press the call button to make sure he got all 10 digits right. Her bare arm pressed against his leather jacket. She smelled of coconut lotion, of freshly washed hair, of coffee and mint breath, of musk.

Julian didn't call her. A few times she called him, left messages. He didn't return them. He stopped going to Coffee

Plus Food and to HomeState. For the first time in many years, he skipped the gym in the mornings and arranged with Buster to meet up later in the day instead. Maybe soon she'd get the drift and stop calling. He really hoped so. Because the next step was going to be changing gyms and getting a new number.

Nearly every night Julian thrashed through dreams from which he would wake drenched in sweat, panting, sometimes even screaming. He became afraid of closing his eyes at night.

He kept disturbing Ashton with his dementia at all hours. He dreamed of Riley shaking Ashton's body, shrieking at him as if they were in a fight, not realizing he was already dead. Everyone was in the ditch with Ashton—ice babies, Riley, Julian. He dreamed of dragging what he thought was a man's corpse through London streets, looking for a place to dump him, but when he threw the man in a ditch, it was Mirabelle. And sometimes, it was Ashton. And sometimes it was Julian himself. He dreamed of being choked, of being pelted with rocks and glass, sometimes with parachute mines, and sometimes with babies.

He dreamed of Normandie.

Pushing, pushing, pushing past the backs of people, like he just had to see what was there, and on the street lay a dead Ashton. And a dead Mirabelle. Unsayable things happened on Normandie, the street he had never been on before last week and which now was a boiling river of blood.

In the middle of one especially smothering night, he and Ashton climbed upstairs on the roof deck, sat in their shorts with jackets draped over their naked shoulders, sat shivering in the dark, high in the mountains, and stared at the gleaming lights of Los Angeles valley, listening for the sound of the coyotes, trying to make sense of things.

Julian hid his face from his friend. He didn't know what was happening to him. Everything had been all right for years. Since the craniotomy and the induced coma, he had lived mostly dream free. It's true, when he had been under the coma's evil spell, he dreamed then, too, though he'd forgotten about what. Something unbearable. In some ways it was worse than this. At least now he could wake up. Then, he was forced to keep dreaming until the circle-jerk doctors deigned to bring him out of it. He had been at their mercy, they never gave him a choice. Had they asked him, he would've told them what to do with their fucking induced coma.

He had told Ashton about some of the dreams, about the embattled, endangered girl whom he had just met, whom he barely knew. He didn't tell him about the worst of the worst— the infant boy in the fire and the heart eaters—which he simply could not put into words. But he had told him about the great burning city and the black screaming caves.

Tonight, Julian told him nothing.

He couldn't confess to Ashton about the bloodied ice babies shattering like glass over his corpse.

"Please, bro, I don't need your penance stare in the middle of the fucking night. We have four meetings tomorrow. I need to be sharp, I can't deal with this."

"I think you need to make peace with your father," Julian said.

"What?"

"I know. It's not easy. He hasn't been…you're the child, and he's the parent; you're not supposed to make the first move. But he isn't going to. He's only the way he is because he lost his own father too young, and he doesn't know how to be a dad to anyone past the age of twelve."

"I don't know what you're talking about. I told you my dad didn't have a dad."

"The one-armed man who raised him."

"You're nuts. And how did you know he was one-armed? Did I tell you that?"

"I don't know," Julian said. "Did you?" The one-armed man walked through nearly every vivid street of Julian's dreams. Someone in his dreams was always without arms, or fingers, or eyes. Especially Julian. In his dreams, he was always one-eyed and mutilated. He took a breath. "Ash, do you remember how you once told me you wished you could live your life over, so you could live it without regret?"

"I never said that. Live your life over? Now *that* sounds like a nightmare."

"You said it. You said you wanted a rewrite."

"Jules, I promise you, it's not even close to something I think, much less would say."

"Your dad lives with a lot of regrets. Let him know who you are. You'll be glad you did."

"Yeah, 'kay. I'm going to get right on that. Can I go to bed now?"

"Trust me, Ashton, there comes a time in every man's life when he says or does something that surprises the shit out of him. The regret thing may not sound like you, but in a few years, you won't recognize yourself. You'll stop being the person you are and become a person who says shit like that."

"So have I said it to you or not?"

"One hundred percent you said it to me. What has your story been so far? You've been wandering like most of us, living in all the long minutes of your life. And you'll continue to have your bright days before you end up alive in the horror."

"What are you talking about, what horror?"

"Despite your hard knocks, you don't hate the world or God or the moon, and that's *good*. In one of my dreams," Julian said, "I drifted down a very long river, and at the end of it you were saved. I don't think I've ever felt happier in my life."

"In the dream or in real life?"

"Yes," said Julian.

"So now they're happy dreams?"

"Now," Julian said, "you'll go on, like you've been going on. You'll make new friends to go drinking with and for years you'll sit with them, ceaselessly talking about nothing."

"Jules, I swear…"

"Look, I know you're a mule, but shut up and listen. I can't answer all your questions, and trust me, you don't want me to, but I'm begging you, stop doing the thing you always do. You think you can wade ankle deep in your life, and that everything will somehow work out fine because it has so far." Julian shuddered. "But, Ashton, some things are not going to work out."

"What things?"

Julian wouldn't say. Couldn't say.

"Is it possible to be slightly less, oh I don't know—crazy?" Ashton said.

"You want me to be less crazy?"

"Yes—fuck—*please*."

"Give Riley back her life." Like Julian was giving Mirabelle back her life.

"Riley?"

"She needs to be free of you," Julian said. "I don't know how else to say it." *Ask him to do something*, he heard a wise man's voice in his head say. *If he obeys, he can be healed. If he doesn't, he cannot.*

"Riley and I are great, we made up, we're all good," Ashton said. "You do understand that I can't operate in the real world because you saw something idiotic in your phantom world, you do understand that, right?"

"You will hang them both like puppets on a string," Julian said, "and the string will break. And everybody will break with it. There will be *nothing* left." At last, Julian stared into Ashton's face. "*Nothing*."

"What the *hell* are you talking about?" Ashton exclaimed. "You need to have your head examined. I think all your old injuries have resurfaced. Who's *them both* in that scenario?"

"Maybe she hasn't come yet. And maybe she has."

Ashton said nothing.

Julian nodded. "You're playing it cool. I'm used to it. You act as if nothing is real, or will last, or has meaning. Eventually you'll be right. By not choosing, you're choosing. You're choosing not to choose. You're choosing nothing, not even yourself.

Remember how you wrote that your heart searches all your days for something it cannot name?"

"I *never* in my life wrote that or said that!"

"You did. You will. It's written on your grave." Groaning, Julian looked away. He couldn't bear to see his friend's face. "And just so we're clear," he said, "in case there is any doubt, I like Riley, I love Riley, but you know that *you're* the one I'm trying to protect. You are my ride or die. I'm begging you, Ashton. Let her go—and save yourself."

43

The Julian by Diane von Furstenberg

A WEEK LATER AROUND NOON, JULIAN AND RILEY WALKED out of his gym together. She was draped around his arm, and they were laughing at some private joke. Mirabelle was waiting for him near his convertible. Julian didn't want his shoulders to slump when he saw her, but he couldn't help himself. The heaviness he felt every time his heart said her name would not lift. It was like fog with cement in it.

"I'll see you later, Riles," he said, leaning in to kiss Riley's cheek. "I gotta…"

"Yeah, yeah, you gotta," she said, kissing him back with a smile. "Don't forget to gargle with coconut oil when you shower. It's called pulling."

"Oh, to be sure, my next stop will be for some coconut oil."

"It should be," Riley said. "Coconut oil has many uses. Teeth whitener. Skin moisturizer. Personal lubricant."

"Shut up," he said, poking Riley in the ribs, and walking up to Mirabelle.

She wore a silky floral wraparound dress, high heels, red lips. Skimming the length of her thighs, the dress fit like a second skin over her narrow waist, her slim round hips. The neckline ended in a deep v between her breasts.

"Hey," she said. She wasn't smiling or bubbly.

"Hey." Julian waved to Riley who honked as she drove off.

"Can we talk for a minute?"

"Sure. What's up?" He stared at the pavement.

"I mean...can we go sit down somewhere?"

Trying not to sigh, he took out his keys. "You want to grab a cup of coffee? I have a few minutes. Are you hungry?"

They went to the Griddle Café on Sunset and sat at a table on the sidewalk, across from the Laugh Factory and down the street from the white Chateau Marmont rising on a hill over Sunset. At first they avoided any real conversation by discussing the merits of red velvet pancakes and The Golden Ticket—banana nana originals for the dreamers of dreams.

When the food came, Mirabelle fiddled with her undrunk coffee, stabbed her pancakes with a fork and didn't eat. "Look, I understand you don't want to be with me," she said. "You've made that pretty clear. I get it. And I'm okay with it. Really. It's for the best, anyway, because I auditioned for that London part I was telling you about, and I have a really good feeling about it. So I'm not going to be around much longer."

Julian winced.

"But I need you to explain to me what I did," she said. "This isn't kind. I need to know, so that next time, like when I'm in London, and I meet someone else, I don't do the same thing or will at least try to do things differently. If I can work on it, I want to."

"There's nothing to explain," Julian said.

"I thought you and I had something."

It was Julian's turn to stab his food with a fork. Of course, at that moment, the waiter came over to ask if everything was all right with their food, since after all, it was the *Griddle Café!* and they hadn't taken a *single* bite. To get him to leave them alone, they nibbled on their food mindlessly.

"You don't think we had something?"

"Maybe. I guess," he replied with as casual a shrug as he could muster. "The timing's just off."

"Why? Are you engaged to someone else?"

"No." He and Gwen kept talking on the phone, but they both knew it was over.

"Because I'm not. That guy I wrote you about before, he's old news. I've gone out with a couple of guys since, but nothing serious. I live with Z, honest."

"I believe you," Julian said. "Why wouldn't I believe you?"

"So what is it, then?" she said. "Is it because I'm broke? I'll make more. I'm always working. I'm a hard worker. I go on a dozen auditions a week. I'm always trying. You said yourself trying again is the important thing. I'll get there."

"I know you will, and what do I care about your money?" For some reason he cringed at that, too. What was with him?

"Is it because I'm an actress? Some people don't like to date actresses. Is that it? Because you think we're selfish, always me, me, me?"

"No."

"Performing has been my whole life, ever since I was a kid working with my dad. I can't explain it. It's in my blood."

"You don't have to explain it."

"It's not because I don't drive, is it? I failed my test last year, but I've signed up for lessons again. I'll get my license."

"No."

"So what is it? Don't make me play twenty questions. Just tell me."

Julian didn't know why his soul filled up with such unrelenting horrors. He was sure it had everything to do with her. "Something happened to me when we were up in the mountains—"

"I knew it!" Mirabelle exclaimed. "You hate that new age mumbo-jumbo."

"That's not it."

"Z warned me not to take you there, and I didn't listen!"

Reaching out, Julian took her hand. "Mia," he said, squeezing her lightly, "you keep guessing, but let me finish. Let me tell you what you asked me to tell you."

She fell quiet but would not let him release her hand. He couldn't hold on to her and tell her what he was about to tell her. The expression in her eyes—vulnerable, full of yearning, in a teary communion with him—was making him incoherent. He pulled away. Her eyes welled up.

"When we were up in the mountains," Julian said, "I saw things that I didn't want to see, that I wish to God I had not seen. It made me feel so bad, it hurt me so deeply that I still haven't recovered. I wanted to wait to call you until after I've calmed down. The trouble is…" He paused. He knew she wasn't going to take the next part well. "Not only have I not calmed down, I've gotten worse. What I briefly felt in the mountains has spilled over into my nightmares. I can't sleep anymore. I'm a zombie during the day. Ashton is ready to pack up and move. He says I'm ruining his life, too."

"But how is that my fault? I didn't do that."

"Because every time I so much as think your *name*, Mirabelle," Julian said intensely, "I feel such crushing despair that it makes it nearly impossible for me to live my life. I don't know *why*. I can't explain it. But I need to get away from you, not get nearer. Otherwise I'm going to lose my mind."

She started to cry.

"I'm sorry," he said, taking out a pack of tissues from his jacket pocket and handing them to her.

"Aren't you the hero, carrying around tissues in case somebody cries."

"I'm sorry," he repeated. "Trust me, I can't be any good to you like this."

"Who says I want you to be good to me?"

"Come on…"

With shaking hands, she put on her sunglasses. He put on his. They still stared at each other but now through black barricades.

"You asked me to be honest," he said.

"Yes, and thank you very much." Her lip quivered.

"You're a nice girl." *Very* nice. "Any guy would be lucky to call you his."

"You mean any *other* guy."

"Yes," Julian said. "That's what I mean."

"But I don't want *another* guy to call me his," Mirabelle whispered.

"Are you not listening to me?"

She rummaged through her bag and pulled out the crystal necklace. At the sight of it, Julian flinched as if she had hit him across the face with it. "Do you remember this?" she said.

"Oh, yes," Julian replied, looking down into his plate. "I keep seeing it in my nightmares, exploding like a tactical nuke, its shards slicing up everyone I care about until we all bleed to death."

Gasping, Mirabelle stood from the table, marched across the short sidewalk to the curb on Sunset, and flung the crystal quartz into the storm drain. It dinged when it hit bottom. She came back to her seat. "It's been in my family since the Second World War," she said. "But I don't care about the stone. I'm sorry I ever showed it to you. What happened to you up there has never happened to me. I stand inside a festival of color and I make wishes, that's all. It's harmless fun. I thought you and I could make a wish together. I didn't know it was going to be so upsetting, honest."

"I know you didn't."

"But thank you for telling me," she said. "Because now I won't make the same mistake with some other poor schmuck who might be into me. I was trying to entice you, not drive you away."

"I know." Julian's gaze was turned to the street. He couldn't take his eyes off the grate through which the crystal had fallen. It's like the stone had a life of its own. He was going to be picturing the quartz in that storm drain for the rest of his life. The crystal lying there, eventually splintering apart, the glass ashes melting into the water table, rising up with the wind, being carried through the air, forever infusing the earth and the plants and the fruit and the atoms of all living things with its great and terrible power.

Not looking at each other, they sat stabbing their pancakes until they were dead.

"Do you want to tell me about your dreams?" she said.

"Absolutely not."

"Sometimes talking helps."

"This is not one of those times."

"Why?" she said with a sniffly chuckle. "Are they about me?"

He didn't look up.

"Wait," Mirabelle said. "Your dreams are about *me*?"

"Not like that."

"Julian, can you please look at me?"

He looked but he was hiding behind his shades.

"You *dream* about me?"

"Not like *that*." Though sometimes like that, too. Not often enough.

"Like what?" Her soft breathy voice lowered a notch, the tempo of her words slowed.

"It's nothing good." Though sometimes it was.

"But just so I'm clear—you see *me* at night in your bed when you take off your clothes and go to sleep?"

"Nothing *good*, Mirabelle."

"You dream of *me*," she said, relaxing slightly. "Not about that tall blonde supermodel you left the gym with."

"Who, Riley? She's Ashton's girlfriend. No, I dream about her, too," Julian said.

"Does your best friend know you're seeing his girl on the side and dreaming of her?"

Julian almost laughed. "I'm not seeing her on the side. She's my friend."

"Do all your female friends look like her?"

"No. Just her." Behind the sunglasses, his eyes twinkled lightly. If this was a normal brunch, they would have twinkled long ago. There would've been teasing and flirting and joking. "She likes to watch me box."

"I bet," said Mirabelle.

"She thinks she's my life coach. She gives me health tips."

"I have a health tip for you," Mirabelle said, leaning forward. "Smiling for sixty seconds triggers the serotonin in your brain and makes you feel better. Even if you're in a crap mood and don't want to smile, it still makes you feel better."

"Huh."

"Try it now. Like this." She took off her sunglasses, wiped her eyes, and shined her shining shine on him.

He grimaced.

"Not good, Jules," Mirabelle said. "Not good at all." She sat quietly, pondering something. He motioned for the check. But she shooed the waiter away after asking for some fresh coffee and a chocolate shake, and continued to sit, still mulling, still thinking.

"Mia, I gotta go—"

"So here's my question," she said, interrupting him. "How do you know your dreams won't stop as soon as you take me to dinner?"

"Why would they stop if I took you to dinner?"

"Why would they not?"

"You think dreams can be bribed?"

"I don't know how dreams work, I'm not Freud," she said. "But how do you know it's not your suppressed desire to take me to a movie and dinner that's causing them? I mean, what have you tried so far? Sleeping on the other side of the bed? Leaving the lights on? Pfft. Piker. Maybe the answer is a movie and dinner. With me."

Julian shook his head as Mirabelle's drinks arrived.

"That's fine," she said, examining her nails. "Clearly the dreams must not be that bad. Because if you *really* wanted them to stop, you'd try anything."

"I don't think that's how it works."

"If you know how it works, then why are you still having nightmares?" She took a long slurpy sip of her milkshake. "This is clearly a problem in search of a solution. Personally, if it was me, I'd try everything until they went away."

Julian took a breath. "Everything?"

"*Everything*," she repeated, lowering her voice another notch.

What was a man to do?

Her freshly washed long-flowing hair, her musky floral perfume, her slinky snug summer dress, the scent of coconut (!), her lovely face, all of her was stirring the swirling hot molasses inside his body.

He remembered that in his dreams she died. And he watched her die, knowing every second until her death that she was dying.

She rolled up a piece of napkin into a spitball and blew it at him from her straw.

"Are you thinking about how much you want the dreams to stop?"

"Something like that," he said.

"So much that you're finally willing to take a nice girl out to a movie and dinner?"

"Something like that. But you mean dinner and a movie, right?"

"No," she said. "Movie first. Then dinner. You pick the movie." She could barely keep her voice from exultation. "As long as it's something vaguely superhero-y. And I'll pick dinner. That's only fair. But I pay for the movie, and you pay for dinner."

"That's only fair," Julian said.

They went to ArcLight on Sunset to see a matinee of the latest Marvel flick. Mirabelle said she didn't want any popcorn, and then munched on his the entire movie, sitting pressed against him, half turned to him, taking up his entire armrest, and constantly leaving her hand inside the bucket. "Popcorn's good here," she kept whispering. Of course it was freezing in the theatre and he had to give her his jacket. Now it smelled like her.

For dinner she chose the Chateau Marmont. She'd never been, she said, and always wanted to see what it was like. "Plus," she said, as they were driving back west along Sunset, "it's like the boxer Jack Johnson says—just because you have muscular strength and the courage to use it in violent contests with other men does not mean that you should lack appreciation for the finer things in life. I don't know if you know this, Julian, but Jack Johnson was the first black heavyweight champion of the world."

Julian suppressed a laugh. "You're quoting Jack Johnson to get me to take you to Chateau Marmont?"

"Whatever it takes."

"A simple 'I'd like to go' would've done it." He didn't want to add that even a smile and asking nicely wasn't necessary.

The valet at the Marmont said, "Are you staying with us tonight, sir?"

"No, no, just here for dinner," Julian quickly replied, ushering Mirabelle up the steps to the elevator before she could make a joke out of it.

"Am I dressed okay?" she asked, applying bright red lipstick in the elevator mirror.

"Yes, you're fine."

"It's a Diane von Furstenberg." She twirled around. "Cost me a month's rent, but it's called a *Julian* chiffon wrap dress. Some coincidence, right? How do I look?"

"Fine."

Shaking her head, she rolled her eyes. "You may look fly, Jules," Mirabelle said, sauntering past him as the elevator doors opened, "but you got no game."

Julian had never been accused of that before. "I meant, you look very nice."

"Yeah, yeah."

They walked up to the hostess podium. "It's pretty here," Mia whispered, looking around. "Swank. Art deco."

The hotel lounge was long and dark, lit by fake candles and lined with velvet couches that were at the moment empty as it was still early. She said she liked it. She took Julian's arm, pressing her body against his jacket. "Okay, Mister Smooth Talking Romeo, let's go dine with the beautiful people."

Under the glass ceiling of the outdoor veranda they sat in the back near the bar and watched the glitzy world fill up the restaurant, the famous filtering down into the center lounge, draping themselves carelessly over the low-backed chairs.

"Only celebrities can sit in the center, huh?" Mia said enviously. "Look at them, like they all live in *The Great Gatsby*. Don't they know *Gatsby* was an indictment to their shallowness, not a tribute?"

"It was a little bit of a tribute, too," Julian said. "No one wished harder or worked harder than Gatsby to turn his dream into reality. If only the beautiful people hadn't been so shallow."

The Avett Brothers kick-drummed their hearts and approached her door, and the Moscow mules went to Julian's head. They must have gone to Mia's, too, for she was half his size and was matching him drink for drink.

After they sat for hours, and he paid the check, they strolled to the darkened lobby lounge, where they ordered more drinks and she too draped herself carelessly over the arm of a red chair, her chiffon dress riding up, uncovering her thigh. "What do you think, do I look beautiful and shallow?" she asked, throwing back her head.

"Yes."

"Yeah, yeah."

They sank into the plush velvet couches. The glam of Hollywood filled up the rooms. Tipsy hours drifted by at the castle on a hill, while the chic celebrities bustled past them in their designer faded denim, wearing their rehearsed indifference like jewelry. The night was hot, and the fans failed to cool the stars whose skeletal bodies tottered by in their flamingo heels, the dazzling women with their fake casual men by their sides. Julian's dazzling woman, dressed in petals and daisies, was neither skeletal nor indifferent, and he was neither fake nor casual. Z once took her to a bar downtown, Mia said; did he want to go? Julian said no. Too many Moscow mules for him to drive, and she said that was fine; and why would they leave here anyway when they had a lobby like a fantasy, and he said, yeah, *that's* the reason.

"Well," she said, bobbing sideways and affecting a serious tone, which was difficult considering her intoxicated reclining posture. "Aren't you going to ask me what my favorite movie is?"

"Sure. What's your favorite movie?"

"*When We Were Kings*. I don't know if you know it. It's about Muhammad Ali's fight with George Foreman in Zaire."

"Um, yes, I know it," Julian said, his amusement rising, his tenderness rising, his lust rising, everything rising along with his heartbreak.

"Ask me what my favorite book is," she said. "Besides yours, of course."

"Of course. What is it?"

"*The Fight*," she replied. "It's Norman Mailer's account of the Zaire match between Ali and Foreman."

"I'm aware. It's one of my favorites, too."

"You don't say."

"When did you read it?"

She waved her hand around to some nebulous past. "So what's a boxer's favorite part of a joke?"

"I don't know, what?"

"The punchline!"

And Julian laughed.

"Oh, and I have a life hack for you," she said, languidly turning her head to him. "Did you know that alcohol is a fire starter?" She let her words linger.

"I knew that, yes," Julian said, his head already turned to her. He let his words linger.

"Okay, now you tell me a life hack," she said.

Not quick enough on his feet to come up with something more suggestive, Julian told her to put the little soaps she took from hotel rooms into her dresser drawers at home to keep everything smelling fresh and clean.

"What little soaps?"

"The ones they give you in hotel rooms," he said.

"I don't know anything about that," Mia said. "I've never stayed in a hotel room."

"You've never stayed in a hotel room?"

"Never," she said nonchalantly. "We lived on the ocean. My dad and I worked the boardwalk. Where would we go, to another ocean, to other Luna Parks? After my dad died, my mom and I lived carefully and never went anywhere. She had money, but she was saving it for my Ivy League education—joke on her."

"But not even later, by yourself? With..." Julian circled the air alluding to the guy she'd written to him about.

"The guy who wouldn't watch my favorite movie with me?" she said. "Nah."

Julian stared at her, unable to say all he wanted to say. Or anything, really.

Mirabelle waited, saying nothing herself, slurping the last of her icy drink, gazing around the dim lobby. The velvet place was dark, alit with firelight and chandeliers blue, and glimmering with L.A. goldlust.

"Mia, would you like me to ask if the Marmont has any rooms avai—"

"Yes," she said before he was finished. "I've dreamed about seeing one of these rooms ever since Dominick Dunne lived here when he covered the OJ trial in 1994. It sounded so romantic."

"The OJ trial?"

She giggled. "No, living in this hotel, writing copy on the balcony."

They meandered to the front desk. The hotel had only one kind of room left—a two-bedroom suite on the top floor overlooking Los Angeles.

"That sounds nice," Mia whispered. "And two bedrooms is perfect. One for you, one for me."

The clerk trained his slow-blink stare on Julian.

"Thank you," she said to Julian as he was paying. "I hope it wasn't too expensive. It'll be worth it if your dreams go away."

"And if they don't?"

"Tough break, then."

"Do you have any luggage we can help you with, Mr. Cruz?"

"We have no luggage," Mia said, holding on to Julian's arm, swaying from the booze, her breast pressing into his tricep. "Not even a toothbrush."

"Very well, miss. Have a good evening."

The suite was spectacular. The stucco balcony, part of it covered by a striped awning, was forty feet long and lined with red-flowering planters. They could see the last of the dying sun streaking violet and pink over a million palm trees. The view took their words away, and for a few minutes they stood in silence. For some reason, even that felt painfully familiar to Julian—standing with her on a balcony, looking out onto the beauty beyond.

She slipped off her strappy sandals and walked around barefoot, excitedly examining the dining room table, the TV, the fully equipped kitchen. She checked out the two bathrooms, the two bedrooms. "I call dibs on this one," she called to him from the master. He saw her bouncing up and down on the bed. "I could live here. It's the nicest place I've ever been to."

Julian's fists were clenched, and he said nothing. His visions showed him she had been to many places.

She bounded out to the balcony and stood by his side. "Is your house nice like this? Does it have a view like this? How many bedrooms do you have? Four? Hey, so I could stay with you, too, in one of your spare rooms. What do you need so many rooms for? So, what do you dream about? Come on. You know the first fight we'll have, you're going to attack me with those dreams. You're going to use them against me as a weapon. So why don't you neutralize their power by telling me about them now, when you can use them on me not as vengeance but seduction."

Mutely he regarded her. Was she joking?

"Don't give me your penance stare, Ghost Rider," she said, leaning back on her elbows against the stucco balustrade. "I can't be shamed, I've done nothing wrong. Just tell me what you dream about."

"No."

She dropped herself into a chair, crossing and uncrossing her legs. "Okay, so what *do* you want to do?"

"I don't know." He stared out onto Los Angeles. "What do *you* want to do?"

"I wanted to talk."

"Okay." He sat down. "But not about the dreams."

"Fine, about anything."

But Julian couldn't form words. She undid him. There was no sun in his bones, no light in his body. Free of gravity he flew above the moon, his soul broke loose. She was some terrible mutated sexual wandering spirit, almost whole. And then a different thing—an intoxicating, breathtaking thing—but death still came for her. All those graves, and a million miles of her to fill them all.

In silence they remained like this, sitting apart in their wicker armchairs. Music played somewhere down below, over the sound of dim laughing voices. Other voices.

Mirabelle inhaled like she was about to cry. "I don't know why you're acting like being here with me is the worst thing that ever happened to you," she said, her soft voice breaking. "Do you want to just take me home?"

"I think I do, Mirabelle," he whispered. "I'm sorry."

"What are you so worried about? What makes you think if we got together that we'd even stay together? We wouldn't, most likely. Nothing is permanent, especially in this town. Everything is just another set, waiting to be dismantled and hauled to the dumpster. We'd hook up, have some fun for a few weeks, a few laughs, nothing wrong with that. And then we'd go our separate ways." Her lips quivered. "It would end the way most things end. I'd think about you for a while. Maybe you'd think about me. I'd ache for you a little bit, the way one does when things are over, even things that aren't meant to be. I'd get busy with my life. You'd get busy with yours. We'd say we'd keep in touch. But we never would. And when people asked, we'd say we had a thing once, you and me. One minute it was, and the next it wasn't. It didn't mean it wasn't real. It just wasn't forever. And years later maybe we'd run into each other on the street somewhere, and you'd barely remember my name. And I'd barely remember yours. I'd say to you, hey, remember how you once loved me? And you'd say sorry, not really. And I'd say yeah, me neither."

Julian's eyes welled up. He couldn't look at her.

Her shoulders were quaking. After a few moments she shrugged, like it was all never mind, got up and went inside. He heard her put on some music, a smoky R&B playlist. It sounded like Ginuwine. Yup. There was "Pony."

"I want to take a shower before we go," she said. "Our hot water tank broke. Is that okay?"

She showered with the door half open while Julian sat on the balcony and stared at the sky. He may have cried.

∞

Barefoot she came out and sat in a wicker chair away from him.

Julian said nothing to greet her. He barely acknowledged she was near. But he smelled her. She smelled of coconut verbena.

"You said to always leave on a joke," Mirabelle said.

"Let's hear it."

"Do you ever sit on the bus, and the driver announces that the bus is being held at the station, and you think, gee, I wonder what it's like to be held?"

Julian sucked in his breath at the suddenness of that, at the fragile look on her face, but said *nothing.*

"I don't know what's wrong with me," she said. "What kind of girl am I to come with a man I barely know to a hilly dark chateau where people die?"

"People live here, too," he replied.

"Yes," Mia said. "Other people. Who aren't so blue. They come together under the stars, dance a little, maybe hum 'Endless Love' or 'I Hope That I Don't Fall in Love With You.'"

Julian turned away from the night sky, to her. She was damp, wearing her wrap dress loose and barely tied. Underneath the sheer chiffon she was naked. Her eyes stared at him with ineffable longing.

"I hope that I don't fall in love with you," she whispered achingly.

"And I hope that I don't fall in love with you," he said.

"Okay, so don't."

Julian stood up.

Her stretched-out legs parted slightly. "Don't fall in love with me," she said. "But maybe you'd like to touch me?"

Love is modern like a Thursday night, and a black hole swallows every shooting star.

Julian stepped between her legs, leaned over her, his arms locked on the chair rests, and kissed her. Holding on to his forearms, she moaned, her head tipping up. The chair wobbled, out of balance, and they nearly fell back.

He knelt between her legs, wrapping his arms around her. Her arms wrapped around him. Julian couldn't explain how full up he felt. And she kissed him back like she was pretty full up herself.

Let's go inside, he whispered, tugging on her nipples through the silk, listening to her moan, running his hands under her dress.

No, she said. Right here. Under the open sky. The night was hot, a night of the tropics, not of the desert.

He pulled apart her wraparound dress. Her body spilled out.

You smell like coconut.

It's coconut oil. I carry some with me. Do you like it?

I like you.

When his mouth found her nipples, she didn't even try to keep quiet. And he kissed her as if he'd never touched a girl before, spread her open like he'd never seen a girl before. His fingers trembled. Her body trembled. He was still on his knees.

Mia, can you try to be quiet. He lowered his head between her legs.

If you try not to be afraid.

He made no promises.

You're still wearing your clothes, and I'm naked, she whispered.

Yes. He caressed her.

Julian, look at me. Can you see me?

Oh, beautiful girl, I see you.

Put your hands on me. Her back arched.

They're on you.

Put your lips on me. Her legs quivered.

They're on you.

O my God.

O my *God*.

She couldn't hold herself up. Clutching his head, she kept sliding forward. He had to stop. His mouth over her was about to bring the hotel security to their door.

Hoisting her into his arms, he carried her to the bedroom, her clinging to him like a marsupial, her bare buttocks in his palms. His clothes came off.

Finally, his hard body collided with her soft body.

She cried out like she was weeping.

Mia, Mia.

She was too open, too delicious, too defenseless, too willing to receive him, too excited to be touched by him, too fragile. She was *too* everything.

Whatever he did to her, she said was good.

It's good, it's good, it's good.

Yeah, that's good, too.

She turned over for him, let him press his hands into the small of her back, her face in the pillows. She lay flat on her stomach for him, her fingers spread out in the sheets.

Oh, it is *so* good.

Just make it last.

Briefly they lay in a saturated respite.

I've wanted to touch you for so long, Julian, she whispered, her hands stroking him gently, gently, gliding on him, caressing him. I wanted to feel you in my hands since I first met you. Since you wore your Armani to impress the understudy.

An Armani is timeless in any age, suitable for any occasion, he said. What I mean to say is, I'm glad I found my way into your hands.

I can't explain it, she said. I looked at you, and it was like the light came on.

You don't have to explain it, Mirabelle.

She knelt between his legs. I wanted to feel you in my mouth since the first day I met you. I know. I deserve your penance stare for that. It's pretty shameful. She lowered her head to him, her long hair tickling his stomach.

Julian wanted to say he was glad he found his way into her mouth but couldn't speak.

Afterward he asked her to get the coconut oil she carried in her bag.

She gave him the small jar. Will it be enough?

No, he said. But it will do. Rubbing it into his hands, he kneaded and caressed her whole warm moaning glistening body, circling her with his knuckles and palms from her neck to the soles of her feet. He made her slippery all over, as if she weren't slippery enough, and then kissed her where his hands had just been, from her neck to the soles of her feet and everything in between. She moaned with the astonishment of angels. Her abandoned cries were a ratchet in his loins.

You are so sweet, Mia.

My God, it is *so so* good.

He soldered himself to her molten body.

She was gasping, and helpless, and wordless, and writhing. One unbroken rapture, one continuous cry.

Release brought tears that felt like happiness but looked like pain.

Release brought tears that looked like happiness but felt like pain.

Oh, *Julian*, she whispered, kissing his neck, holding his face, how do you know how to touch me like that?

Like what, Mia? Shh. Don't cry, why are you crying? He wiped the tears from her eyes.

Like I *love* to be touched, how do you know how to do that? Who *are* you? Why do you make love to me like you *know* me?

He wanted to tell her it was true: she felt familiar—yet new. He had seen her in his dreams and sometimes, before they turned into nightmares, he touched her. But not like this. Nothing was like this. Because the impassioned drenched girl in his hands was real.

Love me until I say no more, the real girl whispered, giving her body to him over and over. *Take me until I say no more.*

But she wouldn't say no more.

Love me, love me, love me, love me, love me.

What she said was, Julian, my every breath exhales me and inhales you until all that's left inside me is *you*. All that's left inside me is you, Julian. Do you hear me?

I do. All that was inside me is now inside you. He watched her face. Why are you looking at me like that?

Like what?

I don't know. Like I'm all you want.

Do *anything* you want, she whispered in reply, grabbing on to the headboard. Take *anything* you want.

And Julian took it.

Deep in the night, she went to get him water. He looked thirsty to her, Mirabelle said. She rummaged through the shelves in the kitchen to find a tic tac. She turned on the oven. She called room service from the living area, quietly talked to them on the phone, waited for them by the door, and tipped the guy out of her own money. Julian waited on the bed, flat on his back, knocked down but not out. Something smelled good, besides her. A toaster popped. She brought in toast and jam and hot tea with lemon—and warm chocolate chip cookies. I baked them, she said. I asked room service for cookie dough. They were very accommodating. A man needs his strength, she said. You never know what he might be called upon to do.

You mean there is something more he might be called upon to do? Julian said.

She watched him eat and drink, and then crawled into his arms, pressing her body into him, stroking him with her slickened hands.

Why can't I get enough of you? she murmured. I've had so much of you. Too much. I'm raw. Yet I still want more.

He pushed the plate of food onto the floor.

You want more?

Her arms flew above her head. Her body softened, flattened out.

Mia, Mia.

She cried out.

Come inside me again, come inside me, come inside, come.

She makes hungry where she most satisfies.

44

Mystique and Doctor Doom

THE NEXT MORNING THEY STAYED IN BED. SILENTLY SHE gawped at him with an expression you could pour over waffles. She had ordered raw eggs from room service and scrambled them herself; she brought him coffee, juice, toast; she sat in bed, propped up against the pillows, and watched him eat.

"You're not very chatty this morning," Julian said, lying on his side, smiling up into her face. "Surprising, because yesterday, you were an unstoppable chatting force."

"Yesterday," she said shyly, "I was trying to find a combination of words that would get you to touch me."

"Including telling me you watched *When We Were Kings* and read *The Fight*?" Julian laughed.

"They weren't just words. I really did that."

"When did you do that, yesterday?"

"No. Last week, if you must know."

"Last week," he repeated. "What's your actual favorite movie?"

"*Gone with the Wind*. Have you seen it?"

"No. Should I?" He smiled. He was teasing her.

"Only if you want to." She stared into her lap.

He rolled her onto her back and straddled her, threading his hands through her hair, stroking her face. She was gazing up at him like she was ice cream completely thawed out.

"Holy God, you are *so* fly," she whispered, rubbing his arms.

"But I got no game?" Julian liked making the naked girl underneath him blush.

"What, you wanted to prove me wrong?" She pinched him.

"I just want to hear you say it."

"Okay, fine, I admit it—you got a little bit of game. Happy?"

"So happy." He kissed her lips, her face. "So so happy."

They didn't have morning sex, they continued the nighttime sex.

Mia wanted the luxury black cashmere throw, a Marmont exclusive, for a souvenir, and Julian wanted her. He called the front desk and bought it even after he found out how much it cost. He made love to her in broad daylight as she lay naked on it, open and shimmering on top of the soft black wool.

He thought she would tell him not to get it messy, but she said, *get it as messy as you want.*

It was the best seven hundred bucks he ever spent.

They lived a week reclined at the Chateau Marmont.

They rented *Gone with the Wind.* They played Lego Marvel Super Heroes. They sat out on the balcony and watched the world go by. They discovered they were both born on the Ides of March, though on different years, less than an hour apart, she at 11:40 a.m., he at 12:29 p.m. It's almost like we are meant to be, Jules, she said. They danced. From housekeeping they requested toothbrushes. From room service they ordered champagne and steak. He ate around the edges and she ate the raw heart inside.

Julian told her about his life, the stuff outside the dark visions. In the little Marmont kitchen, she made him French toast with extra maple syrup, just like he liked; she made him Cajun grilled cheese sandwiches and lemon cookies. She told him about her life. About the roller derby and working at Sideshows by the Seashore, and how her mom never got over losing her dad. He told her about Topanga, the scar on his head, his lost ambition, his rebuilt career, about staying close to what he couldn't live without. She loved the scar on his head, loved the long wavy hair covering it, loved his eyes, his lips, his jacked arms, his chest, his gentlest hands, loved *everything*. "You are the sum of all your parts, but you are also your parts," she said.

"Is that all you've come for? My parts?"

"No, there is glory to all of you," said Mirabelle.

"Maybe it would be easier to list the things you don't love," he said, and she fell quiet.

"I don't love the dreams."

"Join the club," said Julian.

She told him about the cracked leather purse that was found on the body of her great-aunt Maria who died in the war, died all alone on Christmas on the floor of her house in Blackpool, told him about the contents of the purse: the crystal necklace and the wedding rings and the gold coins that allowed her entire family, aunts and uncles and cousins and mothers, to move to Brooklyn and start a new life. Julian told her he saw that purse in his dreams, but it wasn't in anyone's cold hands. It was hidden inside a wall. And Mia said, you mean a different purse, right? Yours isn't brown leather with gold ribbons. And he said right. But he meant wrong. What he also didn't tell her is that to get to the purse he had to scrape open the wall using nothing but his fingerless hands. What was inside *your* purse? she asked. The crystal, he said. And treasure, hidden in a pool of blood. You see, not the same at all, said Mia, and he said right but he meant wrong.

When she died, Maria's mother, Abigail—who had no other children—left all the gold coins to her sister Wilma and the rings and necklace to Wilma's youngest daughter, Kara, who left them to her daughter Ava, who was Mirabelle's mother. For some reason, Ava did not care for the crystal necklace, "much like you," Mia said, but her parents liked the rings. They wore them on their wedding day. Jack McKenzie was buried with his. "Mom gave me hers, said it was cursed. She gave me the crystal and the ring. I kept the crystal, because it was worth nothing, but sold the ring a few years ago when I was broke. What was I going to do with one wedding ring anyway?" Mia said. "I went to the gold district on 47th Street. I thought I'd get a couple of hundred bucks for it, if I was lucky. But guess how much that sucker was worth. Twenty-five *thousand* dollars! I nearly died. The dealer said it was some kind of rare gold, nearly all pure or something. I had one of the best years of my life living off that gold ring. I went to Mexico, to Puerto Rico, to St. Croix, where didn't I go. Z and I moved out here. All on that money. I can't believe my mom buried my dad with the other ring. I don't think she knew how much it was worth. What's Dad going to do with it now?"

"Not much, I should think," Julian said. "Um, did you say you went to St. Croix and Puerto Rico?"

"Yeah…why?"

"Where did you stay, Mia?" He poked her, tickled her. "Not hotel rooms, right?"

She laughed.

"I'm so easy," he said. "If you wanted me to get us a room at the Marmont, all you had to do was ask." He kissed her. "And not even that nicely."

"You're joking, right?" she said. "Do you remember nothing? I couldn't get you to so much as glance at me while I was buck naked in a see-through dress."

"I'm looking at you now."

"Now you know I'll say yes to anything, and you just want me to be bad."

"You're right, I do want you to be bad."

"Like right now?"

"Like right now."

Mia blew off her auditions. Julian blew off his life.

They spent the afternoons by the pool, tanning, lounging, swimming (in the bathing suits they bought at the hotel shop), playing Marco Polo, wondering which bungalow John Belushi had died in, playing Red Hands, which Julian, much to his delight and her frustration, always won. She asked him if he had ever killed a man. In dreams didn't count. Julian's right fingers twitched when he said no. Could you do it, she said, not accidentally, but like on purpose? He didn't know. He didn't think so. But maybe he would do what he had to do. Like to protect me? she asked with a giggle. Yes, he said solemnly. I would kill to protect you. She liked his answer. Her pupils dilated. Her breath quickened. Can you teach me how to fight like you?

I told you, I don't fight girls.

I'm not a girl. I'm me. Come on. Fight me. I can take it.

No, you can't.

I can. I can take a lot.

That was true. She took a lot. Her crazy sexy body—in a barely there string bikini—showed small suck marks all over, above her clavicles, on her upper back, between her thighs. She was covered with his purple love as with flower burns from an electrocution.

Are you going to stand there and gawk at me, Mr. Olympic boxer, she said, or are you going to fight me?

I'm going to stand here and gawk at you, he said.

She shoved him in the chest. He didn't block her. They say the hand is quicker than the eye, is that true?

It's true.

They say to never take your eye off your opponent, is that true? She went to push him again.

He stepped out of her way. It's true, he said.

Her eyes lit up. Aha! You're dodging me. Well, I'm never taking my eye off you.

She lunged again. He dodged again.

She smiled and skipped closer. He smiled and stepped away. Come on, she said. I'll be your sparring partner. Teach me.

I'll duck you, Mia, but I'm not going to fight you.

You'll what me? Oh, duck. She whacked him on the arm. Didn't get away that time, did you?

Didn't want to.

Yeah, sure. What's the matter, has all the love upstairs made you soft?

Trash talk isn't going to work on me.

So that's a yes? She shoved him. Come on, chicken, show me what you got.

Still no.

She put up her little dukes and danced around him on the pool deck. He weaved and bobbed right back. What are you afraid of, losing to a girl?

Yup, that's it.

She slapped her fists against his open palms. Why won't you make a fist? I know you know how. You rub me with your fists, don't you? She grinned. Why are your hands up and open? Are you surrendering?

Unconditionally, Julian said.

Come on, fight me, she said, bouncing up and down, everything on her bouncing up and down, knocking into him with her body, how can I learn to parry if you won't jab me? All you're doing is blocking and ducking me.

That's all I'm going to do, block and duck you.

Did you say duck? I keep mishearing you. Though I must admit, your reflexes are something else. Or am I just slow, like with Red Hands?

You're just slow.

Don't block me. Jab me. Come on, do it. You don't think I can block a jab?

I don't think you can, no.

Jab me and we'll see what we see. Don't be afraid. I'm tough, I'm tougher than I look.

Stay calm, Mia, he said. The harder you try to provoke me, the harder I'll counter. You don't want that, do you?

I do want that, she said, her smile ear to ear. That's *exactly* what I want.

You could get overpowered.

I'm shook, Mr. Big Talk. So, come on, then. I'd like to see you try. She shadowboxed around him. Jules, what's an uppercut? Wait, I think I know. Is that when you thrust—upwards? Can you show me how you do that—or did you forget?

He blocked her hand, grabbed her fist and pulled her by her wrist through the foliage to the elevator. She was going to ruin boxing for him. He was afraid they wouldn't make it all the way upstairs.

So you *do* know how to thrust upwards, she murmured, blissed out on the bed. You do know how to *fight* a girl.

Is *that* what you call it, said Julian.

Flying high up at the Marmont with the windows open, the sun silver in the sky, sometimes she glowed with inner light, and sometimes she was ink at night.

Why did Julian feel not blessed but wretched?

"Turn, Mirabelle," he whispered from *Paradiso.* *"O turn your holy eyes upon your faithful one, so he might see you, he who's come so far."* He held her to him. *"O splendor of eternal living light, he's drunk so deeply from your fountain. Unveil yourself, unveil your lips to him, so he may see the beauty you've kept concealed."*

"So there *is* beauty, after all?"

"You're the most beautiful thing I've ever laid my hands on." Tenderly he caressed her, lingering here, there. "From the first moment I saw you, you looked like bliss to me."

"Not concealed, O Julian. My body right here. *Take* it," she whispered. "Like you took my heart."

Julian knew: the pageant wasn't the Marmont. It was the girl. The girl with the sparkling face, sitting in a wicker chair, legs splayed, head tipping back; the girl like a sabbatical from life, the girl in whom one night was forever and forever was one night. The girl and not the castle was the dreamland outpost for all the hearts that ever did beat faster, shining bright in starlight above Sunset Boulevard.

∞

But his dreams got worse.

They showed him savage things. They made Julian crawl into other rooms, away from her. She found him like this in the dead of one night, curled up between the wall and the bed in the unused room, rocking. *He is walking around Normandie collecting pieces of her to put together into one whole body before her mother arrives in a cab from LAX, but the cab has turned the corner and he still can't find all of her.*

"Leave me," he said in a rasping voice. "Let me go. Please. Take a cab, I'll give you money. Go far. Save yourself. I promise you, nothing between us will come to any good."

She couldn't lift him off the floor. He wouldn't let her touch him. It took her a long while to lure him back to bed.

She pressed against him, wrapping all of her around all of him to stop him from shaking. And when that wasn't enough, she climbed on top of him, cradling his head in her arms, kissing his face, gently rubbing her large, first soft, then hard nipples against his days-old stubble. *Ouch, ouch, ouch,* she kept whispering.

"So stop doing that if it's ouch." But eventually he stopped shaking. His hands relaxed on her back.

I do it for you. There's nothing wrong, everything's all right, everything is wonderful. Why do you say those mean things to me? Sending me away, getting me a cab. They're just dreams, they're nothing, they're not real. The nipples, now those are real. She tapped them up and down into his sullen, half-open mouth. Come on, suck them. They're like a balm for your lips.

He kissed her nipples and turned his head away.

Don't turn away from me. But she didn't get off him.

Are you Mystique? he asked. Can you be Mystique? *So you could vanish.*

Why do you want me to be her? So I can vanish? Dream on, she said. I'm not going anywhere. But that's an *excellent* question. One not easily answered. Can I be Mystique? I guess first I'd want to know if there was any chance for a normal life if you stayed with me.

What if the answer is no? he said. And is that what you want, a normal life? *What even was a normal life.*

Isn't that what everybody wants?

I don't know, he said. The dreams were black sand in his eyes. Sometimes there was a glimpse of an ordinary life, a pink house, and inside the house there was a ship, and on the ship she lay dying.

I must admit, when I'm here with you, I don't think a normal life is possible, Mia said. Because you make me feel extraordinary. But you have to talk to me and tell me what you're afraid of. I can't answer you until you do. What are you afraid of, Doctor Doom? That I'll betray you? That we're just a passing thing?

She could not even fathom the terror. All the stars fell from the sky into her heart. He couldn't tell her. Sometimes there was a serene white house, and the house was on fire, and inside she lay under a burning beam and no matter how hard he tried, he could not pull her out.

I'm not naïve, she said. You think I don't know your other nickname for yourself, Doctor Doom? It's *Death*, isn't it?

Yes, Mystique. It is.

Is *that* what you're afraid of—that I'm doomed to die?

He didn't answer her, as if he could.

Why? she said. Because you touched me? How can that be? You, with your softest mouth and your strongest hands. You who brings me nothing but ecstasy. It doesn't make sense.

He wouldn't tell her, no matter how much she kept soothing him with her nipples.

Do you want me to be Rogue instead? she said. So I can absorb your dreams and memories and know what you know without any additional words from you?

No, *never*, he said. I don't want you to absorb them. I don't want you to suffer. Haven't you suffered enough? Resist me. I beg you. Be *Mystique*. Julian stared at her with profound sadness. *Vanish from me. Like you vanish in my dreams. Go light up somebody else's life, Mirabelle. Go break someone else's heart.*

I will never resist you, she said. I adore you. I've never felt happier in my whole stupid life than I feel with you. I've never felt closer to anyone than I do to you. I don't know how you did that. Who are you?

Maybe I'm a phantom traveler, said Julian. Maybe we both are. Mystique and Doctor Doom together again, reunited for one last perilous escapade. He tried to joke, to smile, like she taught him.

Oh, Doctor Doom! Now I know how you did it. In one of our past adventures, in another life, you left a trace of yourself in me, so by this trace I could find you.

Maybe you left a trace of yourself in me. He swept up her body, twisting them both into a Mobius fever braid, his limbs around her. You're ageless, he said. You've slowed time inside yourself. In the dreams I see you take many forms, just like Mystique. That's how you defend your soul against marauders.

Marauders like you?

Julian admitted she didn't defend herself entirely successfully against him.

Didn't and don't want to, she said. Tell me one thing from your visions. Come on, just one benign thing. There has to be something.

He thought about it. Sometimes I see us riding white horses through green fields, he said. The horses gallop. We're both dressed the same, in top hats and velvet.

That's weird, she said. I've never been on a horse in my life.

Me neither, said Julian. They scare the shit out of me.

What a pair you and I make. She exclaimed it like it was all fun and games. Mystique and Doctor Doom riding horses in top hats and velvet! What do you think our adventure will be this time?

This one? Julian couldn't help himself. Like all the rest, he said. We'll try to hide from the hand of evil that draws its power from death and sin. The power that wants to consume us, to destroy you, to weaken your power over me until I'm nothing, to take away your power to rule my world, to ruin us.

What about your power to rule *my* world? she said. She thought they were still playing. But in the end we'll prevail!

No, Mirabelle, said Julian. We never prevail. We will fail.

A collapsed Mia, the smile wiped off her sunken face, fell mute. Boy, was I right, she said at last. Your dreams really *are* the darkness. Look at the things they're making you say to a naked adoring girl in your arms. Tumbling off him, pushing him away, she curled into the corner of the bed.

He lay for a few moments with his arm over his face, and then turned her onto her back, climbing on top of her in contrition. I'm sorry. I told you talking about it was no good. He kissed her, the beats of his heart pulsing into her mouth.

Don't hold yourself up, come here, she whispered, her hands on his back. Come closer. You're right about one thing, Jules. Whatever it is that makes you dream these bad things, it does want to ruin us. It's trying to separate us—even now. Especially now. Please don't let it. Isn't it better to lie entwined—to lie as one—as opposed to your way?

What way is that?

The dumb way. All broody and shaky, by yourself on the floor.

Aloud Julian said yes.

If you want to hide from your dreams, Mia said, don't go in the corner. Stay with me. I'm right here, in the ring with you, on center stage with you. She tilted her hips up to him.

I know where you are.

Stay with me, and I'll be Mystique for you or Rogue for you. I'll change for you, cut my hair off for you. Anything you want, I'll be that for you. Please let me. I'll bend your energy to my desire. I can do it. I have enhanced physical attributes, too. Like you.

He didn't think it was enough. Julian kissed her moaning throat.

Squeezing her hips around him to stop him from moving, Mia took his head into her hands, gazing up into his face with everything there was inside her. *Please love me*, Julian, she whispered. *Please*.

I'm trying, Mia. *Let me go. Free me.*

And who knows, maybe our story won't end like everything ends.

Maybe, he said.

Maybe our Marmont lust will become eternal passion. Maybe our brief ecstasy will be remade into enduring glory.

Maybe, he said.

I know you're worried about things, but you don't have to worry about me, honest.

Don't you understand? It's you I'm worried about most.

"But why? I'm yours. Can't you feel I'm yours?" She stroked his hair, his face. "Like Mystique, I'm an actress. I might take on another's outward form, but I *swear* to you, in my heart I will remain true to what I am. I swear, I will forever remain true to you. *Take my life.* I have never felt for anyone what I feel for you," Mirabelle said. "Don't you see that? Don't you feel that? I love you, Julian. I love you with all my soul."

45

Powers Devours

THE BASILISK, THE KING OF THE SERPENTS, WAS ENDOWED with a crown. He was the egg of the cock, hatched under a toad. One basilisk burned to the ground whatever Julian and Mia came near. Another wandered through their lives upright, and when they looked upon the heads of the Medusa, they died from the horror. Unlike other serpents, the basilisk walked arrogant and tall, withering the flowers, breathing death upon the hours and tearing stones like robes.

"She's going to die, Ashton," Julian said. "I feel it. No matter what I do, she is going to die." He and Mia had finally left the Marmont and returned to their lives, and that's where Julian was, returned to the roof deck with Ashton, shivering in the middle of the desert night.

"Dude, it's not true," Ashton said. "Well, I mean, yes, she is, because we all are eventually, but that's no way to live. Just look at you. You're a ghost, haunting my room at night."

"I don't know how to live anymore," Julian whispered.

"Look," Ashton said, "there are two ways you can do it. One is to know that you approach death with every hour of your life. And one is to feel like you're going to live forever. Even if you know it's not true. You and I are a good study in humanity. One way is your way—and look at you. And one way is mine—and look at me." Ashton grinned with all his teeth, flinging out his arms like a triumph on the stage. "So you tell me, which way is better?"

"Like it's even a choice."

"What, you don't think I can be all morbid and miserable like you?" Ashton said. "Well, maybe not. It's like living with a Russian. I had a girlfriend like you once. She was from St. Petersburg. Every single thing was a catastrophe with her. I couldn't run away fast enough. Who can live like that? Well, you, clearly. But who'd want to? If you don't cut this shit out, your angel Mirabelle is going to run from you, too."

"Not fast enough," Julian said.

∞

Julian walks and walks and walks and walks. He is exhausted, but he keeps on. It's cold and hot, it's ice and boiling, the buildings erupt, and the earth shakes. He walks through the caves and black holes, over lava and the craters in the streets. The leaves fall off the trees, and the blizzards come. His body gets thin, then emaciated, his hair grows long, then gray, then falls out. He bleeds from his arms, his legs, his back, and still he walks. He catches a reflection of himself in the black water. He is nothing but a skeleton. He looks at his arms. Radial bones. He looks at his legs. Femoral bones. Long bones in his feet, and his ribs are like cages, and still he walks. The bridges look familiar, the buildings, the river. Another once around the scorched earth, and another, and another, a circle he can't break out of. In horror he realizes that if he doesn't wake up and do something, he'll be walking in circles like this for eternity. It feels as if he already has. Julian stops moving, stretches out his arms to make his body into a cross and screams.

That's when he woke up.

"Oh, honey, you poor thing. Not again."

They were at the MGM Grand. He and Mirabelle drove to Las Vegas to watch Buster "The Exterminator" Barkley lose a heartbreaker to a knockout in the seventh. As consolation, they were comped by MGM with a corner suite with a view of the desert and the strip. Julian was crouched in the corner of that suite, by the windows overlooking the city that never slept.

"Come back to bed, Jules. Please."

"Come here," he said.

"Really? Instead of us spooning all cozy under the blankets in a warm bed, you want me to get down on the hard floor with you?"

"Yes."

She hopped off the bed and came to stand naked by his side. "Okay, now what?"

"I wanted a fairytale," Julian said, "and instead I'm down on my knees." He stared up at her in the pale crescent moonlight. He kissed her stomach, her thighs. Either he was in the midst of death or he was in the midst of life.

"Mia, marry me."

"*What?*"

"I love you," he said. "I didn't know it was possible for me to love someone like I love you. Please, will you marry me?"

She swayed.

"You think it's too soon," he said.

"Yes."

"I know. There are a million reasons not to do it."

"I said *yes*, Julian." She fell to her knees in front of him. "What took you so long? There's nothing I want more, *nothing*. When?"

"Well, we *are* in Vegas, the capital of classy weddings," he said. "How about tomorrow?"

"I can't *believe* I have to wait that long," she said. "Okay, fine. Maybe that'll give you time to buy me a ring."

Julian opened his clenched fist. Inside the palm of his hand, like an ancient relic, like a crystal of souls that had once been inside her palm and was now in a storm drain on Sunset Boulevard, lay a two-carat princess-cut sparkling diamond.

Mirabelle wept.

∞

"Chapel of the Flowers?" Julian asked her. "Or Chapel of the Bells?"

"I hope that's the hardest decision I'll ever have to make."

"We could wait," he said, brooding in a chair by the window. She got upset. He was backpedaling already.

"We could wait to get married in a real church," he said, half-explaining.

"Chapel of the Bells *is* a real church," she said. "It's got the word *chapel* baked right into the name. Why would we wait?"

"I don't want your mother to think it's a fake wedding."

"Who cares what she thinks," Mia said. "And who's she to judge? She and my dad got hitched on the Coney Island boardwalk during the thirty minutes between end of confession and start of Mass."

"Haven't you dreamed of a perfect wedding?" he said, looking up at her standing over him, arms akimbo. "What did you wish for? Whatever it is, I want to give it to you."

"I *have* dreamed of my wedding, of course I have," Mia said, planting herself in his lap. "What girl hasn't? Do you want to know what my idea of a perfect wedding is? Okay, I'll tell you. One in which I become *your* wife and *you*, Julian Cruz, become my husband."

That took his breath away. "Okay." He patted her bare hip. She was wearing his boxer tank and a barely there thong, just a silk thread between her buttocks. "So which one? Bells or Flowers?"

"I'm trying to imagine which answer I'd prefer to give people when they ask where in Vegas we had our fake wedding," Mia said. "They're both so good! I can't decide. You decide."

"No matter what I do, you keep saying it's all good." He patted her hip again, a little harder.

"Because everything you are and everything you do *is* good."

"Chapel of the Flowers, then."

"Why'd you pick that one?" she said. "I liked Chapel of the Bells."

"*Aaaand* it starts," Julian said. "Not even married, and already it's not all good."

She laughed. She just wanted to know why.

"Because Flowers is harder to rhyme," he said. "Therefore, flowers will make a better story because the words will be less common."

"Powers devours," she said, rocking on top of him back and forth. "Speaking of rhyming, we need a wedding song."

"How about 'I'm So Afraid' by Fleetwood Mac."

"*Aaaand*, you see, he *can* be funny, ladies and gentlemen! He's here all week. Try the veal. Make it real."

She rocked so hard against him, the chair tipped back. They fell over.

Don't get hurt before the wedding, he said.

I won't get hurt before the wedding, she said.

46

Hey Baby

Ashton talked Julian into waiting a few days.
Mirabelle saw some wisdom in that, too. She admitted she
couldn't get married even in a tacky Vegas chapel without her
mother. Julian agreed to wait until the following Saturday if
Ashton would do him a favor and give Zakiyyah a ride to Vegas.
Riley was in Chicago on business and would fly into McCarran
straight from O'Hare. Ashton refused. "I'm already your best
man. You can't have my intestines, too." Julian said Zakiyyah
had sprained her ankle and wasn't comfortable driving all that
way by herself and besides, it didn't make sense for both of them
to take separate cars.

"It makes perfect sense," Ashton said. "What doesn't make
sense is for her and me to be in proximity to each other, ever."

"Please, bro. For me."

"What, I don't do enough for you?"

"One more thing."

"You want me to drive across the desert," Ashton said,
"across Death Valley..."

"Not Death Valley, Mojave."

"With Attila the Hun?"

"Come on."

"Death Valley, Julian. That's most appropriate. *Death. Valley.*
With Attila the Hun."

∞

The following Thursday, the day of the bachelor party and two days before Julian and Mia's wedding, at seven in the morning, Ashton pulled up to the curb on Lyman in front of Zakiyyah's house and honked the horn. No one came out. He honked again and, receiving no reply, switched off the engine and walked up the stairs to the landing, where he gave a surly double knock and stood back, nearly kicking over the damn petunia pots.

Zakiyyah opened the door. She was wearing a gray cotton knit dress and a pink ribbon through her halo of corkscrew hair.

"Hello," she said.

"Hello, did you not hear me honking?"

"That was you?" Zakiyyah said. "I was about to call the cops to report a disturbance."

"You didn't see my car?"

"How would I know it's your car?"

"You didn't see me sitting in the open convertible? You didn't recognize me?"

"Odd, isn't it," she said, "I didn't recognize you without your Free Licks shirt."

Ashton wore an ironed, thin cotton buttondown, sleeves rolled up, and jeans. He was done speaking to her. She hadn't invited him in or offered him a drink or asked him for help, so he stood like a pillar.

"Ready to go?" he said.

"Hold the door for a second," she said. "I have to get my suitcase. Come in, I guess."

"Thanks, I guess."

She held open the door as he walked past her. It irritated him that she smelled good, of something warm and woodsy, irked him even more that the dress, even though it had a square neckline, could not contain her voluminous cleavage.

He tried not to look around as she hobbled in her ankle boot to get her suitcase. It was a cute, girly apartment. Comfy.

It smelled nice. All tapestries and film posters and funky lamps and scented candles. It even had a plant, like she wouldn't kill it instantly with her death glare.

Limping, Zakiyyah rolled a large suitcase out of her bedroom.

"What's that?" Ashton said.

"It's a conveyance for carrying clothing and sundries."

"Why are you bringing it? We're barely going to be there two nights."

"Just in case," she said.

"Just in case *what*?" Why was Ashton raising his voice?

"Anything. Brush fire. Earthquake. Flood."

"Flood," he said slowly. "In the desert?"

"I don't know," she said. "Anything. Everything. Have you not read your best friend's book, his chapter on survival? Clearly not. He said to always be prepared."

"Prepared for what, the siege of Las Vegas?"

She matched his antagonism. "And I suppose you brought nothing but the keys in your hands and the beanie on your head?"

"I brought a tux, and what does my beanie have to do with anything?"

"Well, it's 90 degrees out," said Zakiyyah. "Wearing that in 90-degree weather makes it seem like you don't know what temperature is."

Ashton swiped the beanie off his head. "Better?"

"Saner, certainly."

"Ready to go?" he repeated through his teeth.

"Just a minute." Zakiyyah stood in the middle of her open living room, appraising the kitchen, the cold stove, the latched windows, the killed lights.

"What are you doing?"

"Hang on," she said. "I'm having a silent moment. Or trying to."

"Having a what?"

"A moment right before you leave the house when you don't talk and don't move, you just stand or sit completely still and try to make sure that you've brought everything, done everything."

"Great. Ready?" he said.

"I can't tell. You keep talking through it. Did I mention what it's called? A *silent moment*. What you're supposed to do is built right into the name. It's another one of your friend's life hacks."

Ashton snapped his mouth shut to keep himself from speaking so they could finally leave the house.

"Okay, now I'm ready," Zakiyyah said.

"Let me help you with your suitcase," Ashton said. "Do let me get that for you. By the way, have you seen my car? Take a good look at it while I carry this downstairs. Appraise it in silence."

On the sidewalk they stood in front of his BMW two-seater convertible.

"That's small," she said.

"That's what I've been trying to tell you."

"Clearly you're pretending not to compensate for something," she said.

Ashton didn't respond. He had nothing to prove.

"Is there a trunk?" she said.

"Yes. The top of the car is in it. And my tux."

"Well, put the top up."

"I'm not putting the top up," Ashton said. "We're driving through the desert. You have to have the top down in the desert. We're not eighty."

They stood in the street at an impasse. His arms were crossed. Her arms were crossed.

"Well, what am I supposed to do with my suitcase?" Zakiyyah said. "Hold it in my lap?"

"There's an idea."

"Fine," she said. "I won't go. Call Julian, tell him I won't be able to make the wedding because you have no room for me in your car."

"I have room for you," Ashton said. "Just not your steamer trunk."

"So is that the choice," Zakiyyah said, "a zero-sum game? Choose the luggage, then. Be my guest. I'll stay home. The suitcase can be maid of honor."

Ashton tried not to swear under his breath. "Give it here." He moved the passenger seat all the way forward and stuffed the luggage as best he could behind them.

"Wait, I forgot one thing," she said.

"Suitcase looks like it has your entire wardrobe in it."

"I'll be right back."

"Why even have a silent moment, then?" he muttered.

"Oh, I had a moment," Zakiyyah said. "It was anything but silent."

A minute later, she limped back outside, holding a guitar in her hands.

"Are you kidding me?" Ashton said. He had to restrain himself from saying are you fucking kidding me.

Zakiyyah gave him her phone. "Mia asked me to play at her reception, to sing her and Julian's wedding song. Call her and tell her I can't because you refuse to help."

Ashton took deep breaths. "What's the song?"

"What, if you don't approve of their choice, my guitar's not coming? I don't even want to tell you now." Zakiyyah took deep breaths herself. "Tom Waits, if you really *must* know every detail of every single thing before we can drive away. 'I Hope That I Don't Fall in Love With You.'"

"That's their wedding song?"

"By all means," Zakiyyah said, "when you see them, let them know what you think of it."

Somehow Ashton squeezed both the guitar and the suitcase behind their seats. "There," he said. "You don't mind sitting with your nose to the dashboard, do you?" He closed her car door, taking care not to *slam* it.

In aggravated silence, they drove out onto the 101 and a half hour later, onto Highway 10. Out of Pasadena and San Gabriel Mountains, it was a straight pass through the desert to Vegas. Six hours. Five if he drove like a maniac. The hot wind was fierce, even when they were stuck in traffic and were barely moving. Zakiyyah took a black thermos from the bag between her legs, popped it open and took a deep swig.

"What do you have there?" Ashton asked.

"Lemon water with ice."

"What kind of thermos is that?"

"The amazing kind," Zakiyyah said. "Your best friend recommended it. Japanese technology. Incredibly light, yet keeps any liquid ice cold or very hot for over twelve hours."

"Huh."

"It's another one of his life hacks," she said. "It's in his book."

"Whatever."

"I don't want to insult you by offering you some of my lemon ice water," Zakiyyah said. "Can I get you your own drink? I'm sure you brought your own. I mean, you being Mr. Prepared, you wouldn't commit to a six-hour drive through the desert in the middle of summer in hundred-degree temperatures with the top down without bringing something to drink, would you? That would just be crazy. So, where's your water, Ashton?"

"I see," Ashton said. "This is going to be one long mother of a drive."

"And getting longer every minute," said Zakiyyah.

After a few miles of silence, Zakiyyah offered him her thermos, and Ashton grudgingly accepted. "Do you want to listen to some Apple music?" he said, taking a long welcome swallow and handing it back to her.

"I prefer Spotify," she said. "Better playlists."

"Shame that your Spotify is not hooked up to my car, sweetheart."

"My name is not sweetheart. It's Zakiyyah. My friends call me Z."

"Your phone is not hooked up to my car, *Zakiyyah*," Ashton said. "But you know whose phone *is* hooked up to my car? Mine. With my inferior Apple playlists."

"Whatever."

He tried again. "So what would you like to listen to?"

"Some classical? Early Bach, or Chopin?"

Ashton groaned.

"Fine, how about some Simon and Garfunkel, or Sam Cooke?"

He made a small whimpering swearing sound under his breath.

"Just forget it, then."

"How about some Kendrick Lamar?" he said. "Or Chance the Rapper?"

Zakiyyah made a face.

"How about Rihanna?"

Zakiyyah made a face.

"You don't like *Rihanna*?"

"I like her fine, but why?" Zakiyyah said. "Do you think I *should* like Rihanna? Because I'm black?"

"No, not because you're black," Ashton said. "Because you have two ears and can hear. *That's* why you should like her."

"So put on some Rihanna, if you know everything. We'll take turns. And after her, I'll put on some Sam Cooke. Because I have two ears and can hear."

"Do you want us to crash?" Ashton said. "Do you want me to run off the road because I've fallen asleep listening to your narcoleptic music? Do you know anything about car music? It must be in 4/4 time. Its tempo should be faster than 80 beats per minute, faster than the average beat of a human heart. It needs to keep me awake. That's also in my friend's book, or have you not gotten to that part yet? It's a long book, and that bit is at the end."

"It's nine in the morning, why would you fall asleep?" Zakiyyah said. "It's literally the beginning of your day."

"My day already feels like a year long," Ashton muttered, adding louder, "and that's not the point. Is Cooke's tempo even 15 beats a minute? He's not upbeat enough for a wake."

"I'm done." Zakiyyah crossed her arms. "Put on whatever you want. Just close the top. It's too windy and hot."

"The AC is on."

"Yes, you're cooling the outdoors admirably. Maybe that palm tree over there likes your AC, but inside, where I am, I'm *hot*."

"Why don't you take a sip of your ice water to cool yourself down if you're so *hot*." Ashton grumbled, but he pulled into a gas station, closed the top, took her suitcase and stuffed it into the trunk. He laid his garment bag on top of it, moved her seat slightly back so she'd be more comfortable, bought himself some bottled water, some Coke, and got back on the road. He put on Rihanna's "Only Girl," the only girl in the world, and Zakiyyah put on Sam Cooke's "You Send Me" as Ashton flew a hundred miles an hour across the Mojave while Cooke slowly warbled that she sent him, she thrilled him.

When it was his turn again, Ashton put on "Hey Baby" by Stephen Marley.

"Now *that's* more like it," Zakiyyah said, and actually smiled. Her dazzling smile lit up the desert.

"Aha," said Ashton. He stared sideways at her beaming face. "You like Stephen Marley?"

"*You* like Stephen Marley," Zakiyyah said. "I *love* Stephen Marley."

Ashton turned his eyes to the road and the volume up. At the top of their lungs, together they sang "Hey Baby" along with Marley, afterward expressing a reluctant surprise that they'd finally found a song they both knew and liked.

"It's one of my favorites," Zakiyyah said.

"Mine, too," Ashton said. "I love all the Marleys."

"You do?"

"Yes, why? A white boy can't like reggae?"

"Stop getting defensive every five seconds," she said. "You don't look like the type who would like Stephen Marley is all I'm saying."

"What type is that, Z? The white type?"

"Why don't you put on the song again instead of speaking. That would be best."

"Couldn't agree more."

They sang along to "Hey Baby," three more times, and then to UB40's "Red Red Wine" and "Please Don't Make Me Cry." They sang along to everything because they knew it all. They argued about who was better, Sean Paul or Jimmy Cliff, agreed that Ziggy Marley was amazing, that Bob was in a class by himself, accepted that Third World and UB40 were fun to listen to, especially in the car with the top down, but both confessed to a particular weakness for Stephen Marley's hip-hop/reggae brilliance. Next time they stopped, Zakiyyah asked for the top to be down and Ashton said, "Make up your mind, will you?" but he put it down happily, and they cruised down Desert Inn Road, cranking Marley all the way up and turning him down to passionately disagree about which album was better, *Revelation Pt. I: The Root of Life* or *Revelation Pt. II: The Fruit of Life*.

If, at the start of the trip, Ashton had been breaking every speed limit trying to get to the end of the journey faster, by the end, he was dogging it on Highway 15 at forty an hour, still trying to persuade the infuriatingly unpersuadable Zakiyyah that he was right and she was wrong.

They stopped at a watering hole in the Mojave to gas up and grab a quick snack. The food was gross. Old wrapped burritos, nachos with dried-up cheese, dubious-looking tuna sandwiches.

They got sodas and Doritos and brownies and potato chips and sat at the picnic table in the desert dust under a canopy, continuing their ardent conversation. The topic veered off to the horror genre.

"Your ignorance of classic horror, Zakiyyah," Ashton said, "leaves you woefully unqualified to run my haunted house."

"I have a job," she said. "Why would I *ever* want to run your haunted house?"

"I didn't say I was going to pay you," Ashton said. "You're not even qualified to run it for free."

"I wouldn't run it even if you paid me," said Zakiyyah.

When their lunch at the decrepit picnic table on the side of the gas station convenience store in the middle of the desert began, Ashton knew he was sick in love with her. By the time it was over, he knew he couldn't live without her.

Why are you looking at me like that? she said.

He waited to answer. Like what?

I don't even know. Like I got something on my face.

Is that how I'm looking at you?

I don't know. That's why I'm asking.

He said nothing.

What's wrong with you? she said.

Everything's wrong.

Ugh. What is it now?

Ashton didn't say anything, he just stood up. He lifted himself off the bench, leaned all the way across the table, over their garbage train wreck of travel mart food, and kissed her.

For God's sake, what do you think you're *doing*, Zakiyyah exclaimed, breathed out. She dropped her drink. Her arms wrapped around his neck.

I really don't know, he said. He came around the picnic table and pulled her up. His hands were in her hair, his lips were on her. His arms slipped down her back, down her cotton dress, pressing her breasts against him. Her hands rose in supplication.

Ashton, what are you *doing*, she kept repeating, her eyes closed, her face up.

I really don't know, he said.

Their fevered fumbling in his miniature car could've been filmed as a climax of a screwball farce. He couldn't move the seats far enough back, not his, not hers. Before he could even get her inside the car, before he could pull down her dress or expose her breasts, he had to remove the boot cast from her leg *and* put the top up. He sat in his seat, she in hers. He leaned over the console. Finally the tinted windows got steamed up. He pulled down her dress, unhooked her bra, bared her glorious breasts to him. He didn't have enough hands for all of her, enough lips for all of her. He didn't know what to touch first, what to do first. He knew where he wanted his hands and lips, he knew where he wanted his everything. Why do you smell so good, he murmured. Why are you so hot? They made out like wild kids on the beach.

Off to the side at the rest stop, they remained parked, her trying not to make a sound, and every five seconds a new car would pull in and some joker would get out, and peer across the dust at his lightly shaking BMW.

He pressed her against the car door, fondling her, kissing her, the heat off his body melting her down, the heat off her body making him rock solid.

Ouch, she said.

That's not me, he said.

No, it's the door handle in my back.

He took her hand and put it over himself.

Whoa, she said.

That's me. Let's get out of here. Quick. Let's go find a motel.

Are you out of your mind?!

Yes. He was panting.

She was panting. Everyone is waiting for us in Vegas, said Zakiyyah. Julian's family, Mia's mom, my mom—oh, and *Riley*!

Ashton pulled back slightly. How do you know about Riley?

Mia told me.

You asked Mia about me? That is *so* hot. His mouth was on her breasts.

It was a question, not an invitation, she said in a moan.

How wrong you are. Let's go. Motel.

Ashton, we can't!

I didn't say we had to stay *overnight*, he said. We're not *moving* in. But I can't drive like this or stand aright. I can't move or breathe or live until—

You want us to go rent a motel for an hour? Please, Ashton, *do* continue with the romance. But he was making it difficult for her to berate him and moan at the same time, his fingers and palms and mouth on her topless body so insistent.

Z, this is the most romantic thing I can give you, Ashton said. I want you so desperately that I can't wait until later. I can't wait another *minute*. He tried to move his entire body over the stick shift into the passenger seat to get closer to her.

You cannot fit into this space with me! she said.

Watch me.

It's physics, Ashton. Two people can't occupy one space at the same time.

Watch me.

I think your idea of romance and mine is quite different, Zakiyyah said, gasping it out, pressing his stubbled mouth harder against her nipples. Suck them, she whispered, suck them. Wait, she kept saying, *wait*! This isn't going to work.

Even the motel that rented by the hour was about to become out of the question.

You knew what you were doing, he said, when you wore this unbelievable dress. You knew how I'd feel about it.

The $20 knit pullover from Amazon?

Yes. Sitting there tantalizing me, seducing me. You'll think twice next time.

I'm thinking twice right now, but what does the dress have to do with it?

His hand was between her knees.

Ashton!

Now you know. Because the dress is nothing but flimsy fabric, nothing but a bit of cotton between me and your bare—

Ashton...!

Now it was really too late.

Somehow Zakiyyah held herself up and he slipped under her from his seat into hers, somehow he unbuttoned his shirt and unbuckled his belt. While Marley's "The Lion Roars" played through the car speakers, he sat in the passenger seat, moving it as far back as he could against her guitar, and she climbed astride him, her underwear off, the dress bunched up at her waist. His mouth tried to remain on her nipples as she fit over him and slid up and down, but she weakened too soon and was unable to hold herself up, breathing out his name *O Ashton* followed by *I can't, I can't, I can't*. He had to keep her steady and move himself, breathing out her name followed by the words *I can,* her hips clamped between his hands. Both he and she tried desperately not to make any sounds that would make the people putting gas in their cars 50 feet away call the cops. The convertible heaved. The shocks made a sound, hissing in, hissing out. Stephen Marley made a sound. The guitar behind their seat made a sound. The bass strings vibrated their humming rhythm pounding on every half beat, then every quarter beat, then every semi-quaver. And then Zakiyyah made a sound.

"Well, you were certainly right about *one* thing," she said after it was barely over, still on top of him, clutching his wet neck.

"What's that?" Ashton murmured, his head back. "Oh, yeah. If you see something that needs doing and can be done in under two minutes, do it immediately."

They both laughed.

He opened his eyes. "I saw something that *really* needed doing." Her body was in his hands.

"And you did it immediately."

"Woman, I think I love you," said Ashton.

She gazed at him. "You're very fickle. A minute ago you hated me." She rubbed her breasts back and forth against his bare perspired chest.

"Do that for two more minutes."

"Ashton!"

He fondled her, he kissed her.

"Do you know when I knew I loved *you*?" Zakiyyah said. "When I stepped into your store and you were wearing your stupid Free Licks shirt and I was yelling at you for it, as you deserved to be yelled at, and you opened your arms like you could do no wrong—and I realized even as I was infuriated that all I wanted was to be in them."

"That's why I opened them."

Eventually, they got going. With their lips pulpy and Zakiyyah's neck and chest inflamed from his stubble, they got themselves dressed and sorted, got cleaned up as best they could, and pulled out onto the highway, but not before Ashton leaned over and put his face into her outrageous breasts, pulled down her dress, kissed her nipples again, kissed her lips. *You're a goddess*, he whispered. He drove with one arm. His other arm lay in Zakiyyah's lap.

"I hope Mia and Julian don't kill us for what we're doing," she said.

"For what we just did," Ashton said, "or for throwing them a surprise wedding with a hundred people, not twenty?"

"Yes," she said. "Wait, did you get the right flowers? Mia said he's really…"

"You don't have to tell *me*. A bear. Ridiculous. Nuts. They nearly wiped out my bank balance, but yes, I ordered them some white asphodel. He keeps telling me the asphodel is the forever flower."

"That he even knows that is weird."

"He knows a lot of weird shit, pardon my language."

"Oh, when you spoke to him yesterday, did he tell you he punched a guy?" Zakiyyah said.

"If Julian told me about every man he punched," said Ashton, "we'd have no time for any other conversation. What did the guy do?"

"Oh, great. Sure. Defend Julian."

"Um, did you want me to defend the *other* guy?"

"Whatever. Mia said they were in the casino and some drunk said something to her. She said the words had barely come out of the man's mouth when he got his shit quaked. Julian hit him so hard, he knocked him out. MGM had to comp the guy like two years' worth of visits so he wouldn't press charges."

"What did he say?"

"Mia said something like *aren't you a sight for sore eyes.*"

"Come on," Ashton said, "there had to be more."

"That's the thing—there wasn't. Julian couldn't explain it. He told Mia the phrase just set him off."

"Well, the drunk should've kept his trap shut."

"Oh yeah? What if Mia says something that sets him off?"

"Let's all calm down. You know she can do no wrong in his eyes." Ashton cleared his throat, let a mile of road go by. "But he has been having really bad dreams lately."

"I know. She told me."

"I don't think she realizes how bad it's been," Ashton said. "She'll know soon enough. Several times a week, I find him sleeping on the floor in my room. I had to put an air mattress in the corner."

"Because *that's* not weird," Zakiyyah said.

"You know what's weird? That the dreams only started *after* he met your friend."

"Um, do you know what the word coincidence means?"

"Julian says there's no such thing. First time coincidence, second time happenstance, third time enemy action."

"Then this is coincidence even by his definition," said Zakiyyah. "You can only meet someone for the first time once."

"Jules says otherwise," Ashton said.

"Does he remember what he dreams about?"

"Unfortunately for me, yes."

She waited. He drove. "Are you going to sit there, or are you going to tell me?"

"The dreams are so bad, I almost don't want to tell you."

"Oh, then by all means, *don't* tell me."

"Dreams in which," Ashton continued, "I die, and Julian dies, and Mia dies."

"So he tells me anyway," said Zakiyyah.

"Dies not just once. But over and over. In the most unimaginable ways. He doesn't come right out and say what happens to me. It's so bad, he won't tell me. I've had to extrapolate. But no matter what else happens, Mia *always* dies. Don't tell her I told you this."

"Oh—not to worry."

"I'm serious, Z. *Ever*," Ashton said. "Or I'll actually be dead, because Jules will kill me. It will ruin our friendship."

"Do *I* die?" Zakiyyah said.

"I don't think so. You just vanish."

"Thank *God*."

"Are you going to take it seriously or what?"

"You want me to take seriously the screwed-up dreams of some guy I hardly know?"

"Yeah, some guy who's about to marry your oldest friend."

"That's *her* problem."

"Nice."

"What do you want me to say? What do you want me to do? Why did you tell me?"

"Because I'm worried about him," Ashton said. "I couldn't keep it to myself anymore. I couldn't bear it on my own."

"Well, now we both can't bear it. Happy?"

"Happier," he said, "knowing I've made you a little bit miserable."

"A little bit?" Zakiyyah said, bringing his hand to her lips.

She's not the one.

Ashton said that about every girl he'd been with. And it didn't matter. Every silk designer-bejeweled beauty from Pasadena to New Orleans made him shake with joy, but he'd also shake his head and say, Jezebel, Delilah, Grace Kelly or Marilyn, I love you, girls, I love you all, but you're not the one. You're pretty, foxy, you smell good, you sing, do cartwheels, laugh at my jokes, you like morning sex and swimming naked in my pool. But you're not the one. He and Julian had a decade of sun and fun pretending to search for the one.

And then the bell rang on a Friday morning, and she walked into his Treasure Box with her ripe body and her perfect face, judging him even as she herself was falling, falling, falling. Before she spoke a word, Ashton knew. He knew it in his gut.

And when that happened in a man's life, the man had to come clean with everyone else, and make good on his human promise to struggle toward perfection, to try to be good, to try to do good, and hope that his puny effort would be enough.

Ashton finally understood what Julian had been talking about.

He and Z were quiet the rest of the way into Las Vegas, listening to Marley's "The Fruit of Life," listening to "Babylon" and "Paradise" and "The Lion Roars," on repeat. Half a mile before the Wynn, Ashton pulled into a 7-Eleven. "Look, Z," he said, taking her hands in his, "my Julian and your Mirabelle are getting married at the Chapel of the Flowers. It's an incredible momentous day. Even my dad, whom I haven't seen since my college graduation, is flying in for the occasion."

Zakiyyah nodded. "And Mia's mom, Ava, who's been a widow for sixteen years, is bringing a plus one! Some Vietnamese guy. She met him on her last trip to London. Had lunch at his place, and they hit it off. Mia doesn't even know about this yet."

"Yes, and your girls from Brooklyn are flying in to meet my boys from UCLA and Jules's boys from the gym," Ashton said, grinning. "It's going to be one hell of a party. My point is, I don't want anything, not one single blemish, to ruin this for Jules and Mia. Okay?"

"Of course. But why are you telling *me*? How are you planning to ruin it?"

"What I'm trying to say..." Ashton regrouped. "Is that I can't speak to Riley until after the wedding. I promise you, it will be the next private conversation she and I have. I will do right by you. But I also have to do right by her. I've been with her a long time, and I owe her that."

"Okay," Zakiyyah said, looking at him with deepening emotion.

"I just don't want you to be upset that I have to stay with her, and sit next to her, and dance with her. That for the next few days, I'll have to *be* with her."

Zakiyyah leaned forward to kiss him. "Thank you for being honest with me. Besides, the maid of honor always dances with the best man. So I'll get to dance with you, too."

"Yes. Because you're my maid of honor."

"And you're my best man."

He gazed into her face. "You are so familiar to me," Ashton said. "I don't know why. You're like my favorite song."

"And you are mine," Zakiyyah said. "Don't worry about me. You do what you need to do. I'm playing the long game. I'll stand aside."

"And if at any time during the wedding and dinner and dancing, you hear me say the words *Hey Baby*," Ashton said, "know that I'm thinking of you." He smiled. "I'm thinking of the next time I can *romance* you again."

"Ashton!"

"Yes, Z?"

"Hey, baby," she whispered.

"Hey, baby," he whispered back.

47

Pink Palace

"Jules, the original girl they hired broke her leg in a freak accident, and I got the part!"

Mirabelle had gotten the call while they were in the morning ocean learning how to surf in the gentle Waikiki waves. She took the phone to the lobby where the reception was better and ran back to their cabana on the beach to tell him. They were staying at the Royal Hawaiian, "The Pink Palace," for their honeymoon.

"What's the part?" Julian said, sipping his breakfast cocktail and looking up at her, blocking the sun, jumping up and down in her Marmont minimum-coverage bikini. She'd gotten crazy tanned in the lethal tropics by using one of his hacks: one day heavy SPF, next day light SPF. "Don't tell me—Medea, the vengeful mother, in London?" Judging by how excited she was, what else could it be?

"No, sadly. Though that would've been *so* great."

Julian shrugged. "Not *that* great, newlyweds being separated while the wife is wooed by another man in a foreign city."

"Okay, *that* part might not have been great," she said, "though I do like to be wooed, but—*London*! And why would we have been separated? You would've come with me, of course. To keep an eye on me. You know how you like to keep an eye on me." She smiled. "You would take in the sights while I rehearsed."

"London is not all it's cracked up to be," Julian muttered, glad they didn't have to make that decision. "So what part *did* you get?"

"The part of a chick named Josephine—in a horror flick!" she said in a thrilled voice. "I tried out for it a month ago and had two callbacks." She plonked down on the edge of his chaise, rubbing his leg. "You probably don't remember; it was during that heady period in our courtship when you were contemplating moving continents so you wouldn't have to make dreaded love to me." She tickled his knee.

Julian kept a straight face. "What's the film called?"

"The Dungeon of the Haunted Warlord!"

"Now *that's* great."

"Isn't it?" She took a sip of his drink, their own invention—or so they thought—in honor of the Pink Palace, gin and tonic with angostura bitters, making the gin pink, hence their moniker for it: Pink Gin. "And get this, the film shoots right in the hills at Warner! Both soundstage and backlot. It's a block away from the Treasure Box. You could come visit me on my lunch break. If you're good, I'll let you be my fluffer."

He threw back his head and laughed. "I don't think that means what you think it means," Julian said, pulling her on top of him. "But how about if we go upstairs and I'll let you be my fluffer."

"What, again?"

"Yes, I believe they call this part the honeymoon. Did they email you the script? We can kill two birds with one stone. Ask the front desk to print two copies for us."

"Don't use my coveted film script to lure me into your dungeon, Haunted Warlord," Mia said.

Post love and lunch, they returned to their cabana by the water in the late afternoon to drink Pink Gins and read the script. She sat on the sand, propped up by big cushions, and he lay on his back with his head in her lap.

"Okay, so it's not going to win any Oscars," Mia said, when they were finished, "but it's my first leading role."

"It's awesome," said Julian. "You can do a lot with this Josephine."

"Josephine, the poor doomed maiden! I love how the killer is so obsessed with her, he stalks her everywhere, and no matter where she hides, he finds her and carries her off to his dungeon." Running her fingers through his hair, she leaned down to kiss him. "In my first scene, I get hit by a bus! Isn't that tremendous? You think it's an accident, but who's driving the bus, in disguise?"

"The Haunted Warlord!"

"Yes! Shall I call them back and tell them I'll do it?"

"Like it's even a question."

Mia managed to get a signal on the beach. He lay in her lap, gazing up at her as she spoke to Marty Springer, her agent. When she got off the phone, she was even more excited. She eased out from under him and jumped to her feet. "Apparently, rehearsals are next week and shooting begins the week after, can you believe it? Life is really looking up."

Giving him her hand, she pulled him into the water.

The early evening was Julian's favorite time on the beach. The crowds thinned out, the high tide increased the size and frequency of the waves, and the entire half-moon coast from Diamond Head to Kahanamoku shimmered and dazzled like an animated postcard. They dived in, cooled off, slicked back their hair and bobbed in the waves.

"Here's another kicker," she said. "Marty said they need an extra to sit and watch me in the first scene as I get whacked, and he suggested you."

"What? No, not me. I'm not an extra."

Mia rubbed his hard shoulders with her soft hands. "You're so extra." She kissed his chest. "What's the big deal? You sit at a table like a passer-by, I walk and then BAM! A bus comes out of nowhere, and—"

"No, I get what I'm supposed to do."

"Come on. I'll introduce you to Florence, the casting director. You'll be up and running in no time. And you'll get to go to wardrobe and pick out your costume. You know how much you like cosplay." Grinning, she splashed him.

He splashed her back. "A costume for sitting at a table? Isn't that called wearing clothes?"

"Hardy-har-har. And you'll get paid. $150 big ones."

"Well, they named my price."

She jumped him in the water, trying to knock him under. It was her favorite game, next to him tackling her and *actually* knocking her under. She flung herself on him, wrapped her legs around his waist, her arms around his neck, rubbed her cheek against his stubble, kissed his face with her wet lips. In Hawaii, Julian shaved only before dressing for dinner. "Come on, say yes." She rocked back and forth, trying to unbalance him. "Say yes so they can say of us, look at those two. They're unstoppable. Everything they do, they do together."

"How about if we find out what we can actually do by living together," he said, "and we'll see about the rest." Their love affair had been so whirlwind that her stuff was still at her apartment on Lyman. Since they met, they'd been a week apart, a week at the Marmont, a week shuffling from his to hers, a week in Vegas, now a week here. Five weeks and not even a drawer for each other in his place or hers.

"Can you believe we're *married*, Jules?" she said. "Sometimes I can't even."

"Me neither. But I carried you over the threshold of our Vegas suite, so I know it must be real."

"Go us, right?"

"Go us," said Julian.

48

Big Ben

BACK IN L.A., ASHTON THOUGHT IT WAS THE GREATEST THING he'd ever heard, Julian being an extra in a horror movie. Though he wanted to know why Julian couldn't audition for the part of the haunted warlord.

"Because I already have a day job."

"Dayjob shmayjob," said Ashton. "On the one hand Mr. Know-it-All, on the other—HAUNTED WARLORD. Like it's even a choice, Jules, you lucky bastard."

While Julian and Mia were in Hawaii, Ashton had ended things with Riley. Julian had a commiserating lunch with her at the Whole Foods café in Beverly Hills after Mia started rehearsals. They chatted about the wedding, the honeymoon, the *Haunted Warlord*. Toward the end, Riley finally brought up Ashton. "Did you know anything about it?" she asked. She was composed if shell-shocked. "Did you have anything to do with it?"

"Why would I?"

"Because this has you written all over it. First you and Gwen break up, not five minutes later you're marrying some chick you barely know, and five minutes after that, Ashton is sayonara. It's not his MO. He is not the type to make a decision like that, he is such a go with the flow guy. That's one of the things I loved about him."

"Riles, who are you kidding?" Julian said. "That's what you hated about him."

"I know," she said. "But why does his wandering nature seem so appealing to me now?"

Julian took her hand. "You deserve better," he said. "You will have better."

"Is there anything better than him?" Riley's elegant, fine-featured face had sadness etched on it as if she didn't think so.

"Yes—me for one." Julian smiled.

"You're taken. And not for nothing, but why does Mirabelle get to have you? Who the hell is she? The rest of us have put our time into you. Years. She bats her eyes at you in a coffee shop and suddenly she's Mrs. Know-it-All? How is that fair?"

"I'm saying," Julian said, "plenty of other fish in the sea. For instance, did you notice how Mia's mother's companion, Devi Something, was smitten with you in Vegas? You stand a real chance with him."

"I've had enough of your jokes," Riley said, but she was smiling. "But, you know who does keep texting me from the wedding? Liam."

"Liam Shaw? From Freddie's?" Liam was a good guy, a tall welterweight.

"Yeah, he was pretty drunk at the Wynn. Kept asking me to dance. Got a little handsy. Now won't stop texting me."

"Riley, you can't hook up with him," Julian said. "Both your last names are Shaw!"

"I know! He told me he's a thoroughly modern man and if I marry him, I can keep my name."

"So he's funny, too?"

"All you men think you're damn comedians." Riley glanced at her watch. It was time for her to get back to work. She walked Julian through the sliding exit doors and before he left, said, tearing up, "Are we still going to be friends, Jules? If you were a girl, you'd be one of my best friends. I think that's another reason I'm mad."

"Come here, Riles," Julian said. "Come in for a therapeutic lean." He embraced her. "You and I are not breaking up. We'll always be friends. Who else is going to regale me with the benefits of a colonic cleanse?"

"Not to mention the benefits of coconut oil," Riley said, giving him a kiss. "Or have you already discovered those?" She grinned into his grin and strolled back inside Whole Foods in her high heels and pencil skirt, her silky blonde hair swinging.

∞

Julian's dreams had lessened in their viciousness, but not in their murky vividness. There was less of her melting in fires or being shelled with empty bottles, less of his helplessness, but more of the heaviness. She kept appearing to him on a stage. She stood high in red lights or low on some door. Sometimes this door would open like a trap and she'd vanish. She wore headscarves and bonnets. Sometimes she was a boy. All her hair was cut off. Once she was in *La Traviata*, dying of a wasting disease. And sometimes she looked like a Russian babushka, in black clothes, with a kerchief tied under her chin, standing on a stage that froze under ice floes, reciting words he couldn't hear.

In recent days, the dreams had become less about Mia and more about something else troubling and indefinable. He kept hearing a dull distant toll of ringing bells. He walked, trying to get closer to the sound. The tolling was constant, ringing every few seconds. He felt a man's mangled hand on him. It was Devi, the Asian man Mia's mother had brought to their wedding. In real life, shaking the man's half-hand on the receiving line after the ceremony had flooded Julian with the oddest sensation, like stinging salt water filling up his body from his feet to his head. And the way Devi had stared at him...Julian didn't know *what* that was about. In the dream, the man gave Julian something to drink. It was sweet. After Julian drank it, the tolling got louder.

He looked up. It was Big Ben. London again. It kept ringing and ringing.

49

Everything Forever

JULIAN KNEW WHY HE NEVER WANTED TO BECOME AN ACTOR. All the waiting around on sets made him want to drive off a bridge. It was no way to live.

The one-minute scene of Mia wordlessly walking down the street before getting hit by the bus was taking days to set up. They were still building the sets. They kept telling Julian to come back, that they weren't ready for him. Maybe the next day. Or the day after. Finally, they promised him that tomorrow would definitely be the day.

The night before the shoot, Julian dreamed of Big Ben again. He stood, looking up at the Great Clock, trying to see the time. He turned his head to see if he was alone in the street. But no, a crowd of people, familiar and strange, had gathered around him. The armless man, the fingerless man, tall men and dwarfs, prostitutes, thieves, men with Bibles and manuscripts, in suits and bandages, albinos and giants, they all stood, and, like him, everyone was looking up at the Tower. The bell kept tolling. He heard someone say, start over, Swedish. He wasn't Swedish. Why did he think that was meant for him? The bell stopped tolling. They stood in the silence. No one spoke. Then it began again. This time Julian counted.

The bell tolled 49 times.

When Julian woke up, around four in the morning, he couldn't get back to sleep. He began the day with a feeling of dread so heavy he could barely get out of bed. He tried to chalk it up to exhaustion, wishing he could take four sleeping pills and pass out until the day was over.

But it wasn't exhaustion. When Mia woke up, she looked pale. She wasn't her bubbly self. She was dragging and running late. She added cream and sugar to his normally black coffee. She called to him from the bedroom. "Jules," she said, "how much time do I have?"

He stood in the door. "What did you say?" He spoke in a shaken voice. Why did he remember her saying that to him?

"How much time do I have? When is the absolute last second we can leave so I'm not late?"

Why did so many things with her—things they said, they felt, they did, they looked at—fill him with such a relentless sense of déjà vu?

His anxiety would not abate. He drove them to Warner's, braking for every yellow light. When another driver cut him off, Julian actually jumped out of the car and started screaming at the guy. "Hey, buddy, what the hell is *your* problem? Watch where you're going! You nearly crashed into us!"

Inside the car, Mia was staring at him. "Is the bloom off the rose?" she said. "Was that the real you you've been hiding? Or is there something else going on?"

Julian wouldn't answer her. Both options condemned him. Either he was a jerk, or there was something else going on.

He was glad he was on set with her today, because, boy, did she need to be watched over. As she got out of the car, her silk scarf got caught in the door. "Just like Isadora Duncan," she said as a joke, but it wasn't funny. She tripped going up the stairs to her trailer and hit her shin on the metal step. As she was walking across the soundstage, she didn't see a thick wire coiled in her way. She would've fallen had Julian not caught her. She took a sip of coffee, scalded her tongue, and dropped the cup, spilling it over her wrist and hand. She got a small burn. A corner of a desk ripped her stockings and left a bruise. With mounting unease, Julian watched it all.

Just when things couldn't get any worse, the AD sent Julian home. They couldn't shoot today after all, despite the promises. The weather was terrible. Miserable windy gray clouds swirled overhead. There were even a few drops of rain. *In Los Angeles.* No one knew what to do. If there was one thing you could count on in L.A., it was clear skies. It's why the film industry moved out west in the first place instead of to a rain hub like Florida. Yet today, when they needed full sun to shoot, there was this.

As they said goodbye, Julian begged Mia to be careful.

"Of course, but what an odd thing to say. Why wouldn't I be careful?"

"Odd, really? You've been spilling, burning, tripping, falling the whole morning." He brushed the hair strands away from her eyes.

"Jules, nothing bad can happen to me today." Mirabelle gave him a marital hug and a mistress kiss. "Don't you know that today is my lucky day?"

"Why is that?"

"Today is exactly 49 days since we met! Remember I told you 49 is my lucky number?"

"No, and I didn't know you were counting."

She smiled at him full of love, but Julian didn't think it was possible to feel worse. Big Ben tolling 49 times in his dream was as vivid as she was in his arms. To get rid of his pulsing anxiety, Julian drove to Freddie Roach's and pounded the speed bag until it was a blur, until he could barely lift his hands. He pummeled the heavy bag, turning into it with his whole body over and over until he thrashed every fucking Big Ben thought from his mind. He took a Comedy Central meeting with Ashton, for which he was physically present but mentally a million miles away and spent the rest of the day at the Treasure Box, finally driving to pick up Mirabelle at seven.

She was in one piece, but quiet as a struck bird. She said everything was fine, she was just tired. She wasn't hungry. She wasn't thirsty. She didn't want to go for a drink, she didn't even want dinner. She just wanted to go home. He asked if she wanted to go look at some furniture. A month ago, after they had climbed down from their Elysian outpost at the Marmont and returned to the world, Mia requested new sheets before she would stay at his place. She said she didn't want to sleep on sheets, even laundered ones, on which a parade of other women had been entertained. Julian did one better. He took her to Cantoni on La Brea and they picked out a whole new bed, a leather pampas king-sized beauty with an adjustable base and a plush headboard you could sit up against when necessary and grab on to when necessary.

But now a full spousal remodeling was in order. They were planning to repaint the house, redo the floors, get new kitchen cabinets, and a wine fridge. She wanted to get a 75-inch flatscreen TV. He offered to take her shopping for it.

She said no. "Maybe tomorrow, my love," she said, taking his hand as they drove. "I don't feel up to it today, even though it's my lucky day and everything, I'm sorry." She tried to smile.

At home Zakiyyah had made buttermilk chicken and a summer salad, but Mia had no appetite. Ashton invited them to go swimming. Mia didn't want to. Zakiyyah wanted to go dancing; not Mia. They brought out Taboo, Mia's favorite game, and she didn't want to play. She asked for a cup of tea, but when Julian brought it to her, she had fallen asleep on top of their bed. He couldn't watch TV or work on his website.

Mirabelle slept, and Julian sat in the chair by the open French doors and listened for any change to her breathing, and to the laughter and guitar-playing and arguing and singing coming from Ashton's house.

Eventually the joy died down, and Julian lay down by Mirabelle's side. Rhythmically, deeply, completely asleep, she continued to breathe and live.

He fought his own sleep all night, searching her body for signs of destruction. How could he defend her from threats both mystical and mundane when he didn't know what his dreams meant? Were they what had been, or what was yet to be? Were they memories or premonitions? Were they nothing but irrational fears? Though that was a fuckload of some pretty specific fears. He'd never been on a ship, or in a fire, had never seen bombs fall, or watched anyone stoned or choked to death. He had never killed a man. Had never been to London, yet London was so clear in his dreams like his mind's eye had drawn a map of the city, with every well-defined street etched in bold.

Why London?

And why Big Ben?

What did 49 mean?

Nothing made sense, nothing.

Julian stayed awake, afraid of things he couldn't express. He covered Mirabelle with the black cashmere throw from the Marmont and left his hand on her until dawn. His eventual sleep was brief but not dreamless. He saw Mirabelle as when he first met her. But it wasn't at Coffee Plus Food. He saw her bathed in red lights, in a garden, naked in a house, in a crowded square, next to a field gun in a room with no ceiling, in a tavern, and on top of the horizontal door. Different stage, different life, but it was always Mia's face and Mia's eyes and Mia's shining smile.

50

The Dungeon of the Haunted Warlord

THE NEXT MORNING SHE WOKE UP EARLY, SPENT A LONG TIME in the bathroom, and informed him she wouldn't be needing a ride to work because she was running off for a quick appointment with Zakiyyah who would drop her off at Warner's afterward. "But you better show up at eight," she said. "It's beautiful out. We're definitely shooting today."

"I'll believe it when I see it. What appointment?"

"I don't know, Jules," Mia said. "I don't ask questions. Z needs me to go with her, I go with her."

"Like a doctor's appointment?"

"You know what, we are going to respect other people's privacy," she said, "and not put them on the spot."

"Me asking you a question is putting Zakiyyah on the spot?"

"Privacy, Jules. Boundaries." She texted her friend. "Oops, gotta go, see ya." She gave him a peck, ran out, got into Z's Chevy Cruze, and off they sped.

At nine she was back on set but, before Julian could say a word to her, was whisked into hair and makeup. Because she was late, they were scrambling to get her made up and dressed so they could shoot before noon. Julian paced outside her trailer. There was some commotion, back and forth, walkie-talkies, the costume designer in and out. They were looking for something for Mirabelle to wear that would pop in the scene, but they couldn't find the right thing. Shoes, umbrellas, belts. "How about a beret?" Julian said to the stressed and out of ideas assistant director, castigating the befuddled costume girl.

The AD perked up. "What color?"

"Red. Red leather. Gucci. Vintage."

"That might work. I'd have to see it. Do you have it?"

Julian called Ashton. In ten minutes, Ashton was on set, holding out the red beret to the AD. "It's not for sale or for keeps, though," Ashton said. "It's a free rental to the production. Sign it in, but I need it back as soon as you're done." The AD and the costume girl carried off the beret on a tray in front of them like the head of John the Baptist. Ashton and Julian waited outside Mia's trailer. Mia loved it, the director loved it. It was a go. It was the final touch they'd been looking for.

Ashton was beaming, in an unusually good mood even for him.

"It's a beret, dude," Julian said, rolling his eyes. "Calm down. It's not a holy relic."

"It is literally a holy relic, you incorrigible misanthrope," Ashton said. "It carries the physical remains of a holy site and a holy person. It was given to the man who saved my father from a burning house during a world war, given to him by someone else for whom it had been a sacred object. And then I gave it to you, and it saved your stupid stubborn cynical ass. It's like you know nothing. Relics contain spiritual links between life and death, between the soul and the body. A relic is a sacrament. Every church must contain a relic on its altar. Way to go, Jules, way to respect the treasures of the faithful."

Shaking his head, Julian crossed his arms on his chest. He didn't want to tell Ashton how unfathomably often he dreamed of that one-armed man and his vagabond throng on the war-torn streets of London.

The two men stood shoulder to shoulder, watching six people primping Mirabelle's hair under and around the beret.

"I must say," Ashton said, "I admire their attention to detail. Every fucking thing has to be right." He knocked into Julian. "I gotta go. We've got somebody coming in fifteen for the Donkey Kong machine. And I sold another Jeannie bottle this morning. Can't keep them in stock. Later. I'll be back for your ten-second close-up—maybe even with Z." He smiled wide. "When do you think, maybe five, six hours?"

"Kill me now. How do they do it?"

"How? Because it's so much fun. Look how much fun it is."

And it was, it was fun.

The worst day on a film set is still better than the best day anywhere else. Julian would be wise to remember that as he chafed outside Mirabelle's crowded trailer.

"Okay, ladies," the AD called, "let's hurry with that makeup, we gotta shoot sometime this century. Julian, come with me."

He took Julian over to the finally finished set. The director wanted him sitting in place until Mirabelle was ready. One less thing to worry about.

The set was built as somebody's idea of a modern London street, yet with something old in it. A somebody who'd never been to London, or seen London in a film, or maybe even a photograph. The windows in all the shops were tall, like in Century City, except for the quaint rustic coffee shop in the middle of the street, a coffee shop that was supposed to be uniquely British but which still sported L.A.'s skyscraper-height windows, though the production department had fitted it with a golden awning. Was that British? The street was built wide so that the fake red double-decker bus—all frame and no engine— could be rolled down it on a pulley. At the end of the set there was a hint of a fake park, a dress shop façade, and a florist. Shae the production assistant was lovingly arranging the flowers for maximum dazzle. The bus and the chunky black cab stood in the corner, waiting for their own close-up.

There was something uncomfortably recognizable about the street. Julian's sense of déjà vu was never stronger. He had no idea why. He was sure he'd never been on a street like this before. On the way to the bistro table, Julian assessed the familiarity. What was it? Did he catch a glimpse of something like it in one of his dreams? He would've remembered. The London of his dreams—messy, clanging, enormous, full of life, sometimes under punishing duress—was never this clean, this sunny, this empty.

The director and the cameraman surveyed the scene, analyzed it through their lenses and remained unhappy with it. They said it didn't look true. They obsessed about the red bus. Something was wrong with it. After twenty minutes of their hand-wringing, Julian had to step in.

"This isn't the story of the bus," he said to them. "This is the story of the girl who gets hit by the bus."

"What are you saying?"

"Emphasis," Julian said. "Priorities."

The director and the AD agreed with Julian in theory, but they still couldn't let it go. Something didn't feel right. They couldn't figure it out. They had a bus, a cab, a green bag from Harrods, what was missing?

What was missing? White granite townhouses, a river, twenty bridges, the dome of St. Paul's, a Roman wall, chip shops, newsagents, roundabouts, bookies. And ten million people. "Rain," Julian said, rubbing the bridge of his nose, trying to find his patience. "When is the sidewalk ever dry in London? You're not making a fantasy. You're making horror. And horror has to be solidly grounded in reality. Rain is a must."

They extolled him for the suggestion. As if by magic, a water hose appeared. They asked Julian to step away while they sprayed down the metal table, the sidewalk, the road, the vehicles. They sprayed the awnings and the flowers. It looked much better, and Julian's sense of déjà vu got stronger. He returned to his table and sat in his toweled-down chair, the metal legs scraping against the fake concrete.

"Well done," the director said to him, coming over to adjust the collar of his jacket. "Thanks for the consult."

"I'm curious," Julian said, "why did you set the film in London, if you've never been?"

The director, a young eager kid named John Pagaro, making his film debut, smiled. "It's supposed to be a magnificent city, that's why. I once read a Sam Johnson quote and have never forgotten it. *When a man is tired of London, he is tired of life, for there is in London all that life can afford.*"

Julian shrugged. He wished his nightmares weren't so squarely set in London.

"How's Mirabelle feeling?" Pagaro asked.

Julian was instantly on edge. "Why? How should she be feeling?"

"Well, she fainted yesterday. You didn't know?"

Julian stood up. Unsteadily he sat back down.

"I'm sorry," Pagaro said. "I shouldn't have said anything."

"Did she faint," Julian said, "or did she faint and fall?"

Pagaro admitted she fainted and fell. "She was sitting, so she didn't have far to go, but she did hit her head a little. But just a little," he added hurriedly, off the expression on Julian's face. "She didn't bleed or anything."

Julian's hands shook. He looked down into the full cup of coffee.

"How was she this morning?" the director asked.

"Okay, I guess." Julian wouldn't look up.

"Well, she's back at work, and looking spry, so everything must be fine. Don't worry. I'm sure it was nothing. She's going to be great in this."

"Yes," Julian said. "She's great in everything."

"We're very excited to have her on board. And you're doing great, too, by the way, sitting there."

"The job I was born to do."

"I like your costume."

Julian was wearing jeans, a white shirt, black shoes. And a jacket, to show that it was a cool rainy day, not sunny and 90. "Thanks." He'd picked out the ensemble from his own closet this morning.

Pagaro stood up. "Hang tight. We should start soon." Crossing his fingers and then himself, he rushed away.

Julian texted Mirabelle. *Hey.* What he didn't write was, *I knew you had a secret. I could taste it on your lips.*

She didn't reply. It was nearing noon. Julian watched Pagaro on the sidelines, with his full crew, tearing his hair out. This was the first scene in his movie, and they were already running four days behind schedule. It didn't bode well for the future. But then what did.

At the far end of the street, Mirabelle appeared. She was ushered into place.

Her gaze searched for Julian, and when she caught his eye, she smiled.

And finally—ACTION!

He sits in a chair at a metal bistro table on a wide sunny street. The noon sun is blazing. He sits and he waits.

A cup of coffee stands on the table. The cup is full and cold. He hasn't touched it. He never does.

There she is, gliding toward him. Her dress shimmers. In her swinging hands is a pink umbrella. The red beret is on her head, tilted to the side.

She waves to him when she sees him, her fingers splayed, a jazz hand. She floats forward, joyous and smiling, as if she's got news she can't wait to tell him.

He smiles back.

He can hear her heels click on the pavement—

"CUT!" Pagaro yelled. "Good, but let's try that again, Mirabelle, this time without the jazz hand. Just the smile will do. Places, everyone! From the top. Take two. ACTION!"

The set was so hyper-real, it felt realer than life. Everything in it was as it should be, every bronze standpipe gleaming, every prop in place, the flowers misted and the tall windows wet, reflecting the red double-decker bus and black cab.

After five more takes, they were done with that camera angle, and a glowing Mirabelle walked up to Julian and sat at his table.

"How was I?" She was flushed and in heavy makeup. Her expertly tousled chocolate hair was held into place by a pint of hairspray.

"You're a very good walker," Julian said. "But, Mia, why didn't you tell me you fainted and fell yesterday?" Intensely he stared into her eyes.

Looking sheepish, she was about to answer when the director interrupted.

"Okay, girls and boys," Pagaro shouted, "we're resetting, and then we go again from a different angle. Mirabelle, Julian, stay put, we'll be ready to go in a jiff. Shae!" he barked to the nearby production assistant, "don't just stand there, get them some water, will you?"

"Jiff is film-speak for five hours," Mirabelle said, with a conciliatory smile.

"Aren't you an optimist," Julian said, not smiling.

Chewing her lip, she considered him a moment, then got up from her chair and went to him. Standing behind him, she gathered his curly hair away from his face into a small tight ponytail and secured it with a rubber band, leaving a bit of hair out at the nape of his neck. She kissed the back of his head, murmuring some endearment, but her hands on his shoulders were trembling. She sat in his lap, draping both arms around his neck. "I'm sorry I didn't say anything, Jules. Yesterday you were so jumpy. I didn't know *what* was going on. I didn't want to worry you."

"You fell and hit your head. That's cause to worry, no?"

"It was an accident. I hit my ankle, put my head down for a second, next thing you know, bam."

"Bam." If she told him she needed brain surgery, he would not have been surprised. If she was knocked down by the double-decker in the next scene, he would not be surprised. He patted her hip. She pressed her face against his head.

"Mirabelle, please!" the AD yelled. "Stop that! Don't kiss him! We have no time to reapply your lipstick or wipe it off him. And now your beret is all askew! Ugh. Just take your seat—*please*. I'll send Gladys to fix you in a sec."

She returned to her chair but was agitated. Her face was flushed; her eyes blinked rapidly; her hands were fidgety.

"How do you feel now?"

"Great!" she said too loudly. "Amazing."

"Amazing," Julian repeated. Was she overcompensating?

"But, listen…I *do* want to tell you something."

He hid his clenched hands under the table and gave her his best poker face. All the broody silence from him in the past. It was like he'd been training his whole life for this moment.

"Jules, *please*, don't look like that."

"Like what," he said in a leaden voice.

"Like a brick fell on my head. I'm fine."

"Okay, you're fine."

"Can you calm down, I beg you."

"I'm calm," he said.

"I'll admit, Pagaro was a little worried," Mia said. "His star—that would be me—hitting her head and all. He asked me to go see their doctor this morning, get checked out, just in case. That's where Z and I went."

Julian's features were frozen like they'd been dipped in stone.

"I would've had you drive me, Jules, but I didn't want you to panic. I only went to appease them, for their insurance, you know how they get. Don't be upset with me."

"I'm not upset with you, Mia. What did the doctor say?"

"He poked and prodded. Took some blood, shined a light in my eyes, asked me if I had breakfast, you know, life and death questions."

"What did the doctor say?" Julian repeated slowly.

"Nothing." Mia took a breath. "But, Jules, guess what he told me."

"I thought you just said nothing."

"I mean he said nothing about my fainting."

"Don't make me guess. Just tell me." Trying not to look away from her face, Julian clamped his hands together.

"He said, congratulations, Miss McKenzie, you're going to have a baby!"

The sound left Julian's head.

"Jules, can you hear me?"

I can hear you.

"I know, right? Can you believe it?" She inhaled, then let out a thrilled laugh. "I can't *even*. My mom's gonna have a heart attack. Julian, you're *white*—are you shocked? But shocked like *amazed*, right?"

Did he nod? Or did he just sit there? He swayed.

"I'm feeling so many things at once, I don't know what to feel first. I hope we can finish shooting this thing before I become blimp-like, though the way this is going, the Haunted Warlord is going to be dragging a huge-bellied, knocked-up matron to this dungeon, because *maiden* certainly won't be the right word for me…my mother's gonna *die*. As soon as I have my lunch break, I have to call her. You want to call her with me?"

Did he nod? Or did he just sit there?

"I know your mom has like seventy grandchildren, but mine only has me and she's waited her whole life for her baby to have a baby. It took her so many years to have me, trying and trying again, and you and I have been married five minutes, and we didn't even have to *try!*" She emitted an elated cry, and then lowered and thickened her deathless voice. "It's because I'm *drowning* in your love, Jules." She blushed. "Oh my God, how do you feel, you're not saying anything."

Julian opened his mouth to say something. She didn't let him get a word in.

"I know it's a lot to process. Look at you, seven weeks ago a carefree bachelor—and today! No wonder I kept falling all over myself yesterday, tripping and slipping and sliding. Literally the gravity in my body was shifting, and I didn't know it." She chortled. "I told you 49 was my lucky number, and you didn't believe me."

Julian opened his mouth to say something.

"My body was telling me my life was about to change. Oh my God, I'm going to be a *mother*," Mirabelle said and burst into tears.

She wiped her face. The foundation came off on her hands. Her cheeks were streaked. "They're going to be so mad; I was three hours in makeup today. Oh, whatever, I can't help it, I'm completely overwhelmed." She laughed. "One second crying, the next laughing. Now I know why we couldn't get around to buying any furniture. It's like the universe knew we were going to be needing different kinds of furniture. We'll convert one of your offices into a nursery? You don't need two offices and a work-out room, do you, Jules? One of those rooms can be for the baby? Or we can keep it in the bedroom with us at first, my mom did that with me. Oh—but I'm warning you, she's going to want to move in. She'll need her own room. Maybe she'll marry Devi, and they'll both move in." She laughed again. "A wife, a baby, a mother-in-law *and* a step-grandpa. You're pretty shocked, aren't you?"

He tried to nod.

"I know—it shocked the hell out of me. I said to the doc, it can't be, it *can't*, it can't be *con*ception, I'm using twelve kinds of *contra*ception, I'm being responsible, in control, dependable, I told him I'm like the Fort Knox of anti-baby *protection*. And do you know what he said? There's no protection against a miracle. If it can, the good doctor said, life always finds a way. For our baby's sake, I hope the dude has a degree in medicine as well as philosophy. Oh, no, Jules, I just realized—you and I have never even *talked* about whether you wanted kids. We've had absolutely no time! Too late now, I suppose, to have *that* conversation, and it does seem kind of soon, but—you do want children, don't you?"

There, he knew what to do. He nodded.

"Should we find out if it's a boy or a girl? I don't think I want to, is that okay? I can't wait, I just want to have it right fucking now—no no, I don't mean that, I *want* to be pregnant, and also we're going to need at least nine months to learn to control our potty mouths, the poor kid can't be around parents who curse like sailors—oh, hey, if it's a boy we can name him after you. Jules Junior, hah! Or that name you said you've always liked, *Sam*? You said it means lucky. Well, if this is not a lucky baby, I don't know what is. Sam Cruz. I love it. And if it's a girl, we can call her *Juliet*. Oh, yes! *Juliet Cruz*, it's a stage name already—a star in the making. *The sweetest flower in all the field*. Or we can name her anything you want. You gave me my Viennese dessert bar at our wedding and took me to Hawaii. In return you get to name all our kids. I really want to call my mom, though. Do you think I have time? They have to redo my makeup anyway. I know I should've told you tonight, but I couldn't wait. You know what they say—good news must be shared at once. And you sure looked like you could use some good news. I'll Facetime my mom later. I have to see her expression when I tell her. I hope it's as priceless as yours. She's going to want to take the next plane out, oh, my love—I simply can't believe it. We are going to have a *baby*. Everything in our life is changed."

Behind her, they were wheeling the red bus and black cab into position, wiping the glass on the windows for a streak-free reflection, hosing down the sidewalks and the flowers...because it was always raining in London. Julian hoped his face didn't look like he felt, like he was about to break down. He wanted to look like a man who was simply outranked by the good news flanking him. The tension had fled his body. While he had been doing his own thing, panicking, fretting, dreading the worst, the universe was doing *its* own thing, loading the dice, dealing the cards, breaking the crystal quartz. Relief flooded him, and joy. He knew everything was going to be okay, at least for a while. He felt it in his gut.

Mirabelle was gazing at him expectantly. Something demanded to be said. What's my line? Please give me my line.

Ad lib, Julian.

He closed his eyes and spoke the only words to say when there was nothing left to say.

"Oh my God, thank you," said Julian.

There was familiar noise, and Ashton and Zakiyyah strode across the fake street, both of them grinning from ear to ear, as if they had already known. Grabbing two chairs, they fit around the small metal table, Ashton next to Julian.

"We were *dying*!" Zakiyyah said. "Jules, Ash and I stood over in the corner the whole time, watching her tell you!"

"Z was right, it was better than any horror movie has a right to be," Ashton said. "Now we know what kinds of shenanigans *really* go on in this so-called dungeon."

Zakiyyah waved her phone through the air. "I taped the whole thing," she said. "It's going viral, baby, I'm posting it on Instagram in five minutes."

"Look at my poor buddy, it's like a bomb has gone off." Ashton threw his arm around Julian. "Has he managed even a single word, Mia? What's the matter, Jules? How do you feel, happy or scared shitless?" Ashton laughed. "Hard to tell, right? Both emotions feel about the same."

"Ashton!" said Zakiyyah. "Anyone can see—he's so thrilled, he's been rendered speechless."

"Oh, Z, quick, you have to get pregnant, too," Mia said, "so we can have our babies together."

"Well, if anyone can be quick about it," Zakiyyah said, winking at Ashton.

"Thanks a *lot*, Jules," Ashton said.

"Places, everyone!" the AD yelled, "it's almost time—all non-essential personnel *off* the set! Wait," he said to the director, pointing at the four of them, "maybe we can have those two sit at another table? Instead of just the one guy sitting by himself. We're trying to make it real. Plus, look how flash they're dressed, like they're already in costume."

"Fine," Pagaro said. "Call Florence. Ask her to bring the paperwork right away." He addressed Ashton and Zakiyyah. "What do you say—want to be extras on your friend's movie?"

"I dunno," Zakiyyah said. "Who's got that kind of time?"

"Oh, let's do it, Z," said Ashton. "We can always go to Disneyland tomorrow." He smiled at Mia. "You two want to join us?"

"*Disneyland*? Ashton, are you out of your mind?" Mia said.

"You'll be fine, we'll put you on It's a Small World with Z," Ashton said. "I'm not telling you to go on the Tower of Terror, am I?"

Across the table, Julian and Mia gazed tearfully at each other.

"Florence! Sometime this century, please! She's got one job—casting. Why isn't she here doing it? Does she even understand the concept of time? Florence!"

In you is every woman I have ever loved.

Julian reached for Mia's hand, looking at her with all the emotion there ever was on the prefab streets and painted sets of this fakest and realest of cities. Their time for irresistible grace had come. And they were both in place to receive it. Turned out there *was* something stronger than death. Their brief ecstasy had been remade into enduring glory. Love is the only perfection, Mirabelle, Julian wanted to say but was too overwhelmed to speak, and it wears the shiny robes and swaddling clothes of immortality.

Their story continued. It wasn't finished. Julian knew all too well: only the storyteller was left behind, only his telling of it was finished. Yes, the curtain fell, but the story itself never ended, the story of what it was to live a life, and to love another.

That's it, ladies and gentlemen! Thanks so much for joining us!

Make it real.

Make it last.

Make it beautiful.

Acknowledgments

I spent so many years alone in my room, working on making the *End of Forever* books come to life that I forgot how many people were outside that room, advising, cajoling, inspiring, bolstering, believing. I'd like to gratefully acknowledge their help and support.

Many thanks:

To Carl, my first husband, for introducing me to London and for giving me my first child, Natasha, when we were both so young.

To Natasha, who has brought me so much joy and who has grown up into such a remarkable young woman, who, among many other things, kept the running lists of hundreds of titles we considered for the *EOF* books, and who very early on said, "I *love* Julian," when she read *The Tiger Catcher*, and I knew then we were going to be okay because she is a tough critic.

To my last child, Tania, who kindly allowed her mother to drive her to school every morning at 7:30 and therefore get to her studio early; otherwise these books might have taken another five years to finish.

To my sons, Misha and Kevin, for banding together and keeping the household machinery running and the jokes flowing.

To Lee Sobel, for his friendship and advice in good times and dire, and to Declan Redfern, for his invaluable counsel.

To Jennifer Richards of Over the River PR and to Fiona Marsh and Kate Appleton of Midas PR, my U.S. and U.K. publicity teams, for their tireless efforts on behalf of the *End of Forever* books.

To Lorissa Shepstone, my website, graphics, and design guru, who's created some real artifacts from my imaginary places.

To Nicole and Sissi, my constant devoted readers and friends, for running my fan club, my social media support groups and for being my cheerleaders both online and in life.

To Zakiyyah Job, a beautiful young woman who appeared on my driveway in 2015 as if by magic because she loved *The Bronze Horseman* and lent me her name for *End of Forever*, enriching my fictional world by her real-life presence.

To Kasia Malita, my Polish translator extraordinaire and my friend, for mailing me chocolates to keep me going, and for weeping when she read *A Beggar's Kingdom* and calling me "a sorceress." I hope she means the good kind.

To Shona Martyn, my publisher for fifteen years, who said to me in 2016, "You write it however you can, and whatever it will be in the end, we will figure out a way to publish it."

To Michael Moynahan, who in 2011 spent considerable professional and personal resources to start me on this remarkable journey.

To Brian Murray—who made it all possible.

To Kevin, who for the last five years, the last 25 married years, the last 38 "best friends" years walked every day of both the real and creative life with me, which so often amounts to the same thing. Kevin is the one who said the books are everything. Just have faith.

Sometimes I joke with my readers that the only true happy ending to a Russian is when at the end of her journey, she finally learns the reason for her own suffering.

Well, these three *End of Forever* books are the reason and the end of the story of the last five years of my life.

I hope they bring you some happiness.

Paullina
2019